A TEAR BETWEEN WORLDS.
A WAR OF ETERNAL PROPORTIONS.
A CHOICE.

OMNISCIENT

ALAINA GRAY

TW

Published by Twisted Words Publishing, LLC

twistedwordspublishing.com

Paperback ISBN # 979-8-9934106-0-9

Ebook ISBN # 979-8-9934106-1-6

Book Design by Christian Bentulan

www.coversbychristian.com

Illustrations by Twisted Words Publishing, LLC

First edition: October 2025

ALSO BY ALAINA GRAY

The Kalpanian Prophecy

1. OMNISCIENT

CONTENTS

For that one substitute teacher who convinced me this story was worth sharing.

ON JULY 17TH, 2099, approximately 1 billion people were spontaneously found deceased during the early morning. Like a thief in the night, this pandemic sidled by, stealing the souls of unsuspecting dreamers and the joy from even more ignorant survivors. The mystery thief did not discriminate between the old and the young, nor the sickly and the healthy. The victims' bodies were unscathed, without so much as a bruise to show signs of struggle. On the contrary, many wore expressions of bliss at the moment of their untimely death, leaving their faces frozen in a permanent, unnerving grin. Mass hysteria broke out among the human population as realization spread, which resulted in a bloodbath so violent it would spark the deadliest war known to man. One so grotesque that those living would grow envious of the dead.

The only lead in the aftermath was reported sightings of "a Man of Light" in the dreams of numerous people that same night, accompanied with a large search for one called the Anima Genus. However, these sightings and ravings were brushed to the side as madness born from grief of loved ones lost. There were no further details of what could have caused this phenomenon, and to this day, there have been no explanations found.

This day became known as *The Harvest*.

History of the West World, p. 901

July 17th, 2106

A WOMAN STEPPED AWAY from the bullet train onto the platform with a grace only the wealthy could possess. The wood creaked beneath her three inch heels, as if threatening to break from the weight of her grief. However, it must have felt pity for the woman, arising from that same overwhelming sorrow, and so it resisted the urge to falter and held its own strength.

The train departed as soon as she exited and whipped her coat around with its speed. Teeth chattering, the woman wrapped it back around herself, cursing God for the frigid weather, despite knowing it was the weapons of man that had made it so.

In front of her stood the meeting place she had meticulously prepared: a small coffee shop that would calm the mind. A setting that would not draw too much attention. However, as the lady gazed around, she assumed that she could have arrived on an elephant, belting at the top of her lungs, and no one would have spared her a second glance. The inhabitants that passed her all studied the ground, as though the dirt's grooves held the secret to immortality. Even children, grasping the hands of their parents, shared their gloom, with not a spark in their eyes as they gazed upon the stranger in their town.

The woman could not blame them for their bleak mood. Along with the atrocious state of stores lining the dirt road, the town of Chesterfield was one of the hardest hit during the ongoing famine. Most of the survivors left as soon as the Western Government had lifted the outdoor curfews. Those that remained stayed either because of financial issues, or pure stubbornness.

Kicking an empty can that had rolled by her feet, the woman huffed a breath that could be seen in the air. She, for one, could not imagine how anyone survived here, without the environmental control and radiation absorbers. She, seeing how thin the inhabitants were, could not fathom how each of them could carry the heavy portable blockers on their backs.

She stepped onto the dirt road, paying no mind to the old man who had collapsed against the store's brick wall, and opened the door to the coffee shop, its sign hanging sideways by a thread. A bell went off as it swung open, announcing her presence to the servers, who didn't offer her a second glance as she searched for her companion. The sudden temperature change warmed her bones and she stuffed her mitted hands into her coats' pockets.

The woman had managed to keep her anxiety under wraps until she spotted a man sitting in the middle of the room at a table set for two. He was younger than she had expected; not as young as her, but only appeared to be in his mid-fifties, with mild work done to keep his face from aging. He was slightly overweight, filling in his seat nicely, but most of the fat gathered within his arms and legs. The top of his head was void of any hair, but a gray well-kept beard grew from his face. His navy blue suit embroidered with gold was what confirmed her assumption that this was the man she had contacted, as only a high-ranking government official would be able to afford such attire.

Forcing herself to keep her breath steady, she assumed her natural smug smirk and made her way over to the table.

"I appreciate your patience," the woman started. "And I apologize for my own tardiness. Although, I am sure you are more than aware of the precautions that must be taken when dealing with an issue such as this." She placed herself behind the chair, waiting for the man's permission to sit. When he nodded, she pulled the seat out and sat down gently, legs crossed over one another.

The man had already gotten his cup of black coffee, mixing it rhythmically while gazing at her. A shine from his multiple rings infiltrated her peripheral, but she refused to drop eye contact with him. She had to demand respect. To treat him as an equal, if she ever wanted the man to agree to her lofty request.

"An unfortunate day you chose to meet." The words implied a solemn tone, but the man's expression hinted otherwise. He raised his eyebrows as if to test her.

"Seven years since The Harvest," the lady answered. "The start of all this madness. I thought it was a rather fitting date to have this conversation."

The man then leaned back, not quite smiling, but harboring a twinkle in his eye. "I presume it is." He summoned one of the servers with a wave of his hand, who refilled his coffee and brought her own. Not bothering to thank the young waitress, the woman blew on her drink before taking a sip. The man's gaze still did not leave her. "Well? I believe you have procrastinated long enough. And I must admit, I am brimming with curiosity. Tell me what this genius plan of yours is. You've already made me wait two weeks, and my patience is wearing thin."

She licked her lips and put the mug down slowly. It had been a six-month endeavor to come up with a way to approach her plan, but even what she had prepared would sound insane to any rational person. She only hoped the man in front of her was as mad as everyone had gossiped about. "What if I told you I have found a method that would guarantee the West World's victory, punish the East World's atrocities, and leave *all* people of our nation without endangerment?"

He didn't miss a beat. "I would say you are farcical. Keep going."

Steadying her nerves, she held her chin up high. "Last night, you dreamt of a house of bare stone and glass, which turned to steel once you touched it. A figure, whose face switched from that of a middle-aged woman to an older man, followed you around the walls."

The man's eyes were blown wide, not with unbelief, but intrigue. "And then?"

"You hid in a dark room and locked the door, but the figure phased through it with ease. Its hands grasped you and froze you where you stood, and that was where the dream ended."

"Fascinating," he whispered to himself, tilting his head as though to pull the thoughts from her mind. The woman mentally scoffed—unlike him, she herself knew attempting such a feat would only ever be successful in Kalpana. "I wasn't aware such psychic abilities existed outside the realm of entertainment. Consider me impressed." He took a small sip of his black coffee and raised an eyebrow. "And yet, I still fail to understand its tie to your plan."

So the woman outlined her story, her motivations, her plans, and her unsuccessful attempts. She told him about how she discovered Kalpana—the realm existing beyond dreams— and what remarkable things were possible there. She voiced her solution in light of the peace treaty, knowing that the agreement between the East and the West was only temporary. Finally, before checking to see if the man had believed her, she made her lofty request—a 10 million dollar loan.

Her lungs would not release when she finished her story. While maintaining eye contact, she slowly twisted her wedding ring that brought along the familiar feeling of loss. The man in front of her had not said a word during her entire speech, which made it all the more terrifying when he broke the silence with a laugh. It started with a slight shake of his shoulder, which transformed into a cackle so violent it turned the heads of even the most depressed townspeople. All color drained from her face. As his wheezing finally slowed, she winced in preparation for his rejection that was sure to come.

To her ever-growing bewilderment, he reached over and shook her shoulder roughly with a tight grip, an unnerving grin reaching ear-to-ear. "A miracle, that's what this is. That which seems like madness to the blind is genius to the wise. If what you say is true, then you have just changed war forever. No, not only war, but the entire world."

"It is true, sir. I will prove it to you tonight."

He released her shoulder and extended his arm, bringing extra attention to a large ruby on one of his rings. "Call me Mr. Chance."

Biting back a smile, she shook his hand in a robotic way. He continued to speak. "I'll tell you what I'll do. If, come morning tomorrow, you can tell me every detail of what I have been thinking during this conversation, I will give you all you ask for and more."

Struggling to maintain composure, she straightened her back. "That will not be a problem, Mr. Chance."

"Well then, I look forward to being your accomplice." With that, the man stood up, chugging the remainder of his scalding drink before setting it down. He smoothed out his gold-embroidered coat and bade her farewell.

However, just before the man walked out the front door, a quiet, submerged voice of her subconscious suddenly spoke. It was the last bit of morality that had squeaked its way through the cracks of her soul—a part of her that still resisted its dark encasement. "It would require children." Her motherly side fought against what she would become. "Young ones. Project Lucid can only be successful with them, even if it meant subjecting them to unimaginable pain–"

"Worry not about the details," Mr. Chance interrupted, the first sign of aggression exposed as he fastened his coat in a violent manner; though, his smile was regained so fast that the woman could have imagined it. "You focus on your research. As for potential candidates, leave that to me."

Chapter One

"Guardian Angels Don't Always Stay"

The ground shook. A train howled. Her sister screamed.

It was just *a dream.*

"Wake up."

Maya's heart hammered in her chest as she jolted forward. Her hands were clammy, gripping her thin blanket so tight her fingers started to cramp. Sweat trickled down her forehead and she wiped it away as she tried to remind herself repeatedly that the scenario was simply a horrid fantasy inside her mind, no different than every other night the same nightmare played out.

Still, images of the terrible explosion and the disappearing bullet train stayed etched in her brain. A mixture of echoes from the past and fears of the future, all fused together. The dream had become so recurring that by now Maya was sure she could describe every little detail of it.

It was expected. Normal, in its derisive way.

But when Maya saw the person responsible for her awakening, she remembered with a deep sense of foreboding that this was *not* a normal day.

It was one she had been dreading since the second the idea became a plan. Every birthday leading up to it served as a painful reminder of the day to come. It weighed down on her like boulders in her pockets. A gravitational pull that threatened to drag her under. The one thought offering the slightest reassurance was that there was still time. But time bolted by like a jet against the futile wind, and before she knew it, the date had finally arrived.

Her sister's eighteenth birthday.

The day Amarie would leave the old farm for good.

"Maya, get up!" Her sister showed no mercy as she yanked on her arm, gripping a ticket in her hand. "I have to catch the train before it leaves!"

In a daze, Maya reached for her worn out slippers, rubbing the sleep from her eyes. She had wondered why the nightmare hit so much harder than it had all the times before, but now the reason was obvious. After all, it was the day part of that dream would come true.

"I slept in," Amarie rambled to herself. "How could I have slept in? We need to sprint. Hurry!" Amarie tugged on Maya again, and she shrugged her off.

"Just give me a second!" Putting the final slipper on, she picked up her flashlight and followed her sister out of the room and to the back of the house, past the wooden dinner table and stone fireplace, where a lone seat and coffee table were placed.

The chain of keys in Amarie's hand pinged against one another as she stepped purposefully on the maze that was the hardwood flooring. Maya copied her steps, both of them having memorized the exact spots to place their feet in order to create the least amount of noise possible. Maya noticed Amarie's hands shaking as she searched for the correct key to open the front door, and she felt her lingering irritation melt away. Amarie's breaths were ragged, more labored than usual. She pushed her hair—a brown mop of untamed curls lacking the blond highlights of her own— behind her ear. It was little things that others may have not noticed, but the fear from these stressful moments was all too familiar to be hidden.

Maya unhooked her and Amarie's jackets off the coat hanger. She threw the bigger one at her sister while putting on her own. Amarie managed to open the door, a whiff of frigid air sending goosebumps all the way up her neck. Maya flinched as a loud creaking noise was made, looking over her shoulder to the room of old man Broth, located just down the dark hall to her right, to make sure he was still asleep. But before she could see, her sister pushed her along, shutting the door behind them and sprinting forward.

Mr. Broth's dogs barked as they sprinted by as if proclaiming the girls' presence to the world. Maya felt herself instinctively increase speed, despite knowing that the faster she moved, the more likely the sheep dogs would chase them. Though she ran with all her might, Amarie's strides remained longer. Just as she was beginning to fall behind, her sister grabbed her hand. Amarie dragged her through uncut grass that reached all the way up to their abdomens. The sharp thorns from the weeds grazed and scratched Maya's skin, but the adrenaline made all pain unrecognizable.

She turned her head back to the house. Its porch light had been switched on, making Maya's blood match the temperature of the incoming breeze. The old crude wasn't asleep after all.

"We're almost there," an unfazed Amarie whispered. "Come on!"

Up ahead stood the barbed wire fence outlining the entire property. It hadn't been fixed in years, corroded by rust and covered in dead vines. A portion of the fence had broken down, making it easy to step over, and, gripping her sister's arm for support, Maya took extra caution not to scratch herself on the wire.

The barks of the dogs were getting louder, as was the pounding in Maya's chest. Amarie seemed to notice the canines too, a brief moment of fear flashing through her eyes, which she quickly shook away. The setting became more forest-like and roots jutted from the ground. Maya had to point her flashlight directly down to prevent herself from tripping.

The two of them had gone down the trail countless times, making sure they'd never forget the way when the time came. But never in all their treks had the journey to the train stop felt so long.

The sound of a train's whistle echoed through the air, causing her to jump. Ones just like it had been placed all around the countryside after the Nuclear War in an attempt to fight access outdoor exposure, reaching speeds faster than any car could dream of. This one, however, served a different purpose. The green train wasn't for the general public. Only people with chips in their wrist would be permitted to board, and while SCRO, the Sectionalized Children Relocation Operation, had made sure both sisters got one, it also meant that all their information would be on display with a quick scan. Their age, their history...and their caretaker. One failed attempt, and Broth could flag Amarie, blocking her from using the train despite her age.

Fear surged through Maya. *If we miss the train, Amarie will never get this chance to escape again.*

Of course, they had known this for years, it being the reason why they were waking up the midnight she turned eighteen, unbearingly early, but that didn't expel the fear surrounding the consequences of failure.

She studied her sister's face for any sign that the same worries were circulating inside her mind, but her expression remained as stoic as ever, not a hint of doubt on her face.

The whistle went off again. Amarie let out a cheer and pointed ahead. Through the trees stood a shack made with loosely nailed in planks, a lantern hanging from the ceiling. Maya couldn't contain her apprehension as they neared the contraption. The train let out a third whistle, the loudest one yet. Amarie darted forward, dragging her along, and with a final burst, they jumped onto the wooden platform.

Amarie pulled Maya down before she could catch her breath, putting a finger to her own mouth to silence her. They listened closely for the sound of the canines. When nothing but the distant train was heard, Maya released a sigh of relief, sinking to the ground.

Amarie slid down with her, eyes closed and relief evident in the relaxing of her shoulders. Maya pulled her into her arms and squeezed her tightly.

"You made it," she told her while burying her face in Amarie's shoulder.

"I made it."

They sat there without saying a word, the sound of the approaching train filling in the gap. Only then did the reality of Amarie's success settle in.

Maya struggled to maintain composure as she pulled away to look at her sister.

This could be the last time we see each other.

"I *really* want to come with you," Maya found herself whispering, but she knew Amarie's response before a word even escaped her mouth.

As expected, her sister shook her head. "You know better than me that you'll be given right back to Broth when they scan you. You have to wait." Amarie reached in her pocket and pulled out the key to the house, plopping it in Maya's hand.

The ground started to shake as the train drew closer. Maya pulled her jacket to herself, eyes transfixed on the key chain.

"I don't know if I can do this," she admitted with a quiver.

Amarie grasped her face in her hands and turned Maya's head to her, eyebrows pinched together.

"What are you talking about? Of course you can. You're the one who came up with the plan in the first place! We've spent years preparing. I'll move into the city, find a place to live, and when you turn eighteen, you'll escape and move in with me."

"I know, but—what if you get caught? What if I can't escape? What if Broth traps me inside the basement forever? What if I *do* make it out but can't find you? Gosh, there are so many ways this could go wrong. How would I make it if we never found each other again?"

The train's light came into view and Amarie momentarily turned toward it before facing back, placing her hands on Maya's shoulders. The lights from the train's windows swept over the two of them numerous times, its speed decreasing with each second.

"You *will*. I know you will. You and me? We're *survivors*, Maya. If there isn't a way out, you'll create one. You won't stop fighting until you're out of that cursed place. You've survived eight years with Broth. I *know* you can survive two more. And as soon as you turn eighteen, you book it out of there, okay?"

Maya couldn't help the doubt that crept inside of her despite her sister's overwhelming confidence.

The tears that had collected in Maya's eyes finally spilled over. There were a million different thoughts and emotions she wanted to express, but no words formed, so as the train slowed to a stop, she pulled Amarie into one final embrace. "I...I'm going to miss you."

She could feel the warm smile that stretched Amarie's cheeks on her shoulder. "And here I thought you'd be reveling in the independence."

As if I could ever be independent on this God-forsaken farm.

The green train halted in front of the stop and a light flashed. Maya watched longingly as Amarie pulled out her ticket and pressed it against the screen to the side of the door.

"Ticket verified," an automated voice announced from a hidden speaker. *"Place wrist on the scanner to be identified."*

A cylinder then jutted out from the train. The top half of it rolled back to make a perfect slot for her sister to put her arm in. Without a second's hesitation, Amarie placed her wrist inside and it scanned the implanted chip.

"Person identified: Amarie Shaffer." The cylinder retreated back into the train and the door swung open.

For the first time that night, her sister revealed her own uncertainty with a singular look back at Maya, sorrow in her eyes.

"Bye, Maya," she whispered. "See you soon."

Before she could come up with a response, Amarie stepped onto the train. Not even a moment later, the door slammed shut and the train started to travel across the magnetic railing. The window lights crawled across her frame before turning into a sprint, the last illumination taking a part of her own internal brightness. Bile crawled up Maya's throat, leaving its bitter taste on her tongue as she watched the scene play out in front of her. The train heading away from her continued picking up speed, becoming smaller in the distance. It was all too familiar. No different from her recurring nightmare.

But this time, she knew there would be no waking up and realizing that her sister was still by her side. This time, it was real.

She actually did it.

"Bye, Amarie."

Maya sat by the train stop as the spiders above her head spun their new webs until even they grew tired and weary. She hugged her knees and stared at the train tracks absentmindedly, finding no willpower to start heading back toward the small, secluded farm. To return to the life she resented so much, only this time without her sister there to support her.

Loneliness struck like a powerful wave, smothering her with its force.

Maya's life hadn't been easy. War, Broth, and the evil that was SCRO had made sure of that. Humanity always had an aptitude for pushing the boundaries of reality, but through its fear of the unknown, it had forgotten to fear what it might unveil. Now, the vulnerable were left to face the consequences: the deaths of loved ones, uncontrollable famine, and, above all, the corruption of hope. The pursuit of happiness was nonexistent; survival was the number one priority. It was what had kept Maya and her sister with Broth for all of those brutal years.

Through every hardship, Amarie was by her side, motivating her not to give up. Comforting her at her weak points. Standing up for her when she was too afraid to do it herself. Her guardian angel.

But for the first time in her life, Maya was completely alone.

And it was becoming frighteningly clear that she was not ready.

A jolt of indignation pinched her chest toward her sister. Yes, Maya had made the plan, but it had been Amarie that was so desperate to leave. Yes, it was for a good reason, but part of her wondered if maybe...her Guardian Angel never really cared that much in the first place.

Then Maya shook her head. She *does* care.

When she felt like she cried all the tears she had in her, Maya stood up, finally managing to tear her gaze away from the railroad. It didn't matter how long she waited. Her sister wasn't coming back.

She walked as slowly as she dared down the path back to the farm, but it still ended too soon. The flashlight hung limply at her side, switched off as she watched the house from a distance. Her fear spiked as she noticed a dim light coming from one of the blinds. There was no doubt in her mind that Broth knew what she and her sister had done, and that he was impatiently waiting for her return.

The sheep dogs resumed their barking once she stepped into the open, yet they kept their distance—too transfixed by the chickens occupying the cage next to them to pay her much mind. Maya held her head down, refusing to lift it as she opened the front door.

On a large stained seat in the corner of the living room sat Broth, reclined with his stubby legs propped up. His buttoned up shirt was two sizes too small, with a roll of fat escaping from the bottom. From his mouth hung a large cigar which released a putrid aroma Maya was all too accustomed to.

The light from the fireplace cast the old man in an orange hue as he fiddled with the cigar in his hand. War had varying effects on people, and for Broth, the destruction of the world caused him to be bitter. To resent what little joy earth still had to offer. Life continued to pass him by as he spent hours listening to the news, reminiscing about old times when economic and technological progression seemed unstoppable, before the human population had dwindled down to a lousy 2 billion. Based on the packs of cigars he smoked and the amount of alcohol he chugged, she sometimes wondered if the man believed he was a part of those 7 billion casualties.

Maya momentarily forgot how to swallow as she awaited Broth's next words.

"Good-for-nothin' child actually did it, huh?" the man said without a gaze in her direction.

Maya was tempted to make a retort about how Amarie was definitely *not* "a good for nothing child," but found herself biting her lip.

"She's gonna regret it," he continued. "If ya' think city life's any better than here, you'd be mistaken. Bet in a few days your sis gonna be wishin' she stayed." He finally turned his head and met her eyes with his icy stare. "You not gonna run away too, are ya'?"

"No, sir." *Of course I will, idiot.*

Broth made a grunting noise before he leaned forward and stood up from his reclining chair. Walking over to the burning fireplace, he threw his bud in. "Well, ya' better scurry back to bed. Sun don't come out for a few more hours. In the mornin' you gonna have double the work. You can thank your sis for that."

With those words, he hobbled down the hall and entered his room with a slam of the door. Maya leaned against the wall in defeat. At least one thing hadn't changed; she had no power in front of the old toad, with or without her sister.

Sighing, she headed back to the room she once shared with Amarie. The dull moon outside the window spread its light aimlessly across the bare ground. Two cots were placed a safe distance away from each other, and a small table with only one crossword booklet on top was situated in the middle. Her sister had straightened her bedsheets before she left, leaving no evidence of the sleepless nights they had both shared.

Maya lay down on her own untidy cot, gazing at the ceiling above. As her mind continued spinning webs of hypotheticals of her bleak future, she leaned on her side, staring absentmindedly at her sister's bed. A sharp, familiar feeling of loss struck her chest, and for a moment, the dark room transformed into a red and yellow wasteland, the bed frames black and charred with the mattress almost completely reduced to ash. Then she blinked, and the image was gone.

She pulled her only blanket up to her shoulders, the material so thin that if she brought it into the sunlight, almost all of the light would bleed through. After everything, it seemed like a crime to simply crawl back into bed. The last thing she felt like doing was reentering her nightmare-filled sleep, but gradually the emotional turmoil started to take its toll and unwillingly, she felt her consciousness drift away as she entered the world of dreams.

Chapter Two

"DREAMS NEVER CHANGE, UNTIL THEY'RE SHATTERED"

AT FIRST, THE DREAM was no different than usual.

It started with a memory. Maya's father darted through the messy house while pulling her and her sister along roughly, squeezing their arms to the point where pain extended down to her fingers. Seven-year-old Maya wailed as the ear-rupturing siren blared throughout the house. She had known what the sound signaled, despite the attempts of her parents to shelter her, but the possibility of an attack ever occurring where they lived always had been a foreign concept.

When she would ask why her father was having a bunker installed, her mother would tell her, "Oh, it's just a requirement by the government. But don't worry, baby, we'll never need it."

Her mother's words remained true for months. No one found the need to bomb the outskirts of the West World. Until the horrid day that destroyed every ounce of normalcy in her life.

It was four years into the fifth war that ravaged the world. Humankind had gone mad when The Harvest happened, but comparing the casualties to the losses from the war, the 1 billion spontaneous deaths were nothing but a small blip. Unfortunately, the people who were harvested that night were likely the ones who had been holding everything together.

There was a loud creak as her father swung open the heavy metal door to the underground room, a steep ladder leading to the cemented bottom. His grip finally relaxed as he told the two of them, *"Go."*

Amarie immediately climbed down, but young Maya only cried louder, throwing her arms around his torso. Present Maya flinched at her uncontrollable sobs.

"Let go of me, Maya. Get down with your sister!"

Younger her gazed upon his face, which now had become blurry; his features had deteriorated with Maya's memory as time passed by. *"What about Momma and Rex?"* Ignorance bled into her words.

"Momma is on her way with Rex right now, and I'll be out here waiting for them. They'll be fine. Now, I need you to go down and listen to what Amarie tells you to do, okay?"

He pulled her close to his chest.

"It's okay," her father whispered in her ear. *"It's gonna be okay."*

Younger her had nodded along, but present Maya had seen this event play out too many times to believe his empty words. Current Maya mentally huffed, letting her younger silhouette crawl down the ladder.

She had only just touched down at the bottom of the ladder when her father slammed the door shut above her head. Maya screamed his name and started to climb back up, but her sister, the ever so levelheaded one, pulled her down.

"Put these on!" Amarie yelled as she handed her a pair of black noise-canceling headphones. Maya cried out for her father again, and this time her sister took her by the shoulders. *"Put them on!"*

Maya's hands shook violently as she placed them over her ears. Not even a second later did the room start to tremble ferociously. Even being underground, she could feel the heat of the nuclear bomb. The light above them flickered, and although Maya couldn't hear through the muffling device, she was sure her scream echoed throughout the bunker.

In a blink of an eye, the scene faded before her. And when it reappeared, it was a day later.

She and Amarie walked around the obliterated landscape, Maya refusing to let go of her sister's hand. Charred walls and couches turned to ash speckled the burnt ground. The pool that had been full in their backyard was now as dry as her throat. The brutal sun beat down heavily on the dystopian setting, its rays browning the top layer of her skin.

Current Maya knew what the next scene held and mentally waved her hand in a near bored motion, changing the direction her younger self set her gaze. This, however, did not block out her sister's horrible shriek as she processed the image before her.

The action of avoiding the gruesome scene also didn't stop the memory of their appearances from playing in her mind. Third-degree burns revealed entire skeletons. The skin that managed to remain intact was charcoaled. And the smell—the smell was the one thing Maya was sure she would never forget. The pure stench of death and decay. But even with their near absolute destruction, Maya had immediately known who the victims were.

Her father.

Her mother.

And Rex, her stuffed dog, charred in the arms of her mother's bones..

She was sure her younger self had been devastated, but the Maya of now only felt numb, closing her eyes and forcing the flashback to end so the next scene could arrive.

On cue, a train whistle drowned out the sound of anguish. The nightmarish scenery changed into a railroad and she turned to her side, no longer surprised to see that her sister had vanished.

A bright headlight washed over her and she stepped to the side to avoid collision with the train. Maya looked away, finding no desire to watch it disappear into the distance once again, taking away everything she held so dear.

She waited there for one second.

Two.

Three.

Something's wrong.

The train should have made a final loud whistle after passing by her, followed by her sister's blood-curdling screams. Instead, she was met with silence.

Hesitantly, she opened her eyes and found herself in the same setting she was in before. Only the train was gone, as well as its tracks.

Confusion overwhelmed her. Years of the same dream, and not a single variation. So why had it spontaneously decided to play tricks on her?

A strange noise came from the dark forest and Maya whipped around. It almost sounded like clicking, though something about it sent chills down her spine. Even with her eyes squinted, she couldn't identify the source of the noise.

Click.

Click.

Click.

Abruptly, Maya felt a penetrating searing pain seep its way into her shoulders and she yelped. With a thrash, she sent whatever had injured her flying to the side and quickly flipped around. Baring its teeth at her was an abnormally large canine with saliva dripping from its open mouth, its yellow teeth as large as its crimson-stained claws.

She took a few steps back. On her left, another identical beast appeared. It let out a terrifying growl as it sank onto its hind legs. There was no need to think twice as she sprinted away as fast as she could, though this was much slower than preferred, as if she were pushing through waist-high water. The hounds pursued her unyieldingly. Maya weaved through the trees, trying to get them off her tail.

This task proved easier than she expected. As quickly as they appeared, the beasts were gone. Their barking ceased, leaving the air with a stifling silence. The sudden absence of the dogs, however, did nothing to ease her nerves. In fact, all it managed to do was increase them.

And she was right to worry as she saw the figure that emerged from the shadows. It was old man Broth, holding a bottle of beer in his hand.

"Come here, kid."

He started storming towards her. Maya's lungs constricted, and she frantically searched for an exit, but the setting had changed from a forest to an encased silver box. Her limbs refused to move as the man stalked closer.

"Amarie!" Maya called out, but she knew it was no use. It was just her and Broth.

He lifted his arm, and it took every ounce of her strength to fight the stiffness, forcing herself to the side. The strike narrowly missed Maya and she fell to the ground with a grunt. She scratched the colorless walls. Punched the gray floor. Screamed her throat raw as the man moved closer, arm raised and prepared to thrash down a second time.

"Let me out!"

The scream echoed inside the box. Broth froze, as if he had been paused, with his arm stuck in the air and a sneer imprinted on his expression.

Distantly, she noticed a bright light approaching her. Maya lifted her head up, and while she couldn't see a face, she could feel the heat of its eyes. It wasn't a burning feeling, but a comforting warmth as it came right in front of her. Above the stranger's head spun a strange symbol created with intercrossing swirls. Then, from above, it floated in her direction, stopping just in front of her chest. Her mouth refused to speak, and it was as if she had become frozen in the dream as well.

The figure placed a hand on her head.

Then the room shattered into a million pieces.

Cracks formed beneath her and gave way, hurtling her down a deep hole with nothing to hold onto. The weightless feeling of her stomach gave rise to nausea as she spun in a freefall. With a sickening panic, she stretched her arms as far as she could, and in the back of her mind she sensed strings all around her. In a last ditch effort, she pulled them with all her might.

She stopped falling.

The world faded for a moment before reappearing.

But the next scene she entered wasn't a calm one.

Dark shadows blinded her from every direction. They were alive, circling around in a way that blocked the surrounding area, and when they made contact with her skin, they were ice cold. One must have noticed her, because it stopped directly in front of Maya's face, staring into her eyes.

Maya couldn't begin to describe the appearance of the creature. Its face didn't have a definite shape. Instead, it morphed into a million different features. From long shark teeth to dripping fangs, red glowing eyes to soulless black, each change striking terror right through her heart. It was a manifestation of fear itself.

She had never seen a more hideous thing.

The clicking noise was overpowering now, and it became clear that the fear-inducing monsters were the source of it. Struggling to slow her racing heart, Maya jerked every time one of the creatures passed by her skin.

No, the creatures weren't passing *by* her.

They were passing *through* her.

In a new fit of fear, she jerked her arms roughly. But in horror, she realized her arms were bound to the chair she was sitting on, as well as her feet.

Maya couldn't recognize her own voice as she shouted for help, her whole body trembling. This didn't feel like a dream. She didn't have any control. The terror the monsters caused her to feel was more painful than any physical injury.

Wake up, she ordered herself. *Wake up!*

Another one of the hideous creatures stopped right by her face again, its smell oddly similar to the putrid aroma of her parent's corpses.

Suddenly her feet went numb. Then her hands. Her eyes widened as she watched her body slowly fade away.

She tried one last time.

WAKE UP!

And she awoke.

Chapter Three

"Visitors Aren't Always Saviors"

Maya was drenched in a cold sweat that stuck to her like a second skin. Goosebumps spread across her arms as she removed the blanket from her lap, the temperature of the room reflecting the frigid atmosphere outside. She swung her legs off the bed and rested her head on her hands, trying to shake off the horrifying images of the creatures that were imprinted on her brain, to no avail.

Sighing, she dragged herself up to clean her teeth at the stained yellow sink in the mold-filled bathroom. The ground was wet beneath her feet and she groaned as she noticed the trickle of water coming from the cabinet. The pipe was leaking again. She didn't hesitate to grab the scarf she had learned to keep inside the bathroom and tied it around the leak, logging mentally to fix it up later.

While she moved the brush around in her mouth, Maya forced herself to recall each moment of the previous dream, but even as she tried, some of it remained fuzzy. She remembered with little detail the large vicious dogs and Broth, but the one thing from the nightmare that remained absolutely clear was herself bound to the chair, the room she was in swarming with the terrifying dark monsters. The sound of their clicking still resonated in her ears.

She spit out the toothpaste and looked up at her reflection. The mirror in front of her revealed brown, tired eyes and an atrocious head of curly, matted hair. Maya released a sigh. It would be naive to think that her horrendous night's sleep would earn her a more restful day, especially considering the events of the previous night and the fact that her sister wasn't there to pick up the slack.

The sky was lighter than it had been the night before, but the sun still refused to appear, covered by the permanent blanket of clouds that released a light drizzle. The chickens were wide awake, clucking their tone-deaf morning symphony.

After tying up her hair and putting on her jacket, Maya headed outside to do her first chore. She went around the outside of the house to the power grid and gently flipped on the radiation absorbers, being cautious with the noise she made to avoid waking Broth up, it being too early to deal with the anger he'd most definitely express. Technically, they were supposed to leave the absorbers on the entire time, day and night, but Broth insisted on turning it off the later part of the day because of the cost of electricity.

The absorbers hummed as she walked to the shed, where she picked up the bag of seeds before pouring it into the chickens' eating bowl. All fifty of them immediately rushed to it, sticking their beaks inside the rectangular container. She had names for all of them, even if she couldn't always tell them apart from one another. Then, she walked over to the pig containment. The farm had two pigs—the third had died a month earlier. They oinked loudly when they noticed her holding the sack of corn, and Maya chuckled as she saw her favorite Lewis, who had been born with three legs, roll around in the puddle of mud.

"Here you guys go," she said softly to the pigs while pouring the corn. "Eat up."

Maya went to the shack to put back the bag when she caught sight of a note taped to the wooden door that she'd missed earlier.

List of Chores:
— Feed animals
— Mow lawn
— Sweep porch
— Clean chicken coop
— Clean pig coop
No food until all chores are done.
–Broth

Maya ripped the paper off the door and gripped it tightly in her hands. It was a fairly reasonable list, concerning Broth. At least, it would have been, if she still had her sister to assist her. They'd split up the work and probably be done working around one. But without Amarie? Mowing the lawn alone would take around four hours, and she was forbidden from starting until nine. The cleaning of the coops, considering how filthy they were, would also take a few hours each. She wouldn't be eating anytime soon.

In situations like these, Amarie would track down Broth and tell him how unreasonable his demands were. Threaten to not do the work at all until they both were given something to eat. Face any punishment given with a carefree smile that made the man grind his teeth.

But Maya was not her sister.

With a humph, she took the final sac of corn and dragged it to the far fence, where their fifteen sheep were kept. Their bleating grew louder and they collected together as she lifted the barbed wire to crawl through. She slung the sac around and pulled out a pocket knife, tearing into the bag and pouring it out. After putting the gadget back into her pocket, she petted the head of each one that let her. "Good morning, Debby. Konald. Princess Sparkles." They gave her a small bleat before diving into the food.

Maya felt herself frowning as she watched the animals devour the corn. Almost every single sheep was incredibly thin—not even the wool could hide it. The grass was dead and unappetizing, and she doubted it was healthy for them to snack on anyways. But they only had so much corn, and unlike the sheep, the other farm animals didn't have an alternative source of food.

As she watched them feed, she began to sense something off. She counted the head of each sheep, whispering their names to herself, until she had a headcount. Fourteen. It was Cloud that was missing.

Maya traced the edge of the perimeter, walking at a slow pace. Pushing away the clumps of grass, she searched for the sheep's white coat. Cloud was the newest sheep they had, only arriving about six months ago. Youngest, too. He always rushed to her at the sound of food, so something must be preventing him from doing so. She just hoped he hadn't gotten sick; they already lost five from radiation poisoning, and she had grown quite fond of the little creature.

A blur of white caught her eye and she switched to a jog when she heard a pitiful bleat. Cloud was laying right next to the fence, and started to jerk when she got near. Maya pushed away the tall plants to see his foot caught in a barbed wire that dug into its skin. Blood gushed from the wound, the rusted wire digging deeper with every movement.

"You poor baby." Maya stroked the sheep's coat to keep him still as she flipped open her knife once again. "How on earth did this happen? You're not even supposed to be over here." She cut into the wire, talking all the while. "Be glad I love you, because you sheep must be the stupidest animals I have ever met. Even the chickens are smarter than you!" Cloud bleated, and Maya shook her head to herself, feeling the wire finally snap. "There. You're free."

The sheep did not waste a second and immediately limped across the field to the food, not allowing her to examine its leg. With a sigh, Maya flipped the knife back closed and stared at the gray sky; she vaguely remembered its blue coloring of her younger years.

As she headed back to the farm house, she tossed the bag and grabbed the broom that was covered in cobwebs. Maya shook them off before sweeping in a rhythmic motion. Soon after that, she went to the chicken coop and hosed it out. Then the pig coop. When it was finally nine, Maya hopped onto the lawn mower, it rumbling like thunder as it traveled across ten acres of land, slicing the tall grass beneath.

One might assume the temperature would heat up as the day went by, but since the war, what the News called a "Nuclear Ice Age" ravaged the land. The only times where it didn't feel so cold was when she moved about, and there was very little moving as one sat on a lawn mower. Unlike sweeping, mowing was not the slightest bit relaxing. Monotonous was the best way to put it. She sometimes wondered why Broth couldn't just get a self driving one like everyone—at least before the war—owned. But even so, eventually Maya would settle into a rhythm, and she wouldn't even notice the minutes ticking by.

This was how every day went under the rule of Broth. If you worked for him, you were not a person. You did not have desires or limitations. You were simply a machine that never stopped running. The only thing you required was a touch up of oil every now and then to remain useful. And if you defied this perceived image? If you were no longer a perfect robot and failed your purpose of doing every task without a slip up?

He would fix you. Change your gears and rewrite your code before placing you right back so you could go back to your purpose of easing his terribly *draining* lifestyle.

Maya's mind wandered to her sister, who had finally broken free. Envy swelled in her chest at the prospect of traveling far away, wherever the wind would take her. She daydreamed of her eighteenth birthday, where Broth would not hold any more power over her. She would eat whenever she desired and clean only when necessary. She'd never be in the dark about the newer developments of the world. She'd do all the interesting things she would read about, like jumping from planes and exploring deep craters created from weapons too powerful for humanity to possess.

Maybe she'd even find a romance like the ones in stories. His warm sturdy arms would catch her as she uncharacteristically tripped over her feet. Her cheeks would redden and she'd fumble her words, all while he'd smile at her warmly.

The idea of a romantic relationship couldn't have been more foreign to her. Maya vaguely remembered the way her parents talked and laughed together. There was one situation where she had caught them mouth to mouth with the door open wide. But besides that, all she had were the romance novels she stole from Broth's bookshelf and slid under her bed.

The loud roar of the lawn mower rang in her ears continuously.

Pulling her jacket closer to her skin, Maya gazed at the dead forest. The night made it appear so big and vast, when in reality it was only a cluster of dying trees. Even after six years of peace, war's effects were still as clear as ever. The grass was never green or soft against her feet. Crops refused to grow. Sometimes the rain from the sky would burn her skin. Even the simple act of breathing deeply would cause her head to spin.

Maya had always been drawn to the unknown. Her heart ached to understand the world's secrets, one of those being why Earth's inhabitants had tried so hard to destroy themselves.

Maya was on her last patch of grass when a flash of silver caught her peripheral. She quickly turned off the mower and strained her eyes. Over the hill, she caught a glimpse of a small hover car skidding just barely against the ground, the magnetic rails under the dirt road having lost their strength to keep the car afloat. Its engine was soft as it traveled closer, and it became clear that it was heading towards the house.

Maya watched it in awe. So rarely did she see another sign of human life besides the train. Visitors were more rare than shooting stars, and when they did come, it always sent a spark of hope through her. Maybe *this* person would take her away from the dreadful farm.

After parking the mower and hopping off, Maya jerked her head around when she heard the patio door swing open. With one hand holding a cigar and the other a lighter, Broth caught sight of the vehicle approaching as well. He let out a string of curses before yelling to her, "In the house! Now!" Walking up, he grasped her arm tightly and pulled her along.

Maya didn't resist as Broth shoved her into a small storage closet. She bumped her head against the bottles of disinfectants, and the aroma of ammonia made her dizzy.

"You don't say nothing, you hear?" Broth gripped the door with all his might as he watched her nod. Satisfied with her response, he slammed the door shut and locked it.

Her breaths were deafening in the silent closet. Maya could just barely make out the sound of a knock through the wall. There were footsteps, then the creaking of the opening front door.

"What'd you want, Char?" Broth's distant voice announced. There was a response too faint for Maya to hear, and she tried placing her ear against the door.

"...lost one of them," a feminine voice said. *"Luckily....but..."* The voice faded once again.

Maya could feel Broth's anger through the wall. *"Kid was eighteen. Y'all said you needed kids. She wasn't a kid no more."*

Maya's frustration grew as she strained to hear a single word the woman said.

"...shows promise. Do not forget your oath."

The conversation then seemed to end, and Maya felt her hope drain away.

This was her chance to cry out for help. To make her presence known so that she could be rescued. But something about the woman's words made her lungs constrict. It was more than a gut feeling that told her this woman wouldn't be the savior she desired.

Broth closed the door and Maya sank back into the small cupboard. The more she thought about the conversation, the more she was certain her theory was correct.

The woman knew her sister had run away.

Which meant she must have also known Maya was there too.

Chapter Four

"The Definition of Reality"

THE SOUND OF CLICKING returned before the dream had even materialized. The monsters' presence stifled her breaths. Made her heart triple in pace.

Maya was back where her dream had ended the previous night: surrounded by horrifying creatures and chained to a metal chair. With closed eyes, she thought she could avoid catching sight of them, but the action did nothing to suffice. The beasts were inside of her as well, festering behind her eyelids. There wasn't anything Maya could do to escape them except to wake up, but even that felt strangely impossible, despite never being so in the past.

The scene felt different than other dreams she had experienced. The world weighed her down, as if gravity had decided to act on her consciousness as well. The sensation of the creatures' gelid bodies making contact with hers had a feeling of realism to it. The scene didn't have the cloudiness or airiness that usually accompanied her dreams, rather it was undeniably clear. Maybe it was that realistic feeling that made waking up a forlorn endeavor. The nightmare had sunken its claws into her, and she didn't have the strength to free herself from its grip.

"Help!"

She could barely hear her shout over the noises of the monsters. Maya's body trembled as she focused only on her respiration.

It's just a dream, she repeated to herself. *It's just a dream.*

But if it were, then why did everything feel so real?

She gazed down at her bound hands. A rough brown rope was tied around her wrists; however, when she twisted her arm around, the knot was surprisingly loose.

With newfound hope, she blocked out the creatures that surrounded her, only focusing on wiggling her hands free. Maya yanked at the rope, feeling its fibers scratch her skin as she yanked it as hard as she could until it came loose.

The clicking increased again as she used her free arm to untie her other hand. Visions of her worst fears continued to surface in her mind: her sister disappearing, being all alone, having no control of any part of her life. Her eyes teared up, which made it hard to see, but all the tears did was fuel her inner fire. Maya used her teeth to help pull loose the rope, and once that hand was no longer captive, she bent over to reach for her feet, but a sharp, stabbing headache caught her off guard as she did, and she instinctively gripped her head. Her vision doubled and the monsters blocked her sight, trying to stop her from escaping.

She shouted for help once more, only for her call to be cut off as one of the creatures passed right into her throat. Unlike the others that phased through her, this one stayed lodged inside, stealing her voice and leaving her choking for air.

I want to leave.

Anywhere but here.

Get out.

"GET OUT!"

The ice inside of her instantly disappeared, a gasp of air sucked out of her lungs along with it. And on the ground, a monster withered. The others momentarily stopped swarming, and Maya didn't hesitate. As quickly as she could, she untied her feet and sprang to the back wall. The cage was made of gray stone that extended just a few feet above her head. She banged her fists against the wall as hard as she could. She could hear the clicking starting up again, and she made one final *tug*.

Then suddenly, the scenery changed, and everything went quiet.

A crippling pain brought her to her knees. It wasn't a burning sensation, but an ache that went all the way into her heart. Every body part she could name throbbed, and yet, when she gazed at her arms and legs, they were unscathed.

Of course there aren't, she thought to herself. *This is only a dream, after all.*

Then again, in a dream, the imagined pain would usually cause her to wake. But Maya was still trapped inside her mind, experiencing it as if it were real.

She placed her arms on the ground and lifted herself up. Blinking multiple times to clear her vision, she took in her surroundings.

Underneath her feet, thick green grass grew just past her ankles. Numerous trees towered over her, casting everything in a darkened shadow. Leaves gave in to the earth's pull, spinning a few times before gently landing on the ground. The air was moist, and a thin layer of fog hovered right on top of the grass, completing the aesthetic of a mystical forest.

Maya wrapped her arms around herself, looking over her shoulder to make sure nothing could sneak up from behind her. Every direction she peered at was the same. Just more and more trees, roots hidden by the undergrowth.

But it did not stay that way for long. Something appeared in the distance, and Maya took a step back.

A figure stood on two legs. The cover of trees and the dense air made it difficult to see from her distance, but it wandered without any purpose, changing directions so frequently that it was almost traveling in circles. Maya's curiosity got the better of her. Slowly, she drifted closer while making sure she'd be prepared to run if the figure was dangerous.

It's a man, she thought to herself as she approached him. The stranger wore rags for clothes and had shaggy hair. His features made him appear around the age of forty, a little on the thinner side. But those were not the details that caught Maya's eye. As she headed closer to the man, she noticed a small black shadow circling around him as he walked, and when she was finally able to get a clear view of the man's face, she saw his closed eyes. The man wasn't even awake.

Sleepwalking.

The man moved right past her, and Maya had to quickly step to the side. She gazed around once more to see if there was a home nearby that he had been sleeping in, but there was no such place in sight. Maya turned around and brought her attention back to the sleepwalker who continued heading forward, barely missing the trees. She stayed close and prepared herself to pull the skinny man back before he ran head-first into one of them.

That was when she heard a faint noise come out of the stranger's mouth. Maya noticed the way his upper lip shook and beads of tears trickled down his cheeks. The black shadow increased speed as it traveled around him.

Maya almost didn't notice the tree until it was too late, and in a quick motion, she yanked the man out of the way. The action sent them both tumbling to the ground, but at the contact, a weird sensation overtook her. She lost all feelings associated with the dark forest, and when she gained them back, it was no longer grass beneath her feet.

She rubbed her head, the familiar light, cloudy feeling of a dream rushing back through her. She opened her eyes to see a plain white sky with no detail whatsoever. The ground was flat, the same color as above. Maya groaned and squeezed the bridge of her nose. *Couldn't I have just stayed in the forest?*

After regaining balance from the constant change of scenery, she looked ahead and there stood the man, curling up in an attempt to appear small while on the ground. His eyes were glued to the figure in front of him; it was a middle-aged woman wearing a tight pink satin dress, a large red stain just over her heart. She held a knife tightly in one hand. Only the whites of her eyes were visible and her teeth were sharper than the weapon she gripped.

The scene appeared to be a bedroom. Bookshelves and tables were knocked over. A glass of wine lay shattered on the floor, staining it dark red.

The man's quiet sniffles immediately stopped as the woman approached him, placing a hand on his cheek and pressing the knife against his neck.

"I love you," the woman whispered. Her voice held a sweetness to it, yet still managed to sound threatening. Maya felt the man's fear as the lady lifted her knife and–

"Stop!"

She covered her mouth with her hands, but the word had already escaped. She held her breath, cursing internally for her outburst.

The woman's knife stayed hovering right over her victim while the man trembled under her gaze.

Then the woman's head snapped in her direction.

Maya's lungs caught as she made eye contact with her white empty eyes, whimpering at the sight.

She tried stepping back, but the woman started stalking toward her, the previous interest in the man no longer present.

"S-stay back," Maya pleaded.

The lady continued forward.

There was the sound of crashing and she looked up to see the white scenery deconstructing. Falling apart and shattering into a million different shards, the damage exposed endless holes of darkness that threatened to swallow her entirely.

The man in the dream flickered in and out of reality. The ground vanished beneath her and she lost her footing. The woman lurched forward, and Maya let out a cry.

She felt herself start to fall into the void.

Then another pair of hands grabbed her.

The sensation was so real that she could have sworn someone had actually caught her. The arms pulled her up, dragging her safely to solid ground. Maya's head spun and she rubbed her eyes before opening them.

She was back in the forest. And in front of her stood a boy, gripping each hand.

The boy appeared to be around Maya's age and had black, tightly-curled hair that frizzed in all directions, which allowed him to barely reach her nose. He wore a maroon shirt that hung off his torso loosely. His eyebrows furrowed and his eyes displayed a swirl of emotions Maya couldn't name.

"Who are you?"

It took a moment for her to register that the question had been directed at her, and the best Maya's mind could come up with was, "What?"

The boy stared at her for a moment, only pulling away his gaze when there was the noise Maya had grown to despise.

Click.

Click.

The boy cursed under his breath. "Nightdweller."

She didn't have much time to think before the boy stood up, still clasping her hand. "Come on," he told her. Without wasting a second, he took off running toward a large tree. Maya strained to catch a sighting of what the boy had called a nightdweller, to see if it was the same creatures who had joined her in the cell, but he didn't give her the chance to as he pulled her along. When they arrived behind the tree, the boy pinned her against its bark, placing a finger on Maya's mouth to signal her to be silent. She could feel the warmth of his breath as he kept her close. The boy reached down and grabbed a strange weapon from his pocket. It was the size of a sword, but built like a spear with a tip that glowed a ferocious red.

The clicking grew louder and Maya sank lower against the tree, catching a glimpse of the monster's black fog. Next to her, the boy got the weapon ready in his hands, peeking around the trunk.

Maya held her breath as they maintained that position, keeping her eyes glued to the boy in front of her and waiting for him to make a play against the creature.

She didn't have to wait long. In a swift movement, he jumped out with a roar, jabbing it and rolling away to avoid contact. A horrid sound came from the beast as it dematerialized and faded away into the atmosphere. The air around them became ten degrees warmer and the boy's weapon lost its red glow.

After a few more seconds, Maya came out from behind the tall tree, watching as the boy stood up and shoved his gadget back into his pocket. Her next words, however, stuck to her throat as the stranger stormed toward her, a hostile look in his eyes.

"Well?" the boy demanded.

Maya didn't respond, prompting him to let out a groan as he grabbed his head tightly.

"Look, I don't know who you are or where you came from, but you *must* have a death wish. Entering a dream without a recouper? Are you *crazy*? If I hadn't risked my butt pulling you out of that man's consciousness, you would have been dragged into the Void forever! Does that sound fun to you? *Does it*?"

The only thing Maya could think to do was shake her head.

The boy turned around to grip one of the trees and banged his head against it repeatedly, muttering something incomprehensible.

"Sorry?" The boy stopped to look at her as Maya uttered the apology. She wasn't quite sure what *exactly* she was sorry for—she still had no idea what half of the boy's outburst had meant—but whatever she had done seemed to upset him greatly.

Shaking his head in disbelief, the boy dug through a satchel swung across his side and pulled out a gadget before plopping it into her hand.

He took a deep breath. "Whatever, you're fine. *It's* fine. Just be glad I have a spare." Maya lifted the trinket up to eye level in order to study it. It looked like a watch, but instead of a clock, there was a small button in its place.

"What's it for?" Maya asked him, and he looked at her like she had sprouted another head.

"A *recouper*?" The boy answered with such disbelief that she might as well have asked him what color the sky was. "The only way to escape someone else's dream—how do you *not* know what a recouper is?"

"Escape their dream..." Maya stepped back, swinging her head around to gaze upon the surroundings. It was all so clear. She could see details in everything—the leaves, the fog, even the dewdrops stuck to the tall blades of grass. But it also felt *off*. The trees were too green. The air was too crisp. Everything was too *alive* to be real.

And so, as she looked into the boy's eyes, she had no doubt in her voice as she proclaimed, "I'm still in a dream."

Maya was expecting to wake up right then, like every other time she became fully aware of her sleeping state. She even closed her eyes and imagined herself lying in her uncomfortable bed, waiting to be yelled at by Broth. So she was surprised to see the boy still staring at her when she reopened them, an expression of disbelief and feigned amusement dawning on his face. With a fabricated chuckle, he said, "Okay, very funny. Seriously though, which pocket are you from? Sipapu? Venemo? Pity if you are from Hel; if that's the case, maybe we can make an exception to let you stay here."

His fake smile then started to drop as he studied her clueless manner, and while Maya remained speechless, she could sense the moment when the boy understood her proclamation was really what she believed to be true, and his eyes widened as far as it was humanly possible.

"*That's impossible,*" Maya heard him mutter under his breath. The boy looked at her, then over his shoulder, then at her once again. "You *really* think you're dreaming?" The accusation in his tone almost made Maya retract her statement, but she stopped herself. Surely it was her own mind tricking her into believing its self-formulated fantasy.

The boy must have noticed her resolve as he continued talking before Maya could say anything. "You see that guy over there?" he asked, "The one you ran into?" Pointing to the middle-aged man who had been (and still was) sleepwalking, the boy waited for her to nod. "*He's* dreaming." He walked over to where the man was standing, waved right in front of his face, and snapped his fingers a few times. Meanwhile, the sleepwalker didn't even flinch.

Without warning, the boy then turned around and snapped in front of Maya's face, causing her to jump back. She covered her ear as though the noise had caused physical pain.

A prickle of annoyance filled her as the boy watched her reaction with a smug look. "And *you* are not."

Bringing her hand down, Maya shot him a glare. "That doesn't prove a thing," she argued. *Here I am, fighting with my own mind.* She shook the thought away. "If this really were a dream, which it *is*, I would react to certain situations as if they were real, because in the moment they *feel* real. And yet it isn't reality because the real world doesn't have healthy forests and air that doesn't smell like pig manure—at least where I live. So I'm 100 percent certain that this is a dream. And I'd like to wake up now. Please."

Maya held her breath as the boy squeezed the bridge of his nose.

"That's a lot of words," he mumbled. He paced back and forth with his eyebrows furrowed, kicking the grass with his feet. After a few seconds, he said, "What do I have to do to convince you that this isn't a dream?"

The question took Maya off guard. "Nothing," she said. "You don't have to do anything because I *know* this isn't Broth's farm. It's not logical for me to sponta-neously transport somewhere else, so the only explanation is that I'm still dreaming."

The boy scoffed. "*That's* not logical, but being aware of your dream and still not being able to wake up is?"

The dream boy did have a good point, Maya reluctantly had to admit. She tried one last time to return to the real world, closing her eyes and thinking herself out. When that didn't work, she felt doubt start to creep up, as well as a growing panic. Maya *always* had control of her mind; it was one talent she had developed throughout all of her nightmares. No matter how bad they got, she could always escape them. But now...

Maya turned her gaze to the ground at the soft grass. She bent down to feel it and let the blades brush against her fingertips. The dew left her skin damp, a sensation as clear as day.

"So what you're saying is that... I'm awake?" She asked quietly. "This is all real?"

The boy's expression softened slightly and he patted her back. "I never said you were awake. I just said you weren't dreaming." Maya waited for him to expand on that statement, but he continued on. "And as for real, I guess it just depends on your definition of what's real and what's not. Is anything only real because it happens in *your* reality?"

Maya crossed her arms. "That doesn't make any sense."

"Trust me, none of this makes any sense. You're obviously omniscient, but based on your blank expression, you probably don't even know what that word is. Meaning you either just became an Omni—which is impossible—or you have amnesia. My bet's on the latter."

"I don't have amnesia."

"Ah, and how would you know if you forgot?"

"Don't you think I'd notice a big gap in my memory?"

He thought for a moment. "Fair point." Heading over to the sleepwalking man, the boy tied a rope around his waist. Maya also noted that the man now sported a band around his head that hadn't been there before. The boy adjusted his grip and pulled the rope sharply.

He then turned his head to look at Maya, blowing a tuft of hair out of his face. "Well stranger, I have to take this guy back to camp before he wanders off to an even more dangerous place. You have somewhere else you need to be?"

"I don't even know where I am."

"Of course you don't," the boy said. "Better take you back to camp too. Maybe Halo or Talon will know what's wrong with you."

She scoffed at the way the boy had phrased her situation, but she couldn't deny the fact that she was completely and utterly lost. Maya wasn't sure if she fully believed this wasn't a dream yet, but even so, she was desperate for answers. And if this really *was* all in her mind, she couldn't see any harm in following the black-haired boy to wherever he planned to lead her.

So Maya trailed behind her new companion as he pulled along the sleepwalking man, wishing for this all to make an ounce of sense.

Chapter Five

"Undeniable Truths Can Become Deniable"

"Why was it a risk to you?"

The walk through the forest had been silent in nature, with the setting of evergreen trees refusing to change no matter the distance they walked, and without proof of progress, time proceeded to inch by even slower. Despite being so chatty in their earlier encounter, the boy had become lost in his own thoughts. Because of this, Maya finally worked up the courage to ask one of the many questions that plagued her mind, and the boy turned to look back at her with an eyebrow raised, questioning the context of her statement.

She took the opportunity to repeat word for word what the boy had said to her during his first tangent. The words flew out easily; in their quiet trek, Maya had made it her mission to decode every sentence that had escaped the boy's mouth, her mind focusing on the clearest sign of danger. When she finished, he let out a quiet snort. "That's observant. What are you, a spy for Tenebris or something?" The sleepwalker started heading off course and the boy yanked him back.

"I'm not a spy for Teni–tere...um, whatever you said."

"So you're a spy for someone else then."

"*What?*" Rubbing her temples, she stated, "No. I'm not *any* type of spy."

"If you say so."

Maya waited impatiently for a response to her previous question, but he paid her no mind as he remained on his forward course. Frowning, she jogged up next to him and prompted him to answer.

He shrugged. "That's for me to know, and you to figure out."

Frown growing deeper, Maya huffed. "Okay, then what is Tenebris?" The sleepwalker made another groan which switched her attention. "And why are you abducting a sleepwalking man with a band around his head?"

A teasing grin danced along his lips. "Again: me to know, and you to figure out."

"What's your name?"

His tone was infuriating as he said, "Nope. I'm not going to be answering anything until we're at camp, and that's that."

Maya then crossed her arms and stopped walking. The boy took a few more steps before noticing, turning around with a confused look. "What are you doing?"

It was a good question. Maya wasn't quite sure where she had discovered this pool of confidence, but she decided to wade in it a little while longer. "I am not moving until you answer my questions."

"Funny. But that's not gonna work, so come on."

She held her chin high as she plopped to the grassed-covered ground, defiant. The boy rolled his eyes. "*Very* mature."

"Answer my questions."

He groaned. "We don't have time for this." "*Answer.*"

Letting out a dramatic sigh, he said, "You *really* aren't gonna move?"

Maya shook her head and, gazing up at the canopy of trees, the boy finally relented. "*Fine.* Which one do you want me to answer?" She did not hesitate. "All of them."

"*All* of them?"

"Every single one."

With his free hand, he pulled on his hair. "What did you want to know again?"

"The risk. Why was it a risk?"

"Get up first, then I'll tell you."

Maya squinted at him, trying to decipher if he was telling the truth. Hesitantly, she stood up, wiping the grass off her shorts—a new outfit that she had no recollection of changing into. The boy nodded in approval when she was no longer sitting before sobering, looking into the distance. The sudden shift in tone took her off guard, and she could guess that it was a touchy subject.

"Well, for one, the dream was already deconstructing," he started. "That's what happens when the dreamer becomes aware of something *other* in their dream. Like you, for example. And if you are in the dream when it falls apart completely, then..."

"You fall into the Void," Maya recalled.

"Yeah. But the fact that this sleepwalker is unregistered makes it even more dangerous." He went quiet for a moment, and Maya had to push down her overflowing curiosity as she waited for him to continue.

It felt like decades before he elaborated. "'Unregistered' means that they haven't been identified as Passive or Lucid yet. Count yourself lucky that this guy happened to be a plain old dreamer. Otherwise...well, let's just say that things could've been *much* worse."

"Worse than the Void?"

A darkness overtook his eyes. "Last I checked, the Void doesn't steal your free will or erase your consciousness if it's aware of you." He clenched his teeth. "Lucids could torture you, control you, even turn you into a pile of goo if they so desired. But you can't even get mad at them because *they* don't know what they did. *They* don't know that they were dealing with actual human life and just murdered somebody. They think it's 'just a dream.'" He gave her a targeting look before adjusting the rope around his wrist once again, pulling the sleepwalker forward.

Words refused to form as Maya searched desperately for a response. That couldn't be real, she thought. No one could manipulate reality that way. It was impossible.

Still, Maya wasn't quite sure if this really *was* reality. And if it was, then clearly there needed to be an adjustment of what she believed to be in the realm of possibility.

"I'm not going to be telling you about Tenebris, so don't even try to get that answer from me," the boy said after a minute had passed. "But as for your other question, the band around the man's head is so that he stays dreaming. I put it on him while you were still in his consciousness. To bring him back with me, he needs to be completely inside Kalpana, not flickering between realities. Plus, it stopped his dream from fully deconstructing, giving me more time to get you out."

Maya took the information in, trying to make sense of it all. She was surprised at how logical it all sounded. Much more so than the events that occurred in her dreams regularly. It was getting harder and harder to deny the fact that maybe—just *maybe*—the boy was telling the truth. That this was all really happening, and not just a dream.

And nothing surprised Maya more than how calm she felt about it.

She half-expected herself to be freaking out, questioning the very fundamentals of life itself. After all, another realm could open the door to countless other discoveries and possibilities. And yet, learning about this other world the strange boy had dubbed "Kalpana" was more of an awakening moment. Similar to all the pieces of a puzzle finally fitting together just enough to begin to see the whole picture.

It was an escape from the farm into an entirely different universe where she was *free*. A new adventure of discovery.

Maya had never felt more awake than she did in that moment.

Then she rolled her eyes at herself. *I can't believe I'm actually considering this. Amarie would say I'm crazy.*

The scenery finally began to change as the forest thinned, allowing light to pour through its gaps. The grass was now revealed to be a vibrant green—so bright it almost appeared to be glowing.

Ahead, the line of trees ended, unveiling rolling hills that seemed to extend for eternity. Various creatures Maya couldn't identify roamed the land. Bears with long tails. Birds with red-colored feathers. Even horses with long horns extending from the top of their heads.

Unicorns, she thought with a growing smile.

But the one thing that stood out above all else was the sky. The clouds swirled and spiraled around each large star. Inside the strange clouds were trillions of twinkling lights, illuminating the setting with a golden hue—just like how the sun used to transform the land before disappearing behind the horizon. The resemblance of the clouds to The Starry Night painting by Vincent Van Gogh was uncanny, and Maya wondered if *this* was where the man had gotten his inspiration. If she were an artist, she'd be itching to transport the scenery onto paper as well.

A sound of awe escaped from her mouth, and the boy next to her let out a genuine laugh for the first time. "You know, I was having my doubts about you not knowing anything about Kalpana. But I don't think even the best actor could pull off that level of surprise."

Maya felt her cheeks burn as she sighed and turned her head before noticing a small settlement tucked into a small valley. A large gate surrounded a building a hundred times larger than Broth's farm house. The design of it resembled an elegant castle, slabs of gray stone stacked on top of one another and a pointed roof with a statue of a bird on its tip. It had numerous stained-glass windows that shimmered all sorts of colors, and yet the castle's grandeur was diminished by the overgrowth that grew up its walls. Vines covered the windows, in some cases even breaking through them and entering inside. The bushes in the front were untrimmed and wild, and from Maya's distance the walkway up to the door was nearly invisible underneath all the weeds.

"There's camp," the boy said, noticing the way she was studying the building.

"It doesn't look much like a camp," Maya noted. In her mind she had pictured a few small tents all situated around a fire, perhaps with at least two trees to tie up a hammock. Certainly not an actual castle.

He shrugged. "It's where the people of Neshama Valley stay. What else would you call it?"

She could think of *many* more accurate descriptions of the so-called "camp," but she forced herself to refrain from arguing and copied his shrug.

A beeping noise resonated from the band around the sleepwalker's head, causing Maya to whip around. The boy turned toward it as well and said a curse under his breath as he tapped on the gadget.

"Our friend's due to wake up soon," he muttered. "A few minutes, tops. Well then, no time to waste. Let's go."

Maya followed wordlessly as the boy increased pace. Soon enough, they were traveling at a light jog, the poor sleepwalking man continuously tripping over his own feet. At one point, he had fallen straight on his face and Maya bent down to help him, only for the younger boy to push her hand back and say, "Are you *trying* to be stuck in his dream again?" So they resorted to dragging him for a while until Maya found a stick to prop the sleepwalker back up.

Soon they neared the castle's gate. It was much bigger up close—at least twenty feet high. Plants grew over its rails as well, and some bars were rusted through. Maya waited for the boy to pull out a key of some kind to open it, but when they arrived, he simply pushed the gate open. A loud, squeaky noise erupted from it, and a flock of the red birds that had been calmly congregating in the unkept garden within the fence's walls flew away at the sound. From behind one of the shrubs, a large, frazzled woman who couldn't have been much older than Maya's sister appeared. Her wavy blond hair reached just past her shoulders and her tight pink dress was dirt-free, despite working on her knees. She dropped whatever had been in her hands and rushed over to where they were standing.

Her eyes remained fixated on the boy next to Maya. "Finally, you're back! I was wondering what was taking you so long. I need help bringing some of the sedaflors"—she held out a handful of purple flowers—"down to the Underdwellings, but I'll let you handle that. Wow, two wanderers! That's—wait a minute." She then turned to examine Maya, her eyes widening. "You aren't Passive." Pointing at the boy again, she started scolding him, though her voice sounded too melodic and high-pitched to be intimidating. "Where were you? Who is she? You *know* you aren't supposed to–"

The black-haired boy cut her off by placing the rope tied around the man in her hand. "Here," he told her. "I need you to get the sleepwalker to Halo before he wakes up."

The woman narrowed her gaze. "No way, Jose. Remember last time I covered your butt? If you're causing problems, you can fix it yourself."

Waving her off, the boy said, "Come on, Jane! I'm not even causing problems this time. On the contrary: I'm trying to solve them. And as soon as I sort this out, I'll...work garden duty for a few days."

"I don't believe you."

"Jane—*please.*"

With a loud huff, the woman—Jane—wrapped the rope around her wrist. "Talon's not going to be happy, you know!"

The boy let out a sigh. "Yeah, I know. Bye Jane."

Before turning around, Jane's eyes lingered on Maya. She squinted slightly before flipping back around and pulling the sleepwalking man along, much more gently than Maya's new companion had been previously doing.

Maya released a breath she had been withholding while the boy shook his head. "Sorry about her," he said. "She's usually much more...pleasant. Must have had too much coffee before sleeping again." Maya had to bite back her tongue to stop herself from pointing out that *he* had been the one to break the rules. "Anyways, follow me."

The boy led her to the front door. It was a rich dark wooden brown with lines and swirls sculpted into its exterior, mimicking the patterns of the sky. In the middle was a sculpture of a tree with four strange symbols above it. The door stood around ten feet in height and gave off a mystic aura, making Maya's curiosity grow tenfold.

And yet, before he could open the intriguing entrance, she grabbed a hold of the boy's hand, stopping him in his tracks. His surprised expression made it obvious he hadn't been expecting such a gesture, and he looked down to where Maya was grasping him. "And...why are we stopping?"

She tilted her head up. "You still haven't answered one of my questions."

The sigh escaping the boy's mouth almost seemed painful as he said, "And what might that question be?"

"Your name."

The boy raised an eyebrow. "Why is that little detail one of your main concerns right now?"

Maya knew exactly why something as simple as a name held so much gravity to her. A name gave something substance. An identifying factor that created the illusion of realism. Sure, she could *see* the boy in front of her. *Hear* the boy in front of her. Even *feel* the boy in front of her. But it still didn't feel like enough to prove she wasn't going crazy.

"I want a name to go with the face of the boy who supposedly saved my life," she said eventually.

This time, he chuckled halfheartedly. "You know, Omnis aren't too keen on using their actual names. Most you'll get will probably be fake. Privacy and stuff."

"It doesn't matter to me."

The boy smiled as he answered, "Kai. You can call me Kai."

"Would that be your real or fake name?"

"Guess you can add that to the growing list of things you're just going to have to figure out eventually."

With that, Maya hummed quietly and shook his hand. "Well, nice to officially meet you, Kai."

He returned her gesture. "Likewise. Now, as for *your* name–"

Kai was interrupted mid-sentence by the large front door swinging open, accompanied with a deep booming voice.

"Come inside."

Chapter Six

"THOSE WHO STAY HIDDEN FROM THE REST"

THE MAN'S SHADOW PRACTICALLY smothered them. He was tall and strong and had a bald head so smooth that light from the stars reflected off of it. His clothes were clean-cut and professional—straight black pants and a white buttoned up shirt that contrasted greatly with his skin.

The way his eyes fell down on Maya made her suddenly self-conscious about everything one could possibly feel self-conscious about. She rubbed the side of her arm. It was just like Broth, only his actions were predictable—most of the time. This man was as foreign to her as the outside world, and so it took a few moments for Maya to react to the man's demand, snapping out of the haze of worries only when Kai grabbed hold of her hand and led her inside the rundown castle.

It opened up to a gigantic room with towering ceilings that left her gaping. The marble floor was slick and showed the reflection of the large stained-glass window that glimmered red, blue, green, and yellow. Various halls extended from the main chamber, and the mystery of it all made Maya itch to explore every single section of the mansion. For obvious reasons, she refrained from this urge.

The man suddenly stopped to look back at them. Their eye contact made Maya's heart pound out of her chest. However, he only observed her briefly before giving the boy next to her his undivided attention. "Do you wish to explain yourself, Kai?" he asked, his low voice reverberating against the walls in such a manner that Maya started to fear for the boy's safety.

This worry only grew as the boy finally released her arm to run his fingers nervously through his hair. "I found a sleepwalker. Not her," — he gestured to Maya— "She's omniscient and was with the sleepwalking guy. For some reason, she doesn't know anything about Kalpana, so I thought I'd–"

"You found the girl and the sleepwalker inside the Whispering Woods, correct?"

Kai turned his gaze away. "I know, I know. I broke the rules. But I didn't do it intentionally! I was just heading toward the river when I saw something through the trees. Then I heard a scream. How was I supposed to ignore that?"

The man pinched the bridge of his nose. "We'll revisit this later. For now, I'm more concerned about your thought process of bringing a complete stranger with a very questionable story into our camp." At the mention of her, he turned to face Maya.

"Yeah, her explanation was pretty vague," Kai admitted, "but you should've *seen* her, Talon. She looked so...lost. She couldn't have been making it up."

"And what is the name of '*she*'?"

Kai didn't answer, and the man called Talon let out an audible sigh. "Please tell me you at least asked her *name* before leading her straight here."

"I was going to," he mumbled.

His demeanor radiated disappointment. "Have you forgotten all you have learned? For all we know, she could be touched by the Tenebris, and a battle with their kind is the last thing we need. You are grounded. Now, what is your name, child?" It took far too long for Maya to realize their conversation had grown to include her, with her mind spiraling again about what the Tenebris was, so she had to swallow her fear to ask the man to repeat his question.

"What do you wish to be called?"

Maya didn't answer immediately. She thought back to what Kai had told her about the use of nicknames among the people who inhabited whatever "realm" she was currently in. She may not have been aware quite yet of the ways her true name could put her in danger, especially when her appearance should have done that more than anything, but there had to be a reason they remained so secretive.

"Amie." The name rolled off her tongue with ease, all the while stinging her heart. She wondered what her sister would think of her using something so similar to her name.

The man's intense expression did not falter, and Maya started to worry that he could read minds and somehow *knew* she had lied to him.

Kai stood quietly next to her, flipping his gaze from her to Talon. The title for the tall man was fitting; the way he leaned forward at an angle and glowered down at her made it appear like he was getting ready to pounce. In his presence, Maya felt like a mouse moments before being devoured by a hawk.

Talon nodded slowly. "And where, Amie, do you believe we are right now?"

It's a test. She could sense that just by the tone of the man's voice. Her answer would be the deciding factor to see if she were one to be trusted. But at least in this case, she didn't have to lie. "Kai said that I'm asleep," She held her chin up high to exude confidence, "but that this isn't a dream; it's another realm. This castle is your camp, where he told me one of you might be able to give some clearer explanations."

"Kai *told you*," Talon said, "but do you believe him?"

Did she?

She desperately wanted to.

But what if that was the reason why she was willing to believe the words of these possibly fictitious strangers? Because of desperation? How could it be that all of this happened immediately after her sister's disappearance? Was this her way of coping? Was it even possible to cope in such a way that this fantasy could feel so incredibly real? Maybe she truly *was* going insane.

So she said just that, painting out her thoughts without going into detail about her personal life. Maya could sense her story was vague and wouldn't dull any suspicion. When she finished, she looked away, not having any desire to feel like a mouse again under his stare.

There was a moment of silence before Talon said, "If it weren't for the complete and utterly lost look in your eyes, I would have been convinced you were lying."

Maya's eyebrows lifted slightly. "You believe me?" *I don't even know what I believe, myself.*

"Believing you and believing your story are two separate things. I believe you are telling what you see to be the truth with the information you have currently, but I do not believe all of that information to be accurate."

"I told her I thought she had amnesia," Kai interjected unhelpfully.

Talon stroked his chin. "It *is* possible..."

Maya glared at the boy, but quickly regained her composure. "I already told Kai that I don't have amnesia, even though he remains insistent about it. Why is it so difficult to believe that I might have just become aware of this realm now?"

"Because what you are claiming to be true should be impossible." Talon turned around to stare at the stained-glass window. "Omniscient isn't something you become; it is something you *are*. I would explain in greater detail, but considering your arms and legs, your time in Kalpana is almost up."

Maya wasn't quite sure what the man meant until she looked down at her extremities. They were fading right before her eyes, the transparency spreading across her body. She felt herself start to panic as her breathing became more of a struggle.

"If you are still aware of Kalpana when tomorrow comes, we'll start to answer more of your questions." Even as Talon spoke, his voice started to sound farther and farther away until it was nothing more than an echo.

"Do not tell anyone about this realm."

"Don't forget."

"Goodbye, Amie."

And they were gone.

MAYA DIDN'T KNOW EXACTLY when she woke up. She had been fading in and out of sleep for what could have been hours, staring at the dark shadows in her room for so long that her brain started transforming them into those clicking nightdwellers. Then a noise would resound from the darkness and Maya would quickly switch on the light, only for there to be nothing, leaving her mocking herself and her imagination.

She didn't know what to think. What to feel. What to *do.*

Maya, for some silly reason, had been almost entirely convinced that the hidden realm of Kalpana existed when she had her final interaction with Kai and Talon. But the longer she lay in silence, wallowing in the lonely bedroom she had once shared with her sister, the more doubt started to take over, spreading like a tumor.

If only there was proof, she would say to herself. *Not just memories, but material proof, expelling every claim that it was all made up.*

The wish was in vain, Maya knew that. For what evidence could there possibly be of a realm that did not exist in this reality, if at all?

She felt something fall down her cheek and raised her hand to feel it. A tear. Maya hadn't even been aware that she started crying, much less whatever reason as to why. Maybe she was tired. Maybe she was overwhelmed. Maybe it was both. All she knew was that she had never been more desperate for clarity.

Amarie would know what to do.

Checking the clock to her right, she sighed as she read the numbers stating it was 3:51 a.m. Much too early to do anything productive without waking up Broth. She wiped her cheeks dry and tried to fall back to sleep, but her mind's buzzing made the action impossible. It wasn't too long before her throat became itchy, begging her for water.

Eventually, she gave in to the pleas for a drink and got up from her bed, picking up her flashlight and quietly heading down to the kitchen. Making sure not to step on the especially creaky wooden planks, she finally arrived at the dining room, tucked behind the small wall separating it from the kitchen.

A light snore drew her attention, causing her to cast her gaze beside the fireplace. Maya gasped and froze as she saw Broth asleep on his ancient reclining chair, an empty bottle of booze on his lap. He didn't stir, his face tinged with a flush of red.

She swallowed down the dread and slowly started to walk back, only for her eyes to catch sight of a blue light emanating from something on the round coffee table next to Broth's seat. The Messenger—a gadget that received and converted electronic messages to a physical form— was switched on. In it, a scroll had appeared, flashing to signal it was unopened. Behind that one, another started to take shape, the Messenger's lasers creating the words' metal encasement. After a few seconds, it finished with a *click*.

Maya glanced down the hallway before looking back at the scrolls. Like anything that came from the outside world, new messages were extremely scarce. This was no surprise. She doubted many people even knew of their existence.

Maybe it's from Amarie, a little voice inside of her whispered.

The bright blue flashes continued, taunting her.

Her thirst for water all but vanished as she slowly crept up to the table. Broth may have been dead to the world, but Maya didn't have any desire to play with fire and take the risk of getting caught. Each step took more effort than the last. She had to resist the urge to sprint for the scrolls just to make the anticipation end faster. The man's quiet snores echoed throughout the room.

Maya managed to get just in front of the table when the whistles from Broth's nose suddenly stopped. She didn't dare move a muscle, becoming a deer in headlights while watching him with wide eyes.

The ancient clock on the wall marked the passage of time.

It ticked once.

Twice.

He didn't stir, and Maya let out a relieved sigh.

Making sure no noise was made, she quietly opened the Messenger's encasement and lifted up the two scrolls. She pressed the side button of the older one to make it stop flashing before shoving it in her pant's pocket. She lifted the second one to eye level, studying it closely. Maya searched for the name of who sent it. The dark room made it hard to see, but the blue flashing light gave her just enough visibility to make out two initials etched on the side:

C. F.

Her eyebrows furrowed. She couldn't recall anyone she had ever met with those initials. It was also strange how the individual didn't just write their full name, like all the other scroll-senders had done.

The thought of it being her sister resurfaced. It was possible Amarie had made an alias when she escaped to make sure she was never discovered again. Having never sent a scroll before, it could have easily been a mess-up. She could be in danger and hoped Maya would find the letter and—

Something grasped her arm and Maya jumped, dropping the message on the ground. The scroll clanged on the wooden floor, bouncing twice before rolling away. The crash should've been louder, but the sound of Maya's heart and the blood rushing to her ears drowned it out.

She didn't dare breathe as her vision slowly trekked to meet the horrid gaze of Broth, his eyes now open wide and a sneer across his grotesque face.

"Now what were you plannin' to do with that scroll, Missy?"

Words were forgotten as Broth's grip became tighter around her wrist. Maya tried removing her arm, but he twisted it and she let out a whimper as the old man pulled her close to his face, his putrid breath flooding her nostrils.

"I asked you a *question*," he whispered into her ear. Chills trickled down her back.

"*P-Please,*" Maya pleaded. The pain from her wrist grew.

She let out another cry as Broth released her, pushing her back. Maya held her wrist with her other hand, already feeling the bruises that would for sure be there the next day.

She didn't even have time to process before another burning sensation erupted on her left cheek. She raised her uninjured hand to it, blinking back the tears that blurred her vision. Broth stepped away after the slap and bent down to pick up the scroll. He spun it in his hand, the blue light illuminating his face.

"Go to your room," he ordered. "Get dressed. Fifteen minutes I want you down in the basement cleaning the base and checking the Geiger. If you're not, I'll make sure you stay down there till you're old as me, you hear?"

Maya looked down, steeling her chin. "Yes sir."

She turned around with her eyes glued to the ground. Her entire body was shaking. Her throat became itchy for water once more. The one thing she came there to get, and yet the one thing she managed to forget.

But as she placed her hands in her pockets, a small smile formed on her face.

The other scroll was still there. Maya rolled it in her hand.

There was still hope yet.

Chapter Seven

"What Haunts, Pursues"

THE BASEMENT HAD TO have been Maya's least favorite place on the planet.

The steep steps had no railing or support to hang onto. There wasn't one plank that didn't creak as she placed her weight on it. The light switch at the door hadn't worked for years, so the only way to illuminate the room was to walk down the hazardous staircase in total darkness and fumble around until she could feel a switch, hoping it was the one to the lightbulb and not the generator, whose loud noise always made her heart stop mid-beat.

Maya vividly remembered the fear she had experienced when she was younger, being locked in the basement as punishment for attempting to run away. She was nine years old at the time, and naively thought the train would simply sweep her away to the city, no questions asked. But when it scanned her chip, the light had turned red. Two drones emerged from inside the train and forced her all the way back to Broth, who looked more furious than she had ever seen him.

Maya was locked in there for two days before Amarie finally managed to convince Broth to release her.

From that day on, she never went into the basement without her sister by her side. And now she was asked to go down once again, this time all alone.

Yet another reminder of the absence of her guardian angel.

Maya took a deep breath at the bottom of the steps to steady herself. Finding the correct light switch had been easy enough and the Geiger to her right was green (depicting the room's safe radiation level), though that didn't stop the fear that she harbored as she studied the room.

Lead plates had been bolted to the walls, floor, and roof some time before she and Amarie had arrived. The plates gave her the feeling of being in a metal box every time she entered. It had been built during the third world war, when bunkers were only installed by the most paranoid, and nuclear war was still a dystopian fantasy. Broth always made one of the two sisters clean the lead at least once a month, claiming that the cleaner it was, the more radiation it would block from seeping into the house. Maya couldn't ever see the logic in his reasoning. Nevertheless, like every other time she was ordered to do the chore, she walked over to the racks in the corner of the basement and picked up the disinfectant along with a small rag. The movement was almost automatic as she moved over to the wall, sprayed the cleaner three times, and wiped it away in small, repetitive circles.

From above the stairs, she could hear the television blasting at full volume for the deaf old man, who had to get his daily fix in before loadshedding switched off their electricity. The newscaster was yelling about the "good old days" and the abomination that was the World Order. Just like the news channel did every day.

Not that she necessarily blamed them. While she hadn't been alive during the world of nations, even she occasionally found herself longing for a time she never got to experience. For a time before The Harvest or even before countries simply became "The Eastern" and "The Western" world. Sure, it was simpler not to have so many rulers, but that also meant there was one group of people making decisions for literally half of the world. A government wasn't really a "government" when it had so much land that it failed to govern the people actually living on it.

It wasn't as though there were no remnants of the Second Golden Age. The names of many major cities had remained the same, and oftentimes one would refer to a region that had once been its own state. But then again, most of those places had been destroyed in the war, and some names had been lost to history.

The scroll that was still concealed in her right pocket weighed down on her. The temptation to take it out and read the message inside grew more and more overwhelming until it was all Maya could think about.

Not yet, she had to keep reminding herself. *It's not safe yet.*

At any moment, Broth could open the door a crack and catch her reading the scroll. No excuse would save her then; Maya would be entirely at his mercy—or lack thereof.

So she resisted the temptation as she cleaned the basement.

As she swept the floor.

As she fed the dogs. The chickens. The pigs.

Until finally, after what felt like an eternity, there was a moment when Maya was certain she was away from Broth's piercing stare, and she removed the scroll from her pocket.

She had locked herself in the shed where the food for the animals was kept. It was cramped and dark, but had no windows through which someone could spy on her, making it the perfect place to read the message. A dull, ancient bulb hung from the ceiling, casting everything in a faint yellow light.

Maya sat down on the cement flooring, her back leaning against the large sacks of corn. With an eagerness she hadn't felt in years, she grasped the scroll in her hands, flipped it over and pushed in both sides of the metal cylinder at the same time. It made a quiet click before breaking in two and Maya sucked in a breath, the festering feeling of doubt flooding her emotions.

No. It has to be Amarie, she thought. *Who else would send the message?*

Maya pulled the pieces away from each other slowly.

Please be Amarie, please be Amarie, her mind chanted as she opened the scroll entirely, revealing a thin screen that let off a blue glow.

Words slowly appeared, and Maya frantically searched for the transmitter of the message. The text was small and blurry, so she moved it farther from her face, only to lose all traces of hope when she made out the sender's name.

It was the same initials, *C.F.,* that were printed on the outside of the cylinder. But next to it was a small symbol of a crescent moon inside a circle, with a larger crescent that curved over the top and side.

She knew that symbol all too well. It was one she had seen repeatedly during the time between losing her parents and being sold to Broth. It was the symbol for the system she and her sister had been kidnapped by all those years ago: SCRO. Not only was it painted on their buildings and badges, but they had marked every single child they owned with it, tattooing it permanently on each of their shoulders.

Maya lifted up her sleeve, running her fingers over the dark ink. The memories associated with her time in the system had long since been hazy. She couldn't remember any of the faces of the kids that were there with her, or the people who had taken her, or the pain that had been inflicted upon her. And she couldn't decide whether or not that was a good thing.

Rage clouding her vision, Maya threw the scroll down with all her might, pulling her knees to her chest and squeezing her head between them.

She should have known it wasn't her sister. Why would Amarie have sent a message anyway, if she had just escaped herself? It had been a childish, immature hope, with no ounce of logic to support her desire.

Then who is it from?

The question echoed throughout her mind.

The most logical answer was that it was related to the woman who visited Broth the day before. It couldn't have been a coincidence that her arrival and the scrolls were so close in timing. The theory would also explain how the woman had known about Maya and her sister's presence.

"Kid was eighteen. Y'all said you needed kids. She wasn't a kid no more." Those were the words Broth had uttered to the woman during their interaction. If she really *was* working for SCRO, and their mission was to sell children to the highest bidder, then why would they care what Broth did to them after the transaction? And why did he say they still needed Amarie and Maya?

Confusion muffled her hopelessness. She took a deep breath to steady herself and crawled forward to pick up the scroll again.

On the thin screen, words were still forming and shifting, with messages popping up quickly before disappearing. Her eyes couldn't comprehend anything fast enough.

She tapped the screen to get it to freeze, and it suddenly settled on one singular letter with the word *"CLASSIFIED"* across it, and a pop-up with a loading symbol covering the majority of the words.

The title across only revealed the letters, *"PROJECT LU"*.

Project?

The words in the background were faint, so Maya had to squint her eyes to see.

She began to read the letter. *"Mr. Deidre, this is a message–"*

That's as far as she got before a bright light blinded her. Maya lifted a hand to cover her eyes as it moved across her face. The pop-up read, *"Processing..."* as the loading symbol continued to move back and forth.

Then the blue message turned red and flashing.

"Unauthorized access detected," an automated voice announced, and Maya panicked. *"#693 file for Broth Deidre only. Identity of intruder has been reported to SCRO. This message will be erased immediately."*

She furiously tapped the screen to undo whatever nightmare she might have just created, but the message disappeared, leaving only the two halves of the scroll in her hands.

Maya dropped both parts of the scroll with a *clink* and pulled at her hair so hard she could feel some of the strands coming loose.

They knew.

SCRO knew.

She didn't have any clue as to what the words in the scroll could have been alluding to, but Maya clearly wasn't meant to read the letter. And now the organization that had ruined so much of her and Amarie's life, that had been the only reason she hadn't run away from Broth yet, would be alerted of her attempt to read their message.

Maya might not have comprehended any of the details, but SCRO had no way of knowing that. And if they really *were* that desperate to keep whatever they had been planning to tell Broth a secret, then there was no way they would let a possible liability walk free.

They'd be coming for *her*, Maya was sure of it.

And when they found her, who knows what they'd do to her?

Her panicked mind barely registered the pounding on the shed's door until Broth's voice broke through.

"The hell you doing in there, kid?"

Everything inside of Maya froze. "C-cleaning!" she stuttered out. "A squirrel got into the corn sacks again."

There was a moment of silence before he spoke again. "Open the door."

She gazed down at the opened scroll, frantically looking for a place to hide it.

"Didn't ya hear me?" Broth yelled as Maya struggled to stuff the two halves of the cylinder between the sacks. "Open up!"

Her shaking hands refused to cooperate, and the scroll slipped out between them. She couldn't think. All her mind could focus on was if Broth had figured out what she had done, and the consequences she'd be facing if he had.

Or the consequences she'd face if he *did*.

Broth banged on the door harder, causing the whole shed to quake.

Having found no place to hide it, Maya stuffed the scroll in her pocket, hyper-aware of the way it made it jut out.

"Don't make me come in there!"

She reached for the door lock and swung it open, attempting to maintain steady breaths. She looked Broth directly in the eyes, despite the way it made her insides coil.

He looked her up and down, and Maya resisted the urge to cover up her full pocket with her hand. She had gotten away with it the previous night due to the lack of light, but now she was in full visibility. It wouldn't take much for Broth to notice how her pocket bulged out.

He crossed his arms and leaned back. She didn't dare move.

It was too long before Broth finally shifted his gaze away from her and to the inside of the shed, allowing Maya to finally release a breath.

"Don't see no mess from a squirrel," he told her.

She bit her lip. "I finished right before you came."

He studied her a bit before nodding. "Your face is pale. Finish tidying up the shed and then come get some oats."

Maya looked down. "Yes sir. Thank you."

She watched as Broth hobbled away, his once red plaid shirt now a dirty brown. It reached across his belly, the buttons stretching to their max. He scratched the little bit of gray hair he had left and opened the patio door, slamming it behind him.

Maya's legs felt weak as she followed after him. She placed the scroll parts underneath the porch when she got there, tossing some dirt and leaves over them.

Broth hadn't figured out what she had done.

But SCRO had.

And they were coming for her.

It was only a matter of when.

Chapter Eight

"The Secrets That Bind Us"

THE NIGHT REFUSED TO come fast enough.

Maya was suffering through the world's worst headache, stemming from the tension she had been feeling the entire day, her mind constantly on alert as if SCRO agents would jump out of every nook and cranny. It felt like two hands were simultaneously squeezing the sides of her brain, all the while jabbing their thumbs into her eye sockets.

It wasn't as though she didn't *try* to calm herself down. She hummed a made-up tune to herself as she trimmed the dead bushes. Played with Lewis, the three-legged pig. Wrapped some gauze around Cloud's leg. Swept the floor at least three times until every ounce of dust that had accumulated over the years was gone and there was nothing left to sweep.

But every time she started to find inner peace, Maya would be reminded of the threat of SCRO tracking her down that loomed over everything. Her eyes would subconsciously trek to the dirt road that led to the house, waiting for another shiny hover car to make its appearance.

She was almost surprised Broth didn't notice anything off about her. That was until she remembered the stubby man couldn't have cared less about her well-being or anything related to her. Unless, of course, it came to ruining her life.

Careful not to disturb the sleeping dogs, Maya slowly refilled their water bowls and looked up to the sky.

The sun that always hid behind the clouds had lost motivation to brighten up the scene and the night took over. She could almost imagine the billions of twinkling stars stretched across it, a sprinkle of beauty in the otherwise dull world. The sight must have been beautiful on the secluded farm. There would be no light competing with the distant suns and muffling their natural beauty.

She headed back inside, closing the patio door behind her. Broth retreated into his bedroom without a word, and Maya was grateful. She knew she wouldn't have the strength to hold back a breakdown if Broth yelled or hit her once more.

Maya walked slumped to her own room, swinging the door open and sighing. She wanted nothing more than to rant to her sister—or anyone—about all that had happened in the past twenty-four hours. Maybe letting all of her thoughts out would make everything so much clearer and she'd finally put the pieces together. And maybe having someone like Amarie telling her that her strange dream was really just a dream would allow her to finally believe it.

Tomorrow, Lewis will be subject to my ranting session.

Maya got ready for bed faster than she ever thought possible. Before she knew it, she was under the covers, trying to get her brain to go blank and silent. But she was trembling too much in apprehension. But, contrary to the entire day, this type of apprehension leaned more towards excitement. She *needed* the secret realm of Kalpana to be real. To have the little bit of freedom she so desperately desired. Nightmares had held her captive for so much of her life, and she never wanted to be under their grip again.

Closing her eyes, she thought of all the chores she had done that day. Every single reason why she should be incredibly exhausted. With each example, her body grew heavier as she sank deeper into the stiff bed, her mental voice eventually trailing off.

MAYA COULDN'T REMEMBER WHEN exactly she had fallen asleep. It could have been ten minutes, thirty minutes, or three hours. But what she *did* remember was the dramatic chill that went through her body and the smile that broke out across her face as the darkness of her vision suddenly transformed into an entirely different world.

It took a few moments for her pupils to get adjusted to the new light. She blinked and rubbed them, feeling a small laugh escape from her lips as she recognized the stained-glass window and the tiles across the floor. *No nightmares tonight.*

She was back in the exact same place she was the previous night, as though she had never left. Everything, even the vines that came across the floor, were unchanged. With overflowing relief, Maya gazed around the room, searching for any sign of Kai or Talon, but they were nowhere to be seen.

Without the strangers' gazes, she was truly able to appreciate the beauty of the rundown castle. Everything about its tall walls and vaulted ceilings was elegant and grand, and there was no doubt that before Kalpana had weathered it down, it had been a magnificent palace.

It was only her footsteps that echoed as she roamed around the castle, letting the desire to explore its walls take over. It was strange, she noticed, how for a palace so big, there was such little furniture. There were some rooms that were filled with what could have been anything from couches to statues hidden underneath white cloths, so maybe there was more furniture than met the eye, but Maya couldn't understand why the people who lived inside the castle wouldn't use it.

It was easy, however, to figure out what belonged to Kai's people. The few seats they had placed were sleek and modern, and there were a number of gadgets leaned against the wallpaper, which Maya couldn't guess the purpose of.

It wasn't particularly flattering and stuck out like a sore thumb, but it did make Maya wonder if the castle really was their home, or just a temporary resting place. Maybe Kai was right in calling it a camp—not in the sense that she had originally been thinking of, but more the verb of camping. Nothing the people had brought looked settled or like it belonged. They almost seemed to be intruding, hiding in the abandoned palace walls to have shelter from the outside.

She had traveled far down the hall when she found it finally reached an end. A beautifully carved door stood to hide what lay beyond, towering above her head with more strange symbols above what looked like a book. Pulling on its long handle that sprung from the wood like a tree branch, Maya was surprised to find the mysterious door unlocked.

The door carried a heavy weight, and she had to squeeze herself through the small opening she was able to create. Once she was free on the other side, the door made a loud echo in the room that caused her to flinch. Taking a deep breath, she turned around, only for that breath to be stolen from her lungs at the sight of the room.

What must have been millions of books were stacked onto shelves that reached the top of the ceiling, with a glass elevator in the middle allowing their access. Red rugs complimented the wooden tables placed around the room, with candles on each one of them that added light to the very bottom, but the higher areas were lit by the circular sunroof, its brightness hitting floating contraptions that reflected the light in all colors. The massive library had a comforting, almost musty smell, with the smallest bit of sweet that stirred her hunger.

Maya laughed in amazement, doubting there were even this many physical books left in the real world. Dust particles could be seen in the air from a ray of light that managed to reach the floor of the room, and they swirled around with a wave of her hand.

Passing two large vases, she was just about to pick up one of the books when the sound of rustling stopped her in her tracks. Flipping around, she searched for what could have caused the noise. The rustling sound came again. At first she thought it could have been one of the people she had met yesterday, but whatever had created the noise seemed to be much smaller than a human.

She slowly started stepping backwards toward the exit of the room, refusing to turn her back on the sound. Her back, however, bumped into one of the marble vases and she felt it start to fall. In a quick movement she turned and caught it, releasing a breath as she placed it back up.

But when she turned around, she shrieked at the creature before her.

It was about the size of a small dog with black fur and a white belly. It had a pink snout and a tail that resembled a pig's, with black ears that were long and pointy and wisps of white fur on the top. Large, twinkling eyes watched her curiously as it kneaded its white paws on a white sheet. A quiet chirp came from its mouth.

Though Maya had no idea what the creature could possibly be, she had to admit that it was quite adorable. Especially when it skipped over to her feet and rubbed its head against her, chirping all the while. It took its time sniffing her. The creature's eyes sparkled as it stared up at her and went between her feet. A snort came from its nose, and Maya couldn't help but smile. She may not have known much of anything about the little beast before her, but she couldn't imagine anything this innocent-looking to be dangerous.

Once the shock wore off, Maya bent down and the black and white creature stopped momentarily. Hesitantly, she reached her hand forward. It stared at it for a moment before pressing up against her skin, making another snort.

Maya watched in awe as it weaved around her and flipped on its back. She chuckled as she rubbed its belly. "What *are* you?" she said quietly, scratching behind its ears. The way it played with her was familiar, and she could have sworn the animal and her knew each other, despite its unfamiliar appearance.

A cross between a squeak and a snort was her only response. It flipped back on its legs and stepped away to sniff the vase she had almost shattered, as if it had become bored of her.

She tore her gaze away from the creature. To her left, a green board(the oldest movies called it a "chalkboard") was propped up on the wall, with a series of those same strange symbols that were on the door filling up half of it. On the other side, a map of sorts was drawn with white chalk. Through close examination, she made out what looked like the castle—*camp*—sitting on a hill. The triangles most likely symbolized mountains, but nothing else made any sense to her. She stepped back and put a hand on her hip, leaning over to pet the creature who had joined her side. The fur on its back was softer than a pig's, and softer than a sheep's, urging her to pick it up and hold it close to her, feeling the heat against her chest.

"Pretty neat, aye?"

Maya instantly stiffened at the unfamiliar voice, and the animal jumped out of her hands. Reluctantly, she slowly spun around to see an old, haggard man with white hair, frail and hunched over. He leaned on a cane that reached right past his hip, his expression without judgment, as if her presence was to be expected. The creature ran up to its master, who leaned down and scooped it up.

Her mind spun as she struggled to recall how to form words. "Um...yes. Yes, it is, sir."

He sighed in admiration, walking to her side and tracking his finger over the symbols. "The ancient language of Kalpana. I've spent my whole life trying to decode it, just so I can read these books. Some of them thousands of years old! And yet, here I am, shriveling up like a dried grape, and this is all I have managed to map out."

In hopes the man wouldn't realize she was an intruder, she nodded stiffly without saying a word. The creature in his arms chirped as he stroked its fur. "Seems like you already met my friend, Revere. A little rascal, this one is. But I'm surprised! He usually stays away from unfamiliar faces."

"Mhm."

The man then side-eyed her, tilting his head to get a better look at her. "You're not supposed to be here, are you?"

Crap.

"I'm sorry." She stepped away towards the door. "I didn't mean to intrude. I was just looking, and I thought...well, nevermind. So sorry for bothering you sir."

Maya heard him yell after her to wait, but she refused to look back as she jogged down the hall, far away from the library. If someone like Talon saw her snooping around, there was no doubt in her mind that she'd be branded as a Tenebris—whatever that meant.

With her breath labored, she tried to find something she recognized from the night before, something that would lead her back to where she appeared in the realm, but nothing of the sort had been found when Maya's ear caught distant footsteps. She immediately stopped. Spinning around, she searched for somewhere to hide. The footsteps grew louder, and in a split second decision, she slipped through a room to her side, closing the door slowly behind her.

A feeling of uneasiness washed over her as she studied her surroundings. Unlike the library, the room was more modern. More lab-like. It had no natural light, and the bulbs hummed as it brightened the room. Two sleek metal desks were pushed against the side walls with spinning chairs placed on top of them. A putrid aroma filled her nostrils, and she recognized it immediately. It was the smell she had encountered when she had emerged with her sister from their hidden bunker: the smell of death.

A tremor made its way to her hands. In the far back of the room, a metal door stood ominously. It was propped open just the slightest bit. Its aura made Maya want to run far away, but she swallowed back her fear and moved closer to the door, equally curious to discover what was hidden behind it as she was desperate to hide from whoever was walking around.

The door creaked loudly as she opened it, causing her to flinch. A steep staircase lay behind it that seemed to never end, leading down into a dark abyss. Maya searched for a light switch on the wall, but the only thing she could feel was a sconce, the torch it once held removed. From the darkness echoed the sound of blowing wind, which almost sounded like soft whispers.

This is a bad idea, she thought to herself as she took a step down the steep stairs. She had not a clue what dangers could be at the bottom, but the sound of someone entering the cold room made the decision for her.

Maya pressed her back against the wall, not daring to breathe as the man from the library walked around the room with his pet Revere in his arms. However, once he started to near the door, Revere squirmed and jumped out of his grasp, sprinting away from the room. The man called after his pet and followed it, allowing her to finally relax.

As she continued down, it took too long for her to notice the chattering wind had stopped. And by the time she did, she had already been spotted.

"Hey!" Maya heard the masculine voice shout from the dark staircase, the stranger's figure illuminated by the faint light of a torch. *"Stop where you are!"*

Footsteps echoed as the man ran up the stairs, and Maya felt fear surge through her. Turning on her heel, she sprinted back up into the room and to the exit. Her heart pounded as she crossed the two tables. She nearly reached the hall, but at the last second, someone grabbed her arm and swung her around.

The man seemed to be in his late twenties to early thirties and had a rugged look. His strength was visible, even through his terribly beaten up and loose-fitting outfit. He was covered with dirt and scratches. His dirty-blond hair was chaotic and short stubble covered the lower half of his face. Thick dark eyebrows glowered down at her, making anger obvious in his features.

"And who might you be, huh?" The stranger squeezed her arm in an all too familiar way. She was transported to the night before, the man's face replaced with Broth's. Terror flooded her veins and before she knew it, she had kicked the man's knee, causing him to grunt in pain and release his grip just enough where she could wiggle out of his grasp.

Maya stepped back, holding her arm with her other hand. The man sucked in a breath, gritting his teeth. He then looked back at her, his anger now a raging fire.

"Why, you little–" He took one step toward her before another, sweeter voice spoke over him.

"Stop it, Griffin."

A lady stood at the back metal door. Soft, light brown waves reached all the way to her lower back. She wore a simple blouse, similar to what Maya's mother used to always wear, and her smile was soft as she made eye contact with her. "You must be Amie."

It took Maya a moment to remember the nickname she had chosen before she nodded slowly.

The man named Griffin jutted a thumb at her. "You know this kid?"

"Not officially." Walking with her arm stretched out, the woman shook Maya's hand. "My name is Halo. Talon and Kai told me a little bit about you. And I have to say, I've been pretty excited to meet the girl who managed to become omniscient."

Griffin's jaw went slack. "You're joking." Maya's attention was then drawn to another pair of footsteps running up the stairs. The metal door swung open, revealing a panting Kai.

"Every single time," he said with a dramatic flare. "Next time you guys leave me down there, I will–" His irritated rant was cut off when he caught sight of Maya standing on the other side of the room. "Oh, hey, stranger. Glad you made it back." He waved to her.

Maya offered him an awkward wave in return.

Griffin pinched the bridge of his nose. "Nice to know everyone already heard about this little development and didn't bother telling me." The more the man spoke, the more Maya noticed what she thought to be a strange accent she'd later learn to be South African. He turned around to face her. "So, *maatjie*, why are you really here?"

Maya cleared her throat to speak, but Kai talked for her. "For once in your life, could you not be such a brute?"

"Oh, don't be a suck-up. It is an entirely appropriate question. Someone new comes in and you're ready to kiss their *gat*. If this kid really has become an Omni, what's to stop her from having been a Lucid before, huh? From being a Lucid now?"

Kai's face paled slightly and Griffin crossed his arms. "You didn't think about that, now did you?" Kai's silence answered for him.

"He may have not," Halo interjected, "but Talon did. That's what I'm here for."

The woman moved to her side, smiling all the while. Maya, on the other hand, stepped back at the sudden movement, wrapping her arms around her chest. Noticing her discomfort, Halo said, "Don't worry, this won't hurt. All I'm going to do is run a test in your mind that will tell us whether or not you are Lucid."

"And if I am?"

Griffin stepped forward. "Then have fun in the Pit."

She had no idea what the Pit was, but she didn't get the chance to ask before Halo blocked her vision and pressed the tips of her fingers against Maya's temples, shutting her eyes and delving into her mind.

"I am just looking for your memories." Maya jumped when Halo's voice appeared loud in her mind. *"If you are passive, then there will be no resistance."*

It was an odd feeling, having someone dig through your mind. There was almost a tickling sensation as Halo poked and prodded. While Maya wasn't experiencing her thoughts like a dream, she could visualize what the woman was doing. The itch had moved to the back of her brain when in Maya's vision she pictured something similar to a doorway, leading to the depths of her consciousness. She knew all her memories were back there, the good and the bad—mostly the bad—and she felt herself squirm at the prospect of someone seeing such a raw part of herself.

"She's taking too long," Maya heard Griffin mutter under his breath.

"It's different for everyone," Kai defended. "Chill out, Griffin."

The pressure got stronger as Halo's mind shoved against the door, and Maya had no control when she pushed back, the force in her mind instantly disappearing. Halo came back with a gasp, as though she had been submerged under water.

"Halo!" Kai ran up to help the woman steady herself while Griffin demanded to know what happened, keeping a piercing gaze on Maya, who struggled to swallow. She and Halo made eye contact, and her face paled. There was no doubt; she failed the test.

Griffin then stormed towards her and jutted a finger into her chest. "What did you do?"

Maya's panicked thoughts spiraled as she waited for Halo to answer Griffin.

"She did nothing," Halo said. "I'm just a bit lightheaded after such a long day. You have no need to worry, Griffin. She was a passive dreamer prior to becoming omniscient."

Maya forced herself to hold back her shock as Kai released a relieved sigh. The statement, however, didn't seem to bring any assurance to Griffin. The strong man grunted and stormed away, muttering under his breath, *"Still don't trust her a bit."*

After Griffin left, Kai moved up next to her, nudging her playfully and said, "Knew you weren't dangerous."

Maya had to swallow back her guilt. "Right."

She tensed up as a hand was placed on her shoulder. Halo squeezed it gently as she asked Kai to leave the two of them alone for a bit. The boy shrugged before exiting, and when Maya was sure Kai was out of hearing range, she turned her attention back to the woman who had previously entered her mind. Halo wore an expression that couldn't be deciphered.

"Why did you lie?" Maya spoke softly. She didn't know how she'd done it, but Maya knew that she had stopped Halo from viewing that specific memory. Something only a Lucid could do.

She still had yet to know exactly how dangerous a Lucid could be, but even so, she knew that even the possibility of being one terrified the people of Kalpana almost as much as the Tenebris. So how could this woman keep something like that a secret?

Halo placed a hand on top of hers. She sat in silence, pondering before she answered. "There has been...history here. Terrible things have happened because of Lucids. Lives had been lost. And for a Lucid to be aware of this world and still have the power to control it? It scares them."

"It doesn't scare you?"

She smiled lightly. "You don't strike me as the dangerous type. Even if you have this ability, I don't see you intentionally using it in ill-will."

Oh, Maya could guarantee that. Then again...she didn't even know how to use this so-called ability. Blocking the memory had been a subconscious effort, just as escaping her dream had been. Whatever Halo believed she could do, Maya clearly didn't have control over it.

And that brought along another, even more worrisome thought.

"I won't tell the others about this," Halo continued, taking Maya's mind off of her ever-growing worries. "If I were you, I'd do the same. The ones out there are good people, but even good people can make poor decisions out of fear. If they learn that you have kept this secret, they would think you, and even I, are Tenebris." The woman must have noticed the way Maya's posture sank and Halo's tone softened. "I'm so sorry you have to keep a secret this big, especially being so new. It's not fair to you. But it is very important to not tell anyone you are Lucid, for your own safety. Do you understand?"

"Yes."

So much for an escape.

Halo then stood up, straightening her pale yellow blouse. "Well, you better head over back to Kai. I may have been excited to meet you, but he's been ecstatic. Something tells me he's a little more than happy to have someone new to talk to in this realm." Maya bit her lip, not knowing whether to tell her that he seemed more annoyed toward her than anything.

"Thank you," she told Halo as she got up herself, having no better way to express her gratitude.

The woman only smiled. "If you ever need answers or just relief from this secret, I'll be here."

Chapter Nine

"WHERE REFLECTIONS DON'T EXIST"

KAI WAS LEANING AGAINST a large vase in the garden when Maya walked out of the castle. He sported a frown and watched disinterested as the bigger blonde pulled weeds from the soil. His face, however, lit up at the sight of her, only for the hand he was using to support himself to slip and the vase to fall over. The boy barely caught it before it hit the floor.

Maya covered her mouth with her hand to hide the smile at the klutzy boy. Jane didn't share the same courtesy, with a high-pitched noise between a snort and a giggle escaping from her nose, and Kai sent her a glare before he stood up, straightening out his maroon shirt.

The boy cleared his throat. "Well, um. Follow me, Amie."

"Have fun on the tour!" Jane said as they walked away, and it took all of Maya's willpower not to chuckle when Kai's nose scrunched up in detestment. That—paired with his tight, stiff movements—made it look like he was holding in a large stool as he led her away.

It was in that moment that Maya's brain helpfully decided to remind her of the earlier revelation with Halo, and as quickly as the urge to laugh had emerged, it vanished.

Maya followed Kai around the side of the palace. She felt the cold rough stone under her fingertips and she was once again amazed of how real the dream world seemed to be.

Obviously, she now knew that Kalpana wasn't simply a "dream world" but another realm or dimension in its entirety. Meaning it *was* real...technically. But it still baffled her when a sensation like running her hand against a stone wall would be just as vibrant as it was while she was awake, with not a hint of cloudiness hovering over the scene.

Maya let herself become distracted with the thoughts and implications of Kalpana. It was much more appealing to try and solve universal puzzles than to dwell on the possible consequences of her being as dangerous as Kalpana's inhabitants believed.

Her existential problem-solving was abruptly interrupted however when Kai stopped, causing Maya to run into him. She quickly snapped back to reality and stepped away, feeling heat spread across her face.

Her mouth was already forming an apology when Kai spoke. "So, stranger, now that we're away from Jane, how do you feel about doing something fun?"

Maya shook off her embarrassment and raised an eyebrow. "I thought you were supposed to give me a tour?" *A tour that is very much needed.*

Kai sighed loudly, looking up dramatically to the sky. "Yes, I know. But a tour of the camp—which, I must tell you, is extremely disappointing—can be done any day. What I want to do is only possible at a certain time of year. And considering spring is almost over, it might not even work tomorrow. So please?"

Maya was about to comment on how it was autumn—not spring—until she realized that it was more than possible for Kalpana to have different seasonal changes than Pennsylvania.

"Do you *want* me to get in trouble?"

The boy didn't comment and continued to stare at her with pleading eyes. Maya didn't know what it was about it that made her falter, but she found herself yielding despite her internal protests. A loud groan escaped her lips. "I guess I could wait a day..."

A grin broke out across Kai's face and he shoved his hands in his pockets, pulling out a handful of round cream-colored pebbles that he plopped in her hands. Maya's jaw hung slack as he dug into his pocket again and somehow pulled out even *more* of the small oval-shaped rocks.

"What–"

"Nope. No questions until we get there."

"Get *where*?" she called out as Kai walked around the overgrown gate. Maya did a slight jog to match his pace.

"Nuh uh. That's a question!"

She huffed under her breath.

The two of them walked to where a field of tall bushes had been hidden. They weren't brown or stiff nor did they scratch her legs as she pushed her way through them; they were a dark purple and soft to the touch. A scent akin to fresh rain sinking into a dirt road filled her nostrils, bringing about memories of the times when Mother Nature's strength would give her an off day from farm-work. Its leaves were so thick and tall that soon the bushes were all she could see.

Panic filled her for a brief moment when Kai disappeared, only to dissipate when she heard him call out, "You coming or not?"

Rolling her eyes, Maya followed the sound of his voice and parted the purple leaves. The thick bushes ended, opening up to a scene that left her awestruck.

It was a sea of a thousand crystals that reflected the magnificent starry sky. They varied from appearing almost powder-like to being as tall as the pecan nut trees her parents used to own. An ever so slight tint of purple could be seen in the otherwise clear gems. A few feet ahead, Kai stood just before the breathtaking landscape, watching her with a stupidly wide grin on his face. "You sure are easy to impress," he said teasingly, and Maya immediately closed her agape mouth.

"Not everyone gets to see a crystal forest every day," she retorted.

"Well don't worry, now you'll be able to gaze upon it whenever you're here. And this isn't even the impressive part. Come on." Kai grabbed a hold of her hand and pulled her into the reflective crystals. The ground transformed from grass to glass, slick under her feet. The sound of their footsteps ricocheted off the tall prisms.

They made it nearly two meters before Maya's foot slipped from underneath her, sending her falling face-first into Kai's back, which sent him tumbling down with her. She landed on top, bumping her jaw against his elbow and wincing.

The boy groaned in pain beneath her. "Did you forget how to walk too?" He managed to wheeze out and she rolled off of him.

"I don't" —Maya attempted to stand, but lost her grip, falling back down onto the slippery surface. She blew her hair out of her face—"have amnesia," she finished.

"If you say so." Standing up with relative ease, he straightened his clothing. "Oh, and a quick tip: you should be on your toes. Makes walking a whole lot easier."

Kai held out a hand for her to grab and brought her to her feet. Maya instantly turned away, muttering a quick thank you. She shifted her weight to the balls of her feet and held onto Kai's shoulder for support. His frame was sturdy and strong and moved with a confidence that spoke of experience walking on the glass-like floor. He remained her brace until they finally stopped before a large black rock structure. Its knobbly texture grew up from the ground like stalagmite. The sharp difference from the crystal sea made it stick out like a false chord in a piano concerto.

"*This* is supposedly more impressive than the crystals we just passed?" Maya said skeptically.

Kai tsked. "You'll be apologizing for ever doubting me in a second. You still got those pebbles I gave you?" She dug through her short pockets and revealed them to him. He grinned and took out his own stash, pulling Maya level with him as he crouched down. "Okay, now you're going to aim for the tip of one of those rocks and throw one of these at it. The closer to the tip, the better."

Maya raised an eyebrow, but did what he said. Winding her arm back, she watched the pebble fly through the air as it left her hand. It made contact with a quiet *ping* before falling to the ground.

She drew in a breath when the black stone instantly shattered as if it were the shell of an egg. Behind the layer of rough skin was hidden beauty. The pebble transformed the rock into another purple crystal that shimmered brightly in comparison to the others around it. It cracked all the way down until it reached the ground.

Kai nudged her. "Satisfying, isn't it?" Maya was sure her jaw was hanging open once again, but this time she didn't feel the need to close it. Taking another small rock in her hand, she threw it at the black structure. This one landed closer to the base, so she aimed and threw it again. And again.

"Hey, slow down!" Kai told her as she started rapid firing and shattering stones left and right. "Leave some for me!"

Maya laughed as he began throwing the pebbles as well. The two of them made it their mission to see who could hit the tallest pillar first. She worked her way up from the base and slowly narrowed the target down, only for Kai to make the perfect throw that shattered the stone entirely.

"Yes!" He cheered, and Maya groaned and leaned back, turning her gaze to the sky.

For a moment, all the pain she had experienced the past couple of days became a distant memory. For a moment, a rare sense of pure unfiltered happiness swelled in her chest. There was no Broth, or SCRO, or fear. Maya could create a different story for herself here. She could be an entirely different person and no one would have to know the truth. Suddenly, the thought of lying felt much more attractive.

"You have no idea how long I've been waiting to do this with someone," Kai said with a sigh. Maya sat up, giving the boy her full attention.

"No one else wanted to do this with you?" she asked.

He brought his knees up to his chest. "Everyone only has about two hours in Kalpana every night. They each have their own work that needs to be finished before waking up. With such a short window, there isn't much time for hanging out and having fun. You'll probably get your own job soon too. So it's better to do nice things like this before Talon decides to put you to use."

Maya gazed down at her hands, feeling the joy she had felt slip away. She didn't want this part of her life to become just like what she did for Broth, where she spent hours doing different chores to earn her stay. Couldn't this be different? Didn't she deserve at least that?

"Work like what?" she asked quietly.

Kai gave her a smile. "I never told you what we do here, did I?"

Maya shook her head, and he rested back on his arms. "You know the man we brought back yesterday? He's a regular person, just like you, except he's not aware of all... this. He doesn't see the trees or the grass or the sky. He only sees the fantasies his brain makes up. His dreams. And because of this lack of awareness, sleepwalkers are vulnerable to nightdwellers and other slaves of Tenebris who can enter their minds.

"I don't think humans were ever meant to be aware of this realm, but we are. So we do what we can and protect those who can't protect themselves. If we run into a sleepwalker, we bring them to camp and shield them away from what gives them nightmares. If we run into a nightdweller, we make sure it doesn't escape. And if there's ever anyone new, we make sure they won't pose a risk to those we are trying to keep safe. That's why Griffin was so tough on you earlier. Not saying he was necessarily right to act the way he did. He always assumes the worst of everyone and is hard to soften up, so I won't be surprised if he treats you coldly for a while. But don't take it personally. Unless you're some kind of sinister manipulator that has a hidden agenda"—he chuckled, as if the prospect of her having that ability was impossible to imagine—"you'll be fine. And while I might not fully understand how you got here, I believe you. For now."

Maya felt a lump form in her throat. Such words she assumed were meant to be comforting, but the strange boy didn't know what she really was, and when he did, he would leave her faster than a cat tossed in a bath. Because she was dangerous. Because she was Lucid.

Halo had told her to keep it a secret, and now she understood how necessary it was. They were trying so hard to keep everyone safe. Any threat would be immediately removed. They would banish her, even if she tried to explain how she didn't have any desire to hurt anyone. Just when Maya had started to imagine a future here, the inevitable outcome made itself known.

Griffin may have been bitter. Talon may have been intimidating. Jane may have had her suspicions. But she could handle them. Maybe even grow closer to them. Halo—and even Kai—had already shown more friendship to her than she had experienced in years. It was only the second day of knowing the other world existed, but she already had formed a connection to it. Maya wasn't ready to lose it all just yet.

"Thanks," she said. "But..." *Why the heck would you believe me?* "You've only known me for a day."

"I mean, I did say for now. But to be fair, you're not exactly the most intimidating specimen." Maya rolled her eyes—an action the boy continued to cause her to do. "And—well, ulterior motives aren't hidden very well here."

At the last statement, Maya tilted her head in confusion, and he elaborated. "Look down at the reflections on the ground. Notice anything off?"

Her perplexity grew as she looked at the glass-like floor. The swirling clouds and yellow stars were cast back so clearly, it was as if she and Kai were sitting on the sky. The large black rock and crystals were there as well, just as vibrant. Everything in her line of sight reflected off the smooth ground.

Everything except them.

Maya hovered her hand just over the surface, but nothing was mirrored. It was as if she wasn't even there.

"How is that possible?" Maya murmured. She looked back at Kai, who was playing with a metal chain necklace she hadn't noticed before. He rolled the coin at the end of it between his fingers.

"It's because you aren't from here," he said. "Only things created in Kalpana have reflections. The people you see here are just subconscious projections of themselves. Well, I say subconscious. Some say it's their soul. But either way, their bodies are still in the other realm, sleeping tightly.

"No one has control of the way their subconscious displays them. Someone could look completely different in their mind than in reality. They could be a different size, a different age, a different anything. Then there are some who might look very similar to their actual self."

"So you could be an old man, and I would have no idea?" Maya interjected. The idea of him being an elderly man brought a surge of amusement.

The boy laughed and answered cheekily, "I don't know, I could be." Maya gave him a light shove, and he laughed again. "Luckily for you, I happen to look pretty similar all the time—based on the descriptions I've heard of myself." He shook his head to get back on track. "The point is, it's impossible to hide your true perception of who you are. If you plan on doing anything harmful to anyone, or have done so in the past, it will be noticeable. Because even if you don't think you feel guilt, your subconscious does. You will look filthy, torn up, ugly. And *you* can't have any ill intent because, well…" He coughed.

The left side of her mouth tilted up. "Well?"

Now it was his turn to look perturbed as he rubbed the back of his neck. "N-nevermind."

"Describe me," Maya said after a moment of silence. "Then I can see how similar I look to my actual self."

The request had taken him off guard. Kai cleared his throat and ran his fingers through his hair. "Well…you're a girl…"

She chuckled at the uncertainty in his tone. "Go on."

His shoulders relaxed and a playful smile rested on his face. "You have brown curly hair, but there's streaks of blond here and there. And it's so messy that it looks closer to a lion's mane than anything else." He snickered at that. "You've got a loose purple shirt and brown shorts on. Both kind of dirty and wrinkled, but the hardworking type of dirty, like you were working in a garden. Your skin tone is tanner than me, though that's not the most impressive feat. And your eyes…"

He made eye contact with her and she was immediately tempted to look away. "They're brown, but they're not dark. They're big and bright." A crease formed between his brows. "You look tired though, like you've been single-handedly holding up the sky. You got bruises under your eyes. And there's a scar that goes across your cheek."

"A scar?" Maya felt the side of her face. The rest of what he said had been more or less accurate, even if stated to poke fun of her, but she knew for sure that even though she had many scars across her body for various different reasons, her face had always been spared.

"Okay, now it's your turn," Kai interrupted her thoughts. "Describe me." He slouched back and crossed his arms with attempted formidability, causing Maya to blow out a breath.

"You are a boy," she said. "Your hair is black and curly. Your eyes are blue. You have a silver chain necklace around your neck, and your shirt is a strange mix between red and brown. The sleeves are rolled up, and the hole you fit your head through is folded open. Lace is used to tie it closed. The lace actually runs halfway down your shirt..."

Maya was aware of the way she was rambling on about his shirt, but she had just noticed the surprising amount of muscle the boy sported, despite appearing skinny. His shoulders were strong and wide and his exposed forearms had a slight bulge. The lace of his shirt was loose enough for her to see a small amount of his chest, which also sported a fair amount of muscle. It was something Maya was not used to seeing, and she found herself staring before snapping out of it.

Blush covered her cheeks as Kai noticed what she was focusing on and he snickered. "Don't be ashamed," he teased, "I've been told I have the peak physique."

Maya cringed at the statement, annoyance flaring back up. "I'm starting to think your subconscious projection is just a representation of your ego."

He put a hand to his chest in an immensely dramatic fashion. "I'll have you know that I am an incredibly humble human being."

She snorted. "Obviously." Maya was about to follow it up with another retort when a putrid smell filled her nostrils. The temperature dropped and an irrational sense of fear reached her nerves. She tensed up, her heart rate doubling in pace.

She looked over to see if Kai was feeling what she was experiencing. He looked around frantically, hands balled up into fists.

Without warning, Kai grabbed her arm and pulled her behind the black rock, crouching down and motioning her to do the same. Maya bent down next to him and tried to steady her breathing.

"Is it a nightdweller?" she whispered.

Kai nodded, eyebrows furrowed. "But this doesn't make any sense. They're never this close to camp. It would only be here if..." He peeked around the rock to see where it was before quickly turning back. His eyes widened when he turned his gaze to her. "Your two hours are nearly up."

Maya looked down at her disappearing hands and then back at him with a worried expression.

Kai was digging through his pocket, pulling out the small spear from the first time they had met. Its red glow emanated off of his face. "I'll be fine," he assured her. "Go live your other life. See you tomorrow, lioness."

"Seriously? You are not—"

Her response was cut off. Swinging the weapon back, his eyes focused past her. He started swinging it forward and Maya braced herself by putting out her hands and shutting her eyes.

The next thing she knew, Broth was tossing away Maya's covers, waking her from her sleep.

He glared down at her with cold eyes, a scroll tightly gripped in his hand.

"Get up, kid. We're moving."

Chapter Ten

"The World That Lays Beyond"

MULTIPLE EMOTIONS ERUPTED AS a reaction to this statement.

Whiplash—she was still dwelling on what happened to Kai.

Shock—not in a million years had she imagined moving someplace else.

Disbelief—Broth had always vocalized never wanting to leave the home his wife had lived in

Apprehension—she would finally be able to see the outside world after years of being sheltered.

And then realization—she knew why they were moving.

Maya had seen the letter they sent.

Broth was taking her to SCRO.

Instantly she was awake, sliding on her slippers and tying up her hair. She followed as Broth hobbled out of her room, throwing the remains of the scroll in the garbage. The living room already started to appear more barren, with every small trinket removed. The faded red walls bore no paintings or portraits. The unwashed blankets that always lay on the reclining chair were nowhere in sight. On the rug was an open suitcase, packed with plaid shirts and worn-out jeans.

Broth was in the kitchen, packing utensils faster than she'd ever thought possible. A frantic look was hidden behind his eyes, and Maya started to wonder if he was in trouble with SCRO as well. And if it had anything to do with the escape of her sister.

"What ya' doing just standing there?" he scolded her, bringing Maya back to attention. "Get all the junk ya' need to survive. No extra stuff. Then you're gonna let out all the chicks and pigs into the wild. We're leaving right after."

Maya studied his face for any indication that this was all a ploy. Sure, it was a day's travel to the nearest town, and they'd have to stay overnight, but that didn't require bringing everything they could take from the house. And to let go of all the animals she had tended to for nearly eight years?

"Why?" The question weaseled its way out of her mouth before she could swallow it back. She flinched prematurely, knowing questions wouldn't leave her in Broth's good graces.

As expected, he looked towards her with blazing eyes. "'Cause I said so. Now get to work!"

Without turning back, Maya hustled to her room. She folded her thin blanket and placed it neatly next to her bed, her stained pillow on top of it. She then bent down onto her knees, reaching underneath the mattress and pulling out a crossword booklet. A thin layer of dust was scattered on top of it and Maya blew it off.

Broth had said not to bring anything that she could live without, but the book stuffed under her bed was more than just paper and puzzles. Inside were feelings. Memories. Holding it, she could still see Amarie and herself solving the questions when Broth was either drunk or asleep because he was drunk. It was the one thing she was better at than her sister, and she had always cherished that small victory.

Stepping back, Maya observed the room one last time. So many moments had been spent inside these walls. But she wouldn't miss it. And when she found her sister, this house would hopefully be a distant memory.

Maya placed her three outfits folded on top of the blankets. In an old brown cinch bag, she shoved in her toothbrush and toothpaste, and then placed the booklet inside as well.

Trying to avoid Broth's attention, she gently put down what she packed against the wall next to the things Broth planned to take with them. In a container, he had brought along a framed picture of him and a woman Maya had never met that was previously hanging above the fireplace. Broth rarely ever talked about her, but sometimes when he was drunk he would go on rants about a woman named Susan who had once been his wife.

Maybe we truly are moving, she thought to herself. For what other reason would there be for Broth to bring along such personal items?

Either way, that didn't change the fact that whether he was planning to move permanently or just temporarily, she would soon be given to SCRO. *One thing at a time.* Maya could worry about escaping the organization on the way to the city. Right now, she needed to complete the other task Broth had given her: release the farm animals.

She swung on her jacket and took a step outside, shivering at the chilly temperature. The sky was a dark gray and a thin line of snow covered the ground, with flurries falling from the sky—the first sign of the approaching winter, surely to be full of powerful blizzards and unbelievably low temperatures. The screen door was loud as it closed shut. Maya rubbed her hands together and shoved them in her jacket pockets before heading over to the shed, grabbing as many sacks of chicken feed she could hold.

Her heart sank in her chest as she opened the chicken coop door and made a trail of seeds leading outside. They wouldn't last very long without her bringing them food and water. And with the increasingly low temperatures, it wouldn't be long before they froze to death. Maya wanted to shove them all back into the cage and stay with them forever when they started pecking at the ground and leaving their containment. Still, she restrained herself, turning away from the sight and to the sheep.

Out of all the animals, she was least worried about the woolly creatures. She only dumped out one sack, and left the wire gate open. Cloud, who was faring well despite his injury, was the first at the food, barely looking at her as he ate the food. She gently stroked his wool, already feeling that sense of loss for the sheep.

Finally, she made her way to the pigs. Her eyes formed tears as she watched them squeal at the sight of her, running up and scavenging her hands for food. A painful laugh came from her chest as she threw her arms around Lewis and squeezed. Maya could still see him as a baby, struggling to walk with his three legs. She could see him as he grew, playing with Bernard and Russell. She could see him as he mourned, resting against the body of his friend. At that moment, Maya had seen herself in the animal. They both were victims of the war. They both had someone stolen from them that they loved.

Amarie used to make fun of her for having such a strong connection to a pig, but her sister could never understand. Amarie was always so strong and skilled at hiding her emotions—so skilled that sometimes Maya would forget that she had lost her parents from the war as well. But whenever she felt alone or like she was the only one who struggled, she would play with Lewis, who bore his suffering on his skin.

"I'm sorry," she whispered to the pig as her lip started to quiver. "I'll miss you guys."

Bernard nudged her side and she wrapped an arm around him as well. She sat there for a moment, struggling to find the energy to abandon the only friends she had in this world.

"Maya!" Broth's shrill voice caused her to flinch. "Hurry up!"

With one last look at her two pink friends, Maya moved away and stepped outside of the coop, hanging her head low. Two open sacs of corn were left next to her, which would hopefully last them a week.

She choked as she tried to swallow down the enormous weight of guilt. She couldn't look back. Couldn't bear to see them for the last time.

Over the next hour, she and Broth packed everything they needed into his truck until each square inch was filled to the brim with everything from pillows to wall decors, save for the driver's seat and a small opening in the passenger's. The truck was gray and run down, paint peeling off. It had no shine to it. Mud splashed on the sides. The vehicle was so ancient that it still used wheels to move.

Maya slipped into the open spot, pulling up her knees to avoid stepping on the boxes at her feet. Broth slid in next to her, slamming the side door shut and starting the vehicle with his keys.

The house disappeared too fast for Maya to comprehend, and she twisted her neck back to observe the miserable dwelling in all of its inglorious solitude. Maya may never have to see it again, but the pain and fear she had experienced on its property was permanently instilled within her.

The road's bumps jerked the car roughly and Maya quickly put her seatbelt on. It had been so long since the last time she had ridden in a car, herself being eight and her sister ten. They had spent the months prior to Broth in the hands of SCRO, constantly being moved from one side of the country to the other. She could remember a mask of some sort being placed over the faces of the workers as they would present the two of them to different individuals. Amarie would always make such a fuss, however, that they would get rejected each time and replaced with another, more polite young lady or gentleman.

Eventually, their journey led to the grouchy old man with his vile breath and unwashed clothing, who stuffed them in his old pickup truck without a single word. Even from the start, Broth made it abundantly clear how much he despised his new burdens. Her sister had said a snarky remark about him taking care of them on the first car trip to his house, which cost her a slap across the face. And there, Maya knew that this new caretaker wouldn't be the slightest bit like her deceased parents.

Her eyes focused distantly on the foreign scenery that lay beyond the window's glass. Rolling hills extended as far as the eye could see, but it wasn't like the breathtaking green hills of her dreams. Save for some spots of snow, it was brown. Dead. The trees that peppered the landscape weren't much livelier. It created the same pang in her chest that she would feel any time she'd read about the nuclear war or see its effects on the farm animals. Maya couldn't remember much of her life before the war destroyed it, but surely the world was once healthier than *this*.

Time passed by like stone being eroded by water. The car hopped with every small rock in its path. Boxes in the back would topple over each other, and utensils inside would spill out. But besides that, the trip was soundless. There was no small talk, or even a radio, to fill in the silent void.

It had been around an hour since they left when ice rain started falling from the sky, which made it impossible to see into the distance. Raindrops trickled down the window and Maya watched them race to the bottom. The windshield wipers ticked back and forth, lulling her to sleep. But it wasn't restful. She would merely close her eyes before a bump on the road would cause her head to bounce against the window seal.

When the rain finally stopped falling and the wipers stopped going, it was once again quiet, leaving her thoughts louder than ever.

I need to escape before SCRO captures me, her mind whispered. *But how,* was the question.

It became clear to her as they continued down the road that she was incredibly oblivious as to where they were heading, or what they were heading into. After all, Broth had never explicitly stated why they were moving.

He was the only one that could answer Maya's questions, but bringing up such a topic to him terrified her just as much as the nightdwellers did. She was certain the only way she had survived this long in his care was by flying under the radar and only interacting when absolutely necessary. Sparking up a conversation would be a terribly immature move.

But I need to know.

A debate ensued between the voices inside of her head. One choice would keep her safe for now. The other would possibly keep her safe in the future.

It took Maya another hour before she finally managed to summon enough courage to bring up the topic.

"Where are we going, Mr. Broth?" Her voice was slightly more high-pitched than usual. She waited in apprehension for Broth's response.

"Blacksburg," he said bluntly. Broth continued to keep his eyes trailed straight ahead as he had the entire car ride. But that quickly changed when Maya asked her next question.

"What does SCRO want from me?"

His neck snapped her direction, wide eyes staring at her with the same panicked look she saw earlier in the kitchen. The truck skirted to a stop and Broth turned his back completely to face her.

"How'd you know 'bout SCRO, kid?" His tone was low. Dangerous.

Maya swallowed down her fear. "The woman that visited yesterday. I didn't try to hear her—I promise. But her voice carried and I was able to figure out where she was from. It was an accident, but please sir, why do they still want me?"

A flash of anger was seen in his features and Maya gripped the seat's arm rests tightly.

She released a breath of relief when Broth slouched back and turned the truck back into drive.

"No reason to concern yourself with."

She bit her lip, knowing very well that there was indeed a reason to be concerned. A sweltering fire of hatred erupted in her chest. How could this man act as though nothing was wrong when he was handing her over to child abductors? *Criminals*? Maya wasn't stupid, she knew the man never cared about her or her sister's happiness. But she couldn't imagine anyone being *that* cruel.

She opened her mouth to speak again, then closed it. Broth wasn't going to answer her questions, and provoking him more than he already was wouldn't do her any good.

Her gaze was once again brought to the scene outside the window. She rested her elbow on the sill and put her head against her hand.

It was around two o'clock when Maya saw the first sign of other human life. Buildings could be seen in the distance, with expansive areas of cement ground. Granted, it didn't seem like it had been occupied by anyone for quite some time. The fences around the parking lots were filled with holes and brown with rust. Weeds grew untamed, and graffiti even more so, with the statement, *BEWARE OF THE FREAKS,* written in large font. She assumed it was a spook—a town abandoned by people in search of better resources. Most of the population was now concentrated in larger cities, like Blacksburg, leaving spooks like the ones they passed home to misfits, criminals, or those who simply couldn't afford the cost of city-life.

There were a number of spooks as they drove. Sometimes the towns looked nearly modern, with solar panel powered buildings and hover car charging stations. Others looked so broken and unruly that Maya doubted even the most desperate persons lived there.

After a few more hours, Broth must have decided they'd traveled far enough. He turned into one of the more upkept spooks and parked into an empty parking lot, the loud and severely aged engine going silent in a shaky, abrupt manner. A large, dilapidated building stood in front of them. The sign above the glass doors was unreadable, but Maya could tell it had been a supermarket. On cue, her stomach growled; she hadn't realized how hungry she was.

Broth slammed the car door with a full-armed swing so violent that Maya was surprised the old piece of metal did not fall apart. She turned her attention to the old supermarket with a hop in her step as they walked forward. She could picture herself biting into a cheese sandwich. Or a bowl of cereal. Or a cookie. Or any of the wonderful treats her parents had once fed her.

Maya stopped in front of the doors, waiting for the old man to give her permission to enter. But Broth didn't pay her any attention. Instead, he stomped towards another door to the side. The sign above that one was less faded, and Maya could make out the word, "Liquor".

Fear spiked in her chest. Broth was angry enough. The last thing he needed was to be drunk. But there was nothing Maya could do to stop it.

She took his lack of care as approval, stepping into the supermarket.

But the sight wasn't what she had come to expect.

Isles were knocked over, and while some cans lay on the floor, the majority had been scavenged. Wires from lights hung from the ceilings. Empty shopping carts were rusty. There was a quiet squeak and Maya let out a yelp as a large rat skittered over her feet, and that was when she noticed the smell: the rotting of food after months of being unrefrigerated.

She knew even before searching the bakery that she wouldn't find anything like the cookies she loved when she was young. Maya kicked the moldy box of brownies as hard as she could. Anything that had once been edible was gone.

If only that had been the case for the alcohol.

BROTH SAT ACROSS FROM her, a weak fire and their jackets the only things keeping them warm. Maya felt herself shiver and hovered her hands as close to the flames as she could without burning them.

They were in a dark small alleyway. A brick wall blocked them from behind, but they were completely exposed from the front. Broth didn't seem to care though. In his current state, Maya doubted he cared about anything.

A melody fell from the man's lips as he rocked back and forth, pouring the remains of the liquor bottle down his throat. Maya had no idea how he had managed to find any bottle of the vile drink, let alone *three*. And somehow he had finished every single one.

Maya was used to the angry Broth. The one that would scream. And yell. And throw empty bottles at her and her sister. She knew that Broth all too well. But this Broth was new. He was singing. Laughing. *Smiling*. Which somehow scared her even more.

"Too far away," he moaned, slurred. Maya peered up, hoping the man was talking to himself and not her. She should have known better.

"Come o'er here." He flimsily gestured her over. Maya's legs trembled as she stood up and walked around the fire. She sat down a foot away from him, hugging her knees, not daring to look at the man.

"You listen," he muttered. "You always listen."

And I hate myself for it.

Without warning, he grasped her hand. Maya resisted the immediate urge to yank back.

"Look at me," Broth said. At first, she didn't comply. Then he said it again, a hint of that angry Broth shining through. "*Look at me.*"

Tears pricked her eyes as she reluctantly met his gaze. In it was longing. *Hunger.*

"Just like Susan," he whispered, rubbing her arm with his thumb.

Where was her sister when she needed her? A singular tear fell down her cheek as he moved his hand to her face, caressing it.

"Why'd the radiation have to take her, huh?" Broth asked as if she was the one who had the answer. "Why'd she hafta die?" His questions morphed into almost incomprehensible blubbering, a melancholy tone seeping through every word. "We-we were happy. Why the war gotta ruin everything, h-huh?"

Maya could sense his mood change once again, in the swift way that would only occur in a muddled and confused mind. It chilled her severely, especially when his crying suddenly stopped. "You-you can help me," he said quietly, that hunger filling his eyes again. Heart rate speeding up, Maya attempted to wiggle free of his grip, but Broth grabbed her other hand, pulling her close.

"You can help me." She felt his breath on her neck, the smell causing her to gag.

"Let me go," she pleaded. "P-please."

Either he didn't hear her or didn't care. She felt every touch of the man as though he was pricking her with needles. The press of his chest against her side as he drew a ragged breath. The growing pain as he dug his large fingers deeper into her arms. The rough bump of his head as he rested it on her shoulder. Maya let out a whimper.

"Mr. Broth, *please-*" she stopped. Broth's head had gone limp. As had his grip on her arms.

Not bothering to be gentle, Maya scurried away from the man as fast as she could, throwing off her jacket, which now stunk of alcohol. The air was frigid, but she couldn't get herself to put it back on. Her entire body shook uncontrollably as she studied the man from afar. He was out cold. Maya wasn't even sure he was still breathing, and her tattered heart wretchedly hoped he was not.

She fell to her knees, sobs racking her body.

I have to leave. Far away. Where Broth can never reach me again.

Half aware of her surroundings, she searched for any way to escape. She felt her way around the fire, feeling metal under her fingertips. *The car keys.*

Her heart leaped in anticipation, and Maya wasted no time picking them up. She grabbed one of the spare fire sticks and lit the top.

She didn't think as she ran down the cracked sidewalks, or through the abandoned parking lot. She didn't think as she pressed the button on the car keys, causing the truck's lights to flash twice. She didn't think as she threw open the door, sat on the seat, and turned the keys.

There was no sound.

She tried again. And again. And again. Each time more frantic, until she was yelling at the truck to work.

Maya screamed as she stepped out, slamming the door shut. *Somehow*, there was no gas left, despite being some earlier.

She grabbed her burning stick and stomped around the truck, only to find a trickle of oil flowing from it, all the way down into the gutters. And when she looked in the back of the car, the spare gas jug was gone.

The spookers had robbed them.

The stick in her hand burned out, the light disappearing along with the rush of energy she had felt. She was sure she should've felt furious. Distraught. Sad, at least.

But she felt none of that. In fact, she felt nothing at all as she walked back to the alleyway, laying on the small blanket she had brought from the house and closing her eyes. A numb sensation swept through her, a shield against a hidden torrent of emotions and tears that were writhing inside like monsters lurking in the dark.

Then there was the quiet, broken thought that echoed through her drifting consciousness. *I'll never be free.*

Chapter Eleven

"What Frees Can Conceal"

"You're back."

The beautiful world of Kalpana appeared gradually. Maya blinked her eyes rapidly, revealing a sitting Kai who wore a gentle smile on his lips. He walked over to Maya and helped her steady herself as she gripped her head with the sudden change in lighting. The touch caused her to flinch, bringing back the memory of Broth, but she hoped Kai hadn't noticed.

The scene was just how she left it—the crystal pillars standing tall on top of the reflective glass ground. A deep sigh released from the depths of her chest. If only she were as free in the awoken world as she was in this one.

Maya straightened in realization as she asked the boy, "Are you okay? What happened to the nightdweller?"

Kai waved her off. "Nothing I couldn't handle. But thank you for caring." His nonchalant tone, however, changed as he observed her closely. "Are *you* okay? You look upset."

At the boy's keen observation, Maya looked away, cursing her subconscious for allowing her emotions to be so visible. "Nothing I can't handle," she rebuked. Studying the scenery around her, she tilted her head. "Have you just been sitting here this whole time, waiting for me to come back?"

Kai cleared his throat. "Well, I haven't been here *too* long, but...yes?"

She raised an eyebrow. "A little creepy, don't you think?"

Secretly, she was slightly touched. Maya wasn't used to being cared for by anyone besides her sister, and the odd affection the boy showed, however reluctantly, was something new. Something Maya didn't know if she would ever get used to.

The thought of affection, however, caused her mind to think back to Broth holding her in a death grip. His face, so uncomfortably close...

"For your information, this is a wonderful place to hide away from responsibility," he claimed, "and I was bored."

So maybe she had gotten ahead of herself.

"We should see if Talon is here yet," Kai changed the subject, which allowed Maya to refocus. "Here." He held out his elbow and prompted her to grip it. Maya wrapped her arm around his for support and together they glided across the slick earth. They raced through the purple leaves hanging on branches of silver, color exploding through her vision in a display of unfathomable beauty. For just a moment, she forgot her fears and cast them away, leaving them littering the soft grass under her feet. Was it so impossible to stay inside Kalpana until time itself died? Where she would be sheltered from every evil that tormented her?

She knew the answer. The strangeness of its beauty and the absurdity of its entire nature only served as a reminder of what she was: an outcast. This wasn't her world. Her world was void of any sort of vibrancy, wretchedness and woe corrupting even the purest of things.

Her heart fell from its momentary altitude, joy as fleeting as a shooting star. So fragile that the softest hands could break it.

But she would be caught dead before Kai discovered the reason for her off character.

Crossing through Jane's gardens, they searched for Talon's figure inside the castle's walls, but he was nowhere in sight. They did manage to find Halo, her long light brown hair falling down her back as she watched them with caring eyes. She told them that the bald man had not made his appearance yet, but he would most likely be materializing soon. Managing to rope Maya and Kai into helping her check on the passive dreamers, she led them to a large room with a clear dome, revealing the breathtaking sky. Numerous white circles glowed from the floor. Some were empty, while others contained figures with their arms pinned to their sides and their eyes closed. Towards the back were rows of people—all different sizes, shapes, and appearances. All standing next to each other, but not registering any of their surroundings.

"This is where you bring the sleepwalkers you find?" Maya guessed, and Kai nodded.

"They are safe from nightmares here. In the dome, they can sleep in peace."

Maya looked down and found herself standing in one of the glowing circles. Moving her hand across the light absentmindedly, a rush of sadness smothered her. She had suffered through years of terrible dreams. Every night she spent reliving her worst fears with not a day's break, until she had finally gone numb. Where had she been in this realm where nightdwellers attacked her relentlessly? Where was the cage that imprisoned her located?

Kai tapped her shoulder and gave her another concerned look. "Hey, you *sure* you're okay?" This time, Maya could not find the energy to respond, which led to the crease between his eyebrows to deepen.

Halo taught them how to check if the slots were functioning correctly, which was a much-needed distraction. Each standing dreamer had a band around their head, just like the one that Kai had put on the man she had run into on the first day in Kalpana. On it, a small bulb glowed either green or red. The red ones required one of them to press the button next to it and hold it until it changed color. According to the woman, the red bulb meant that the person's actions were crossing over to the other world. While only dreamers wandering around outside of the containment could sleepwalk, they could still sleep talk, and the band was meant to prevent that.

Maya and Halo snuck a glance at each other, causing the mucous in her throat to thicken. Halo was a painful reminder of the secret she was hiding, and a part of her still worried that she would eventually reveal it to the others. Even so, she had to admit that, out of everyone in the realm, Halo was the one person she'd most prefer to know she was Lucid.

The woman offered her a reassuring smile, as if she knew what Maya had been thinking.

It was then when she noticed something shimmering just in front of the dome's entrance. It slowly grew, until she could make out an arm. Then a leg. Then the entire figure's body she could identify as Talon's. His eyes opened and he rubbed them, taking in the setting. When he made eye contact with Maya, his expression hardened, and she had to remind herself to breathe.

"Oh, Talon!" Halo moved up next to the man and gave him a light peck on the cheek. "Just on time."

Talon seemed to relax slightly as he pushed her back gently to look her in the eyes. "I assume all the dreamers have been accounted for?"

"As always."

He gave her an approving nod and turned his view to Maya and Kai, the latter offering him a fleeting wave with a quick, "Hey, Talon."

"Don't you have more important things to do, Kai?" Talon said with a stern gaze.

Kai huffed. "I was just helping—"

"I don't want to hear it. I gave you an assignment, and I expect you to complete it. Understood?"

The young boy groaned. "Fine."

"*Now,*" Talon prompted.

He put his hands up in surrender. "I'm going. I'm going." Kai turned to face Maya and gave her one last minuscule smile before exiting the room with his head down.

Talon's eyes tracked him until he was out of sight. A frown was painted on his face. He closed his eyes and took a deep breath, shoulders drooping, and Halo looked upon him with concern, placing a soft hand on his shoulder.

"I must speak to Miss Amie alone," he told Halo, not offering her a glance. The woman understood and stepped back.

"I will leave you two to it." Giving Maya a pat of reassurance, Halo left without another word.

A shiver ran down Maya's back as she played with her hands. Talon and her stood in silence for what felt like an eternity. Every second that passed heightened Maya's anxiety. She didn't dare move, nervously awaiting his next words.

Maya snuck a glance at the tall man who was staring out into the distance.

"What I am about to tell you is something that is vital," Talon stated. "Not just for you, or for us Omnis, but for everyone who inhabits this realm and the awakened one. I need you to heed what I say. Can you do that?"

Maya was slightly taken aback by the directness of his tone, but she responded nevertheless with a slightly trembling "Yes."

He gave her a brief nod before gazing upon the sleeping humans inside the glowing circles. "Look at all the dreamers that occupy this room. All of them entranced by their mind's hallucinations. Blissfully ignorant of their true vulnerability.

"Even us who have been aware of Kalpana our whole lives don't fully understand this entire reality. Among the few things we have discovered is that dreaming appears to be a way of keeping this realm hidden. Whether it's the human mind's doing or the realm itself is another matter, as is why some of us have broken through this barrier, and others have not. We must respect the fact that we are intruders—beings never meant to become self-aware inside of Kalpana. But even though this is the case, that doesn't mean we don't have a purpose here."

"That's what Kai told me," Maya noted.

"Kai is a smart boy," he agreed. "Although he tends to lack much critical thinking." Talon adjusted the cuffs of his sleeved shirt before resuming. "You, on the other hand, seem to be someone who thinks about everything profusely. I could explain the exact implications of what this obliviousness means for dreamers, but I am sure you have already created multiple scenarios where this would be an issue, as well as I could tell you exactly what you need to heed in my words, but I am sure you have already inferred that too."

Maya held her hands behind her back to prevent the temptation to fidget with them again. Of course, the man was right. From the first time she learned about the weakness dreamers had, she had been playing different ways it could place them in danger. Anything, from their darkest secrets being revealed to them wandering into an unreachable place in Kalpana to being tormented by nightdwellers for eternity, could result. And that wasn't even including the possibility of someone able to control or manipulate someone's thoughts. Maya was tempted to ask if that was something that could be done, but it didn't take much pondering to come to the conclusion that such a question better be answered by someone like Halo.

"These people are at risk, and you need to be certain I won't be a part of this risk," Maya said to answer his second assumption. "I don't know exactly what I should say to convince you that I'm trustworthy, but I can promise that I will never do anything to harm them."

Talon peered at her from the corner of his eye. "It isn't a matter of spoken words. Griffin, who it seems you have met, told me about your snooping around our camp last night."

So the older man in the library hadn't *sold her out.* Maya resisted the urge to immediately defend herself, taking a calming breath. "I know how that must have looked and your suspicion is completely justified, but I swear that I meant nothing by it. I was curious, that's all. I'm sure you can understand that."

"I do, which is why I am giving you a warning." Talon, for the first time in the entire conversation, faced her fully. "I am willing to overlook the issue this time. But this will be the *only* time. There are certain locations inside of Kalpana that are off limits, and if I catch or hear of you exploring any of them, you will be banished from here. Thrown into the Whispering Woods and into the Pit, where you will be left staring at the carved art on its walls and wondering what fate had become of the previous unfortunate souls who had ended up trapped in the same caves."

Maya's hands shook as he adjusted his sleeves again. "It may be harsh, but it is necessary. Everything in this realm works because of a delicate balance. Anything that threatens this balance must be dealt with as swiftly as possible. Have I made myself clear?"

"Yes, sir."

"Good. Now, Jane will be showing you around this place, since Kai supposedly forgot to do so yesterday."

Talon started to walk through the room's exit, but must have noticed the terror in Maya's eyes as he slowed down and sighed. "I am sorry if I scared you, Miss Amie. But I can assure you, if you listen to what I have said and follow my rules, you and I will have no problems."

She gave the man a slight nod of the head, not mustering enough courage to form words.

Jane was messing with her blond hair when Maya met her outside. A smile spread across the young woman's face when she noticed her, which took Maya by surprise. A few feet behind, Kai and Griffin were having a seemingly heated argument. Kai turned his head to look at Maya, but Griffin placed a firm hand on his back and guided him away.

Maya's eyebrows furrowed in confusion, but her focus was suddenly changed to Jane as she reached her head into her line of sight.

"Hi!" Jane said in a cheerful tone. "I know *technically* we've already met, but I don't think I made the best first impression. So let me try again: I'm Jane." She held out a hand for her to shake. "Not a nickname, my name is actually Jane. I don't see the point of making a codename for something so basic. I mean, I'm sure there are *millions* of women called Jane. Oh, and also, I love your hair."

Maya took her hand slowly, overwhelmed by the energy that radiated off the woman. "Um, thank you. My name is Amie. Again."

A good-natured laugh erupted from Jane. "You're funny." Brushing down her pink dress, she tsked. "So, that tour Kai was supposed to take you on didn't really pan out, did it?"

Maya offered her a small shrug. "He showed me the crystal formations behind the castle. But as for the castle itself, not so much."

Chuckling to herself, Jane shook her head. "That kid is truly something else, let me tell you. But anyways, since I'll be the one giving you the tour, let's go back inside, shall we?"

Jane led her back through the grand castle and down the halls, pointing at the doors and telling her what lay behind each one.

"Most rooms are just for storage," she told her. "Or filled with furniture from centuries ago. There's only six of us that live here, so there's not really a need to fill every room."

They passed by the room Maya had explored the night before, where she had encountered the strange creature. She wondered if it would be hiding in there again, or if the hybrid had found a new place to inhabit after she discovered its home.

As their tour continued, Maya was once again drawn to how out of place certain objects that belonged to the Omnis appeared. Now, she was almost certain that they hadn't constructed the castle, but that brought along another set of questions.

"How old is this place?" Maya asked. "Do you know who it belonged to previously?"

Jane said a curious, "huh," as if the thought of the castle's origins had never occurred to her. "That's probably a question better suited for Talon or Hypnos. The palace has been here in Neshama Valley since way before I was born. As for the people who lived here back then, not a clue. But there must have been a lot of them, because it would take a *ton* of strength to meld out an entire castle. Melding is—well, I'll leave that up to Talon to decide whether or not you're ready to learn about that fun trick. I'm not very good at it, but Griffin's a master."

Maya bit her lip and looked towards the white and gold wallpaper. There were too many questions left unanswered. She was hoping the people who lived in Kalpana would have all the answers, but in many ways, they seemed just as lost as she was.

"You know, you must be someone really special," Jane's statement yanked Maya out of her thoughts.

"What makes you say that?" Maya flinched as her voice raised in pitch, dread filling her stomach. *Keep calm, idiot. She couldn't know anything,* she tried reassuring herself.

"Well, because of what Kai did," she said, and Maya's shoulders sagged in relief. "Did he not tell you?"

"Tell me what?"

Jane's expression sobered. "That feat he pulled saving you from that collapsing consciousness was no easy task. Especially for him. Before that night, Kai refused to enter anyone's mind. Ever since..." She trailed off. "Actually, it's probably more Kai's place to tell. Just know that he had to break more barriers than one to save you. And you should be incredibly grateful."

Maya's eyes widened at the revelation. "I... am."

She thought Kai had been mad at her the first time they met. But instead, he had been scared. And worried.

A spike of emotion hit her chest, probably a sense of fear. Who was this boy to care for her in such a way before she had even known him? What did he desire in return?

"I can tell," Jane teased, playfully elbowing her. Maya blew out her cheeks and looked away, deciding not to engage in an argument about her emotions and focusing on the cold room up ahead that she had been in the previous night. Chills ran down her back as she recalled the way Halo had placed her hands on her temples. How she had been immersed inside of her own mind. How she had prevented Halo from entering the door where she had hidden her memories. And once again she was reminded that she was living a lie.

"Yeah... probably best to avoid that room at all costs," said Jane. "There's places Talon doesn't ever want you, one of those being the Underdwellings." She then pointed down the seemingly endless hall. "A bit farther down is a big locked door. You probably couldn't even go in it if you tried... but still. Don't try." Maya coughed, realizing that was another rule she'd already broken. "There's also the Whispering Woods. Avoiding that is more a safety issue. And you should never venture out to the point where you can't see the castle.

"Besides that, pretty much everything is free to be explored. Just make sure to do your share of work and let us know where you are. So, any questions?"

Only an endless stream, her brain retorted. But instead of asking them, she simply smiled and said, "No. Thank you, Jane."

If she wanted clear answers to her questions, she wouldn't be getting it now. She'd have to put it all together herself. Just like the apple falling on the head of Isaac

Newton, sometimes a small piece of evidence is all that is needed to spark a discovery of the secrets of the universe.

And if that apple never fell down on her own head, well, she'd just ask Halo.

Chapter Twelve

"A Blink Of An Eye"

MAYA WAS AWAKENED BY a bright light. The sound of Broth groaning followed it.

She struggled to shake off the heavy cover of drowsiness. Her eyelids were crusted shut and her cheeks were sticky, the tears from last night leaving their mark. Rubbing it away, Maya was finally able to open her eyes to see where the light was coming from.

The sun was undoubtedly preparing to burst from the horizon, the cloud gaining a blue hue, but that wasn't what brightened the alleyway.

No, the source of the light came from the headlights of a vehicle which stood just at the entrance, blocking the only way out.

The cover of sleep was immediately lifted away as Maya jumped back, holding the light blanket to her chest. Next to her, Broth noticed as well and released a string of curses. He turned to look behind him, only for his eyes to widen as he gazed upon the towering brick wall.

Trapped.

The car lights dimmed slightly, which allowed Maya to see a silhouette behind the windshield. The figure opened the van door and stepped out slowly. It was a tall man, sporting a navy blue suit and black sunglasses, despite the miniscule amount of light in the early hours. When he put his hand on his hip, Maya's attention was brought to the gun strapped to the man's side and she felt herself freeze.

More men dressed in black stepped out of the vehicle, all gripping large weapons. She made her way up to her feet and moved back. Broth suddenly grabbed her arm and hissed in her ear, "Don't move." And for once, Maya felt inclined to listen.

The man in the navy-blue suit stepped in front of the black van, holding up a badge of some sort. "Secret Services," he said with authority. "We must ask you to come with us."

Broth released his grip on her and walked forward. "Men, please. No need for the antics. This is all just a big misunderstandin'! I've done nothin' wrong."

"We both know that is far from the truth, Broth Deidre. Where, may I ask, were you heading off to?"

"Town. Food was getting scarce."

"And it just happened to be today of all days, didn't it?"

"Yeah."

A hollow laugh escaped from the man's lips. "Unlikely." He made a hand gesture. Immediately, the other agents who had been standing back enclosed Broth and her, holding their guns to the side threateningly. Maya clutched the blanket tighter.

"Don't make this harder than it needs to be, Mr. Deidre," the man said in a low voice.

Broth practically growled as he told him, "I'd die before goin' with y'all."

"Then I guess it's a good thing we're not here for you then, is it?"

Maya connected the dots even before Broth said his next line.

"The girl ain't going with y'all either."

"Really? Oh, I'm sorry, did I miss the part where you suddenly gained the ability to inhibit us from doing so? Honestly, Mr. Deidre, don't start pretending now that you care about the girl."

The man then lifted his glasses—a small ounce of his intimidating aura diminished. He was no longer looking at Broth, all of his attention now on Maya. He moved closer until he was no more than a meter away. Holding his hand out, the man said in a gentler, softer voice, "Come with us, Ms. Shaffer. We'll keep you safe. Promise."

Two of the men held Broth back as he lunged forward. He struggled to break free, his spirit short-lived in his hungover state.

"Don't go with them, kid," he strained. "They're gonna hurt ya'."

"As if anyone could hurt me more than *you*." The venom the words held would've guaranteed her a slap to the face, spat with all the fury she had felt for eight years. All the times she wanted to speak up, to yell, to curse, and yet was too afraid. But she wasn't afraid anymore, because from the moment she saw that van, she knew she would be leaving in it. Whatever it took to get away from the monster who had been the bane of all her nightmares.

Maya grabbed the man's hand and dropped the blanket, finding satisfaction in the twisted look on Broth's face. Her heart continued to swell with complacency as she was led to the back of the vehicle, ignoring Broth's vocal protests.

"You ungrateful child!" he called out as she was fastened to the seat. "Ungrateful! I was tryin' to save ya', ya' hear me? *I was tryn' to save ya'!*" His voice was then silenced with one of the special force agents knocking him out with the back of their gun.

She wished it had been the last time she saw Broth.

It wasn't.

THE VAN SKIDDED SMOOTHLY over the road, hovering just a foot above. The armed agents sat on benches on each side, their weapons hung on the side walls before they buckled up. Above them were racks stuffed with bags and weapons that shifted slightly as they moved.

Unlike the trip with Broth, the soldiers were loud, laughing about life and inside jokes Maya couldn't decipher the meaning of. The man in the navy suit had joined them in the back, remaining quiet, with an occasional glance at Maya through his sunglasses.

A small rectangular window on the back doors was the only source of light. Through it, Maya could see the gray sky. Frail trees. Distant mountains. And that's where she kept her gaze.

Maya had forgotten what it had felt like to be surrounded by humans. How their language would meld together into something indecipherable. How their body heat would warm the room. As much as she had previously desired this type of environment, she couldn't help the terribly uncomfortable feeling that emerged from it.

With the exception of the leader, however, none of the other men seemed to pay much attention to her. She disappeared under the surface and stayed at the bottom, her mind far away from the scene in front of her. A mix of relief and apprehension infiltrated her thoughts.

Broth is gone.

I'm with strangers.

They saved me from being given to SCRO.

But what if they're just as dangerous?

She would remember Broth's heavily accented cries: *"I was tryin' to save ya!"*

Then she would scoff to herself.

Anywhere Broth doesn't want me must be good.

Followed by the revelation.

I'm free from him now.

The thought made her want to cheer and laugh and cry, all at the same time.

One step closer to Amarie.

Her mind became sidetracked when, through the window, she noticed them passing by tall buildings that blocked out the sun. Maya tapped the man's shoulder next to her lightly. Previously engaged in a loud conversation, he flipped around, his cold stare directed at her. A waft of fear seized her captive as she cleared her throat and asked, "Where are we going?"

Irritation flashed in the agent's eyes for a millisecond, but he seemingly shook it off and offered her a smile that was probably intended to be reassuring. "Somewhere safe."

Safe.

It had been ages since Maya had been able to use that word to describe her life. But while "somewhere safe" was comforting, it still didn't answer her question. She was going to ask again, but the agent had gone back to talking with his friends. A sigh escaped her lips. It was as if everyone in her life was determined to tell her as little information as possible.

Maya resumed staring out the window, and a few minutes had passed when she saw a sign: *Blacksburg, Next Exit.* Their black van drove right past it, the town disappearing behind them. She could picture the workers of SCRO waiting for her and Broth to meet them, the disappointment in their faces when they never appear. Meanwhile, she was traveling farther and farther away. Sure, it would be easy for SCRO to track her through the chip in her arm, but she had an army to protect her now. They wouldn't ever lay their hands on her again.

"How long has the Secret Service known about Broth and I?" Maya spoke to the agent again. This time, every conversation between the soldiers halted, and she bit her cheek.

"Uh..." The agent almost appeared to be nervous as he scratched his head. He turned his gaze to the navy-blue man.

"A few years," the leader continued for him. "We apologize for not being able to take action earlier. It doesn't seem like Mr. Deidre took very good care of you and your sister."

"Still. Thank you. I don't know what I'd do if SCRO took me again."

The man's glasses shielded his reaction. The silence in the van was deafening.

The leader leaned back and adjusted his glasses. "Of course. Even though the world's gone apocalyptic, we still have a duty to uphold."

Even after the conversation ended, the agents didn't go back to their energetic blubbering. Their interactions consisted of silent eye contact and small gestures that they each appeared to understand. Maya, once again, did not.

"You know about my sister then." Maya recalled his mention of Amarie. "Do you know where she is?"

A huff from one of the soldiers cued her in on the fact that she was prying too much. Staying quiet was always the safest choice. Talking too much was dangerous, but not knowing enough could prove even more so.

"We do," the leader said.

"Can I communicate with her?"

The first sign of frustration was revealed on the navy man's face, the tip of his lip twitching down. Maya subconsciously squeezed the buckle over her lap as he said, "We have orders to take you to our facility. No detours.""No. Of course not. But a phone call, maybe? Just so I know how she is, and so she doesn't worry about me."

The second part was a lie; Amarie wasn't expecting any calls for a long time. In reality, a call would probably stress her out even more, but the agents didn't have to know that.

The man thought for a while, drumming his fingers on his thigh. "There is a phone station at the facility. I will ask if you can call your sister there."

"Okay, Thank you, Mr..." "Hue."

"Thank you, Mr. Hue."

Satisfied, Maya relaxed back, returning to watching the world through the window. Her heart was still above its normal pace, but she could now breathe fully.

It wasn't too long before Maya felt the van start to slow. The view of the sky was suddenly shielded and it took a second for her to realize that it was a tall metal ceiling that blocked out the brightness of the sky. There was a thump as the automatic door closed shut. Light bulbs turned on. Then the vehicle stopped and the back doors opened.

Two men stood in front of the exit, holding large guns across their chest. The other agents in the van unbuckled and made their way out. Mr. Hue bent over and released Maya's buckle for her before leaving as well.

She stepped out of the hover van slowly, watching her step. The two men with the guns didn't remove their eyes from her, their gaze tracking her even as she walked all the way across the large parking center. Maya, meanwhile, fidgeted as they stuck by her side, as if she would run away if they didn't.

Like I would have anywhere to run to.

Maya was led to a sleek metal door. Mr. Hue strode up to it and put his wrist against a sensor; it flashed green, and a pop could be heard before the door swung open.

"Ms. Shaffer will be coming with me," he announced. "George, Phillip, hold your posts. The rest of you have an off day. Congratulations."

Chattering commenced as the agents began to make plans for their free time and dispersed. The two men with guns didn't share their enthusiasm as they sauntered back to the large automatic door.

"What is this place?" Maya asked, observing the plain hall with white tiles on the floor and ceiling. The lights were too bright, giving it a hospital-esque sense.

Mr. Hue gave her a smile as they made their way down the hall. "You'll see soon enough. But first, as per request." He guided her forwards through another door with the words, *Communications Center,* in tiny font above. Maya's heart skipped a beat.

The room was darker, illuminated only by different color lights from the technology. Ten angled screen tables stood in a row, glowing blue. Maya walked up hesitantly, looking to the suited man for approval. He didn't stop her, so she hovered her hand over the screen, reading the bar asking her to put in a number.

"I... don't know her number," Maya admitted, her previous hope seeping away. She didn't even know if her sister had a phone. Of course, part of their conceived plan had been for Amarie to obtain one as soon as she escaped so they could communicate with each other when she eventually got free, but there was a possibility that she hadn't felt the need to get a phone so early since in Amarie's perspective, Maya was still with Broth for two more years. Plus, it wasn't her 18th birthday, meaning there would be no meeting her by the city train stop. Contacting her through the phone was Maya's only hope.

Mr. Hue didn't seem fazed. "This is the Western government. We might not be what we once were, but we're not completely helpless." Moving to her side, he pressed an icon in the top corner and it revealed a list of options. He selected one and another bar popped up, this time asking for a name. "Go on. Type it in."

Maya didn't need to be told twice. She entered Amarie's first and last name and multiple people appeared. She read each of their information. When she came across the individual that matched, Maya clicked it.

The next screen had a picture of Amarie (appearing fairly recent) and two symbols. One was obviously a call button, but the other one was harder to distinguish. It almost looked like a beacon with lines extending from it—possibly a tracker. Then the government symbol: an eagle with the sun's rays behind it.

She pressed the call button and watched it buzz for one second. Five seconds. 20 seconds. Too many seconds.

Maya backed away, nearly giving up on the ordeal.

But then a static noise came from the screen and she ran forward, hopeful once again. "Amarie?" Maya said hesitantly.

She heard a faint, suspecting voice through the speakers say, "Who is this?" And a smile broke out across her face.

"You don't recognize your own sister's voice?"

More static made it impossible to make out what she was trying to say. Mr. Hue adjusted something underneath the screen and the noise cleared.

"–aya?"

"Hey, Amarie."

Her sister went quiet again, but this time it wasn't static blocking the signal.

"What—how are you calling me?" Her voice came out in frantic bursts. "*Why* are you calling me? If Broth finds you–"

"Broth won't be a problem anymore. I'm free from him now."

There were traces of anger in Amarie's tone as she exclaimed, "You *ran away?*"

Says the girl who ran away. "Of course I didn't! I'm not stupid. This was completely out of my control."

There was another moment of silence. "Did he... die?" Maya couldn't blame the bit of hope in her statement.

"Unfortunately not."

A huff. "Maya, if you don't start telling me what's going on, I will break through this phone and strangle you."

"*Okay,* I will. It's just..." She craned her head to peer at the man next to her. In his silence, his presence had been almost forgotten. Maya made a mental note to heed her words carefully.

"Apparently, Broth had been hiding from the government for a while now. Not sure why. They took me away from him and promised to keep me safe."

"*They,* being the government?"

"Yes." *At least, that's what they claim.* Just to make Amarie aware of the agent by her side, she followed it up by saying, "One of the agents even let me call you. They're standing right next to me." She kept her tone positive and looked at the man, careful not to show her suspicions. It was experience that taught her that if you want someone to slip up, it's best to make them believe you're oblivious.

It wasn't necessarily that she didn't *believe* they worked for the government—they sure sounded and acted like Special Forces. But like Mr. Hue had mentioned before, the Western government wasn't what they once were. Who knows what dark plans they could've been involved in?

Then again, part of her was tired of suspecting the worst. For once, she just wanted to feel relief, with no underlying fear or suspicion. Pure bliss.

"Remember our rule, Maya?" her sister's voice said through the speaker, and as quickly as the temptation came, it was gone.

Whenever you're in a new situation, learn everything. Ignorance is a death wish.

"Always."

A sigh came from Amarie. "I'm guessing whoever you're with plans to keep you there?"

Maya turned to the man and he answered for her. "Just for the time being. They won't have the authority to hold her when she is of legal age. But we will take good care of her. When the time comes, she may not even have the desire to leave."

Maya resisted a scoff. She was sure after two years, she'd be itching to be reunited with her sister.

"Okay," said Amarie, but Maya could hear the undertone whispering, *"You better."*

"How have you been holding up?" Maya changed the subject. "Life in the city any better than Broth's farm?"

Amarie laughed at that. *"So* much better. I don't have a house quite yet, but I've found a few options. There are so many places to go and things to explore. Everyone just minds their own business. And the boys. Gosh, the *boys.* I don't know if I'm just more horny now or what, but it's like every single guy is *hot* now."

It was now Maya's turn to laugh. She was tempted to bring up Kai—an urge that took her completely off-guard—but wasn't quite sure how to explain meeting a cute—albeit annoying guy—from another realm in her sleep, especially with Mr. Hue by her side.

"Well, I'm glad you're enjoying yourself."

"Wait! I didn't even bring up the best part. The *food.* There are so many options and I can eat whenever I want. There's this delicious treat called Iceplops, which is like ice cream, but even better. You just bite into it and–*mhm.*"

"Amarie, I have not eaten in two days, and you are making me extremely hungry."

"Fine, I'll stop. But I'm not joking. Next time we meet up, I'm getting us each an Iceplop and we are eating them together. Got it? No eating one without me there to watch your reaction."

"Don't worry, I won't so much as gaze upon one."

"You better not. And for the man next to my sister" —Amarie referred to Mr. Hue— "you better feed her."

He let out a small chuckle. "Not to worry, Ms. Shaffer. That is our next plan."

"Love you, Amarie," Maya said softly. She didn't want to end the conversation, not knowing when she would have this chance again, but her stomach growled loudly, the desire for food becoming too great.

"Love you too. Stay safe." Then the call disconnected.

A wave of loneliness crashed over her almost immediately, the end of the call breaking the illusion of her sister being a few feet away instead of hundreds of miles.

Mr. Hue patted her on the back in an attempt to be comforting, but Maya involuntarily flinched, curling a loose strand of hair behind her ear. Her stomach growled again and her cheeks flushed red.

"Come on," the man said. "I think it's time you've eaten a proper meal."

Chapter Thirteen

"The 'Better' Alternative"

Maya wasn't sure how, but sometime during their silent but intentful trek, they managed to end up underground.

Everywhere she turned appeared the same—white tiles, long beams, metal doors. If the man hadn't been there, guiding her the entire way, she certainly would have been lost. Although there wasn't much of an angle, Maya could feel the floor slope down, a hall reaching down toward the core of the earth. The only contrivances that reassured her they weren't traveling in circles were the arrows above, pointing down passing halls with labels like *Conference* and *Snack Room*. That, as well as Mr. Hue, whose gait spoke of a confidence familiar with the area.

The man suddenly took a sharp turn down another hall, this one with a sign reading *Elevator*. Loyal to its namesake, a silver elevator stood at the end, and when they reached it, Mr. Hue pressed the upwards arrow next to the sliding door.

There was a moment of awkward silence. Maya played with her hands as she studied the man's piercing blue eyes, noticing something queer hidden behind them. He didn't seem to have any bad intentions, but a gut feeling told her that he harbored many secrets.

"You must have quite a few questions," the man suddenly spoke, as if reading her mind.

"More than a few."

The man smiled. "Then you will enjoy Chance's education profusely."

The elevator door slid open and Mr. Hue stepped in, Maya following suit. The gears in her mind ground together.

"Education? This is a *school*? You're kidding, right?"

The image of secret agents in fancy black attire teaching children multiplication tables made her want to laugh at its absurdity. There were many theories she had gathered about the building's purpose, but never had the thought, *"Maybe the government uses this building to teach displaced children,"* crossed her mind.

Mr. Hue pressed a button with the number six on it and leaned against the elevator wall. "Not exactly. Its official name is Chance Refuge, and it was built to shelter kids like you. Then again, children are the future of the world, and they need to be educated. So yes, I guess you can call it a school. But only the sixth floor, with occasional access to the top floor and basement. The rest are off limits. It's highly selective, so you should be grateful to get in."

"I don't think having no other place to stay qualifies as being selected."

"Then you're in for a surprise." The lift came to a stop. They both exited.

"What exactly does it teach?" Maya asked as they walked down a hall with white brick walls and purple tiles. "Are the grades separated? I haven't gone to school since I was seven, so how will I catch up to the kids my age?"

The man released a sigh. "Being entirely transparent, keeping track of what Chance does and doesn't do isn't really in my job description. All those questions are better answered by the head administrator, who" —he checked his watch— "should be meeting us here any minute."

It only took half a minute for the administrator to make her appearance. She was tall and skinny, with bones showing through her skin. She wore a tight-fitting gray shirt and a long black skirt fit with her slick-backed hair. Her heels clicked on the ground as she walked up to them, a tablet tucked beneath her arm.

It was the way she smiled that made Maya uneasy. It was muted and gentle, but not in a sweet, tender way. It was the smile Maya would make when Lewis would roll in the mud, or when the chickens would rush up to get their food. It was almost in a demeaning way: *"You adorable creature. You think you know everything."*

But it wasn't the woman's grin that sent a jolt through Maya's heart, but her voice. An all too familiar voice.

"Welcome, Maya. I am Mrs. Fondal. It's wonderful to finally have you here." The visitor's voice.

It took Maya a moment to remember how to speak, gulping down the lump that had lodged itself in her throat. "Hi."

She sank back into her dread as the woman dipped her head to the agent. "Thank you for your work, Mr. Hue."

"Of course. Ms. Shaffer is starving, so I promised her a meal."

"That can be arranged."

"And I must speak with you in private."

"We can do that as well. But first, let's get this poor girl something to eat. Does that sound good to you, Maya?"

She nodded, wrapping her arms around her chest.

The three of them continued down the hall, Mr. Hue remaining slightly behind her. Mrs. Fondal made small talk, asking her questions that Maya hadn't been asked in years.

"What's your favorite food?"

Anything edible.

"Do you like sweet or savory meals?"

Depends on my mood.

"When do you fall asleep?"

Whenever Broth would allow me to.

"Favorite color?"

Seriously? *Favorite* color? *What am I, five?*

"Do you strive to learn of the unknown?"

Maya slowed down to study the tall woman more clearly. The way Mrs. Fondal gazed at her was like she was breaking past Maya's outer barrier and entering directly into her brain. Almost as if she knew her thoughts, her story, her emotions and desire for exploration. Her smug look, however, implied that she wasn't aware that Maya had recognized her from two days ago. Right now, she had the advantage. As long as Maya could hide her suspicions, the woman wouldn't feel the need to be overly cautious.

"I do," Maya said and forced her voice to be even, which seemed to please Mrs. Fondal as her smile grew the slightest bit wider.

Maya studied all of her surroundings, reading the signs posted on the walls with different quotes. They were mostly about determination and knowledge, but one caught her eye. It was on a red banner with golden letters, and on it, an anonymous quote that said, *"The world holds many secrets, but the largest ones are hidden in our minds."*

She probably knew better than anyone at the school how truthful that claim was.

There were pictures on the walls of students as well, standing in front of their finished puzzles and holding up towering trophies. All with big grins, as if their whole life had been building up to that moment.

Nothing appeared inherently off putting. If she hadn't been dragged here by special forces and met Mrs. Fondal, Maya would have been fully convinced that this was a normal refuge. She watched the back of the woman's head as she fell more in line with the agent, having been so sure that Mrs. Fondal was a part of SCRO when she first arrived at the farm. It had made sense with the timing of the scrolls along with the woman's awareness of her and her sister, but Mr. Hue told her that they had been aware of them for years, so that no longer proved anything. It did, however, bring up the other side of the coin: why hadn't they been able to free them sooner? What oath did Broth have to remember?

Maya could still play along, listening to their directions and taking whatever classes were required, but couldn't allow herself to relax until she knew *exactly* who those people were and what they wanted from her.

Mrs. Fondal might have not been part of SCRO, but that didn't make her trustworthy. And if she couldn't be trusted, then neither could the so-called "refuge."

So I'm still not safe. Lovely.

It wasn't too long before Maya started to see some of the refugees, and it was a strange experience to see more kids that were around her age. They passed by her—some with judging eyes, others with curiosity, and some appearing even more surprised to see her than she was to see them. Their uniforms were navy blue pants with cream-colored shirts tucked into them. A few students wore suits, typically looking older than the rest, and each child sported a colored band around their wrist; most were red, but she noticed one or two with blue.

There were a number of doors that lined the walls, but a certain one they passed had a large sign over it with a picture of a computer, a cross through the middle, and words underneath that read, *No students past this point, unless accompanied by an admin.*

"Right through those doors is the cafeteria," Mrs. Fondal told her, drawing her attention away from the computer room. "All food is free, and we have plenty of it, thanks to our indoor farming floor, so eat as your heart desires. Lunch A is in there currently, so it may be slightly crowded. I'm afraid I don't have time to talk over a meal, but we'll plan for next time, okay?"

"Yes, ma'am." Maya tugged on a tuft of hair.

The woman gave her a pitying smile. "I know how strange this must be for you, suddenly thrust into all of this. I promise we'll clear things up for you. In the meantime, enjoy a nice warm meal, then head to the screening room. I'm sure one of the students won't mind guiding you there."

Mrs. Fondal and Mr. Hue started to head away, the latter turning around briefly to say, "A pleasure to meet you, Ms. Shaffer." Maya dipped her head, the two of them disappearing around a corner before she looked up again.

Taking a calming breath, she walked up to the cafeteria door. Her heart attempted to escape from her chest, the palms of her hands that pressed against her breast the only thing stopping it. Fear wasn't a foreign emotion, but it had been so long since something as trivial as social interaction had been the root of it.

She reached for the handle when the door flew open, causing Maya to jump back, the scare causing five years of her life to be shaved off. The blue-banded brunette that had been the reason for her startle stood still for a moment, looking her up and down as Maya struggled to regain her bearings. She had piercing green eyes and a sharp jaw that tightened while studying her clothes. Maya's cheeks flushed. The girl then seemed to catch herself staring and grunted before heading down the hall.

Maya mentally slapped herself. *Come on, Maya. Pull yourself together.*

She shook the nerves from her shoulders and turned up her chin. With all the confidence she could muster, Maya opened the metal door and was immediately met with loud chatter. Spread across the first four of eight white round tables, children of all ages commerced amongst themselves, stuffing their mouths with as much food as they could. Chairs screeched as kids took their seats next to friends with wide smiles, as if they had no memory of war, famine, or the Harvest.

The noise softened slightly as Maya moved behind a line of people waiting for their lunch. Maya kept her gaze straight ahead, resisting the urge to tug on her curls.

Don't draw attention to yourself, she chanted in her mind, as if saying so would stop almost all the kids in the room from gluing their eyes to her. The observant part of Maya couldn't help but pay attention to the snippets of conversations.

"A new kid?"

"About time."

"When last did she wash her clothes?"

"Looks like she's been living alone for years."

"Bet she lost her parents from the Harvest."

"Nah, probably from the disease. Or war."

"You think she'd be any good at Cataball?"

"It's your turn, lady."

Maya snapped back to reality, an older woman scowling at her from across the counter. She cleared her throat. "Sorry. I would like..."

Her eyes widened at the display of food. So many options, some she couldn't remember the name of, in an array of color with the freshest fruits and vegetables she had ever seen. Together, they made a magnificent rainbow: strawberries, watermelon, carrots, pineapple, lettuce, blueberries, grapes—*they have mangoes!* Then, on the other side, there was even *more*: wrapped sandwiches, hamburgers, hotdogs, and every kind of topping she could imagine.

She could feel the elderly woman's gaze burning through her skull, so she quickly made a decision, despite her desire to stay and stare in amazement until her eyes fell out. "A hamburger with mango, please."

The woman wordlessly plopped the burger and fruit cup onto the tray, grabbed a napkin, and reached over to hand the tray to Maya.

She said a quick thank you and turned around, her stomach growling as she caught the smell of the meal. The numerous round tables that were spread out across the cafeteria had metal chairs that were just as colorful as the foot. Two tables appeared to be most popular, with multiple kids pulling up seats and crowding them, and while there were a few stray kids occupying the others, it still left quite a few tables uninhabited.

She sat at the farthest one in the back, hyper-aware of the eyes that followed her. Carefully unwrapping the burger, she brought it to her mouth and took a bite. She groaned as her taste buds melted with flavor.

Maya couldn't seem to stop herself as she took another bite. Then another. Before she knew it, she was licking the remnants from her fingers, still hungry for more.

"Hey, new kid." Maya dropped the napkin she was using to wipe her hands and peered around, searching for the source of the accented voice. "You know there's sauce that's supposed to go on the burger, right?"

It was a Latino boy with dark straight hair and a devilish grin on his face, who sat next to a girl who looked almost identical, save for the longer hair and thinner physique. She gazed up from what looked like a tablet and glared at the boy, elbowing him in the side. The boy flinched and rubbed where he had been hit, glaring back at her.

"I didn't see any sauces," Maya said, pushing away the embarrassment.

The boy opened his mouth to speak, but was once again silenced by the girl, who made a strange gesture with her head. The dark-haired boy sighed and stood up with his tray and the girl followed suit. Maya watched with a rising sense of anxiety as they walked over to her table and sat across from her.

"Well, for future reference, all the stuff like extra napkins, condiments, and utensils are on the counter near the door." He handed her an unused napkin and pointed to his face. Her ears turned red as she took it from him and wiped her mouth.

"Don't mind my brother. He's a prat," came from the girl, but her mouth didn't open. The voice came from a tablet in her hands and sounded automated. Robotic. And then Maya noticed that, on the sides of her head, partially covered by hair, there were strange white circles that attached to her scalp.

The boy must have noticed her confusion as he said, "She's deaf. Lost it in the first Mexican attacks. Eardrum replacements are too expensive, so they got a gadget that could talk and listen for her."

"I'm sorry," Maya felt obligated to say.

The girl smiled. *"Don't be. I'm used to it."* She then pressed a button on her tablet and her next words were so deep, it sounded more akin to thunder. *"And it has its perks."*

Maya chuckled at the funny voice. The girl grinned back.

"She *always* does that," the boy complained.

"I'm Camila," the girl said, voice back to normal. *"And this is Carlos."*

"Hola," Carlos greeted her.

Maya hesitantly told them her own name, which was apparently an invitation for the boy to grill her with questions. "Say, Maya, where are you from?"

"Up north. I moved here a few years ago."

"Before or after the war?"

"After."

"With or without parents?"

Maya swallowed. "Without. They died during the battle."

Camila, who had been scanning their words that appeared on her tablet looked up at her with pitying eyes.

Carlos, however, did not share her gentle nature. Raising up his hands, he exclaimed, "Hey, join the club!" which earned him an especially hard shove from his sister.

After the girl was satisfied, her gentle facade returned. *"You must have been alone for a while then,"* she said.

Maya took a fork and stuck it into a slice of mango. "Not completely alone. I had my sister." *And Broth,* her mind unhelpfully added, but she decided to leave that particular detail out.

Carlos raised an eyebrow. "Had?"

"She's still alive," Maya clarified. "We just went different paths. I'll see her again though. Soon." The siblings in front of her gave each other a look that Maya decided not to try to comprehend. "You two are lucky to still have each other."

Carlos shrugged. "If you say so." Camila jabbed him again, and he let out a quiet, "ow!"

The sister huffed. *"He has no filter."*

"Not everyone has an implanted computer to do that for them!"

Maya smiled at their teasing, loneliness poking her in the chest. She turned back to her food and snacked on the mango chunks. The noise in the cafeteria started to pick up again, and the students finally started to lose interest in her. Unfortunately, that assumption only lasted until a stranger walked up to their table and sat down aggressively, causing a mango piece to fall off her fork.

"Uh, hey, could you sit someplace else?" Carlos said to the redheaded boy, who was roughly chewing on a piece of lettuce. "Your *trasero* is clogging up the table."

The redhead scowled at him, shoving another piece of his salad into his mouth. "Watch it, dingo. I can sit wherever I like." He pointed his utensil at Maya. "How old are you?"

Carlos talked before she could speak. "What? You trying to see if you can recruit another person to your team of losers? Well too bad, she's already on our side."

"Sixteen," Maya answered to stop the bickering. She suddenly became aware of the way her leg bounced. "Why?"

The boy's eyes squinted into a glare, throwing his fork down. He shook his head, bundling his hands into fists. "*You.* Of course it's someone like *you.*"

"What is wrong with you, Brian?" Camila exclaimed.

"Stop being sexist!" Carlos accused him.

"I'm not—whatever." Brian stood up with his tray, the chair screeching behind him. He gave Maya one final piercing gaze before turning away, shoving his food into the garbage while Maya watched him stomp away, her mouth gaping.

Carlos said a curse. "That's Brian for you: a jerk to pretty much everybody. Though he does seem to hate you a little more than normal."

Maya gazed down at her plate and Camila rested a hand on her arm. *"Don't worry. You're safe with us."*

The corner of her mouth tilted upwards slightly. "Thank you." *Don't let your guard down, Maya.*

A loud bell caused her to jump, ringing louder than all of the conversations in the room. The siblings got up, the boy with a groan. "Great, now I have to go to Mrs. Jackson. You better hope you don't have her, Maya, or else you're never catching up."

"He's over exaggerating," Camila told her. *"As long as you do your work, unlike some people, you will be fine."*

"Speaking of which," he interrupted. "Where are you supposed to be heading to now?"

Maya searched through her brain. "I was told to meet Mrs. Fondal by the... screening room?"

Camila peered at her tablet. The two siblings shared another look.

"Do you know how to get there?" Camila asked. Maya shook her head.

"Perfect!" Carlos cheered. "I'll take you, and we'll go the long way. Then I could miss, what, fifteen minutes of next period?"

"I'll go too," Camila said. *"To make sure he doesn't go the long way."*

Chapter Fourteen

"Tests Of The Mind"

CARLOS TALKED THE WHOLE walk down the brightly-lit hall, seemingly loving the sound of his own voice. He explained everything from the core classes to the locations of the bathrooms, and when he got off topic to start ranting about sports, Maya stopped listening, only to be reigned back in at the mention of the wristbands.

"What do the bands mean?" she asked, and the boy almost looked hurt that she had interrupted him.

Carlos shrugged and lifted his arm to eye-level, studying his red wristband. "Not a clue. Everyone got assigned their color the day they arrived. That's probably why you're going to the screening place."

"The students with the same color bands have the same classes," Camila continued. *"Hopefully you'll be red, so you'll be with us."*

Considering the redhead from earlier had been blue, Maya hoped so too.

They walked past a uniquely colorful wall, covered from top to bottom with different artistic designs that varied from simple swirls to more skillful contributions, completing the overall piece. But whether it was the work of a two-year-old or a masterpiece on the caliber of the Mona Lisa, it garnered the attention of everyone that passed it, being the only colorful entity in the empty hall.

"Art class," Carlos sighed. "They make every student paint something on the wall, forgetting that being artsy isn't everyone's strong suit."

"Especially not his," Camila's robotic voice said.

"I hate you."

After passing the wall, they finally arrived at what was supposedly the screening room. A large glass window revealed computer screens and white raised beds, with the lights above so bright they were blinding. With the people inside wearing large lab coats and masks, Maya guessed they were protecting themselves from something inside, and this realization only added to the eerie feeling growing within her.

"What do they plan to do to me in there?" Maya asked, tucking the strand of hair she was playing with behind her ear.

"Pretty sure it's just precautionary measures, after you being exposed to the outside world for so long."

"Don't worry," Camila said. *"I don't remember anything the nurses did that hurt."*

"I do," Carlos unhelpfully added, and he expectantly slid to the side, avoiding his sister's slap. *"But,* I'm still alive. So you should be fine."

Maya wasn't convinced, but her attention was drawn to the glass door opening and Mrs. Fondal stepping out. Her heels forced Maya to gaze up at her, which was a motion unfamiliar at her own height. The woman wore a smile on her face, but there was something else gleaming in her eyes. Something that almost looked like... admiration.

What did Mr. Hue tell her?

"Carlos. Camila," she greeted the others. "Thank you for showing Maya to the room."

"What else is a good citizen to do, eh?" Carlos grinned, which generated an eye roll from his sister.

Mrs. Fondal leaned on one hip. "A *good citizen* wouldn't have other motives for helping a person in need, would they, Camila?"

Camila, after reading the tablet, gave her brother a smirk and shook her head.

"Off to class, both of you." The two didn't need to be told twice. With a quick wave goodbye, they headed down the empty hall.

"Did you have a good lunch?" Mrs. Fondal asked her as she guided her into the uncanny room, while Maya reluctantly stepped inside.

"I did. Thank you."

She was met with a blast of cold air as she stepped into the hospital-like setting, goosebumps traveling up her arms. A masked nurse ran up to them, stopping in front of her.

"Hi, sweetie. I'm Margaret. We're just gonna run a few tests, okay?"

Maya noticed another nurse in the back uncapping a syringe and her hands became clammy. Turning around to look at Mrs. Fondal, the memory of hiding in the pantry came across her mind. This was the woman who knew about Broth. Who knew about their situation. Who arrived at their house. And still did nothing.

She wanted to refuse and run back into the hall to Carlos and Camila. Or better yet, escape and hide with her sister forever, eating Iceplops and whatever other treats Amarie recommended. But even through the woman's smile, Maya could tell that this was not up for negotiation. If she wanted to survive, cooperation was the only option.

So with a motion that was barely visible, Maya nodded.

Mrs. Fondal told her she would be back when the tests were over, then walked out to tend to the other needs of the refuge. The relief of being away from the tall woman, however, was muffled by the anxiousness caused by the nurse leading her to one of the white beds.

"Remain still for me, okay sweetie?"

Margaret's ice-cold hands gripped her arm as she took the syringe from the other nurse and stuck it into her flesh, squeezing whatever fluid was inside into the muscles encompassing her upper arm. Maya blinked away the sting. "What's that for?"

"Just a vaccine. We don't want any diseases spreading from student to student, now do we?"

She was instructed to lay down, her body tensing at contact with the cold bed-sheets.

The nurse that had been previously preparing the syringe now held a rectangular device that had flashing yellow lights. It beeped as the woman hovered it over her.

"1.5Gy."

"Drink this for me, sweetie." Margaret handed her a small cup. Inside was a blue liquid with a consistency thicker than water.

I don't want to.

She drank it.

It was bitter. Gag-worthy.

This time, she didn't even get a chance to ask what the vile drink's purpose was before she was directed to stand up and was led to a small chamber covered with black tiles. When Maya was inside, Margaret locked the glass door, and Maya rushed towards it immediately, yanking at its handle. It wouldn't budge.

"Stand still for me, sweetie."

A blast of frigid air came from jets on the walls, spraying her with a white soapy liquid. It entered her eyes, burning into her retinas. Maya rubbed at it, but it did little to ease the pain. When she was completely covered, the white liquid was replaced with water, coming out of the jets so fast that it irritated her skin. The water got hot, and its steam blocked her vision. The putrid smell of ammonia in the water was suffocating.

After an eternity, the jets finally stopped firing and the water was sucked back through the drains. Her wet clothes were ten times heavier, sticking to her skeletal physique. Margaret finally opened the door and handed her a towel. Still shaking, Maya took it. Then the woman handed her something else: her uniform.

The nurse watched as she undressed. Maya curled over to avoid exposing herself completely, but Margaret wouldn't look away. The stark contrast between where the sun's rays had beaten down on her and underneath her shirt was comical. Ribs could be seen through her skin, something Maya never desired to pay any attention to.

Stop watching me! Maya wanted to scream to the nurse.

She remained silent.

She put on the undergarments. Then she put on the buttoned cotton shirt and pants, tucking one into the other, avoiding eye contact with the nurse until her clothes were fully on her body.

"Wonderful. Now, this way, sweetie."

Some other nurse took the wet clothes and towel from her as she followed Margaret into a darker room. Shivering, Maya rubbed her arms to create heat from the friction.

In the middle of the room was a large machine. It had a flat area for her to lay down on with a donut-shaped circle going over it. Just like the gadget that had been hovered over her, this machine also had an assortment of flashing lights. She was once again told to lay down and remain absolutely still. Margaret placed a pair of headphones over her ears. The lights were turned off, and then she felt herself starting to move. Or was it the donut-shaped part that was moving?

A loud humming sound came from the machine, but was muffled by the music coming from the pads over her ears. An announcement from an automated voice said, *"X-ray, in progress."*

The machine went back and forth, examining every part of her body.

"X-ray, complete."

The humming stopped, only to commence again.

"CT, in progress."

The music blasted in her ears as the lights above her flashed. Her head began to ache. She grew tempted to rest her eyes, but forced them to remain open.

"CT, complete."

"MRI, in progress."

This section refused to end. Every time the noise would grow quieter, Maya would grow hopeful along with it, only for the machine to blast its sound above the music and repeat the same phrase: *"MRI, in progress."*

"In progress."

"In progress."

"In progress."

The bed became increasingly uncomfortable. The machine became too cramped. Her muscles ached. Her skin itched. She still couldn't move.

"MRI, complete."

The lights turned back on. The music from the headphones switched off. She could finally sit up.

The sudden brightness was like needles being stuck behind her eyes and Maya brought a hand to her head, rubbing her right temple.

From a room to the side came Margaret, along with two other nurses, and next to them stood Mrs. Fondal. They all wore broad smiles on their faces as they neared her. The latter walked up and gave Maya a hand as she stood up, slightly disoriented.

"A healthy brain you have there, Maya," Mrs. Fondal told her. She remained silent, not sure how to respond to such a statement.

The nurses each held tablets with digital pens in their hands. One of them that Maya did not recognize formed a frown. "You have a small spiral fracture on your right wrist. Does it hurt?"

Maya shrugged. Her wrist had been sore ever since Broth had twisted it, but it had been the last thing on her mind.

The nurse's expression darkened. "Did the person that had custody of you previously ever–"

"Whatever happened with her previous guardian holds no importance now," Mrs. Fondal interjected, placing a hand on the nurse's shoulder. "It's in the past." The nurse didn't seem happy about the school administrator's statement, but for once Maya was grateful that Mrs. Fondal cut off the conversation. After wrapping her wrist, they did more tests in which Maya zoned out for, and unconsciously followed the instructions. Lift your arm. Touch your toes. Open your mouth. Jump up and down. Stand up straight. Then the educational tests. Define. Read. Solve. Explain. Wake up.

The last task proved the hardest.

"You are smart," Mrs. Fondal said, examining her results. "Excellent problem-solving skills, and a surprising vocabulary as well. You do, however, severely lack in the science and history fields. Not that it is your fault. But we'll have to set you up with one of our tutors to help you along with that. Now, hold out your wrist."

Obliging, Maya offered the uninjured one. Margaret held it still and slipped on a band, tightening it.

Maya brought it up to look at it, confusion racking her mind.

Purple.

"No one else has a purple wristband," Maya said to Mrs. Fondal.

"You are... a special case for Chance Refuge. You don't quite fit into either group. For now, your schedule will be split between the two. You will still be in classes with students around your age, and the professors will be lenient on your grading. As soon as I find a tutor for you, I will let you know. Does that sound good to you, Maya?"

"I guess."

The woman smiled and looked at her watch. "Would you look at the time! Already so late. Follow me, I'll show you to your sleeping corridors."

They exited the cold room and walked into the main hall. The lights were switched off, only the numerous signs offering light. Mrs. Fondal led her past the art wall and cafeteria, as well as a few vacated rooms. A closed door stood in front of them and the administrator laid her chipped wrist over a scanner, registering and swinging open.

Each side of the area had a total of six doors, the ones on the right and two-thirds of them on the left having been streaked with a red marking. The remaining one had a blue streak. Mrs. Fondal made her way up to the blue door and pushed it open. The lights inside the room were less harsh than the others around the school had been, with a slight yellow tint. Maya counted four other people in the room, two of them boys she had never met before. They sat on the wooden floor and played cards. The other person was the brunette from earlier that had startled her on her way into the cafeteria, while the last person was no other than Brian.

She held back a groan. *Just my luck.*

They all looked up as Mrs. Fondal cleared her throat, and Maya resisted the urge to turn away as their eyes shifted from the tall woman to her.

"Everyone, I would like to introduce you to Maya," she announced. "She will now be attending Chance's Refuge. I expect each and every one of you to treat her with the respect she deserves. Maybe try to learn a few things from her. If Maya needs something, you will get it for her. If she gets lost, you will show her the correct way. If she has questions that pertain to our education, you refer her to me. Does everyone understand?" A chorus of agreements sounded from the teens.

Mrs. Fondal turned her attention back to Maya. "Everyone has designated tooth-brushes, soaps, and extra uniforms. We take hygiene very seriously here, so make sure you do that. If you have any problems, come to me. I am free until 6:00 pm every night."

"I will," she said. *I won't.*

With a goodbye, Mrs. Fondal left, leaving Maya alone with the near strangers.

Observing the room, she noticed the obsidian-like ceiling. It shimmered with hints of sparkles, almost reminiscent of stars. Bulbs dangled from thin threads, offering light to the otherwise dark surroundings. Three bunk beds were pressed against the navy-painted walls: one to her right, one to her left, and another directly in front of her. Two white doors were placed in the back corners, and she assumed them to be either bathrooms or closets.

The two boys on the floor resumed their game of cards, not sparing her another glance. Letting her vision roam, Maya accidentally made eye contact with the brunette. The girl's face sported a blank expression, green hypnotic eyes staring back at her with not a hint of emotion. If the girl remembered her from earlier, she didn't reveal it.

The brunette held out a hand for her to shake. "Lilith," the girl introduced herself. Maya shook it with her free hand and the girl peered at the wrapping job on her other side. "What happened to your wrist?"

"I fell."

Lilith grunted, unimpressed. She adjusted her shirt—the top of a set of gray silk pajamas. Then she pointed to the bunk bed on the left. "You sleep there. Top or bottom, doesn't matter."

Maya nodded, and the girl headed over to her bed. She was grateful for her spot, it being the farthest away from Brian. Said boy hadn't made a noise since the moment she had walked in. He laid on the bottom bunk, back turned away from the rest. Maya didn't mind.

She was stopped in her tracks when she noticed a familiar brown cinch bag placed on her pillow and slouched against the back wall. Maya couldn't help but run to it, resting the bag on her lap. It was heavy—heavier than it had been when she had filled it. Gently, she opened the top, revealing a new toothbrush, toothpaste, a variety of soap bottles, and a crossword booklet. Her booklet.

Maya held it to her chest, soaking up its familiarity. Mr. Hue and his agents must have gone back and retrieved it. She made a mental note to thank him the next time they crossed paths.

She tucked the book and bag under her bed before examining her own set of pajamas that was laid out over the blankets. Taking it to the restroom, she changed into the silky pj's and placed her uniform into a cupboard. Then, with her new toothbrush, brushed her teeth, followed by washing her face. The mirror over the sink was clearer than any she had seen in years. The pale light exposed her tired eyes. Her sunken cheeks. Her knotted curls. Even the deep wash she had been given by the jets couldn't fix it.

Slowly, she rolled up the gray sleeve of her shirt and moved her fingers over the tattoo that had been etched on her younger skin: the symbol of the crescent moons.

It could be worse, she reasoned with herself. *I could be with SCRO right now, being shipped from one side of the country to the other.*

But the more Maya recounted the day, from escaping Broth to being injected with supposed vaccines, the more she couldn't shake the horrible feeling that she still wasn't *free.*

Mr. Hue had said they could only hold her until she was eighteen. What would happen if she wanted to leave now? This wasn't a normal facility, Maya knew that for sure. Nevertheless, the children seemed fairly normal, but so many questions arose from the lab and academy that she couldn't help but wonder if they withheld countless secrets as well.

Maya rolled down her sleeve and walked out of the bathroom. The room lights had been switched off, a blue night-light allowing the slightest bit of visibility. Lilith was scrolling through a tablet on the bunk on top of Brian, who still was turned away, most likely sleeping. The other two teens on the opposite side were fighting over who got to sleep closer to the ceiling.

She fell onto her bed, the mattress engulfing her. For a moment, Maya felt like she weighed five hundred pounds, her muscles twigs struggling to resist snapping. Gradually, she made her way under the thick covers that offered her more warmth than Broth's ever had, reminding her of a simpler time of family, joy, and peace. She rolled over and let her arm swing, only for her knuckles to hit something hard.

Cautiously unfolding the blanket, Maya found a black buckle. Her confusion only grew when she discovered the other part of it connecting to the opposing side of the bed. Another seatbelt-like contraption was located at the end, where her feet reached.

A clicking sound came from Lilith's area. The girl was fastening the belt around her arms, having put down the tablet. Across the room, the two others were doing so as well.

Her head spun as she said, "What are the buckles for?"

An answer came, but not from the person she was expecting. Brian turned around, face illuminated with the faint blue light. His eyes contained a sense of hatred she could not fathom.

"Nightmares," the boy said bitterly. "There's *always* nightmares."

Chapter Fifteen

"Secrets Of The Dreams"

Griffin seemed particularly irritated that night. Or maybe that was his normal attitude. Maya hadn't known him long enough to make that kind of discernment.

He didn't speak, or greet, or even sneak a glance towards her direction as he marched forward with a hardened expression that didn't so much as twitch. "What are you going to teach me?" she asked the grumpy man. When she had first materialized, Griffin had told her to follow him and that, in his exact words, "Talon wants you to learn this. Don't think it's coming from me." Then he refused to elaborate.

Present Griffin bit his lip. "Melding."

"That's where you bring something from a dream to here, right?"

"Sounds *so* simple, doesn't it?"

He didn't seem pleased with the idea, so Maya decided to sucker up to him. "But I just got here, and that seems like it could be dangerous. Why would they want me to learn that so soon?"

Griffin sucked in his cheeks so far that Maya wondered if the stubble on his face poked the inside of his mouth. "Couldn't have said it better, *kind.*"

Maya took this time to get a better look at the man. It suddenly struck her that he wasn't as old as she originally thought—at least, Kalpana Griffin wasn't. He appeared to be in his mid to late twenties and very fit. But that was masked by his shaggy appearance: the wild matted hair, the not-quite-a-beard, and the crinkled and torn up outfit; then there were the dark circles under his eyes and wrinkles on his forehead and between his eyebrows that shouldn't have been there for a few more years. His skin looked like it hadn't been washed since forever, dirt crusting over it. And then, at the tip of his fingers, there was the red stain of old blood.

She shivered at the sight. Kai's words about the side effects of hidden guilt rang in her ears. The accompanying emotions of regretful past or present actions couldn't be hidden in a subconscious projection. What history did Griffin have that the blood was still visible on his hands? How dangerous was he?

"To be fair, it was more of Halo's idea," Griffin said while gritting his teeth. "Never thought she'd be one to go soft for a newbie. But she also always manages to get what she wants, so here I am, teaching possibly the most hazardous skill to a stranger."

"Hazardous?"

"Not the skill itself, but what someone can do with it. Dreams free from the dreamworld are more powerful than any single person could comprehend. Our imagination is capable of creating terrible things. Melding can make it real."

Maya tilted her head. "I thought it only brings it into Kalpana."

"Take a look around, Amie. Does this feel real to you?"

A breeze blew back her hair. The twinkles in the sky shone brightly within the clouds. The side of the castle they walked beside was covered with vines, flowers emerging from the stems. Birds occupying the garden filled the air with song, with the wind dancing along to its melody.

"The first thing you need to get through your skull is that Kalpana is as real as anything you've ever experienced. You think what happens in this realm doesn't affect Terra? Thousands of babies die every year from failing to cross over to Kalpana. People slip into comas after being trapped in the Void. Hearts stop from the continuous onslaught of nightdwellers, and others become slaves to the will of Tenebris. Then there's people like us that don't have the luxury of being shielded by dreams. Dreamers die, they wake up. Omnis die, we don't. We may only be a projection of ourselves here, but the body can't live without the conscious. There's no reset button for us. Once you realize that, you'll be wishing you never became omniscient."

He turned away, but not before Maya could see the sadness in his eyes.

They entered the palace and Griffin fell back into silence, which left her tending to her own thoughts and worries. The vines from the outside broke through the stained glass, adding a breath of light into the enclosed architecture. And as they marched forward, Maya wondered why the vines were so keen on entering the castle with its caged walls and tall but finite ceilings, instead of remaining outdoors, where there were no such limits.

Faintly, Maya heard a familiar raspy voice coming from one of the rooms they passed. Griffin stopped in front of her, putting out a hand to keep her from moving forward. With a sigh, he said, "Stay here."

He didn't get far, however, before someone busted open the door. It was the old, haggard man with his white hair, frail and hunched over. In one hand, he held the cane that allowed him to support himself, while in the other he grasped a white flower.

"Revere!" The man called out. "Where'd you go, you little rascal?"

"Quite a bit of noise you're making here, Hypnos."

The old man turned his head towards Griffin and his eyes lit up. "Well, good to see you too, son! Revere escaped again, can you believe it?"

"At this point, you might as well let your pet roam free."

"You kidding? Revere's gonna stick with me for the rest of my life, which shouldn't be too long anyways. And..." Hypnos's eyes widened in recognition when he noticed Maya by his side. She slowly shook her head, hoping he could catch that they weren't supposed to have met. "... who do we have here?" Maya almost fell over in relief. "A new member of our humble home?"

"A guest," Griffin clarified, appearing to not notice the obvious tension. "Until further notice."

The man rolled his eyes. "Oh, Griffin. Forever the suspecting one, aren't you?" Hypnos offered her a smile that closely resembled a smirk. "What's your name, little lady?"

His warm expression helped ease Maya's anxiety, and she tucked a curl behind her ear. "Amie."

"A pleasure to meet you." The man gave her a wink, which she hoped Griffin hadn't noticed. Hypnos peered down the hall. "Say, you didn't happen to see any little furballs running around here, did you? He usually comes when he smells me holding his favorite flower, but Revere seems to be in a stubborn mood today."

Maya smiled fondly at the memory of the adorable creature. "I haven't, but I'd love to meet him."

"I'm sure you two would get along."

She didn't even register that Griffin was no longer by her side until she heard a chirp from down the hall. Hypnos let out a cheer and Maya felt a smile form as Griffin marched toward them, holding the restless creature in his hands. It turned and flipped around, pawing at the gruff man's face before hopping down and darting towards them. To Maya's surprise, Revere didn't head straight for Hypnos and instead rammed its head into her legs in a way that demanded attention.

She chuckled, bending down and stroking its back. The same familiarity that had accompanied the first time she pet the creature overwhelmed her, leaving her all the more confused.

Hypnos stood behind her with his free hand on his hip. "And how could I have known that?" The man bent down on both knees and reached his arms out. "Come here you little rascal! Come to papa!"

The creature seemed to be debating for a second before deciding to slowly walk to the man, succumbing to Hypnos picking it up and squeezing it to his chest, like releasing it would spell out the end for all.

Maya was about to ask exactly what the creature was before Hypnos held out the white flower, grinning. "For you, little lady." And with a grateful nod, she picked it up and tucked it behind her ear. When Griffin was turned away, she mouthed a thank-you to the man, who held laughter in his eyes as he whispered, "Don't be getting into trouble, now."

After exchanging farewells, she and Griffin continued on their way and entered the Dome. It was more packed than the day before, with only a few empty spots here and there. In his hands, Griffin held a familiar rope and tied it around a skinny middle-aged woman, who he guided outside through a backdoor and onto a large patch of grass. The plateau made a steep drop off that was blocked off by a brown wooden fence. She peered down and recognized the large purple bushes. If she squinted her eyes enough, Maya could vaguely make out the crystals reflecting the sky.

Griffin tied the rope to one of the poles. "Why do we need to come out here?" she asked.

"Why do you feel the need to ask so many questions?" he retorted, and Maya shut her mouth to stop herself from prying any further. *Why do you give such vague answers?*

The man tightened the knot. "Melding is unpredictable at the start. Rather not be someplace where you could accidentally bump into someone and invade their dream. Here." From his pocket, he pulled out a bracelet that he instructed her to put on her wrist. Maya desired to ask what purpose it served, but refrained. Griffin must have noticed, however, as he said, "Just put it on, *kind*." She obliged.

When she had it wrapped around her wrist, he gave her another bracelet with a large button. This one she knew the function of, but Griffin made sure she'd only press the button exactly when he told her to. They even ran through numerous practice sessions, where he would cue her on and Maya would pretend to slap it. She grew extremely tempted to press the wrong bracelet just to mess with him, but Griffin was currently on her list of people *not* to joke around with.

"We won't use the headbands to keep her dreaming because it makes melding plenty harder. So you have to make sure that the dreamer does *not* see you, got it?" He waited for her to nod. "Good. Now, when you latch onto what you're planning to meld, there's gonna be a lag. Every newbie pulls with all their might and ends up being flung back. The larger the object, the more recoil. That's why we're gonna start small. Not like you would be able to meld any larger stuff yet anyways, but—hey, are you even listening?"

She was, as a matter of fact, not.

In her defense, she had been paying close attention to his instructions to make sure she didn't accidentally shatter someone's dream state again, until her mind had wandered to Kai's silhouette from the other side of the castle. He emerged from the valley, walking side by side with a new dreamer he had discovered along his trek. The dreamer seemed to be giving him issues as he pulled on a rope. His hands slipped as he yanked it and he fell on his back, laid on the ground, and stayed there. Maya chewed on her cheek to stop herself from smiling. *Dork.*

"Ah," Griffin said when he noticed what she had been staring at, pinched the bridge of his nose, shook his head, then mumbled something under his breath.

Maya pulled on her front curl. "Sorry. I'll pay attention now."

Griffin grunted and shoved his hands in his pants' pockets. "Listen to me, Amie. You think that boy is cute over there, huh? You think he's the man of your dreams."

Maya reeled, a snort rising from her chest. "I never said that."

"Eighty percent of all men were wiped out, so you feel the desire to go after the first guy you see."

"*What?*"

"And I don't know how old you are, or where you're from, or if your name is really Amie. But I'm gonna go out on a limb and say you're young. Meaning you got a whole life ahead of you to find the man you love. But that boy over there? Only hurt is gonna come from a relationship with him, so you stay away, got it?"

Maya blinked a few times.

"*Got it?*"

"Yes. Yes, I got it."

She did not get it.

It wasn't like she was actively looking for a relationship, much less with a boy who appeared more inclined to tease her and get her in trouble than anything. Even besides that, right now she more so desired to find her own freedom before being joined with someone else, since there were too many things going on in her life to even consider it. Just the thought of it brought about a hysterical fit of giggles.

Then again, Griffin's order almost made her wish to rebel, because how *dare* this twenty-something going on forty year old man tell her who she's able to be with? What was up with adults always micromanaging the lives of those around them?

"Good," Griffin stated, as if assuming they had reached some sort of consensus. "Now, let's go back to work." He ordered Maya to stand in front of the woman, whose eyeballs were moving rapidly behind her lids. "You're gonna put one hand, *only* one hand, on her temple when I say so. Then you will wait until you see me there, understood?"

After a deep breath to calm herself, she nodded, hovering a hand over the woman's cheek.

"Now."

Maya pressed against her temple, and the second she did, she was transported someplace else.

The mind was quiet. White like a blank canvas. She wondered if her voice would even echo if she called out.

It was unlike the previous mind she had entered, where she had instantly seen the nightmare. In this mind, Maya had to struggle to see the speck of color that was farther along the white chamber. Griffin made his appearance shortly after, removing his hands from his pockets. He raised an eyebrow at her. "You didn't move."

"You told me not to."

He grunted, as if her following his instructions was some incomprehensible idea. She was told to be quiet as they walked toward the dream scene.

The woman was dreaming of butterflies.

They fluttered across the glittering landscape and over the clouds that were created from yarn. Some butterflies dropped down and grew bodies, their faces a mix of human and insect. They made spine-chilling rattles in the back of their throats, a few of them having snippets of human dialogue breaking through that brought along no comprehensible meaning behind it. It had a distinct smell. Not of a particular thing, but of an emotion. Wonder.

The dream was so whimsical. So childish. So... happy.

Maya looked around to see anything they could meld out of the scene, but everything seemed alive. Even the clouds breathed.

"Can someone meld something that's living?" Maya said quietly.

Griffin's facial expression didn't so much as twitch as he told her, "That's complicated. And forbidden. Follow me."

They snuck past a morphing humanoid butterfly. Maya accidentally skimmed its wing and it snapped around, but appeared to look right through her. Uneasy, Maya hustled over to Griffin's side.

Past the dream were two black holes. Light swelled behind the spinning vacuum, a portal leading to the depths of the woman's consciousness, and somehow she knew that everything this stranger had ever experienced lay inside that wormhole. Maya had access to it all.

Her face paled at the sudden realization.

They didn't enter that one, and instead ventured into the neighboring entrance. This wormhole was smaller and darker. Griffin explained how this was where previous dreams were stored.

"Even if a person forgets," he said, "the dream doesn't disappear."

As they entered, a sharp pain erupted behind Maya's eyes from the overwhelming attack on her senses. Thousands of colors burst before her. Emotions like fear and longing, as well as more positive ones like joy, could almost be *seen,* swirling above her head. Griffin, contrarily, didn't appear fazed from the onslaught of colors as he reached for a glowing yellow ball just above their heads. He grasped it and held the stubborn sphere in place.

Lifting it above his head, he told Maya, "Get your *gat* ready for a butt ton of nostalgia."

Then he slammed it to the ground.

Yellow fog sprayed across the floor, transforming the landscape. Towers of coins and ancient artifacts surrounded them, laying at their feet. Rubies twinkled deep inside the piles. Weapons like swords and spears shimmered. Looking up, Maya could see moonlight pouring from a little opening in the sky. They were in a cave.

Under her feet, the coins crunched and rolled down the piles. She nearly slipped, but Griffin caught her by the arm. Her head spun with the feeling of remembrance and longing for some distant experience that was not her own. From the sky fell the dreamer, sporting an exploring outfit. The woman turned her head in her and Griffin's direction, Griffin quickly pulling them out of sight. They slid down the pile of unfathomable wealth all the way to the bottom of the cave. The stone floor was slippery and cold as Maya fell roughly onto her knees and when she finally managed to stand up, Griffin was already spinning a golden coin in his hand. Flicking it in her direction, Maya caught it.

"We start with the coin," he told her as he grabbed his own. "It's a strange feeling that you're searching for. One the brain isn't used to, like forming a new nerve connection. Can you feel the coin in your hand?"

"Yes."

He nodded in a way that almost gave the sense of approval. "A good start. Probably easier because you were a dreamer beforehand. Now, close your eyes and really *feel* the coin and our surroundings."

Maya did, allowing darkness to overtake her vision.

Everything felt hazy, just like her own previous dreams. Even with her eyes closed, she could sense the mounts of coins and artifacts. She could picture the woman in her explorer outfit and Griffin as a bead of light. It was as though everything had strings attached to it, and Maya had the bundle in her hands.

She was in control of *everything*.

All she had to do was *tug*.

Maya snapped her eyes open just as a wave of butterflies surged in from the top of the cave. They blocked out the light of the moon and swarmed the dreamer until she was no longer visible.

"Dreams are merging," Griffin stated. "Happens sometimes. Keep going."

Maya's hands trembled as she stepped back. Her mind was still spinning, her senses still tingling. Even with her eyes now opened, the threads were still there, tempting her to pull them. And somehow, she knew exactly what would happen if she gave in.

Is this what it means to be Lucid?

Is this why they're afraid of people like me?

Griffin's arms were crossed as he raised an eyebrow. "You don't wanna close your eyes? Fine by me. Go ahead, try to latch your brain to the coin. See how much harder it is."

Maya gulped at the way his eyes bore into her. Without being entirely sure what she was doing, Maya felt her mind wrap itself around the coin. Like an invisible hand reaching out, the medallion was lifted up and spun in the air. A glimmer made its way across its reflective surface before stopping.

With eyes as wide as Broth's gut, Griffin stared at her, mouth agape. "I didn't tell you how to do that."

The taste in her mouth was bitter. In some ways, she was just as surprised as Griffin. It felt so *natural* to manipulate the coin. So much so that she hadn't been fully aware of herself doing it, much less how to recreate said feeling. It was as though a foreign entity had taken control, which instilled an even greater sense of fear within her. Not of any outer force, but of *herself.*

Griffin's expression then started to morph into a grimace that reflected her internal emotions. There was a change in the atmosphere surrounding them. The warm presence of nostalgia vanished, changing into something colder. Darker.

The ground shook. The moon hid. Butterflies fell from the sky. From some of the medallions sprouted little black legs that scurried over the pile. They lost their golden sheen and became dark and hairy.

Spiders.

The vile arachnids crawled up her arms and legs. As quickly as she swept them away, more took their place. A scream made its way up her throat, which was muffled by Griffin's hand covering her mouth.

The spiders covered him too, crawling in his hair. He bent over and rubbed his scalp ferociously, his eyes burning with a mix of anger and fear.

"Recoup," he yelled while jamming his thumb on his bracelet. A portal opened up. "Recoup!"

Then he disappeared.

Chapter Sixteen

"Mortality Exists In All Realms"

Frozen, Maya didn't register the sudden lightness on her wrist. A spider crawled across her face and she yelped, smacking it off. She jabbed her finger to the button as well, only for her blood to run cold when she was met with nothing but bare skin.

Peering around frantically, she searched for anything resembling a bracelet. Her vision got darker and a mystical fog started to pour out from the rocky cracks. The spiders that touched the fog immediately flipped onto their backs with their legs curled up. Dead.

She could only focus on one arm in front of the other as she climbed up the pile of medallions. Another hairy eight-legged creature made its way onto her hand, which Maya flung away, but the action caused her hand to slide. She lost her footing, skidding down the side of the heap. In a wild panic, her grip searched for anything to hold onto. Shoving her hands into the coins, she ignored the spiders that stung her and she started to slow down, but the fog was accumulating higher. She wasn't stopping fast enough.

With a final grunt, she grasped onto the handle of a spear that had lodged itself deeply into the stack. Her legs swung around at the sudden stop, her shoulder straining from the shock. She didn't waste any time dwelling on it. Her body moved on its own as she crawled up the pile. The golden spear served as her springboard, bearing her weight when she stood on it and pushed up. Climbing wasn't a smooth endeavor — the coins underneath her kept on rolling down the hill, causing her to backtrack. Hissing came from the spiders that had landed in the fog, boiling and fizzing away.

"There's no reset button for us." Griffin's words played on repeat inside her mind.

I could die.

She kept climbing.

Cries from the woman in the dream grew louder as Maya neared the top. Her eyes roughly skimmed the surface for the recouper. Spiders passed by next to her, beating Maya in the race to the top. And among them, on one of their backs, a quick flash of color.

The bracelet.

She hurried after it, reaching her arms forward. The fog was nearly halfway up the pile. The arachnids were too fast. The top came into sight. With a new adrenaline rush, she ran on all fours. The way out was nearly in her reach. She could almost snatch it–

The spider disappeared over the top, her hand reaching right after it. She panted as she felt the spider squirming under her hand. That's when she noticed the woman's screaming had stopped. Which didn't make any sense to her, until she turned to see the dreamer's eyes fixed directly on her.

Maya's presence had been spotted.

Instantaneously, cracks started to form in the air like glass. The ground quaked again, rougher this time, which allowed the spider to escape from underneath. With no way out, she screamed, watching helplessly as the woman flickered in and out of the realm. The spiders attacked her, covering her like a blanket of needles.

"Stop!" she cried. "STOP!"

And it did.

The cracks stopped growing. The ground stopped shaking. The spiders stopped climbing. And the woman stared blankly, frozen in place.

"You don't see me."

The spiders backed up. The woman blinked. Then she turned away, lost in the nightmare once again.

Maya didn't so much as think when she ran over to the bracelet that now lay unattended among the coins. She fastened it tightly to her wrist, making sure it couldn't fall off again.

Fog was still pouring from the crevices. In a hurry, she pressed the large button, and at the action, a spinning light formed in front of her. A portal back to Kalpana opened up and through it, she could see Kai and Griffin looking at each other.

No, she corrected herself. *Not at each other. Past each other.*

Maya could only watch in horror as two black shadows like those she had been imprisoned with attacked both of them. Kai fell onto his back, prodding his weapon in the air, to no avail. Griffin had managed to remain on his feet, side-stepping the nightdweller, but the frantic movements of his eyes revealed his split attention.

If she went back now, she would be caught in the battle, defenseless.

A reckless plan formulated in her mind as she backed away from the portal, watching it close on its own. If a weapon was what she needed, a weapon she would get.

The opening of the cave was blocked with the fog. The air smelled of fear. Maya rubbed her arms to calm her nerves.

Her mind recalled the spear she had used to hold onto earlier and hustled back to the side of the pile of coins, peering down. The spear was nowhere to be found, masked by the acid-like fog.

Her foot slipped and Maya jumped back, ignoring the way the coins hissed as they fell. The dreamer's screams grew louder. When Maya turned to see what was causing the increase in volume, what looked like a black shadow was encompassing her. The dreamer needed to awaken, but Maya's presence was keeping the lady trapped. She needed to get out, and fast.

Maya ran to the other side of the pile and searched for anything she could use as a weapon. A bling of red caught her eye. A golden sword and its handle jutted out from the pile, a ruby at its tip. And of course, it happened to be over the side of the mound.

But as she gazed around, it became clear that the sword was the only weapon accessible. And with the fog making its way higher and higher, the window of time to grab it would be slim.

So she did what any rational person would do.

She went after it.

Maya skidded sideways, allowing her body weight to take her down. Her hands burned as she gripped deeply into the coin stack, slowing her descent, feet now resting right over the hilt.

The line of fog was directly underneath it, and Maya could already feel the sting of its vapors. Reaching her foot down, she shoved it under the blade. Flexed her toes to hook it. And flicked up.

Maya let go of the pile with her right arm to catch it.

Then she felt herself fall.

Screaming, she instinctively jabbed the sword in the pile to stop herself, but not before her left foot was dipped into the fog. A fierce burning sensation erupted from the limb and Maya cried out in pain, jerking her foot back. Blisters bubbled her skin, a nauseating smell emerging from it.

She pulled herself up, praying to God for the sword to hold. Her foot hung slack as she dragged herself up, racing the growing cloud of acid. At the top, she crawled to the level surface. Gasping for air, she studied the sword in her hands, blinking away the tears that peppered her eyes. Maya tried to mimic the feeling of wrapping her mind around the object, but she was too scatter-brained to focus. She slapped her head and sought out the threads she had sensed earlier. Taking a shaky breath, Maya closed her eyes and instantly felt in tune with her surroundings. The invisible hand of her mind held onto the sword, much heavier than the coin had been.

Maya gasped as the ground shook again, the pile collapsing underneath her. In a panicked frenzy, she punched the recouper and a portal opened up in front of her. Feeling herself sinking, she closed her eyes and took a deep breath.

Then she jumped.

The portal sucked her in with ease, but the sword held some resistance. Maya's fingers cramped from the strain of holding onto it, sensing the grip slipping from her hands. In a final attempt, she pulled with all her might.

It was only as she was sent flying through the air that she remembered Griffin's warning against doing exactly that.

Her body barely grazed the soft grass as she shot forward. Maya couldn't slow herself down, even when the fence blocking the edge of the hill came into sight. Her right heel dug into the ground in vain. She wasn't slowing down fast enough.

The only thing she could think to do was to press her body against the ground. Sliding under the fence, she narrowly missed the wooden plank. A grunt escaped her lips as she grabbed the pole with her free hand, stopping her fall off the cliff. She grimaced. Her hand had somehow managed to hold onto the sword that shimmered in all its glory, but she wasn't able to catch her breath before she caught sight of a familiar black shadow.

The nightdweller attacked her from above. Maya leaned to the side, narrowly avoiding contact. She fumbled the sword wildly around to keep the monster at bay. Swinging her body back and forth, she reached her leg up in an attempt to hook her foot around the neighboring pole. A loud cry came from her as the foot that managed to latch on happened to be her injured one. Despite the temperature drop from the nightdwellers' presence, sweat trickled down her forehead. Like how she had done with the terror of the situation, Maya pushed away the pain and pulled herself up for the third time that day.

The moment she had reached the level ground, the nightdweller slammed into her back, knocking her breath away. It clung to her throat, stopping air from entering her lungs. Her vision became cloudy. A familiar scene with her parents and sister started materializing before her, and Maya shook uncontrollably.

No. Not again.

She sat with her sister. Amarie told her to put on the headphones. They climbed up the ladder. They looked down–

The nightmare then vanished before her and the ability to breathe returned. Maya sucked in the air around her like a vacuum, her lungs constantly screaming, *More. MORE.*

Her hands trembled as the sword fell from her grasp, and after a few seconds she looked up to see Griffin holding a short spear, its tip no longer glowing.

He didn't offer her any assistance in getting up, so Maya did so on her own, avoiding putting weight on her left foot. In the better light, she could see the way the fog had eaten away her shoes and socks, revealing the soles of her feet with even more blisters.

Griffin's expression didn't hold pity. If anything, it swarmed with even more suspicion, but he didn't have time to say a word before their attention was drawn to a shout from across the field.

On the ground lay Kai, who had fallen victim to one of the nightdwellers. The black shadow spun around him, and his eyes were a cloudy gray. His body seized, chest heaving. His mouth remained open, as if he was stuck in a permanent state of agony.

Maya and Griffin sprinted over and the latter lifted his spear. He brought it down onto the black cloud, causing it to be sucked into the weapon. Kai's shaking gradually stopped as his color slowly returned.

Bending down on her knees, Maya hovered her hand over his chest, preparing to wake him. She tried to reign in her terror-struck expression to something more neutral when she heard a groan escape Kai's lips.

"Are you okay?" Her voice trembled slightly more than she would have liked. The boy didn't respond, turning onto his side and moving his hands under himself in order to sit up.

She reached out her hand to aid him, only for Kai to refuse it and state, "I'm fine."

"Are you sure–"

"I'm fine!"

An unconscious flinch racked her body at the elevated volume of his voice while Kai stood up with a wobble, roughly brushing the residue of the nightdweller off himself. Without a word he stormed off, head low, arms shoved in his pockets, then entered back into the mansion.

Maya could only stare for a moment as she hugged herself, as if her arms could be a shield to block the fear from reaching her heart.

"Give me that." Without warning, Griffin snatched her sword, Maya still too distracted to resist. The gruff man lifted the weapon up to his eyes and observed the sword in the light, the stars reflecting from its lustrous coating.

"Not a single imperfection," he spoke to himself with a sense of marvelment, but his awed expression served to be temporary as his gawking features darkened. He turned to stare at her.

"You've done this before." It wasn't a question; it was a statement.

"I haven't."

"Then tell me." He took a wide step towards her. "Tell me how you managed to meld an entire sword *perfectly* on your very first try, when it takes everyone else as long as a lifetime to even come *close* to this level of mastery in melding alone."

"Maybe I'm just a fast learner."

Then Griffin held the sword to her throat.

"I am not stupid, Amie." Maya attempted to step back, but he brought the weapon closer. "Something about your presence here does not add up. I can always tell when someone lies. One way or another, whatever secrets you are hiding *will* come out. And you and whoever you are working for will suffer the consequences, *Tenebris*."

Maya had forgotten the art of ventilation as Griffin lowered the sword. He gave her a final glare before turning away with a sway of his dirty blonde hair and tattered shirt, tucking her sword under his arm.

And as Griffin walked into the distance, there was only one thought on her mind.

I really wanted that sword.

Chapter Seventeen

"First Days, Old Pains"

Maya had assumed the pain in her foot would disappear when she woke up, just like how injuries disappeared when she slept. It didn't.

Her first action upon opening her eyes was curling her body up to her injury, only for the motion to be stopped by the straps around her limbs. Wrestling them loose, she threw off the blanket and studied her foot, but there was nothing. Not a scratch, or a blister, or even a slight discoloration. It was unscathed.

But it felt like hell.

She took deep breaths to stop tears from forming and laid back down on the bed. None of the others stirred, all of them fast asleep in their bunk beds with not a whistle from their noses, creating an atmosphere of unnerving silence. This made it all the more terrifying when the silence was suddenly disrupted by the sound of thrashing.

Maya could only watch in a state of horror-stricken awe as Brian seized in his sleep, stretching the straps to their limit. He didn't speak any words, but the series of grunts omitting from his mouth sounded as though he was in a battle with his own inner demons. Knowing what she knew now, Maya had no doubt that was exactly what he was doing.

As abruptly as it began, the trembling ceased. A final breath came from the boy as he sank back into a more restful sleep, but sweat drops on his forehead that shimmered with reflections of the blue night light made it clear that the nightmare was far from over. *He hasn't found the camp yet.* Despite the boy's sour attitude, she couldn't help but feel pity for anyone experiencing nightmares like herself.

Although exhaustion had placed lead onto her eyelids, sleep remained a foreign endeavor. She fixed her focus on counting the number of dark tiles on the ceiling. Peering through the dim light would strain her eyes and the headache it caused would be enough to dull the pain in her foot. But when she'd rest, the phantom pain would come back with a vengeance. She'd release a sharp gasp and hold it — nothing could soothe the burning.

What must have been hours later, a screeching alarm startled Maya, adrenaline instantly waking her. The four other teenagers were much calmer than herself as they unclicked their braces and sat up on their beds. On the bunk shared by the two boys, the one on top hopped down and was met with a cry of protest by the one underneath. A snicker could be heard as the boy jumped on the bed and held his friend under the sheets.

"Can you two *shut up*?" Brian's gruff voice mumbled. His frizzy red hair was even more chaotic than the day before, and the bruises under his eyes revealed his less-than-peaceful slumber.

The kid on top whined, but loosened up the blanket. The smothered boy's head burst out as he gasped for air, and with a shove to his attacker, he stood up and reached for his pair of glasses.

"Do you feel the need to do that every morning?" the boy grumbled, adjusting his lens.

"Someone's got to loosen you up." His friend stretched his arms upwards and groaned.

Lilith then climbed down the ladder. "Brian's right. A bit of silence would be pleasurable, and I don't believe you two are making the best impression on our new guest."

Dead silence immediately spread across the whole room. Maya felt all of their stern eyes on her, and she rubbed her hand on her bandaged wrist. Gone was the light bickering mood, replaced with hostile gazes.

"New kid." The previously loud-mouthed boy with dirty-blond hair crossed his arms and tossed the name out like it was some kind of demeaning title.

"Maya."

"*Huh?*"

"It's–"

"Irrelevant," Brian interrupted, and Maya bit her cheek. "You're whatever we call you, Mayo."

With a scoff, she retorted, "Really? Bold words for a kid whose name could be 'brain' with a simple letter switch." Thinking back, such a statement didn't seem like the appropriate response. But she was in pain, exhausted, and tired of those around her feeling like they could say anything they wanted to her. She had put up with it for eight years with Broth, and she wasn't keen on allowing herself to be degraded anymore, especially by a freckled boy whose head barely reached her chin.

As expected, the words were not taken kindly. Brian brought his face close enough for Maya to smell his unbrushed teeth and sneered. "I'd be careful if I were you. Chance may have classes and schedules, but it isn't a school. There isn't detention, suspension, or expulsion. The supervisors have their own agendas they follow and couldn't care less about what we do to each other when they're not around. I can hurt you in any way I please, and no one will be there to stop me."

She turned to look at the other kids in the room for any aid, but they simply stared at the interaction with neutral expressions, not the slightest look of concern in their eyes. Brian jerked forward, causing her to flinch. A malicious snicker came from the boy at her reaction and he turned on his heel to head into the bathroom.

Maya was still boring a hole into the back of the boy's head as Lilith shoved her uniform into her arms. "You put this in my cupboard last night." Without another word, she left to her bed, the two boys dispersing to theirs as well.

The outfit crinkled as she curled her fingers, releasing her pent-up fury onto it. Deep breaths allowed her to clear her mind and walk back to her bed, straightening the duvet out of habit. *Whatever. I'm used to this.* If she could handle Broth, she could handle anything.

When it was her turn to get ready, she changed and brushed her teeth so rough that her gums bled. Even in a refuge filled with people, she was more alone than ever. Maya only hoped her schedule would place her with Carlos and Camila so she could have some sort of kind familiarity to latch onto.

It wasn't too long after that an elderly woman with a badge walked into the room and handed her a tablet without engaging in any conversation. Maya's expression of gratitude landed on deaf ears as the lady hobbled out of the room with a shut of the door. With an annoyed huff, she crawled onto her bed with her legs crossed and placed the tablet on her lap. At her touch, the screen lit up; it was a blue screen with her name in all caps at the middle, and the symbol of the eagle underneath. In a tiny font at the top it read, *Press to open.*

It was no surprise to Maya when a beam of light scanned her face at the action. A loading sign occupied the screen, but unlike with the letter, this gadget graciously flashed green. The tablet opened up to a home screen with numerous different icons ranging from electronic textbooks to mind puzzles, but before she could select one, a pop-up filled the screen. *Click to see Schedule.*

It revealed a variety of strange class names, the first one bearing the title "Polemology," though Maya highly doubted it was the study of poles. Colored labels by each name let her know which color bands she would be with. The six courses alternated between red and blue, and while that meant she'd still get half of them with Camila and Carlos, she still sat there grinding her teeth.

Polemology just turned out to be an overly complicated name for history.

In front of the class stood a brown man with hollow cheeks and clearly fake brown hair. His yellow collared shirt had been tucked into his tight jeans, but it must have been in a hurry, for half of it was falling out. With what looked like a fairy wand, he tapped on his wrist impatiently, and Maya was positive the teacher hadn't blinked a single time.

"Class." His higher-pitched voice took her off guard, and if it wasn't for years of practicing self control, she would have laughed. Maya wiggled around to sit up straight in her chair to give the man her full attention. He glanced at her before continuing. "My name is Professor Vincent! Since there has been a... newer arrival, I intend to start this lesson with the event that created the need for Chance."

"The Nuclear War," the boy with glasses said, which reminded Maya that she still had no idea what his name was.

"*Technically*, the three world wars before that also used nuclear power. The only reason the general public calls it that is because it was the only war that used nukes so profusely. For educational purposes, I will be referring to it as World War 5. Can any of you tell me what started the war?"

Silence spread over the students.

"Maya!" At the mention of her name, Maya stiffened. "What do *you* think started the war?"

How should I know? I haven't been in school since before the whole thing started, would not have been the appropriate thing to say.

"Well..." The snicker from the other boy's friend (she desperately needed to learn their names) made her blood boil. "I guess it was The Harvest?"

The professor waved his hand. "No, before that, before that! What happened to society?"

More chuckles came from the class and Maya tightened her jaw. "Before that war was World War 4, and before that was the Second Golden Age. Everything seemed perfect. It didn't seem like there was any reason to go to war."

Prof. Vincent snapped and exclaimed, "Exactly!" which caused her to jump. "Now, why would a world that was near perfect in every way turn in on itself? Medication could cure any disease. Technology made it possible to get whatever you desire instantly. Controlled environments allowed for production of food at an astronomical level. There were no inconveniences. No struggle. So why? *Why?*"

The emotion radiating from the teacher caused fear to spike her chest.

An uncanny smile grew on Vincent's face. "Because humans *need* pain. They *crave* it. And what do they do when every problem is solved? They create new ones, whether that be between their own people, or between countries. I guess one could claim that, in a way, intelligence breeds insanity."

Psychology wasn't any less strange.

To her disappointment, there happened to be many more red banded children than blue-bands, and with her incredibly golden luck, she was placed in a lesson with strangers. Not that it happened to matter who she was with, since everyone was handed a strange contraption that went on top of their heads, inhibiting any engagement with others. When the mass of wires was switched on, a projection of her own brain was revealed, flashes of light representing the nerve connections. With the wave of her hand, she could zoom in closer to see what looked like fireworks going off, bringing her fascination along with it. All she had to do was click on a certain section of the brain, and an automated voice would tell her exactly what the section was responsible for.

Everything was perfect.

That was until an image of a laughing Broth filled the scene.

In a matter of seconds, the contraption was off of Maya's head, her heart beating at an unhealthy rate. Broth's cackles morphed into those of the obese professor.

"Hah! I don't remember telling anyone to take the mind scanner off!"

Maya sucked on her cheek. All around the classroom, students were sitting with their helmets off, a few of them flung across the room. She could have sworn she heard a girl crying in the back.

A series of whines illustrated the children's reluctance as they placed the contraptions back on their heads. Maya sighed deeply, then copied their action.

In Radiobiology, they dissected human eyes. Don't ask her how she knew it was real human eyeballs. It didn't make sense that the way it stared back at her had made her so absolutely certain.

She was back with the small band of bullies from earlier, and they seemed much more calm at the prospect of studying the organ than her as they put on blue gloves. Swallowing back a gag, Maya picked the eye up and tried not to think about the rubbery texture, or who the round ball had belonged to previously. She especially didn't wonder how in the infinite universe the teacher had come in possession of it.

She had never been more glad when the bell rang for lunch.

"You get sauces this time?" the Latino boy teased, and Maya sat down with a hmph.

"No, I decided not to use any sauces just out of spite." She poured ketchup on her hamburger.

"Bad first day?" Camila's robotic voice asked, and Maya slumped her head onto the table.

"It... could have been better. Are the blue-banded kids always jerks to everybody?"

Carlos took a bite of his sub and talked with a full mouth. "Eh, usually everyone stays out of their way. I think they think they're too cool for us. But since you are forced to be with them, well..."

"They think I'm not 'cool' enough," Maya finished for him.

He put his hands up. "Hey, you said it. Not me."

Camila leaned back on her seat as her tablet said, *"Screw what they think."*

Maya grinned. "I'm sure saying 'screw you' to a boy who already took liberty to threaten me would go swell."

Next was Mathematics—taught by the infamous Mrs. Jackson.

All things considered, it was her most normal class. Work was given to each student on their tablet and they were intended to finish the pattern as it was shown on the graph. And while she had no clue what the numbers were meant to symbolize, she took pleasure in discovering what fit in the blank squares. Mrs. Jackson even praised her in front of the class, giving her a sense of validation she hadn't felt in ages.

It was also the class that Camila and Carlos shared, though the latter didn't appear too happy that Maya had found the class so simple.

It got weird again in Interpretive Literature.

On their tablets, they were sent a story about a little dove that followed a tiger everywhere. When the tiger hunted its prey, the dove assumed it was playing tag. When the tiger ate an antelope, the dove assumed it was cleansing it. When the tiger roared, the little thing would chirp with it. But one day, the dove chirped too loud and the tiger turned on the creature and consumed it.

Everyone read the story aloud in unison, which caused goosebumps to prickle her arms. Then there was the professor who was reciting the story, but her eyes remained on Maya.

"Be careful, children," the teacher spoke in a whispered tone. "Don't be the dove."

Don't die, a very helpful sentiment.

Finally, it was the last class of the day: Art.

And what did it consist of?

Covering your entire body with black paint and lying on a large piece of paper.

Everyone from the blue-band crew was given an oversized T-shirt and large pants to shield their precious uniforms, and a net to protect their not so precious hair. With a gallon of black paint, everyone was instructed to splash each other. Maya had a slight suspicion that the others covered her more than necessary.

The five of them stayed pressed with their backs against the paper for five minutes. It wasn't a clean print of her body by any means, and this was made worse when they were instructed to stand up the paper, causing the paint to drip down. Simultaneously, she felt a drop of paint go down her own cheek. She'd be having an early shower that night.

In the future, Maya would curse herself for not enjoying these moments of blissful ignorance, but right now, she wished for nothing more than to be eighteen and leave Chance Academy, or Refuge, or whatever it was supposed to be, and live with her sister.

After the final bell, she followed the lead of Lilith, who was the blue-band who seemed to hate her the least. Maya limped as she walked, the burning sensation in her foot returning with a vengeance. The brunette headed down a familiar cold white and purple hallway and went to the elevator. Lilith only gave her a quick glance as Maya stepped into it next to her. Pressing the top button, Lilith leaned against the metal railing and scrolled on her tablet, though she stopped momentarily to study her, then her foot.

"Did you fall out of your bed this time?" The words implied a joke, but the tone didn't sell it.

"Something like that."

The scene that was revealed when the elevator door opened was not one she had been expecting. Gone was the plain setting, and instead there were bright tiles of every color covering the ground. Each wall had swirls painted onto it, and the ceiling had the same shimmering design as in her room. The back wall was all windows, and while the scene it revealed—the yellow grass and dead trees—wasn't anything special, it was the first view of the outside she had seen since she'd arrived.

Her classes had been with kids around her age, but some of those she could spot had to have been no more than ten years old. They would run from side to side as they searched for a game to play, and the variety of games proved even greater than the expanse of color. Some kids had on VR glasses and were waving their arms freely. Others attempted the obstacle course situated in the middle. Pressed against the walls were large word games, styrofoam bricks, and other mind-stimulating play-things. Large screens with multiple controllers were in between these games. It was every kid's dream-come-true.

But the one thing that struck her attention more than anything was a contraption in the back corner, near the window. She limped past the other toys to study it closer. It appeared to be a maze of some kind, entrapped in a case, with a metal ball at the top. Above it, a sign read, *Complete the maze.*

Beside her was a table with two wands. She picked one up and waved it in front of the ball, which moved with it. A smile grew on Maya's face as she directed the ball down one of the pathways, being careful not to slide it into a dead end. She was nearly to the other opening when the ball suddenly rammed into a wall.

"It's impossible." She turned around to see Brian watching her with crossed arms. "Do everyone a favor and don't make an even bigger fool of yourself."

Don't you have something better to do? She took a deep breath. "How is it impossible?"

More aggressive than what was necessary, he grabbed the other stick and traced each pathway. "Everything leads to a dead end. There's no way to get to the other side."

"If they put the maze in here, there's got to be some way it's possible."

"You want to solve an unsolvable puzzle? Fine, go ahead. Makes my life easier." Before walking off, he knocked the metal rod out of her hand and it hit the ground with a *clank.*

Maya cursed him under her breath before bringing her attention back to the maze. If Brian's intention was to get her to stop obsessing over it, his plan failed tremendously. Curiosity fueled the flame as she stepped back to get a different perspective.

Only her attempt didn't last long, interrupted by Carlos spotting her. She didn't think it to be funny when he laughed at her black-streaked face, the remnants of her failed attempts to remove the paint. He didn't mention anything about her fascination with the maze, but did wrap his arm around her shoulder, an action she hadn't quite permitted.

"You think these games are fun, just wait two weeks. It's—wait, how old are you again?"

"Sixteen?"

"Perfect. *Perfect.* Every year, everyone fifteen and up gets to go in the basement, which is massive, and there's this epic game of Cataball, which is like laser tag mixed with hide and seek mixed with Capture the Flag—I'm a terrible explainer."

"Could be better."

Carlos removed his arm and shoved her while Maya grinned. "Rude. All you gotta know is that it's the funnest thing we get to do here. It's gonna be me and Camila's third year doing it, and they should be picking teams soon."

"They're picked randomly?"

"Yeah, but don't worry. You'll be on our side. The girl that makes the teams fancies me, so let's just say I have connections."

That earned him another chuckle as Maya picked the metal sticks from the ground. "So, what's your favorite game to play in here?"

The smile the boy gave her made her regret letting him choose.

Chapter Eighteen

"THE REASON TO SURVIVE"

SHE WASN'T SUPPOSED TO be there, and she knew that. Curiosity, however, was an incredibly powerful force, and Maya only had a limited reserve of self control when it came to walking past an open door as two people she didn't trust conversed about something she knew nothing about.

The hall was otherwise empty, besides a singular blue bird that had wiggled its way through the cracked windows and chirped as it flew close to the ceiling. Maya walked with a limp, the pain in her foot returning with a vengeance. Still, she tried to make her footsteps soft as she inched towards the open wooden door, the two masculine voices carrying, despite their poor attempt to whisper.

"Second sighting," Griffin's accented voice said. "Two nightdwellers so close to the camp, and you think that's a *coincidence*?"

"I never claimed it to be one," Talon responded. "I simply don't believe that to be Amie's fault." Against the wall, Maya sank down at the mention of her "name", shifting her weight away from her injured foot.

The South African huffed. "I don't know why everyone here keeps on insisting that she's normal. Her story doesn't line up, her eyes practically swell with secrets, and everything in Kalpana has gone awry since the moment of her appearance. There is something incredibly off about her, and I don't want to see anyone getting hurt."

There was a moment of silence. "I agree," Talon said eventually. "And don't think for a second that I don't share the same worries as you. But, despite your belief in Amie being Tenebris, this realm still abides by certain rules. No nightdweller would even dare to come close to us, unless it was after something so valuable that even Jane's flowers couldn't hold them off. Now, what is the one thing a nightdweller desires over all?"

Maya pulled her knees closer to herself.

"You think..." Griffin struggled to finish his words. "A *spirit* caused this?"

"Most likely."

"But why would a spirit be *here*?"

"That's the question that worries me the most."

A hand then squeezed her shoulder, and she barely managed to hold back a yelp as she flipped around to see who had touched her. Her eyes ploddingly trekked up a feminine figure, tracking past the yellow blouse before landing on Halo's face, a quiet smile playing on her lips. Maya gulped.

"Stand up, quickly," the woman whispered, and she obliged without hesitation. The moment she managed to get on her feet, the two men exited out of the room, stopping to converse with them at the exit.

Griffin looked into Maya's eyes and she could have sworn that he could see her internal thoughts. Studying her with judgingly, he asked, "What are you doing?"

Halo placed a hand on her shoulder. "I was just about to treat her foot. Look at the poor girl. The entire lower portion of her leg is full of blisters."

Griffin's gaze held no pity as he looked upon it; if anything, it was as though he was accusing her of faking the wound. Talon, however, was a lot more forgiving as he dipped his head. "I am sorry to hear about your injury. If it offers you any consolation, this type of attack from a nightdweller is unprecedented."

Maya murmured a quiet thank you before the man turned his attention to Halo. "After you heal her, I want her to join Jane in the garden."

Halo nodded. "I will see to it."

Maya waited until the two men had disappeared behind the corner, and then she looked upon Halo's unreadable expression.

"I'm sorry." Her words came out in staccato. "I didn't mean to listen to them. I'll never say anything, and I didn't understand anything either, just...how much trouble am I in?"

Halo, to her surprise, let out a chuckle. "None, but you should realize how lucky you are that I was the one that discovered you. The first rule to breaking rules is to make sure no one finds out you are breaking the rules."

She rubbed her arm awkwardly. "Well...thank you."

"Of course. Now, ask away."

Maya blinked. "What?"

"Ask me," Halo repeated. "I know you are most likely dying to know what they were talking about."

The girl squinted her eyes in an attempt to notice any sign of a test, but the woman gave her nothing, and Maya's question bubbled to the surface. "What's a spirit?"

Halo smiled, as if she had answered a question correctly. "A *spirit*. That is a complicated topic, and it can be a bit much. Are you sure you want to know?" Maya nodded immediately, and she laughed again. "I don't know why I even asked. A spirit, in the most basic sense, is a soul that didn't make the full crossover from Kalpana to Terra during birth, leading them to be trapped in this world. Based on old Kalpanian texts, many live for thousands of years and are thought to have access to information about the world that even we don't have, both past and future." She then bent over and said softly, "Some even say that spirits are soldiers for The Man of Light."

Maya immediately felt chills run down her back that she tried her best to shake off. The Man of Light. Rumors were the extent of knowledge she had about the name. It was from a time where humans still followed religion, before all such practices were banned. Some had believed a being made of pure light that resembled themselves created the universe, and although it was prohibited, Maya had vague memories from when she was very little of people proclaiming said man's return. Then The Harvest happened, and all the religious folks stopped their preaching. But tales of The Man of Light only spread, some even saying they had seen him the same night of The Harvest. A few more went on to say that the man was the reason for the deaths. Suddenly, the name was feared, even by people who didn't believe it. Even by people like her. *But if Kalpana is real, is it really so hard to believe?* She brought her attention back to the spirits. "And they attract nightdwellers?"

Halo then bent over to her level. "Imagine, Amie, that you were a being with centuries upon centuries of memories, past and future, about every atrocity that has ever happened. Then think about what a nightdweller feeds off of."

Halo left her with that, leaving her mind raving in the prospect, and walked in front of her. "Now, let's get that nasty wound healed."

Working in the garden with Jane was a much-needed decompressor.

The flowers were unlike anything she had ever seen, and while she knew that every plant was alive, the way their petals ruffled was just like the rhythmic filling of the lungs. Between the flowers, weeds grew in an even more unique way. As though it had hands, the invasive species gripped onto its neighbors and would only release after being pulled by the roots.

Maya chuckled as the removed weed wiggled in her hand like a worm, tickling her skin.

"How's your foot doing?" Jane asked her, and Maya placed the plant into the bag next to her. "Any better?"

"Much better." Whatever was put on her injury, it helped drastically. She recalled how Halo had taken some ointment from an orange leaf and rubbed it on her foot gently when she'd first arrived back in Kalpana.

"Griffin told me about what happened yesterday," the woman had said. "That must have been terrifying."

"I survived."

Halo nodded thoughtfully. "You must be careful, though. Even with the explanation of a nearby spirit, Griffin is still convinced you are hiding something, and while I will continue to be a voice against it, there can only be so many accusations before Talon begins to wonder as well. When that happens, there will be nothing I can do to help you." Maya brought her gaze away shamefully, but Halo tapped her knee to regain her attention. "Even so, I was more than impressed at what you did. Take pride in that. Never be ashamed of your accomplishments, no matter how they may be perceived."

There were fewer clouds than there had been every other time she visited the realm, revealing more of the orange pink sky. A cool breeze tangled her loose hair, which she swept away with the back of her hand. Maya wished she could've stayed there forever.

A movement across the castle caught her attention. Beside the stones, the elderly man—Hypnos—carried a large ladder, which he took into a side door.

Jane clicked her tongue next to her. "That old man is gonna get himself hurt one of these days."

"Should we go help him?"

"Oh, trust me, even if you tried, he wouldn't let you. Hypnos is a smart but stubborn man. You'd never want to argue with him, nor should you. He's visited Kalpana longer than all of us and knows infinitely more. Hey, maybe you should go to him to ask who originally made camp! If anyone were to know, it's Hypnos."

Maya flipped around to see him again, but the withered man was nowhere in sight, lost inside the palace's walls.

Jane shrugged. "Oh well, maybe next time." Then Maya heard the creaks of the grand front door opening and turned away, in case it happened to be Griffin or Talon.

Who it actually was ended up being much worse.

Kai stood awkwardly by the door, watching her work in silence.

"Do you need something?" Maya could taste the bitterness in her mouth. She clearly remembered the way Kai had yelled at her, and her hurt was just as fresh.

He looked away and coughed. "I, um, actually wanted to talk to you."

"About what?"

"You know what."

Maya sighed and silently gazed at Jane, who was roughly yanking out a stubborn root. She wiped a dirty hand on her tight pink dress. "Didn't Talon tell you not to, Kai?"

He crossed his arms. "Yeah—well, it's important."

A groan escaped her lips. "You're going to get *me* in trouble. Ugh. You guys better talk somewhere else. If anyone asks, I'll make a coverup story, and I'll make sure it's super embarrassing. Like that time you–"

"Thank you, Jane," Kai interrupted. "It's much appreciated."

"And if I don't want to?" Maya put a hand on her hip.

"I'll let you pet a unicorn."

"Fine."

Kai led her down into the nearby valley where the green grass reached her waist, but she wasn't scratched by its rough edges, for there were none. If she were alone, she would have jumped into its soft embrace and buried herself under its dull blades. It made her giddy to walk through such healthy greenery that contrasted so greatly with the brown plants that left her full of scratches.

The grass grew shorter where a gentle river cut through the field, smooth stones visible under its clear flowing water. Contrary to her own excitement at the sight of the creek, Kai slowed down, creeping onto the other side of her with his necklace held in his hand.

"Are you afraid of water?" It was a genuine question.

Kai scoffed. "Of course not."

Maya grinned. "If you say so." Bending over, she reached into the creek and splashed it onto his face, and the expression that resulted from the boy had her cackling. Kai looked at the water. Looked back. Then smirked.

"Don't you—"

He rushed forward and grabbed her waist, and Maya screamed as they fell into the water. Her head dipped momentarily under, soaking every inch of her, even the top of her head. When she resurfaced, she saw Kai throwing his head back, his wet curly hair sticking to his forehead. His cackles were contagious, and soon she was laughing as well.

"You are terrible!" She splashed him again.

"Hey, you got me wet first!"

"Yeah, with a light splash! You rammed into me like a horned bull—" Kai then covered her mouth to silence her, and she resisted for a second until he pointed up to a breathtaking sight.

They sank lower into the water, but her eyes remained glued to the creature. In front of them stood a large animal with the fur pattern of a tiger. However, its shape was that of a horse, appearing especially large from their angle, and as it lifted its head to the sky, a pearly horn shimmered at the top, at least three feet long.

A unicorn.

It tipped its head into the creek, its reflection dancing on top of the water. It was the most beautiful creature Maya had ever seen.

Kai slowly stood up and she tried holding him back in order not to startle it, but he shrugged her off and reached an arm forward. The unicorn started at the action and took a number of steps back, but the boy kept inching closer, whispering calming words. His clothing dripped as he emerged from the water. The animal stopped moving and now watched him with curious eyes. With a slow movement, Kai stroked its back, all the while wearing a gentle smile.

"It's okay, Amie," Kai told her. "You can come now."

Hesitantly, Maya stepped out of the stream and took her place by Kai's side. She ran her fingers through the creature's mane, gasping as she noticed its fur changing color.

"They're amazing, aren't they?" Kai rested his head onto its back. "Did you know they're one of the few animals native to Kalpana? Nearly every animal from Terra has too weak brain waves to transport fully into this dimension, so they become hybrids—combinations of a bunch of animal brain waves fused together. But unicorns are fully Kalpanian, with reflections and everything." He stared into the animal's golden eyes as he stroked its head.

"They're incredible," she said, but even that description could not fully justify their magnificence when she noticed some more further ahead, bowing their heads to snack on the grass. And with the glimmering rays from stars sprinkled inside of the clouds, it was like a glimpse of heaven itself.

Not too long after, Kai took her up the hill at the back of the valley to a collection of orange rocks, and together they climbed onto it. A flat slab allowed them to sit side by side, where they watched the distant palace silently. There was a breeze and Maya shivered, her wet clothing no longer offering warmth.

"Cold?" Kai asked.

"I'm fine."

The boy chuckled. "No need to act tough. Here, picture two towels and bring the image to the front of your mind."

With a brimming curiosity, Maya did what he said.

"Can I enter your mind?"

She raised an eyebrow. "That's the first time I've ever heard that question."

"Can I?" he pleaded, and she reluctantly nodded.

It was once again a strange feeling, like an invader inside her home; it took all her might not to squirm. There was the sound of a pop, and suddenly Kai was holding two towels that were exactly the same as how she had imagined it. He handed her one, and she gratefully took it, wrapping it around her body.

Closing her eyes, Maya felt the wind blow onto her cheeks. The towel fluttered against her skin. She took a deep breath, and wondered once again if all of this could really be true. If her subconscious had truly transported her to a not-so-far-away land that belonged to her, and as far as those in Terra would know, hers alone.

"I'm sorry." Kai's voice took her out of her trance. His blue eyes bore hard into the green setting as he pulled his knees up to his chest.

Maya bit her lip. "It's okay."

"No, it's not."

"So you think I'm a liar?"

He huffed. "You know, you make this whole apology thing way harder than it needs to be."

"Because there's no need to apologize. I overreacted."

"Pretty sure *I* was the one to overreact."

"Well, you had a good reason to."

"Why, because I was a little stressed?"

"That's why I got upset."

That caught Kai's attention, and he sobered. "I make you stressed?"

Maya looked away. "That's not what I meant. I mean, you did scare me last night, but that wasn't your fault. I just... haven't had the best experiences with other people."

Kai studied her for a while, and she felt her facade slowly slipping away. She could hear her sister scolding her for letting someone see the vulnerable side of her, warning her that they would take advantage of it. She waited for Kai to respond in detestment or a scoff, but he did nothing of the sort. Instead, he rested his hand over hers, as if to tell her that he wouldn't cause her that same suffering.

But she didn't believe him.

He would hurt her the minute he knew what she was hiding.

Maya pulled her hand away and tucked it under her other arm with a clearing of her throat, not daring to study Kai's reaction. "The nightdweller had a hold on you for quite a while. It must have been a horrible nightmare."

"It wasn't exactly a nightmare." Maya turned to look at his sunken face. "It was more like a memory."

Just like mine.

There wasn't much expectation for him to continue, but he did so anyway. "I... I never really knew my mom, but my dad and I were really close. He was an Omni, so every night he'd teach me everything there was to know about Kalpana. We'd go hunting for wanderers together, visiting the neighboring camp, that sort of thing.

"But the one thing he loved to do with me more than anything was take me into the consciousness of others and explore their dreams. So one day, we entered the mind of one of the registered dreamers. They had been labeled as passive." A tear threatened to fall from his eye, and he quickly swept it away. "They weren't. That's the hard thing about Lucids. Their dreams can seem perfectly normal, until suddenly you can't move, can't think, can't breathe.

"I was stuck," he whispered. "The dreamer was in control. Eventually, Dad was able to save me, but..."

"Not himself," Maya finished for him.

"It was two years ago, but every time I go into a dream, all I see is *him*. He was so scared, Amie. *He was so scared*."

He lifted his chin up to the sky, stress trapped within his tight shoulders.

Wrapping the towel closer to herself, she said, "It's not your fault."

"Yes, it is."

"My parents died," Maya told him. "Just like your dad. It was during the part of the war where both sides stopped caring where or why they were bombing and just did it. My father locked himself out of the bunker my sister and I were hiding in so that we could be safe." She sat in silence for a while before she continued. "Never start blaming yourself for circumstances you can't control. It only acts as an endless cycle, as long as you keep feeding it. At some point, you just have to move on, and be glad you survived."

Kai pulled his own towel over himself. "What's the point of survival if there's nothing to survive for?"

It was a new way of thought Maya had never perceived before. All her life, it wasn't a question of why to survive in life, but why not to give into death.

It was a question she had no clue how to answer, until another breeze sang by which brought leaves from neighboring trees that danced through the air, while hybrid birds flew overhead. The pack of unicorns trotted below and chased each other all across the meadow in a joyful delight.

Then Maya smiled at him, and the light in his eyes made it clear that he had discovered the answer too. "There's always something to live for."

Chapter Nineteen

"A Friend Amongst Foes"

MAYA WAS STRONGLY CONSIDERING running away.

Chance Refuge had their "chance" to make a strong impression. After all, her expectations of a better life weren't exactly high. But then, by some miraculous happenstance, the school happened to be nearly as terrible as her farm life.

Okay, maybe she was *slightly* over exaggerating, but as she struggled to scrub out a burning chemical mixture from her scalp, her anger couldn't help but boil over, because after a week of going to their classes, struggling to solve their convoluted puzzles, and attempting to avoid confrontations with the blue-band crew, she still ended up with a mysterious solution poured onto her head.

Brian had become the new Broth, directing her to do various impractical tasks. But unlike the latter, listening to Brian's directions only made the bullying all the worse—it only took one instance for her to realize this. So she'd tried to ignore them, though this would only motivate them more. And Brian wasn't lying when he said the adults didn't care. The group had done everything, from soaking her bed to destroying her completed homework, and none of the professors had done a thing.

The most aggravating part was not being able to understand *why* they were doing what they were doing. She stayed out of their way and never did anything warranting their anger(that she knew of), but it was like the mere presence of her offended them. Did they want her to fight back? Is that why they wouldn't stop?

Camila and Carlos were one of the only saving graces the refuge had to offer. They made her laugh with their playful banter and humorous stories about past years, and with them were the only times she didn't feel so alone. But while they comforted her, they also served to make a part of her angry. In their eyes, Chance was the perfect safe haven. They even dreaded the day they turned eighteen and had to leave. As Carlos had beautifully put, "Out there is disease, death, and destruction. In here are friends, food, and video games. The choice of which is better is pretty obvious."

But Maya *knew* something was wrong. She could feel all of the administrators' eyes follow her wherever she went. She could hear them whispering to each other around blocked corners. It was like she was a zoo animal to be gawked at, which made her hairs stand on end.

Not to mention the strange shadow that was cast over every student's face. At first glance, nothing seemed to be off, but after a week of observing, there was a zombie-esque feature in every single one of them, even those she considered to be closer with. It's like the nightmares that they experienced each night bled into their real life, something Maya unfortunately could relate to.

Despite all this, Maya knew she wouldn't really run away. The most miserable part of it all was that Carlos was right. The safer, more logical option was to stay put until she was of proper age. It's what her sister would have done, after all.

Courtesy of her past experiences, her brain had already jotted down each day's schedule. Every day was History, Psychology, Science, Lunch, Math, English, and Art, in that order. The alarm went off each morning at exactly 7:00 a.m., and the first bell an hour later. A woman came to check if they were out of the room at 8:15, a fact she had learned from taking too long to get to class. Each class had ten minutes in between, and in that period, administrators prevented them from stopping their movement. Announcements were right after the last bell, spoken by Mrs. Fondal, and for two hours they got to play on the top floor. Then there's study time. Then dinner time. And after a brief time spent on the balcony—the only time they could obtain fresher air—they headed to bed.

She identified school workers everywhere, no matter how small a task the students were completing. They all had tablets glued to them, where they studied the kids and wrote notes down, and Maya couldn't begin to guess what was written down about her.

The only moments of privacy were in the bathroom, before the morning bell, and while everyone was asleep, but that didn't feel like merely enough time.

At lunch, she took her place next to the siblings (whom she now learned to be twins), and that had become her designated seat. Camila was dangling a grape over Carlos's nose, and he struggled to snatch it with his mouth.

"You two are the strangest people I've ever met," Maya said as she plopped a piece of pineapple into her mouth.

Carlos then grabbed Camila's arm and bit off the fruit, much to his sister's dismay. Before talking, he wiped his mouth with the back of his hand. "I don't think you're the one to talk, Miss Purple Band."

Another detail my oblivious self can't figure out.

Midway through her attempt to respond, however, an announcement came from overhead. *"Students of Chance Academy, today is a special day. We will be celebrating the release of James Presly, who has just turned eighteen!"* There were a few cheers from a table behind them, where an older kid was standing, as the cafeteria door opened and in walked two agents like the ones who had taken her from Broth. They called the boy over, and he walked up hesitantly.

Mrs. Fondal's voice came back on the intercom. *"James, we wish you safe travels as you start a new life. May you take what you have learned from Chance and apply it to your future adventures."*

More students clapped as the boy walked away with a nervous smile lifting his cheeks, slowly making his way to the cafeteria entrance before being engulfed behind the large agents, disappearing forever beyond the metal doors. In the back, however, the blue band table appeared particularly silent. Brian had a solemn look upon his face as he stared out the cafeteria longingly, Lilith wrapping an arm around him in comfort.

Eventually, the group in the cafeteria thinned out, and Maya left with the siblings. She yawned as she thought about the homework she'd have to finish later. It hadn't taken Maya too long to get accustomed to the new schedule, with the class locations already ingrained inside of her brain. She wished she could say the same thing about the course material.

Though today, after the academy wouldn't just be fun and games; Mrs. Fondal had unfortunately kept to her word and set her up with a mysterious tutor. So after Art, there Maya was, without a speck of control in her life, waiting in an empty office for another figure to work her even harder.

Even with her anger, she had to admit the office had a cozy sort of atmosphere to it. It was the first room she had seen in the refuge with wooden floors and a colorful rug, with a brown desk situated in the middle. On said desk were stacks of paperwork and photos omitting from holographic disks, as well as a label that read, *"Henry L. Jeffery."*

Maya bounced her leg anxiously—a habit that had developed from too many hours of sitting—and curled her hair as she waited.

Abruptly, the office door swung open and in walked an elderly man with thickly rimmed glasses and a clipboard in his hand. He leaned on a cane, but was surprisingly agile as he hustled around his desk. "Why, hello there, little lady! Hm, let's see here... Maya, is it? Pleasure to make your acquaintance. You can call me Jeff."

He held out his hand for her to shake, but at eye contact, he froze. And she was pretty sure she had done so as well, because there was something so unnervingly familiar about the man, from his posture to his voice. She only had to imagine him holding a white flower, and then suddenly she was certain of whom the man was.

"Hypnos?" Maya called him softly, and the old man blinked, retracting his hand.

He pointed a wrinkled finger at her. "You–you're that girl. That sweet lady I met in the library." She nodded slightly, and Hypnos—or Jeff—threw his hands up in the air. "Oh, the Light has heard my prayers! An Omni in Terra! Oh, you have no idea how long I've waited to meet one of you here. The last time I met someone from Kalpana in this reality was, well, over fifty years ago! A very special treat, this is. A very special treat." She laughed in delight, sharing the man's excitement. She finally had definite proof that Kalpana was real. And better yet, someone she could talk to about her other life.

"This is amazing!" Maya exclaimed. "You're a teacher here, of all places. What are the chances?"

"Very slim indeed, my dear." Jeff adjusted his glasses and Maya leaned forward.

"So your real name is Henry? How long have you worked here? Did they specifically appoint you or did you apply? How do you balance your two lives? Gosh, I have so many questions!"

Jeff chuckled. "Something tells me we're not going to get much work done today."

With an awkward cough, Maya leaned back down on her chair and rubbed the back of her neck. "Sorry, we can do the assignments, sir."

He waved a hand forward. "Ah, not to worry little one, I can barely contain it myself! And I said to call me Jeff."

She listened intently as Jeff outlined how he had come to work at Chance. He had taught at another school in the state for years before it closed down because of a lack of students. While searching for a new job, he got a federal message inviting him to Chance Refuge. "It was to be a facility that sheltered poor displaced children, while giving them an education not offered anywhere else!" the man said. "How could I refuse?"

Jeff's explanation of the refuge made it sound so absolutely perfect; Maya wished she could have that same faith in it. Whether it be her upbringing or personality, she was not sure, but she just couldn't get herself to believe the facility was as innocent as it pretended to be.

The man then smiled sadly. "I'm sorry for the circumstances that put you here, but I will try my best to make your time in this refuge as great as it can be."

Indeed, they didn't end up doing much of anything productive. Many questions were exchanged, and after Jeff's long rant on the uselessness of test scores, their hour-long session was up.

"Tomorrow, same time?" Maya asked.

"That's what the schedule says, but I suspect we'll be seeing each other a wee-bit sooner."

With one last wave goodbye, Maya walked out with a skip, gravity feeling the slightest bit weaker as she headed over to the elevator to go to the game room. Once at the top, she had a single mission: to figure out the maze everyone claimed was impossible. Maya could feel the judgmental stares by the other kids on her back, but she paid them no mind. They could laugh at her all they wanted, but Maya knew there was no such thing as an unsolvable puzzle. Everything had a solution; she just hadn't figured this specific one out yet.

"Hey, Chance prodigies! May I have your attention!" Maya turned around to see a teenage girl in the middle of the room holding a microphone. Her hair was a chestnut brown and reached to her shoulders, accompanied with a smile that shone big and bright. Students stopped their games and surrounded her while Maya remained farther back. "You all know what time it is... Team Assignment day!"

Cheers echoed even from the tallest ceilings. The girl hushed them. "Now, now. I know y'all are excited, and I don't wanna leave anyone hanging, so I'll make this short. This is my last year running the game, and will be something I remember forever. The connections made through Cataball will never be forgotten. I will miss everyone so much."

A loud cheer came from a boy near the front—Maya later discovered it to be Carlos—and the rest joined in, giving the girl a large round of applause. With tears in her eyes, she waved a hand in front of her face and said, "Y'all are gonna make me cry. Okay, let's get right to it, shall we?"

The crowd went silent as she pulled out a list. "Rand Argyle... Phoenix.

"Ken Bailey... Alicorn.

"Brian Harold... Phoenix."

It went on for a while, each person of the proper age having their name called. Carlos and Camila were put on team Alicorn, and after discovering it to be alphabetical order, Maya waited for her name to be called.

"Maya Shaffer... Alicorn."

After the last person was assigned, the girl up front spoke again. "The game will take place next Friday at 4:00 pm, so don't be late! For the next week, practices and strategy-building will be at 3:00 pm. Good luck, and can't wait to see ya'll there!"

Chattering commenced, but Maya didn't speak a word as she met Brian's eyes from across the room, the fire of the Phoenix already bleeding through his features.

Despite Carlos's attempt to educate her, Maya still didn't know what the game "Cataball" consisted of, but she'd win it, if only to shove victory in the boy's face.

Chapter Twenty

"TRAPPED SPIRITS"

A LUMINOUS LIGHT CAUGHT her attention in the foreign world of Kalpana.

She noticed it while running an errand for Jane, collecting a different type of soil by the river to fertilize the flowers. It came from the trees of the Whispering Woods, which was the land of the nightdwellers, and hand-like roots, and a number of other terrifying things Kai had told her about when she asked to join him in a trip into its trees.

Said boy had been elusive as of late. Ever since that day of emotional apologies, it was as though he purposefully went out of his way to avoid her. Maya would be lying if she said it didn't hurt a bit; she had been almost certain they had ended up on better footing after their conversation, but it seemed like Kai had thought otherwise. Even so, she didn't dwell on it. She didn't enjoy the anger reminiscing about the situation caused, and thought it to be better to just face the issue when she managed to have a productive interaction with him again. If she ever managed such an interaction.

At first, she tried her best to ignore the light. Contrast to Kai's lack of attention, Griffin practically had his eyes glued to her, waiting for her to make a slight misstep. Venturing out again to another forbidden area was her begging to be banished into the Pit—another place conveniently located inside the woods.

But the bright light wouldn't go away. If anything, its yellow hue got brighter. Brighter again. It got to the point where even looking away wouldn't dull the glow, and that was when she came to the conclusion that ignoring it wasn't an option.

Then, with the breath of the wind, she could have sworn a voice whispered her name. *Maya.*

Her *real* name.

Dropping the pot that had been used to collect dirt, she whipped her head around, finally settling in on the light within the forest. She followed it, though it was only when she got to the forest's edge that she heard the voice again. This time, it was louder. More clear. And then she saw it—the source of the glow.

It was an irregular-formed being that could be seen flying through the air, a trail of light following it. Like a butterfly, it fluttered around weightlessly. Maya could feel her mouth hanging open and gasped as it landed on her shoulder, warm to the touch. The memory from the night she broke free of her dream resurfaced, though she couldn't understand why.

It called her name once more, then headed into the forest.

There was no hesitation as Maya ran after it, tracking the being as it went deeper and deeper into the forest. She could feel the grass getting coarser and the atmosphere getting darker the farther she went. Becoming lost was only a distant thought in her mind. The light was trying to tell her something. Something important.

Soon, the only thing Maya could see was the creature. Her feet moved blindly beneath her, and the cold air burned her lungs. Exhaustion started to settle in. Her movement slowed down. Suddenly, her foot got caught underneath one of the roots and she tumbled to the ground, reaching out her hand to tell the light to wait.

But the being had stopped. Around a tree it hovered, spinning around its trunk. Wiping dirt from her knees, Maya stood up and walked to where it stayed.

She didn't notice anything special about the tree. It was just as large—if not more so—as others around it. It had no low branches to allow for a climb. She skimmed her fingers over its bark, which was only slightly rough. The one oddity was a round black dot on the tree that looked charred away.

"What are you trying to tell me?" Maya whispered to the creature, but no answer was given.

From behind her was a rustle, and the mysterious being vanished.

Turning around, Maya bent down and grabbed a stick for defense, but quickly lowered it as she recognized the person standing in front of her to be Jane, wielding a flashlight in her hand. The woman stood still, the contraption held limp by her side.

Maya placed her stick down gently. "Look, I can explain–"

"I can't believe it," she said with an awestruck tone in her voice.

"Can't believe what, exactly?"

The woman then ran up to her and grabbed ahold of her shoulders. "Do you have any idea how incredible what you just witnessed is?" She squeezed her shoulders harder. "That was a *spirit*. Souls! They're eternal, mystical beings, and only are seen when they *want* to be seen. No one has seen one since before Talon was born. But it showed itself to *you*."

"It was trying to tell me something," Maya said. "Something important. I–I need to find it again."

"You can try, but you won't have any luck. You don't find *them*; they find *you*." A high-pitched wail echoed from the depths of the forest, which caused Jane to wince. "I also wouldn't stay here much longer. We're right next to the Pit, and nightdwellers *love* the Pit."

The atmosphere grew colder and Maya shivered, but that didn't discourage her from turning her attention back to the tree in an attempt to decipher the spirit's hidden message.

"Amie, I'm not joking with you. We really should be going. *Now*."

Just then, the sound of clicking filled the air, and Maya froze.

It was already too late.

Jane was rushing her as Maya searched for a distinctive rock, or branch, or *anything* unique as the clicks increased in volume. Her hands felt all around, but there was nothing. Getting on her knees, she crawled, spreading out her arms.

"What are you doing? Come on!" Jane's frantic voice beckoned.

Maya finally landed on a curved stick and she quickly placed it by the tree, running to Jane's side and grabbing her arm to pull her.

"Wait–"

They halted centimeters from the edge of a dark hole, soil trickling down into it as the two of them took a step back. A putrid aroma came from it, and chills made their way down Maya's back.

The Pit.

Herself and Jane could only watch in horror as a cloud of black shadows emerged from the darkness and rose into the sky. It was like how Maya imagined witnessing a tsunami to feel like: a mountain of powerful water growing by the second, and those who are powerless standing underneath it, knowing every attempt to escape would be futile. All one can do is wait for it to crash down with all of its force, pulling them beneath the large tidal wave.

Jane screamed, and Maya suddenly went into a trance. Her mind was hazy, but with vague recollection, she recalled standing in front of the girl, that same feeling of control while in the dream as before flooding through her. She held out a hand, and may have said something that caused the following result, she couldn't remember, but somehow, the wave of nightdwellers subsided, disappearing back into the depths of the Pit. A bright light filled her vision. And Maya stood at the very edge of the cliff, not feeling the ground beneath her feet.

The world began to spin, and she would have collapsed onto the ground if not for Jane catching her. She was too tired to say a word as the woman's hands trembled while holding her. Then, very faintly, Maya thought she heard, in a frightful voice:

"You've been touched."

Chapter Twenty-One

"Lies Bleed Poison"

THE ARGUING THAT SURROUNDED Maya blurred together as she sat to the side of a tiled palace room with golden walls filled with strange markings, her mind still dizzy and her hands placed on her lap. She did not dare speak a word. The red cushion of the seat beneath her remained stiff as she rocked her weight forward.

"This is the third time she's done something like this," the South African accused. "She's deliberately disobeyed one of the few rules we have, and you're just going to let her go free of punishment?"

"A *spirit*, Talon!" Hypnos ignored Griffin's comments. "It showed itself to *her*, and in all my years of living, I only know of one other time something like this has occurred. If anything, we should be celebrating!"

Talon stood deep in thought, hand stroking his chin. Jane knelt down next to Maya with warmth like the presence the sun used to offer on a frigid day. The girl's eyes didn't drift towards her, but the hand on Maya's lap allowed herself to remain grounded.

The journey back to the castle had been a blur, filled with trips over roots and tumbles into the grass. Jane had tried and failed to pick her up, deciding instead to drag Maya along as they attempted to dodge obstacles in the way. Her consciousness had only halfway returned when they reached camp. The faces all fused together, but Maya was certain Kai had been there to help pull her up.

Because of her own mental state, Jane was subject to the grilling of questions. To Maya's relief, the girl didn't answer any of them and went on a jumbled spiel about the soul sighting. No one seemed to know what to do with the information. Halo and Kai situated themselves to the opposite side of the room, avoiding the entirety of the conversation. Griffin was, as expected, harpering on the fact that she had entered the Whispering Woods. Hypnos was ecstatic. And Talon...

Maya usually could read people easily, especially in Kalpana, but the tall man's emotions remained unreadable. The idea of not knowing what the consequences of her actions entailed brought along an almost numbing terror. And after seeing the Pit, she knew she'd never *ever* want to end up in such a place, no matter the effect she had on the nightdwellers.

The interaction continued, and Maya directed her gaze to the boy across the room. Kai's feet knocked against the floor as he rocked back and forth, hands inside his pockets. Adjusting in her seat, she bore her eyes into his features in hope he would notice her staring. She desperately needed to know if he suspected something of her. Or if he hated her. Or if–

Kai's gaze then met hers, and Maya sucked in a breath. Her heart burned, but she didn't look away. With a sense of expectancy, she tilted her head to the side, and the smile that was returned melted the fear from her chest.

He didn't hate her after all.

"Jane, what were you and Amie doing in the Whispering Woods?" Talon demanded, and Maya's attention was once again reined into the conversation.

"Well, I–uh..." Jane's eyes were shot wide as she turned to look at her, and Maya was sure she was wearing a similar expression herself. The woman swallowed. "I thought I saw a wanderer in the woods!"

Griffin raised an eyebrow. "I thought you knew better than to go by yourself."

"And I assume Amie followed shortly after?" Talon said, and Jane nodded.

"We went a little deeper, and that was where we—well, Amie specifically—saw the spirit. It only was there for a bit, and then the nightdwellers came. I think that was the fastest I've ever run."

Talon nodded his head. "And how does Amie's condition play into this story?"

Jane stuttered. "Um..."

"It was overwhelming," Maya answered for her. "Learning about spirits and what they really are. I guess that, along with the influence of the nightdwellers, pushed me to my limit." She could tell no one was buying her story, so she continued on, the lies pouring off her tongue with surprising ease. "I lost my sister, and it made me wonder if she was out there. It was a stupid thought, but I panicked. If Jane wasn't there, I don't think I would have made it. She saved me." It wasn't hard to fake grief; just the thought of Amarie dying brought enough of that to almost result in tears.

Jane watched with an agape mouth and shook her head. "I think it was the opposite way around."

Halo then spoke up. "We are so sorry about you and your loss, Amie." Maya tried her best to hide her shame. "I think it's clear now that no wrongdoing has been committed. Wouldn't you say, Talon?"

He clicked his tongue. "I believe that to be the correct assumption. Jane, Maya, you are free to go."

Griffin glared at Maya one last time before stomping out of the room with a cloud of tumultuous emotions over his head. Kai acknowledged her with a slight nod, but said no words, much to her dismay.

Back outside, Jane stared at her as though she was someone foreign. A strange face she no longer recognized. With a pull to her hair, Maya said, "You lied for me."

A laugh came from Jane, but it sounded forced. "Barely. You did the majority of the convincing."

"But... why?"

"To protect you, of course!" She took a deep breath. "I like you a lot, Amie, but we have a job to do here, and there's no room for mistakes." She tugged on her dress. "I don't know what you did back there with the nightdwellers. I was... terrified. The only reason I'm not rushing to tell the truth is because the spirit tried to tell you something, and if it came to you, then you must be someone very special. But nothing special can happen if you're banished to the bottom of the Pit."

Maya dipped her head at Jane's confession. The girl wiped her forehead and asked, "Did your sibling really die?"

"No."

"Well, you are a very good liar."

You have no idea.

THERE WERE HUSHED VOICES in the hall that night, barely audible through the wall. Underneath the door where the outside trickled through, the light of a flashlight shined through the crevice and two pairs of feet followed it.

"Let's talk in the main hall," an unfamiliar person whispered.

"If you insist." Maya recognized it as Mrs. Fondal, and apprehension fueled her curiosity.

When she heard the door slowly shut, she slipped out of her cot, softly shoving the buckles to the side. The bed creaked as she lifted herself up, which caused her to flinch and stand still, waiting for any sign of the others waking. Thankfully, there was no movement. Her bare feet pressed against the cold ground as she stood up as quietly as she could. The bedroom door whined when Maya opened it, but it was short-lived, and she quickly slid through it.

She crossed the hall and sat by the corridor entrance. The male voice was speaking in a hushed tone, barely audible through the barrier. In a moment of recklessness, she scooted to the other side of the door and opened it just a crack, thanking the world that the door wasn't locked nor was the action loud.

"–performing incredibly well. She has a gift for thinking outside the box, and applying it to all of her studies–"

The man was cut off by the administrator. *"We already knew she would be. The question is how to transfer those qualities to the other students, because obviously our current method is not working. I'm finally told we're making progress, then a girl from an abandoned group ends up being the only success. How is that explained to our sponsor?"*

"We can run more tests," he suggested. *"Maybe we notice something different about her brain waves."*

"What about her sister? Any luck with her?"

"Well, we assumed since she was out of the susceptible age limit—"

There was a fierceness in Mrs. Fondal's tone as she said, *"Based on our recent discovery, there is no room for assuming there are limits. Maybe it is genetic, and she can end up being helpful as well. Maya Shaffer is a peculiar case, and we must come to the bottom of what made her crack."*

At the mention of her name, Maya gasped, covering her mouth too late. The conversation went quiet and Maya shuffled to the other side of the door behind the crease. She held her breath as approaching footsteps echoed in the empty hall. Mrs. Fondal's shadow reached through the crack and Maya scooted back even farther, as if to mold into the wall.

"I thought I closed that," the man said.

Then they shut the door.

Her heart was beating too fast inside of her, attempting to escape from its confinement of bones. She forgot the art of breathing and squeezed her eyes shut, fingers tightly gripping her scalp. The words *test, success,* and *crack* floated around her mind but failed to latch onto anything coherent. The only thing that mattered to her was *sister.*

Whoever these people were, whatever they were doing or aiming to accomplish, it wasn't just involving her. They wanted Amarie too.

Maya could only hope her sister was hidden better than she had been.

Chapter Twenty-Two

"THEIR EVERYTHING, HER NOTHING"

EXPERIMENT.

That was the explanation Maya had settled on. Chance Refuge was an experiment.

An experiment of *what* was the question that plagued her.

Currently, those involved didn't seem to have any intention of hurting her in any way. They educated her, fed her, and gave her a comfortable enough place to sleep. Staying was still the safest option, if only to prevent the chance that resisting conformation would cause her to be punished.

Yet, the louder, more rebellious part of her was screaming to escape the place as soon as she could. The last time she had been so ignorant of her situation was while being shipped back and forth by SCRO, an experience she never wanted to relive. Her instincts and logic continued to war against each other as she went through the day, placing a mask of calmness on herself to hide her internal turmoil. Her first class went by as smoothly as one would expect, and the second didn't prove to be much better. Yet, the one that took the golden crown of complete awfulness was the third.

And no, it wasn't the fact that they had to examine yellow and most definitely human nails, though her imagination running wild with the idea that it belonged to past students of Chance was certainly a terrible thought.

It was because of the woman who walked in mid-way through, holding a tablet in her hand, and wearing an obviously fake smile on her face.

Mrs. Fondal led her down the cold white halls while Maya kept her vision glued down. She counted the purple tiles they passed to distract herself from the terror collecting inside her chest. Could it be that the administrator had found out about her overhearing the conversation? Was this her path to punishment? These theories proved to be false, but the truth was just as worrisome.

They stopped in front of the window, and Maya froze as she watched the nurses working behind the glass. One held a white towel, while the other held a large syringe, poking it into a cup and sucking back in blue-colored liquid.

Maya held back a shutter. "I thought they already treated me."

"Think of this more as a... checkup," the woman said.

A test, more likely.

"What if I don't want to go in?"

Mrs. Fondal studied her for a while, and it took all of Maya's willpower not to break her facade. It might have been anger pooling behind the woman's eyes, or suspicion, she couldn't tell, but Mrs. Fondal made a poor effort to smile graciously and said, "I would never want to make you uncomfortable, but I highly encourage you to let the doctors examine you."

There was a quiet threat behind the words. Without another word, Maya entered the room, the burst of cold air blowing back her hair. She was told to sit on the side of the cot and she obliged, staring straight ahead, not so much as flinching as the nurse who had identified her hurt wrist injected a serum into her shoulder. The opportunity was also taken to rebandage her wrist. Maya didn't know why; she barely felt the pain, and all the bandage did was remind her of Broth.

Drowsiness started to flood her body, and she looked with wide eyes to the nurse, who offered her a pitying smile.

That was the last thing she remembered.

When she awakened, her head hurt worse than she ever thought possible. It was as though someone had removed her brain, sliced it up, and placed it back into her skull. Maya groaned with anger as she struggled to see. Her eyelids weighed a hundred pounds, and what she could see blurred into a mash of white and grays.

She attempted to speak, but the words slurred together. Her attempt to sit up was stopped by a sturdy hand placed on her chest, the nurse shushing her. "Hey, it's okay. You can lie back down." It took a moment for the world to stop spinning, and when it cleared, another unfamiliar nurse looked at her with warmth. But a towelette was placed around her arm, and it was stained red.

Blood.

"What... what did..." The spike of adrenaline that came from her terror lasted merely a second, disappearing before she could even complete her sentence. Rapid beeping came from the machine next to her, and the nurse grabbed her arm, pulling out the needle that had been placed inside of her limb.

"It was nothing harmful." Mrs. Fondal's voice penetrated deep into Maya's ears. She tried jerking her arms, but they hung limp by her sides. "Just something we wanted to try."

I'm not a puppet! she wanted to scream. Every single ache and pain in her body blared loudly while her mind searched frantically for the area that had been operated on. The nurse put a hand behind her back and lifted her up, handing her a cup and tipping it into her mouth. The drink was stimulating and shocked every fiber in her body awake.

"Do you feel better?" the woman in scrubs asked. Maya didn't answer—she was too busy pouring out her hatred onto Mrs. Fondal.

"I'd like to go to lunch now," she said simply.

"Of course," the wretched lady answered in her unnaturally straight collared polo and unnaturally long cotton skirt. The two of them walked by each other in silence, Maya following Mrs. Fondal until she departed into her depressingly colored office.

What did they do to me?

What did they do to me?

What did they–

"Woah, you good, Purple Band? Your face is a little... pale." Carlos asked her with concerned eyes, a look Maya didn't expect to get from him of all people.

"You haven't touched your food." Camila tilted her head to examine her.

Maya shrugged and pushed away her tray. "Guess I'm not hungry."

"Oh no," Carlos scooted back. "You're not sick, are you? If you are, you can sit *way* over there—" He flinched as Camila shushed him.

"I'm not sick." She could tell the boy was not convinced.

Telling them the truth was not an option. There wasn't a way they would react calmly to such a reality, where they were part of a large experiment for something Maya didn't understand yet. *Unless they already know,* a voice in the back of her mind whispered, and she studied the twins again to see if there was some shield over their presentation towards her. Nothing seemed off about them. They looked genuinely happy about where they were.

Maya gathered the courage to ask the following question. "What is Chance to you?"

Carlos watched her like she had grown another head. "The heck is that supposed to mean?"

Rolling her eyes, she said, "What I *mean* is that you two look happy here. Is it like a home to you?"

"Not home," Camila answered. *"México will be the only place with that name. Chance is our safe house. Before we were taken in, our lives were terrible. We had to scavenge for food, sleep on whatever happened to be the softest material... Carlos had to take care of me and protect us from the spookers who sold kids to not-so-good people.*

"When my condition got too bad, he and I walked for days to find the nearest hospital. From there, Chance found us, and for the first time in weeks, we had a proper meal. There were no more freezing nights, or unbearable hunger—"

"Or diseases," Carlos interjected.

"In some ways, Chance is our everything."

The tears that collected in the girl's eyes convinced her that there was nothing but truth in her words. A lump formed in Maya's throat as she asked, "What if Chance wasn't as good as it seems? Would you run away?"

"Where is this coming from?" Carlos shoved a handful of blueberries in his mouth and swallowed it down. "You just got here, and we've been here for years. Don't you think we would notice if something was off?"

"But would you?" Maya pressed.

"I don't know, maybe! But don't start making accusations just because your experience hasn't been the best. Not everyone has a family member outside waiting for them."

Though his reaction was completely justifiable, Maya would be lying if she claimed the boy's words didn't hurt the slightest bit. As if she hadn't also struggled like them, living off of scraps, working day and night to survive.

She wanted to shake them by the shoulders and point out everything wrong with the refuge. To show them how ignorant they truly were. But as her mind flashed back to Camila's teary-eyed, grateful gaze, and Carlos's passionate defense towards Chance, she no longer felt the desire to destroy their illusion. It reminded her of when she was younger and first started living with Broth. It was clear from the start that the man was no gentle fellow, but she had faith that things would get better, and he would end up being just as kind as their parents with time. So she shoved away Amarie's claims and chose to paint the situation in a positive light, as long as she could.

Ignorance *was* blissful, back then. She had been so much happier. So much livelier. She hated the paranoid mess she had become.

She only wished her suspicions didn't always happen to be correct.

Standing up, Maya placed her food on Carlos's tray before walking out, then waited beside the door until the bell rang. The last two classes were so foreign to her mind that she wouldn't have been surprised if the teachers had spoken a different language the entire time. That, or if they had called her name repeatedly, only for her not to respond. Her thoughts were too loud for anything else to be even the slightest bit comprehensible.

When it came time for her tutoring session, her mind was already drained from the worry, and she couldn't even find it in herself to suspect the old man knew about Chance. Jeff was too kind. Too happy. His explanation of how he began working at the refuge had no holes, and he lacked the overcasting shadow all the others possessed. Besides, over their daily tutoring sessions as well as their Kalpanian interactions, the two of them had formed a close bond. With him, Maya found joy despite the misery that surrounded herself, reinvigorating her soul to its brim and giving her a brand new light.

Because of her lack of energy, it wasn't hard to act normal around Jeff. In fact, Maya even found herself nearly forgetting the situation when the man slid across a book with unmistakable Kalpanian symbols embroidered on its cover. Maya picked it up with the realest smile she had worn all day, quickly flipping through the pages with words she could not read before holding it to her chest.

"This will be part of our 'history' sessions," Jeff told her, which reigned her attention back to him. "Now, I want you to bring this book every day, but don't let others see! Don't want to get yelled at by the crude woman again, now do we?"

Maya grinned at their shared memory of Mrs. Fondal stomping in after finding them playing charades to mimic the other workers. The woman's face had become beet red with anger as she pointed at the old man to "talk" outside the room. Maya had been wheezing so much so that it became impossible to breathe and she curled over herself, tears of laughter streaking her cheeks. She hadn't laughed that hard in years.

Holding the dark purple book out in front of her, she said, "How did you even get this?"

The man adjusted the cane that leaned against his chair. "Oh, just my Grandpap. He claimed a beautiful seer that could simultaneously see both realms gave it to him. He was a lady's man, let me tell ya."

Turning it around, she studied it with fascination. Yes, it was physically here with her, but its aura told a different story. She closed her eyes briefly, and there the book was, its hard cover still glowing, just like how Griffin and the dreamer had been during the nightdweller attack.

"Thank you." The words didn't feel like enough; the gift of the book had come at the perfect time, a distraction very much needed in her current state.

"If you're gonna be one of us, you gotta know what we know." Jeff leaned closer to her and said, "You have to know the Light before you talk to it."

"Sorry?"

The man sighed, though in good will, and stood up with help from his cane. He leaned past her and used the stick to close the door all the way shut, then returned to his previous position. "Flip to the third page of the book; if my old memory doesn't fail me, then what I need should be there." Maya did as he said and used delicacy in her handling of each thin paper. The pages were yellowed with time, but its ink had not faded in the slightest.

Jeff's wrinkled finger moved to rest on top of a convoluted symbol that she had not seen anywhere around the camp in Kalpana. It was composed of six lines: five across, one in the middle. It was the only symbol on the entire page—-maybe the entire book—that had no swirls or curves smoothing it out. "This," the man started, "is the mark of Tenebris."

Something about the way he said the word caused shivers down her back, fear grasping her tongue and twisting it. Such a somber tone contrasted so strongly with his typical light-heartedness that for the first time, Maya got the sense of how serious it was for the people of Kalpana to suspect a connection with the symbol. An unrecognizable voice whispered in the back of her mind a single word: "Darkness."

"Yes," Jeff acknowledged, and it took a second for Maya to realize she had said it out loud. "Pure darkness. Everything evil in Terra and Kalpana exists because of it. Like those nightdwellers. Pesky things, they are. And *this*—" he then pointed to another symbol farther down the page. It was composed only of a single swirl that curled at the ends and curved at the top. "This is Lucis. Light."

Immediately, for some reason Maya couldn't understand, the fear had vanished and in its place was an unexplainable joy. She rubbed her chest to get the strange emotions to fade, but the action only stirred what was inside. Shaking her head, she brought her attention back to the page as the teacher leaned back on his chair.

"Ah, what a powerful thing it is to be omniscient. Unlike the dreamers, we are given a glimpse into this fight of light and dark. Unlike all these people fighting an invisible enemy, we can see it! Which means we can also see the servants of the light. Like you meeting that spirit."

Maya shifted in her seat at the recollection of the previous night. "But what would a being like that want with me?"

The old man pointed a finger at her with a grin. "*That* is what I intend to figure out."

How to swallow was lost as her mind overflowed with terrible scenarios of abandonment, punishment, and death. What if the spirit had come to her to get rid of her? What if she really *was* Tenebris and didn't know? Pure goodness, *Lucis*, was after her. She really *was* going to die. And yet, somehow she managed to return his smile, hoping the man couldn't see the terror lying behind her eyes.

That's it. I'm dead.

The remainder of the session was an overview of The Second Age, predominantly AI's influence in creating near supernatural treatments of diseases. These could heal things like cancer and heart complications, which expanded the average age of humans to 125–130 years. Of course, this all fell apart when the last two world wars came about. It took two years after the Nuclear War to get electricity back to the major cities that still stood, and even that was a struggle. Supplying the most powerful AIs required too many resources, so the artificial intelligence system collapsed. Along with this, the majority of healthcare providers had vanished during The Harvest. So, even until this day, coming down with an illness is almost always a death sentence, unless you have an unbelievable amount of money.

After the incredibly positive lesson elevating her extravagantly positive mood, Maya was back on the top floor, in the back corner, fiddling with the maze. She rubbed the sides of the encasement. Tried both of the metal rods. Attempted to put her hand through the bottom. Nothing worked, and the feeling of disarrangement that accompanied it was becoming a well-acquainted sensation.

Behind her, commotion ensued as kids came walking out from the elevator with oddly shaped cardboard cutouts tucked underneath their armpits. They struggled to avoid the various games scattered across the room to get to the very back, where they placed them down.

"Hey!" some older student Maya wasn't familiar with shouted. "The Alicorn team is setting up here! If you're part of Phoenix, you guys head down to the basement!"

"Dang it," Carlos's voice startled her with its closeness. He talked only loud enough for herself to hear. "The basement is a much better place to practice."

Maya watched as the kids turned the cutouts onto their sides, while others joined in with tape. "What are they doing?" she asked him.

"They're creating the setup for Cataball," he said. "Can't play if there's no maze. Of course, it's flimsier and smaller than the real version, but it works. Looks like they started setting up a little late though, so our first practice will probably be tomorrow."

His tone held no sign of anger towards what happened earlier, but Maya still apologized to him.

He punched her arm playfully, and Maya tried to hide her sore grimace. "Hey, we're cool. You're stressed; we all were when we first arrived. Just try to relax. No one's here to hurt you."

The pain throughout her body said otherwise, but Maya still nodded and turned her attention back to the setup. While waiting, Carlos attempted a better, more informative explanation of Cataball.

In the most basic sense, the game took place in a maze-like setting, where the two teams start on opposite ends. In the middle, there was a singular red ball that changes colors based on the team that touches it. The goal was to get the ball to the opposite side, but if right before it crosses, a member of the other team touches it and changes the color, that team would win.

"But there's more," he said excitedly. "Throughout the game, there's lasers that shoot from the walls at any given moment, getting you out if it hits you three times. There's also this thing called the Cataton, but...eh, not important. You have to be on your toes constantly. Practically have eyes on the back of your head."

Cataball *did* sound enjoyable, but the only thought that went through her mind was how the game played into Chance's little experiment. And also what would happen when she returned to Kalpana later that night.

Pick a thing to stress about. Chance or Lucis. Not both.

The first thing Maya did upon returning to her sleeping corridor was head into the bathroom and strip off her clothing, spinning in front of the mirror to see if there was any oddity visible on her skin. But there was nothing that she could see, no matter what angle she stretched her body. There was no pain pinpointing the area; it was distributed evenly from the top of her head to the bottom of her toes.

She leaned defeatedly on the bathroom counter, gripping the back of her neck with her hands. As she did this, however, her fingers brushed against a patch of cloth. A part of her wanted to pretend it hadn't been there, but nevertheless, Maya slowly lifted up her hair and turned to view it in the mirror. Situated between her shoulders, a large bandage was placed, blood already seeping through the cloth. Anger swelled and she took her uniform, crumpled it up, and chucked it at the mirror, screaming without care of the other blue-bands hearing her. Falling to her knees, she allowed herself to break down, punching the floor with all her might before a sharp pain erupted from her injured wrist. Maya yelped and held it to her chest.

The combination of fear and loneliness held her in their grip, and she closed her eyes, picturing herself reuniting with Amarie, the two of them traveling far away from everything in the nightmarish world of Terra.

Chapter Twenty-Three

"The Underdwellings"

In the world of dreamers, Maya and Jane were harvesting flowers.

She had her head on a swivel for the short amount of time she was there, relieved to find no sign of a vengeful spirit, and finally found peace at Jane's side. It turned out that the sedaflors weren't just to elevate the appearance of Kalpana, but to soothe the minds of tortured souls, which gave her an entirely different view of what they had been doing. Jane was rushing as she pushed the flowers into Maya's hands.

"I'm about to leave," she told her. "You're going to have to take these to Halo, okay?"

"I guess—" Maya didn't have time to finish before the girl's form started disappearing in front of her. The flowers smelled wonderful in her arms; she could see why they were used as stress relievers.

Heading to the castle, she searched the rooms, speeding past the one she noticed Kai and Griffin in. The former must have seen her, but she didn't stop as she rushed to the end of the grand hall.

"Amie, are you my gift bearer today?" Halo's voice said from beside her, standing in front of the room with the dark hole. Maya felt giddy as she handed the woman the sedaflors.

"We only picked the best!" Her hands were vibrating, and Halo laughed.

"They do look wonderful. You and Jane did a wonderful job." Maya was beaming until Halo put down the flowers and pressed down on her shoulders. "Seems like Jane forgot to tell you not to directly breathe in the fumes. They are magnificent antidotes for stress, but should only be used in very small portions."

Maya reached up and dusted some of the pollen off of her clothes, bits of the excited tension wearing off. Still, Maya giggled as she said, "Sorry."

Halo smiled and placed a hand on her back. "You know what, why don't you come down with me? I could use the help."

"Won't Talon get mad at me?"

She made a dismissive gesture and grabbed the flowers. "Don't worry about him. As long as you stay with me, you'll be fine."

Directing her to the stairs, Halo reached overhead to grab the lighted torch. The giddiness almost instantly vanished as the frigid atmosphere of the nightdwellers pierced her nerves. Distant howls of pained minds echoed in the darkness and Maya gripped her arms tightly as the two of them headed down.

The sound of their feet on the rock floor reverberated once they reached the bottom. Halo lifted the torch, which revealed the moisture on the walls, black bricks having been stacked with no sign of cement between them. The air felt wet against her skin, and the smell was musty, akin to how it was inside the shed on a rainy day. Though they were closer to those that inhabited the Underdwellings, the cries had gone silent, as if they had sensed their presence. Halo handed the torch to her and Maya held it up, screeching as she saw the figure illuminated in front of her.

"Shh," the woman whispered to her, but Maya's heart thumped out of her chest, eyes glued to what was before her. It had the appearance of a corpse left to rot for years on end. Rotten flesh sagged off the person's face, and their eyes were a soulless black. Their mouth was stuck in a permanent scream, rotten teeth threatening to fall out onto their tongue. A blue-tinted shield was the only thing separating them.

"What is that?" Her voice trembled.

"*That* is what happens when you let nightdwellers take over and you stop fighting your nightmares, embracing them instead. The monsters feed off of one's negativity, and if left for too long, the human and dweller become one."

"Does it affect them in Terra as well?"

"Not outwardly."

Without another word, they moved onward, Maya lighting the way. She tried her best to avoid those inside the cells, but every once in a while she'd hear them shriek and instinctively turn their way.

"This is our stop." Halo placed down the flowers and pressed her face against the force field. This particular underdweller must have been in the very back, for Maya could not make out their face. Shivering, she held the torch close to her chest as Halo put a line of the pink petals by the cell. Her mind wandered, watching the flames dance their unchoreographed way. It eased the cold for a bit, until a whisper cut through. *"Susan..."*

Maya's head snapped up, and the torch fell from her hand.

Halo gazed at her in confusion. "Amie, is everything alright?"

There was the name again. She made her way down the dark path, listening intently. *"Susan... Susan..."*

Maya eventually stopped at the man on the very right. His appearance was just as terrible as the others as he uttered his wife's name, rocking back and forth on the ground. She couldn't move as Halo stood next to her, looking between her and the monster in front of her. "I know him," she whispered. "I know this man."

Halo looked upon her with pitying eyes. "I am finished down here. Let's go back up."

Maya's eyes stayed glued to Broth's disfigured body as she was pulled away. All of her senses had disappeared, replaced only with suffocating, time-stopping terror.

Not recalling walking up the stairs, Maya was suddenly at the top, and the woman in front of her was bent over. Her mouth moved, but no words reached her ears. Eventually, Halo embraced her tightly, and only then did the words start fading in.

"... about to leave. Try and see if Hypnos is still here and if you can help him."

Maya nodded slowly, and she grabbed ahold of her face. "You'll be okay. Let the past be past."

Then she vanished.

The sounds of torment had started back up again, reaching her at level ground. The door stood ominously.

It had been fear that the man had evoked upon her, but it was fury that remained coursing through her veins. The damned fruit of knowledge lay within the mind of her own personal tormentor, and her insides were thirsting for a bite, no matter how poisonous.

Without a moment's hesitation, Maya defied Halo's instructions and headed back into the flight of stairs after snatching a recouper from the metal table of gadgets, then grabbing the everlit torch. The cold aura did not reach through her internal fire as she avoided the other underdwellers' cries and continued down until she reached Broth's encaged self. He was still rocking. Still muttering the deceased woman's name.

Maya searched around for a button of some sort to open up the blue shield. The stones were anything but smooth as they scraped her hands, but eventually she made contact with a switch, and she didn't think twice as she flipped off the shield.

Broth's projection didn't move as his freedom was unknowingly granted, but a whiff of rotten flesh hit her and she gagged. Her steps were slow as she approached the man, and she may have been more terrified than she had thought previously. However, none of that stopped her from reaching forward and putting her fingers to the corpse's temples, making her first step into discovering the darkness that dwelled inside of her.

Chapter Twenty-Four

"Broth"

COLD. THAT WAS THE one word that could describe the state of Broth's mind.

With every mental step she took deeper into his consciousness, she became more sluggish, her limbs turning blue with the freezing atmosphere.

Underneath a cover of black swirling clouds, a younger Broth with brown hair and smooth skin sat next to a woman with red hair who kissed his neck gently.

"Don't leave me," he pleaded to her. *"Don't leave me, Susan."*

Suddenly, the black cloud reached down, taking a hold of his wife and pulling her into the darkness. Then, another black swirl shot through Broth's chest as he said, *"Then take me with you."*

The ground changed texture, and Maya lost her footing as she started to sink. She ran past the dream, ignoring the shuddersome blank expression that had taken over the man's features and searched for the small black holes. Stopping in front of the one that led to the man's memories, she marveled at the explosions of color that came from within. Her hand was about to reach in when she felt a sudden darkness shoot straight into her heart. She looked down to see the nightmare's black cloud, and was no longer able to breathe. Her vision started to fade in and out, replaced with hallucinations of her obliterated home and dead parents and dog, the smell poisoning her nostrils. But those weren't the visions that scarred her. The real terrifying ones were those where she saw herself being revealed as Lucid, and Kai turning his back on her. Then herself being tied to a table and operated on like a lab rat and the nurses trying to see what in her brain allowed her to access Kalpana.

Knees hitting the floor, Maya wheezed as Broth's face came into view, cursed words escaping his lips. *"You will always be beneath me."*

With a forceful shout, she ripped the black spear out of her chest, heaving as she was released from its grasp. Before it could get her again, Maya jumped into the portal.

Peacefulness did not exist on the other side of his mind. Every type of negative emotion could be seen swirling in the air, blurring her vision. Glowing spheres floated everywhere, with dialogue coming from each one.

"Darling, maybe if we had kids–"

"What happened to you?"

"Our president was assassinated again."

"Do you want us, Mr. Broth?"

The last one caused her to flinch, recognizing the sound of her own voice. It was something her younger self had asked him a month after entering his care. A string of emotions from him trailed this memory: disgust, anger, sadness, regret. Then a final, more subtle one: care.

Maya's hands balled up into fists and she scoffed. "Like you ever cared about either of us."

Pushing the ball away, she closed her eyes, listening for a mention of SCRO, or Chance, or even the familiar voice of Mrs. Fondal.

She finally hit gold when a particularly negative memory floated over her head, where that familiar voice she was looking for said, *"I have a proposition for you, Mr. Deidre."*

The spheres were knocked out of the way as Maya jumped up and gripped onto a deep green one. It jerked against her attempt to hold it in place, but she remained stubborn and felt around its smooth texture before lifting it up and slamming it to the ground, just as Griffin had done with the dream.

Maya instantly recognized the scene before her. They were at Broth's house, standing on the deck. The grass grew tall and uncared for throughout the field. There wasn't yet a chicken coup, and there were four pigs instead of three.

It was an odd experience, being in the memory of someone else. Everything was seen from their view, and for Broth that happened to be more blurry and less vibrant. The chair rocked beneath her—*him*—as he whistled a sad tune, smoking a cigar.

It wasn't only those sensations she felt, but his emotions, and most of all, his thoughts.

Sitting outside on the wooden deck, the wind blowing through the little hair he had left and his hand petting his tamed German Shepherd, Broth felt the calmest he had been since the death of Susan. His dear, sweet Susan, who had become a victim of the war, like much of everything had, only existed in the depths of his mind and the photos on his fireplace. Out in the wilderness was the one time he could feel something other than grief or bitterness, which was one of the reasons why he had decided to keep their ever-so-pricey house.

This peaceful setting, however, was interrupted by a silver hover car that made its way across the land, shifting the blades of grass as it drove. It stopped silently in front of the deck and his dog barked at the intruder ferociously. Broth was now on his feet as he got up and grabbed a gun that had been lying next to his rocking chair.

"Private property," he snarled.

The person inside the car—a woman—rolled down her window and held up a card. "Government official. There is nothing kept private from me. So please, if you mind putting down your weapon and taking control of your dog, things can go much smoother."

Annoyance prickled his skin as he slowly relaxed his gun and whistled to the German shepherd, calling it back into the house. When it was clear, the woman stepped out of the sliding car door, her heels sinking into the dirt below. A fake smile remained on her face as she walked up and held out her hand. "Mr. Deidre, I am Mrs. Fondal. It is a pleasure to meet you."

The woman's hand remained unshaken as Broth shoved his hands into his jeans' pockets. "What ya' want? I ain't done nothing illegal yet."

Mrs. Fondal retracted her hand. "I have a proposition for you, Mr. Deidre."

"And what may that be, a new truck for a piece of my land?"

"Oh, we don't have any intention of taking anything from you, as long as you cooperate."

"The hell does that mean?"

Pulling out a tablet, the woman moved closer. "You seem like the type of man that keeps up with the news. Tell me, does the name SCRO ring a bell?"

Broth chewed on his cheeks. "That thing to relocate kids? What's that gotta do with me?"

A smile grazed Mrs. Fondal's lips. "Well, it's actually more than that, and you would be a wonderful candidate."

"Stop talkin' in riddles, lady. What do ya' want? Money?"

"I want you to take in two orphaned children."

A bitter laugh traveled up Broth's throat. "You're kiddin' me."

She scrolled through her tablet. "Amarie and Maya Shaffer are siblings. Their parents moved to Maryland from Egypt years after marriage. They had started a family, but unfortunately lost their lives from a nuke. Their children have been traveling around the country for a while, with no permanent home. For every year you take care of them, $100,000 will be given to you."

The money was tempting, but he still shook his head. "I ain't gonna be taking care of no kids, no matter the money." "It won't be for too long, just until they are eighteen. Then we'll either release them into the world, or we'll take them back."

The statement confused him. "Why would ya need 'em back?"

There was a moment's hesitation before the woman said, "These two children are... unique. They are part of a secret government project, and will be studied throughout their lives. Their level of performance will decide whether or not they are granted freedom."

"So the government's doin' some messed up experiment on kids, and ya' think I want any part in that?"

Broth may have disliked children, but even that wasn't strong enough to will him to aid in whatever this test was.

Mrs. Fondal wore an infuriatingly fake pitiful frown as she told him, "Oh, Mr. Deidre, I'm afraid you don't have much of a choice. You have missed your payments on your land for the past three months. If you don't accept this responsibility, you will be evicted, and will lose this wonderful piece of property you have spent so many moments with your wife on. Do you really want to give this up when all it costs to keep it is eight years?"

Broth's blood boiled at the woman's threat. This house was all he had, and she must have known that. After all the damage caused by the nukes, inflation had hit the price of property especially hard. He couldn't pay; he knew that. But he raged at the thought of no control.

He wished he could punch the woman's grinning expression as he said, "Fine."

"Wonderful! Now, if I could have you recite this oath, and it will be confirmed."

He repeated each word after her in a brash tone.

"I swear to watch over the subjects in my possession until they are of proper age, or they are successful.

"Through my care, no harm will come to them.

"They will be fed, active, and stimulated.

"And, above all, no information will be shared with anyone about Project Lucid.

"Thank you for your cooperation."

The memory ended, and Maya fell to her knees, the emotions of the man flooding her. The fear of loss. The anger of no control. The protectiveness of kids he had never met.

The first thought of her own was the realization; she had never left SCRO. Though, that didn't shock Maya as much as it might have. Deep down, she had always suspected it since the beginning. She just didn't want to believe it.

The second thought, a more impactful thought, was the implication of Broth's emotions; the man cared—or had cared, once—about her and Amarie. It sunk in like a tire through tar. However, when it was finally submerged, her disbelief turned hysterical. "So you did care about us, huh?" she yelled. "Well, you sure did a great job of showing it!" In a mad rush, she got up and felt through the other memory spheres, looking for a particular memory: the moment Broth met the two of them for the first time. Bulbs of all sorts of colors filled the room, and she closed her eyes, strings attaching to each one as she whispered, *"Where we first met."*

From behind the wall of spheres, a pink one appeared, failing to resist Maya's tugging. It floated towards her. When it was in her grasp, she threw it to the ground.

He stood in front of a large modern building, the words "Transportation Unit" plastered onto its silver walls. Nerves caused his chest to burn as he sighed, and he unwillingly stepped into the transport. He cursed at the numerous people who knocked into him, but it lacked his normal fire, the fear of the next encounter prohibiting it. It wasn't the kids he was afraid of. No, it definitely wasn't that. It was more the memories that would resurface because of them. Memories with Susan, talking about children after the war and a family in a beautifully renovated home and what a wonderful life it would be.

He didn't deserve even an ounce of that dream. Not while the love of his life remained six feet under.

The blazing sun poured in from a large sunroof as Broth waited impatiently for the young burdens to be given to him, and after an hour of roaming the premise, finally a black-suited man with a strange mask showing none of his features walked in snobbishly, each of his hands pressed against one of two kids.

"Broth?" the man asked. Broth grunted, and after confirmation of his identity, the man pointed to each child. "Amarie. Maya. Ladies, this is your new caretaker."

The taller one named Amarie studied him with squinted eyes, a fire blazing behind them. Her dark curly hair had been thrown into a messy ponytail that curled around her shoulder. She flinched as the man behind her shoved her closer and reluctantly, the girl held out a hand. "Hi."

Broth couldn't be bothered to offer more than a grunt. Amarie kept her hand out, but after noticing he wasn't going to shake, she flipped her hand over and made an explicit gesture before tucking it back.

The other child was much smaller, with poofy curly hair that covered most of her face. With tiny hands, she swept the frizz away and wrapped her arms around him, catching him by surprise. The kid's hands constricted him and he pushed her away rather roughly, but the girl still stood with a wide smile as she said, "Thank you for wanting us, Mr. Broth." Beside her, Amarie pinched the bridge of her nose and shook her head, much less ignorant than her younger sister.

"Reports about them will need to be filled out monthly. Goodbye, Mr. Deidre."

After seething at the unhelpful government worker, he turned his attention back to the two kids, who were watching him expectantly. Both of them, even the fiery one, remained far too innocent. The younger one had so much hope of the future. The older one had so much will to fight.

It wasn't fair that the kids got to feel so much life.

His gaze went to the younger one again, the wonder in her eyes. Everything about the girl reminded him of Susan. Her smile, her posture, her positivity. A fine, attractive young woman the girl would become.

But not yet. First, they would learn the harsh reality of the world. They'll grow accustomed to his way of life. Amarie's fight will be crushed. Maya's ignorance will be cured. And they will be his.

Maybe Maya could even be his new Susan.

Horrible, horrible thoughts surrounded her, infiltrating Maya's mind through the plugging of her ears. Even after the memory ended, they remained glued to her mind. The awful things Broth had envisioned for them. The terrible emotions she never imagined feeling.

The memory spheres backed away as she crawled out through the portal, her mind feeling as though it was splitting in two.

She had been expecting many things to be going through Broth's mind at their first encounter, but never in her life would she have imagined something so... so... *revolting*.

Scratching at her head, she attempted clawing out what she had seen, but her efforts remained ineffective. Her breaths grew faster as her wrath flowed like red-hot lava, the volcano of emotions amounting pressure. The darkness of the monster's mind wrapped itself around her, but she paid it no attention as her mind reached out, grasping onto the farthest corners of Broth's consciousness. Then, with a scream, she tugged it towards herself.

Maya was weightless as the man's mind shattered in front of her. His dreams, his thoughts, his memories. They all fell into the black void that lay beneath it all.

And then, with a click of the recouper, she was back in Kalpana, and her legs gave out on her.

Horrified cries escaped her lips as she realized what she had just done. The Underdwellers were shouting along with her, but Maya's was easily the loudest, riddled with more pain and regret and self-hatred than any human should have been able to feel.

She had called Broth a monster.

But she was the one that shattered him.

Through her sobs, she didn't hear Kai's calling of her name. She didn't hear him when he asked her why she cried, or why she was down there. For all she knew, he may not have asked anything at all. His arms wrapped around her, holding the pieces of herself that had gotten caught in the damage of Broth's mind together. She felt sick. Ugly.

But Kai didn't seem to think so as he pulled her closer, giving her room to cry on his shoulder.

"It's okay," he whispered in her ear. *"I got you."*

In the Underdwelling cell, they remained in their prolonged hug until Maya's time ran out, her sobs finally turning into mere hiccups.

"I'm sorry."

Chapter Twenty-Five

"Reality Is Often Disappointing"

Breathe. I need to breathe.

She didn't kill him.

Nothing's wrong.

She was fine.

He's not.

Maya swung the thought away as fast as it had come, watching it fly into the back corners of her mind. Denial was the only thing holding her together, and the last thing she wanted to do was give the blue-bands another reason to bully her. Not like they needed a reason in the first place.

In Maya's history class, Prof. Vincent projected a 3d map of the West World, stretching from the tips of Canada to the lowest points of South America, then had the four kids, as well as herself, stand around it. She bent down for the map to be eye-level as the names of different cities floated above. From behind, someone bumped into her back and she fell through the hologram, landing roughly on the tile as multiple soft laughing fits erupted. The shoulders of all of the kids, save for Lilith, shook as they struggled to hold back their outbursts. Like usual, the professor continued on with his lesson without a single hiccup.

"This is a map from the time before World War 5." Prof. Vincent said in his typical nasally voice. "You can tell this by Washington DC still being the capital of our nation. And—Maya! What are you doing in my presentation?"

"Sorry," she mumbled, which only served to increase the boys' laughter. With her hurt wrist, Maya struggled to get back on her feet, but was shocked to find a hand being held out from none other than Brian. She scowled, but accepted his aid in order to stand. Though, as soon as she had regained balance, she yanked her hand away, feeling a sticky goo-like substance on her palm. Turning it over, she saw that same green substance they had put in her hair a few days ago. Maya fumed. Without a second thought, she grabbed a chunk of the boy's red hair and wiped the liquid all over it. He tried ducking away, but Maya had the advantage of height and held him in place. Once his hair was greased, she wiped the rest on his shirt and gave the boy a smile in response to his gaping expression. The boy with glasses looked worried as the other held back his chuckles, this time aimed at Brian. Lilith still remained quiet, but Maya thought she could see a flash of hostility cross her features.

The professor sighed at their antics before continuing his lecture by clicking a button. The map then changed, many of the major cities vanishing, while different patches of color emerged: red, yellow, and green. There was no longer Washington DC, and the star that had been floating above it now resided over western Texas.

"Fast-forward to now," Prof. Vincent continued after a hard glance at herself (as if it was her own fault the kids were being jerks). "You can see just how power-ful—and widespread!—the effects of the atomic bombs were. Only twenty bombs were dropped, but that was all that was needed for our destruction. They attacked our most concentrated states, maximizing casualties indiscriminately, those barbar-ians! And that's not even the worst part. No, not only did they destroy our cities, but they also sent different weapons to destroy our food! And so came the famine. Everywhere you looked. Everyone. Dead. Dead. *Dead!*"

The memory of Maya's parents resurfaced at the mention, their bodies burnt to a crisp. And then all those other corpses they would come across. Some slouched against walls. Others away on the road. Some already appeared to be dead with their glassy eyes and withered body, grasping for one final snack, only for their hands to turn back empty. Each day she would witness another loss of life during her time with SCRO. Although, now that she had discovered Chance had been alongside the cursed organization the entire time, it seemed like she had always been trapped with them. Maya never was free. Not like those other people. They didn't have to suffer anymore. They were dead. Dead. *Dead-*

The professor startled her out of her trance with a loud guffah, his sarcastic laughter filling the room. "And yet, there still managed to be a government! Never underestimate humanity's desire to be ruled. The politicians, or those that were left from around the nation, came together to keep the Western Government from falling apart and ran their own election to elect a president for president's sake. Not like that title had any power now! But those civilians remaining clung onto the nor-mality of having a ruler. They established new major cities and marked which areas were still habitable, shown by this map. The red areas will kill you in hours, and the yellow in weeks, without any gear. The very little land that remains green will allow life, but radiation blockers are still required. Then, through various connections the presidential cabinet had, funding for powering labs gave rise to more food.

"But not for everyone. Oh no. But only for those that paid taxes to the government! The people, who had nothing! Nothing, nothing, nothing! Food should be free, yes? No! Because after all the fighting had ceased, only the most cruel were left, greed ravaging their wretched souls! And you, children, you ungrateful children! All of this given to you, and yet you throw it away like dirty rags! Ungrateful"—he threw his remote—"Ungrateful! Every single one of you!" His eyes glowed with devouring fury. "This nation should have burned! The Man of Light should have harvested all of us!"

She glanced at the blue-bands beside her, surprised to find her own expression of terror portrayed on theirs as well. The professor was trembling at this point, repeating the phrase, *"harvest, harvest, harvest"* until it no longer sounded like a word. Slowly, Maya began inching her way to the door, while the others hustled past her. They tried closing the door in front of her, but she rushed forward, kicked it with her foot, and squeezed through the crevice. When she was finally through, Lilith shut it behind her and locked it by placing a stunt underneath the door. Maya panted as she studied the teacher through the small window. Prof. Vincent was entirely lost in his mental breakdown, falling onto his knees.

It had been around twenty seconds of silence before the soft sound of chuckling came from the rowdy dirty-blonde boy, but his friend elbowed his arm and cleared his throat, which cut him off quickly. The others continued to watch their trembling teacher, remaining a distance away from the wall. Prof. Vincent soon got up, albeit with a wobble, then made his way to the door and lifted his head to see them through the glass. His eyes were still glossy, as though he had not fully returned, but he tapped on the window with an expression of terror. His one-finger knock eventually turned into a fist, and he punched with such force to rattle its hinges. The attempts grew more extreme with every second, but none of the blue-bands made an effort to free him. When the man began screaming, Maya felt her own tears start to form. She knew what he was feeling. She knew it all too well.

Without thinking, Maya rushed over to the door and struggled to remove the stunt from underneath. She felt hands try to pull her back, but she slapped them off and, finally loosening the metal stunt, swung the door open. As soon as she had done this, the professor fell into her arms, almost sending her toppling to the ground. Maya tried to hold him up, finding it difficult when he began to dig his nails into her arms. She flinched, but still held him as he met her gaze, once again mumbling something she couldn't comprehend. His trembling increased, and he spoke:

"Only those who have been touched by the Man of Light will survive His fury, for Lucis is pure and just. When He returns, this world will cease to exist, and all of Tenebris will be forever destroyed.

"Before this time, may we watch out for the Anima Genus, who will prepare the way for Light's victory. Whose strength will not be their own, but the power of Lucis. For Lucis to thee will reveal the truth, and thus many will be brought before the Man of Light. And then, the soul child will be consumed by the embers of their own darkness."

At this point, the man began seizing, and Maya had to let him fall to the ground. Those things he said...those terms she had only ever heard in Kalpana. How could the man know those words? Was he an Omni as well? *Wasn't being omniscient supposed to be rare?* And what was the Anima Genus?

The moment the professor was on the floor, there were already nurses surrounding them. They opened a syringe and injected it into the shaking man's arm before tying him to a stretcher and rushing him down the hall. No one bothered to ask what had happened; they had no need to ask because, as Maya gazed down the hall, she noticed another one of the Chance workers studying them intensely while writing on her little tablet. She felt her cheeks flush in anger and bit her cheek. Had what just happened been just another test in their messed up experiment?

Of course, she never got an answer to this, as after the episode, the professor was never to be seen again.

"Okay you five, head to your next class," ordered a nurse, who had trailed behind the others. The blonde boy groaned, while the one with glasses thanked him hurriedly. Brian and Lilith did not say a word, but Maya found her mouth gaping at the couple when she saw their hand-holding. It wasn't as though she was *actually* shocked—she had assumed the two of them had something going on—but they were showing it so *openly*. The two lovebirds locked eyes with Maya, causing her to quickly shut her mouth. Lilith didn't seem impressed by her surprise, but Brian snorted and gazed down the hall before saying, "What a desperate attempt for extra credit. Even for you, Mayo."

At the comment, Maya growled under her breath. She had to bite her tongue to prevent her retort, and still, the nicest words she could manage were, "You must be jealous, given your grades."

She headed the opposite way before he got a chance to respond, walking to her next red-band class. However, as she passed the worker with the tablet, she peered over her shoulder. Maya didn't get to see what was written, the woman pulling it to her chest too fast. Maya sighed before leaning back and saying, "I hope you're writing good notes about me. I wouldn't want to disappoint." The lady glared at her, but Maya simply turned on her heel and paid her not a single thought, instead putting her energy into decoding what Professor Vincent had said.

Later that day, she barged into her tutoring session, ranting all the while to Jeff, not caring if he ever responded. "I figured out what the blue bands stand for: the biggest divvys in the entire school! It has to be that, because there is not *one* red-band in this entire stupid place that are such big jerkwits! They dumped an entire gallon of black ink on me! Who *does* that? This stuff will never come off!"

The man seemed to be holding back a grin as he said, "I can see that."

Maya groaned loudly before falling into her seat, slouching all the way down. With her finger, she slid the Kalpanian book across the dark brown table. She still had the terrible taste in her mouth. Half of her wanted to get some kind of poisoning from the ink to require the administrators to have *some* kind of response.

"I'm already on my second uniform too," Maya mumbled, and this time the old man did laugh. Against her will, she also felt her mouth twitch up.

"Ah, they'll get what they deserve. One day," Jeff promised, and Maya sighed and sat up, resting her elbow on the table. "And *we* have work to do."

"Actually..." She looked away from the man for a second. "I do have something to talk to you about. Well, two things."

"You always do," he said, and Maya gave him an exasperated look. "So? I'm all ears!"

She contemplated which problem to address first. In reality, there was so much she wanted to tell the man, but the last thing she wanted to do was scare her friend away. So she started by asking, "Do you know what the... what Anima Genus is?"

At the name, Jeff stared off into the distance, stroking the white hairs that grew from his chin. "*Anima Genus.* Now where did you hear that name?"

"It was something a teacher of mine said. Do you know what it is?"

Her response led to more confusion plaguing the elder's features. "There has only been one time I've ever seen those words. It was in Kalpana, though I can't remember what it said about it or in what context. Oh! But I remember which book! At least, I have a pretty good idea. Tonight I will show you, yes! Does that sound good to you, Maya?"

"That sounds perfect," she told him. *Then at least one thing would be answered.*

And now it was time for her other topic. But how do you tell someone, *"Hey, so you know the nice organization you joined to help orphaned kids? Well, it turns out it's actually tied with this evil thing called SCRO, and it itself is experimenting on children like me. What are they testing? No idea. Why are they doing all this? No clue. Is it a coincidence there are two—possibly three—Omnis that are a part of it? Most likely not. Do I have proof? Nope. You just gotta trust me."*

She realized her prolonged silence, but Maya couldn't find a way to start. It turned out she didn't need to, because right as she opened her mouth, Mrs. Fondal entered through the door. Maya felt like ice-cold water had been poured down her back. She turned the spinning chair around, secretly pushing the thick book closer to Jeff so that he could hide it. Meeting the lady's gaze, she lifted her chin and kept her face neutral.

From behind her, Jeff kept his perky tone. "Ah, Mrs. Fondal! Lovely to see you, as always. Tell me, what can we do for you?"

The head administrator narrowed her eyes at the man, but made no other comment than that. "I've come to collect Maya. She was outside for many years, and we must do some more examinations to make sure she remains healthy."

Of course you have to.

Jeff couldn't object, so Maya found herself following Mrs. Fondal back to the nurse's office with a sneer. "Let me guess," she said, "you still can't say what they did to me last night?"

The woman side-eyed her. "Do you truly want to know?"

"Why I happen to have a big incision at the back of my neck? It would be preferred."

Smiling that same demeaning smile, Mrs. Fondal turned her head back to ahead. "During one of the scans, a malignant tumor came up that was situated on your spine. Without treatment, it would have spread."

Oh.

She stuttered, "Am...am I okay now?"

"We caught it very early. So yes."

She fell behind instep with Mrs. Fondal, struggling to process the fact that they actually *had* been treating her. *Thank God the government is rich.*

Having one less question, she felt a momentary sense of relief, and it nearly made her audibly laugh. She had gotten to a point in her life that a diagnosis such as this offered her *relief.*

It didn't lessen the hate she felt towards the woman, but it allowed her to be *slightly* less confrontational. At least, that was until she recalled what she was about to tell Jeff before she had been interrupted. No matter how they healed her, they still had a singular motivation. She was a guinea pig in their experiment, which they needed to be in tip-top health. And she still did not know what it was all for.

However...as she walked with Mrs. Fondal, a plan to answer exactly that began to form in her mind.

Chapter Twenty-Six

"A Helpless Plea"

"Do you want to talk about it?"

Maya had been sitting in silence on the orange rock formation in Kalpana, staring absentmindedly at the hybrids that roamed the field below. Her curly hair tickled the back of her neck as the wind blew the clothes of her subconscious, as loose as the threads of thought flowing around in her brain. Being back in Kalpana refreshed the events of the previous night, down to the moment of Kai seeing her at her lowest. There's no relief from the struggles that infiltrated her life. Whether awake or asleep, the emotions were the same.

Though tonight, she felt different. There wasn't a way to see if she had changed physically as well, but Maya wouldn't have been surprised if she did happen to look ugly, with all of her guilt and shame. It was funny, the way her mind worked. In one way, what she had done to Broth was nauseating. But at the same time, hidden deeper in her mind, was a sense of accomplishment.

That side scared her.

Kai had just sat next to her, gazing upon her with a look that creased his brows. His features held concern and worry, but nowhere in there did she sense pity. It was an empathy that was warm and accepting. It was an expression that caused her heart to beat faster.

With her head lifted to the sky, she said, "I don't know how."

There was too much to unpack—too much painful history to unveil. She could barely handle thinking about it, much less telling her story out loud.

"Well, I won't force you." Scooting closer to her, he leaned over and wrapped his arms around her, his heat spreading over her body. Her face must have been red from the initial fluster of the action, but soon after she melted into the embrace.

It was then when she realized how much she had missed the boy and their conversations. They hadn't known each other very long, but already it felt like a lifetime.

She squeezed back, afraid his presence would be as fleeting as the breeze.

Kai was the first to break, clearing his throat and shuffling farther away, and that action alone caused Maya's chest to ache. "You looked like you could use that," he chuckled as he brushed back his black hair, and she could have sworn there was a twinge of pink decorating his cheeks. Standing up, the boy rubbed his hands. "Well, I should probably head back before–"

"Kai—wait." Without realizing, Maya had grabbed ahold of the boy's hand. Slowly, he sat back down, knees turned toward her. "Just..."

"... Amie?"

"My real name's Maya," she blurted out. Kai watched her for a while before a cute—albeit teasing—smile spread across his cheeks.

"That name fits you."

They stared at each other in tranquility, and Maya took in every feature of the boy's face. The light freckles that peppered his cheeks. The red lips that contrasted with the paleness of his skin. The black, tightly curled hair that reached as far as his nose. And then his blue eyes that should have been cold, but held more warmth in them than a million suns.

Her mind flashed back to where he held her the night before, preventing her from falling apart completely.

He cared for her. Really, *truly,* cared for her.

Maybe I could tell him the truth–

No. I can't risk it.

"You've been avoiding me," Maya chose to accuse him instead. "Why?"

At that, he shifted uncomfortably. "What makes you think I was avoiding you?"

Maya scoffed. "Oh, please. All I've gotten from you for the past week is a passing greeting and a sentence if I'm lucky. I thought after the last conversation, we were better."

"We are," he stressed. "It's just... I've been busy. With work."

As a certified liar, Maya could confirm the excuse didn't hold a single ounce of truth. And yet, she couldn't be upset. Not with everything she was withholding from everyone. There was, however, one thing she held onto that could be shared.

Reaching her arms forward, she grabbed onto each of Kai's hands and brought it up to her temples. "Here, you can see."

Shaking his head, Kai said, "Maya, you really don't have to."

"Yes, I do. You were there for me, so you deserve to know. I trust you with this."

He looked at her as though he didn't recognize her. But by the way his gaze lit up, he must have liked the new person he saw. Kai closed his eyes, and Maya closed hers with him, making sure to bring up only the memories about Broth and her childhood, and not those that exposed herself.

Kai went through multiple emotions while he watched. Curiosity that sparkled in his eyes. Confusion that pinched his brows. Then, at the end of the flood of memories, a starking realization. She could see the exact moment his heart broke in two, and when tears started streaming down his cheeks, Maya pulled away, feeling guilty for putting him through what she had gone through herself.

Putting a hand behind her neck, he pulled her forehead to his, whispering apologies on her behalf.

"I'm pretty sure I'm the one who needs to apologize," she told him softly, and he groaned.

"Not this again." He laughed, wiping his tears away roughly before sobering. "Are you okay, though, after all that? Well, of course you're not okay. That was a dumb question."

"No, it's fine. I really am okay, and I have you to thank for that. I don't know what would have happened if you weren't there for me last night."

Or any other night.

The longer they sat next to each other, the more the warmth in Maya's chest grew. What had started off as a pleasant, although sudden feeling, had morphed into one that burned her heart. She rubbed it in an attempt to muffle the pain, but it stayed there.

However, the more she understood what the feeling was, the more she was brought back to Broth—his memories as well as her own. Kai must have noticed her change of mood and reached for her arm, but out of pure instinct, she jerked away. There was a look of pain on the boy's face. "I'm sorry," she said. "I don't know why I did that."

"You're hurt." Maya looked upward to see Kai now standing. "Whoever that Broth man is, he deserves whatever comes for him for making your life miserable. But here in Kalpana, you can be free from him. Don't let him control you."

He reached his hand out to her, as if to give her another chance. Her mind quickly flashed between Kai and Broth, causing her to flinch, but after a second of closing her eyes and taking a deep breath, the ghost of her past disappeared.

And she put her hand into his, allowing him to pull her up.

She didn't look away as the boy led her back to the castle at the other end of the valley, not even to look at the unicorns in all their beauty. Before she knew it, they were back at the castle. Emerging from the doors, Griffin appeared, and Kai abruptly dropped her hand, said a quick goodbye, and walked into the palace, leaving Maya struggling to figure out the puzzle that was Kai.

Griffin had his arms crossed, watching her with dangerous eyes. Swallowing, Maya forced herself not to flinch as he got closer and said, "I thought I told you to stay away from him."

"Kai was just cheering me up." She tried to sidestep him, but he blocked her from moving by grabbing her upper arm.

"You still think I'm stupid, like I didn't see the way you two were looking at each other. Did my warnings last time mean nothing to you?"

At the tightening of his grip, Maya became furious and jerked her arm away. "So what if I do? What do my feelings have to do with you? If he wants me to back off, then so be it. But he *doesn't*. So you have no right to break up a friendship that makes both of us happy just because you hate me so much!"

Griffin studied her for an extended moment before scoffing. "You really think I hate you? I'm doing this *for* you. There's no trust, don't get me wrong, but you better listen to me when I say only hurt is going to come from that boy. And then you're going to cry, because when he finally decides to tell you the truth, you'll realize that you guys *can't* be together. And when that happens, don't say I didn't warn you."

With that, the man stormed away, and Maya was beckoned over by Jane to make a flower delivery, still chewing her cheek raw in frustration.

Whatever. I have bigger things to worry about.

And yet, topics like Broth somehow wormed its way into her conversations again when she ran into her other friend, not thinking before asking, "Halo, is it possible to destroy someone's mind?"

Maybe it wasn't the best way to start a conversation, but the question had been haunting her ever since she started to review what *exactly* happened the previous night. And a theory was beginning to manifest. One that terrified her even more than the Man of Light.

Halo hummed as they continued to walk side-by-side after Maya had delivered more sedaflors to the woman. Maya held the flowers behind her back to prevent the high it had given her before. Humming in wonder once again, Halo responded, "Now, why would you want to know that?"

Maya gazed off to the side. "No reason. Just...curiousity."

Halo raised an eyebrow before answering. "Not for an Omni."

"But–" The weight of the question choked her. "For a Lucid?"

The walls appeared to grow in size and height, the broken windows creaking with the wind. Her shadow that was cast across the marble tile shrunk in size, while Halo's only grew. Even the minute smell of the sedaflors did nothing to ease her apprehension, despite herself already knowing the answer. The woman's steps slowed as she slowly turned towards her, Maya holding herself together by a thread. "What did you do, Amie?"

That was all it took.

At her words, she felt herself break down, as though a dam had shattered. Her voice was stolen, and, placing her head in her hands, she began to tremble. "It was an accident. I didn't mean to, I–" Halo didn't let her finish before bringing her close to her chest, silencing her with gentle shushes. A sob came from her throat when she stroked her hair. It had been years since Maya had thought of her mother, but in Halo's arms, she found herself longing for that type of relationship once more. Maya sank deeper. While holding her, the woman said, "Oh, dear. Don't blame yourself for this. We both know you had no intention of hurting him."

"But what if I *did*?" Sobs shook her chest, and she struggled to free her encased fears. "What if I did but didn't know? I hate him, Halo, I do!"

The woman pulled her even closer, embracing her with an all-encompassing warmth. At the action, Maya felt her sobs begin to dissipate and her breathing begin to calm. Softly, Halo said, "The workings of the mind are complex, but love is even more so. I don't think you reacted this way because you hate him. I think you love him."

Maya attempted to blink away her tears as she lifted her head to meet Halo's gaze. Halo was one of the few women she had ever met that looking up was necessary, which might have been part of the reason why Maya felt such a strong respect for her.

The woman carried herself with such poise and purpose. But, despite her stature, she never looked down on her. Now, even after stating her observations, Halo watched her with anticipation, as though eager to discover what Maya believed. *Broth never cared about what* I *believed.*

With the thought brought about a surge of anger, surprisingly at herself. "How could I love him?"

"Who knows the way love works." Finally, Halo released her, taking in her hands the purple flowers. "The cruelest of actions have come from it." Leaning forward, the woman tucked the strand of hair Maya usually curled behind her ear. And without another word, she walked through the door to the Underdwellings, Maya having no idea how they got there in the first place.

Footsteps echoed from down the hall and she quickly wiped away her tears, half tempted to follow Halo down to see Broth's state. Nevertheless, Maya turned around and even managed a smile when she identified Hypnos hobbling towards her. He gave her an exaggerated wave and Maya headed his way. Inside her mind, she pushed away anything to do with Broth. She would address those worries tomorrow in Terra.

One worry at a time.

THE LIBRARY WAS JUST as majestic as it had been the first time she entered, with millions of books reaching all the way to the circular sunroof. The spheres of light glowed a dark orange today and surrounded her like fireflies. Maya sat on her knees with Revere on her lap, stroking its soft pelt. Her hand reached around one of its long ears and it leaned into her hand, chirping excitedly.

In front of her, Jeff—Hypnos—balanced on a ladder as he traced his fingers down the fifth shelf. He mumbled softly beneath his breath and continued to do so until suddenly he released a shout of accomplishment. "Here it is!" He waved it across his chest, but at the movement, the ladder slid forward, causing it to fall back. Maya didn't hesitate before hopping up and darting to it. She crawled beneath the wooden ladder and grabbed its sides, pulling it down to the floor. It stopped wobbling and she sighed in relief, her heart still thumping with adrenaline. As if nothing had happened, Hypnos slid down its steps and, patting her shoulder, said, "You are a wonderful young lady."

The old man moved to one of the wooden tables and an exasperated Maya made her way beside him. The book he had found was black with golden print and embroiderment. Hypnos then opened it and flipped through its pages, eventually settling on a section near the end. Like all the other books in the library, the words were encrypted, but he scanned through the words like it was his native tongue. The only symbols Maya could make out were the ones representing Lucis and Tenebris, and just as the previous night, the paranoia of Lucis coming after her stimulated her senses. She gripped the ends of her shirt, struggling to resist gazing in every direction, in case a spirit was coming after her.

"This is one of the oldest books we have in Neshama Valley," Hypnos said. "A book of prophecies."

Maya couldn't hide her skepticism. "How do we know if any of it is true?"

"Well, it did prophesy The Harvest, so I would say it is explicitly truthful!" He gave her a wink when her jaw dropped.

"You mean this book *knew* a billion people would die, and yet no one sent a warning? If people knew, then the war could have been stopped! Maybe people could have taken actions to prevent all the deaths, and the world wouldn't be so surprised. And yet, here the book is, collecting dust when it could have saved the human race!"

With a nod of his head, Hypnos told her, "I share your passion, young one. But you must understand that even if the world had knowledge of the words of this book, it would have made no difference. Prophecies stand forever. There is no changing a prophecy, for it comes from a place beyond time, unable to be manipulated. And, speaking of prophecies, here is what you were looking for! The *Anima Genus*. Right here! Come see, come see!"

Maya did as he asked, though a closer look didn't do much to aid her in making sense of it all. However, the specific symbol did remind her of something. Something that was important, but she couldn't remember what.

"What does it say about it?" Maya asked him.

Squinting, Hypnos traced the words with his finger, reading the page as if it was in his native tongue, mumbling the language under his breath. "It is incredibly cryptic. But it is a prophecy, so that's its nature!"

Then he recited the same words the teacher had:

"May we watch out for the Anima Genus.
Who will prepare the way for Light's victory.
Whose strength will not be their own, but the power of Lucis.
For Lucis to whom will reveal the truth.
With it, many will be brought before the Man of Light
Before thee loses themself."

A ringing grew in her ears as he spoke the prophecy, becoming muffled while Maya's vision remained glued on the symbol. It appeared to grow, spinning in the air and then floating to her. That was when she realized why it looked so familiar.

"The Man of Light," Maya whispered, mostly to herself, but Hypnos had heard her. She couldn't elaborate, for fear had taken hold of her throat. The memory had been buried so deep inside her mind that reliving it was like trying to relive a dream. But she knew it had happened. That same night she had broken through her dream, *He* had been there. The one who had apparently been responsible for the deaths of a billion people. He had *touched her.* The Man of Light. He was the reason she was omniscient. He *knew* she was lucid. So...so what did that mean? Was He after her to kill her? Enslave her? Infiltrate her life in Terra?

"Little one, are you okay?" Hypnos reached out to soothe her, but Maya scooted back faster, her eyes not straying from the book.

"Who is the *Anima Genus*?"

The man gave her a concerned gaze, but answered her nonetheless. "We don't know who it will be. Or even when, for that matter. It could be thousands of years before the *Anima Genus* appears. Personally, I'm hoping it is a *very* long way away."

Maya ran a hand through her hair. "Why do you hope for that?"

Sighing, Hypnos stretched his arms above his head. "According to this prophecy, their appearance means the end of the world is very near. Which in itself doesn't bother an old lad such as myself. *But,* it does make me worry for everyone else, especially when you read the end of the prophecy. *Thee loses themself.* So they must die, and whoever kills the *Anima Genus* must be profoundly powerful to defeat them."

"*This is crazy,*" Maya told herself as she gripped her head with her hands. The Man of Light had shown her the Anima Genus. What did she have to do with that? Louder, she said, "It doesn't matter, since this isn't true. The Man of Light was made up by those who went mad. And I'm not mad!"

Hypnos held pity in his eyes. "You may choose to believe that, if you please. But it is true, whether or not you have faith. Though, you have now seen Kalpana. Is it really such a stretch to believe in a God?"

Maya groaned and pulled on her hair. "Yes! Because I can *see* Kalpana. I can't—I mean, I *did*, but I—no! It doesn't mean anything. It wasn't *Him.*"

"Maya?" The use of her real name immediately sobered her, and she met Hypnos' gaze. "Little one, did I hear you right? Did you see The Man of Light?"

He whispered the last part so softly, but its impact was just as violent. "No, I didn't!"

Yes, you did.

Stop denying the truth.

To you will be revealed–

"Just *STOP!*"

At the word, a powerful jolt went through her body, and Maya collapsed to the ground. Her vision faded in and out as she struggled to regain consciousness. Blinking rapidly, she started to notice the familiar strings that trailed from her fists. A sharp headache caused her to flinch. Finding it odd that Hypnos remained quiet, Maya turned her eyes to the man, only to let out a cry. The man's entire body remained impossibly still, with not even his chest elevating. It was only his eyes—his gray, panic-stricken eyes—that moved. Hypnos directed his irises downward to where Maya struggled on the ground, which made her overflow with shame. She stood up with shaking legs and limped over to his side, forcing her vision to remain as she gripped his shoulders, searching for a way to unfreeze him.

"I'm sorry," Maya cried. "I'm so, so sorry! I didn't mean to, I promise!" The strings were still knotted tightly around the man, and she tried with all her might to undo them, but she no longer had the energy.

Still, Maya tried and tried until finally she was brought to her knees, sobbing at his feet. Everything just kept getting worse. SCRO—Chance—Broth—and now Kalpana. What was *wrong* with her? Why did curses keep following her? What was she being punished for?

She had no answers for those questions, but there was one thing she knew: Hypnos did not deserve this.

"I don't know what to do," Maya whispered to the air. Looking up through the sun roof and to the heavens, she called out to The Man of Light. "I'm sorry! I'm sorry I denied you! Punish me in any way you please. Take me like you took all those people during The Harvest! But *please*, do not hurt Hypnos because of my mistakes. Please, help him! Because I *can't*."

The utter hopelessness of her plea manifested another series of tears that fell to the rug beneath her knees. *Lucid.* The reality almost made her long for her nightmares, where terror only lasted through the night. Maya flipped over the palms of her hands and noticed the slight fade that was coming over them. With great sorrow, she looked up at Hypnos, but let out a cry of relief when she saw the strings begin to loosen and twitching begin in his arms and legs. A small light the size of her hand rested on the knots before snapping the ties, and instantly the man stumbled forward, the strains released.

The light then floated towards her and rested in her palms, speaking a voice only she could hear: *"I will be here to fix your messes, so long as you trust me to do so."*

Maya began to tremble as the light dimmed along with her body, Kalpana signaling that her time was up. She refused to look at Hypnos and tuned out his voice until it was barely an echo behind the void which her emotions resided within, its encasement being the only thing preventing her from truly going mad.

Chance is an experiment.

SCRO has always had me.

The Man of Light is real.

I may be part of the Anima Genus.

I shattered Broth's mind.

Hypnos knows I'm Lucid.

I'm dangerous.

One thing at a time.

Chapter Twenty-Seven

"Understanding Brings Peace"

Step one: figure out how to get out of tutoring.

Maya tapped her tablet pen rapidly on her desk, earning her a glare from the blue band with glasses. Pushing up his spectacles, the boy tracked his eyes back to the tablet. Its glow illuminated his face, the glass around his eyes reflected the words on the screen, and it seemed like he was the only one of them actually taking the art exam. Why did art even have an exam?

She didn't even notice she was still fidgeting with the pen until the teacher cleared her throat. And, in a moment she wasn't too proud of, Maya flicked up the instrument between her middle and ring finger. Thank the Light(she would thank Him in the very far future) the teacher had turned around, but the other blue band she-still-didn't-know-the-name-of did see, which surprisingly earned her a chuckle with a thumbs up.

Shaking her head, Maya felt the anxiety crawl back up. She could not face Jeff now. Not after what she had done the previous night. And even though she had attempted to push away all thoughts of it, Maya still didn't understand how she had done what she did to Jeff inside Kalpana. It wasn't as though she intended for *him* to stop, and she definitely didn't try to pull any strings, but...and the Light, too. What *was* that? It glowed like a spirit, but it was smaller, with a familiar voice she had never heard before, which didn't make sense in itself.

Stop thinking about all that. One thing at a time.

Maya could try to hide inside the gaming room and in the maze, but she wouldn't be able to stay there very long. She could go in the bathroom and stay there for as long as she could, but a scanner on the bathroom door marks and times how long everyone is in there, so she'd be caught. There was no privacy anywhere, so her best bet was to stay within the group.

After the test, they were excused from class, and Maya hurried to catch up with the four blue bands, following them with wide steps. She kept her head low and put her hands inside her pockets. Hope started to build up that her plan may work, until a stern voice spoke her name. Sighing heavily, Maya turned her head to the voice and said, "Yes?"

The administrator who called her gripped tightly onto her tablet. "Mr. Jeffery's office is the other way."

Then, with a groan, she was escorted to Jeff's office, the administrator refusing to leave her side until they reached the door.

The session with Jeff was tense, to no surprise of her own. Jeff, the ever easy-going one, now shifted his cane in his hands and gave her an obviously forced smile. Maya pulled out the chair across from him and sat down in silence—shame engulfed her at the sight of the man, paired with an overwhelming fear and guilt. She wasn't ready for this.

"You gotta talk to me sometime, little one," the old man tried to joke, but Maya sank into the chair and wrapped her arms around herself. How was she supposed to weave her way through this, especially when she still didn't know what exactly had happened? Maya probably could have figured it out, but she still refused to think about everything to do with her lucid abilities and The Man of Light. Having that crowd her brain along with the rest of her current problems would surely shatter her own sanity. Just like she shattered Broth's.

Don't think about that. Later. Jeff first.

Said man was nodding slowly when she looked up again. "Okay, well, I may not be the smartest man, but my old brain is occasionally able to put two and two together. A lucid Omni. Ah, Maya, aren't you full of surprises."

If possible, she sank even lower, her face heated with shame. After realizing she wasn't going to respond, Jeff continued speaking. "No one else knows, I figure. The people of Neshama are some tough fellas, let me tell you. But guess that's a good thing I was the one to find out, aye?"

"Halo knows too," Maya mumbled as she played with her hands. "She told me to keep it a secret because of that. But I didn't—well, she told me, but I didn't know what it meant. To be lucid, I mean." She then buried her head in her hands. "I'm so sorry for yesterday. I don't know what's wrong with me."

Suddenly, she felt Jeff's hand on her shoulder and his voice much closer. "There is nothing wrong with you, little one."

Lifting her head up, she felt the tears in her wet hands. "No one else can do the things I can. And when my emotions get the better of me, I can't control it. I don't know what to do. Why am I like this, Jeff? I hurt people. Everywhere I go, bad things follow. I thought I could escape it in Kalpana, but it finds me there too. Asleep or awake. Then there's the Anima Genus. What do I have to do with that? I just—I can't deal with it all. It's too much!"

"Darkness attacks hardest those who have the most potential for good."

Maya let out a bitter laugh. "Trust me, Hypnos, I am *not* good."

"Ah, I highly doubt that," he said. "But even if that were true, mere potential can cause resistance. Now youngin, why do you believe you are tied to the Anima Genus?"

And so Maya explained herself meeting The Man of Light, as well as the prophecy her teacher said that felt directed towards her. She told him about the familiarity of the Anima Genus symbol, and the voice that spoke to her after Hypnos had been released from her grasp.

"I don't want any of this." Maya gripped her hair. "Why couldn't I be back on my family's farm, growing pecans and oranges and mangoes, with nothing to worry about except deer eating the crops? We were happy. *I* was happy. I—I'm saying 'I' a lot, aren't I? Sorry Jeff, you don't need to hear all this. Are you okay from yesterday?"

A grin spread across Jeff's face as he said, "You are asking if *I* am okay? And you are not good, you say." He stopped her from retorting by cupping her hands in his own. "Little one, you have grown up too fast. Do not worry about me. You do not need to fear all these things. The Man of Light has a purpose for you, and the best part about that is Him leading you. If you are right and you have something to do with the Anima Genus, then there is no reason for worry, because it will happen either way. So relax! You have too much on your shoulders to worry about what-ifs. Focus on what you can change."

Maya sniffled and closed her eyes. Jeff was right, of course. There are some things in life that can't be changed, no matter how hard one tries. But that doesn't stop the search to understand the meanings behind it.

They moved on with the lesson, Jeff gratefully choosing to focus on history and science rather than Kalpana, and when the session was over, Maya got up with slightly less shake than before. Before leaving, she stopped at the door, faced back, and said, "Hypnos?" He lifted his head from his paperwork. "Will you tell the other Omnis I'm lucid?"

Then the man smiled at her warmly. "Your secret will lie only with me and Revere."

Weight lifted off her shoulders, Maya returned his warm gaze and stepped out of the room. Not with less anxiety, or hatred, or regret, but with a plethora of confidence and determination. She would unveil the secrets. She'd focus on what she could control. And right now, it was this: somehow, in some way, she'd escape the project that had destroyed her life.

STEP TWO: DISCOVER WHAT Chance was up to.

If she wanted answers, there was one person who would have them for sure, and that was Mrs. Fondal. The visitor. The head of the refuge. The only direct tie she had from Broth to the experiment. And also someone Maya was really, *really* starting to hate.

But her intense hatred for the woman still did not outweigh the overwhelming fear she caused to course through her body. Unlike Brian, Mrs. Fondal had nearly all the power in every aspect of her life in Terra, and even Maya herself wasn't quite sure how far that influence reached. She was exactly the type of person she had been taught to avoid confrontation with and obey without question if she wanted to survive.

But if Maya had learned anything the past few weeks, it was that dangers are hidden in every part of life. And, comparing the risk and reward, the revelations

Fondal would give her earned the struggle it would take to obtain them. As Amarie and herself always said, "ignorance is a death wish."

Now she just needed to find her office.

Based on the lock she had seen during the previous walk-by, it seemed likely that the only way to get into the woman's office was by her own chip, so there was no way Maya could get in herself. The next best plan was to have Mrs. Fondal open it for her, somehow. And a plan was already starting to formulate in her mind.

After her tutoring session, she absently listened to the Alicorn team leader go over their plan to get the ball to the other side for what felt like the hundredth time, and still no one seemed to be getting it. Maya didn't know why they bothered with strategic planning. The listeners clearly weren't understanding the directions, so the leader should make it simple: turn the ball purple and get it through the exit.

Simple. If only everything else was so cleanly put. If only she could actually *understand* and *overcome* all the mess in her life without causing pain and—

Stop thinking about it! Focus on what you can control.

Camila tapped her on the shoulder and Maya quickly turned around to see the girl wearing a large grin on her face. Flipping her tablet over, she pointed to the screen, which had on it a statement making fun of Carlos as he gazed heart-eyed at the announcer girl.

Maya shook her head and forced a chuckle. "You're despicable." But her conversation with her friend remained detached; it didn't take priority over the retracing of her steps to find the office in her mind. Camila most likely sensed this, as she soon walked over to bother her brother.

The practice session was somehow too short and too long simultaneously. She had been practically vibrating as she stood, but when the bell finally rang, Maya suddenly wanted nothing more than to stay back and head to dinner along with everyone else. Nevertheless, she had already committed to her extraordinarily risky plan and separated from the group, heading in the direction she hoped was towards Mrs. Fondal's office.

The topic she was going to discuss with the woman could easily bring suspicion to herself. Not only was it a sensitive subject, but it involved admitting she sensed something off with the refuge. However, she knew it *had* to be this topic. It was the only thing she could think of that would be a believable reason for her coming to Mrs. Fondal. And this way, if the administrator tries to convince her that everything is normal, which she most certainly will, she would pretend to take her words as though it was Scripture.

A few adults she passed noticeably traced her up and down, but thankfully said nothing as she made her way further down the hall. It was as she passed by the screening room when she remembered the path they had taken. Finally arriving at the door, Maya knocked on it three times before putting her hands in her pockets, twisting a paper clip from art class between her fingers.

It took around ten seconds for the office door to open, where Mrs. Fondal stood in front with widened eyes. "Maya. What a pleasant surprise. What do you need? Are you lost?"

"No," she cleared her throat. "I actually came here to talk to you."

The woman's predatory smile stretched across her face. "Well, in that case. Please, do come in."

Inside, the office was just as cold as Mrs. Fondal's aura and lacked any of the character of Jeff's. Gray walls, a white desk, and black metal shelves were the expanse of the color. The only personality the room had came from the photos that displayed strangers. Mrs. Fondal must have noticed her observing the holograms as she said, "My children. And my husband. I lost them eight years ago. A cruel thing, war is." Watching the woman now, Maya couldn't imagine her with a family, holding her children in her arms and giving a kiss to her husband, but she nodded her head still. Mrs. Fondal then sat down on her desk and placed her folded hands in front. "So, what can I assist you with?"

Maya took a deep breath in preparation. "Broth. Not the meat stuff, but...well, the man."

The woman's eyebrows raised in understanding. "I've heard about your poor experience with him, and I am terribly sorry for that. But that is in the past. You are safe here, so there is no need to dwell on it."

Heated anger swelled inside Maya at Fondal's performance of innocence, as though she hadn't known all this time, or better yet, had been the very *reason* she was put there in the first place, if her assumptions proved to be correct. But that wasn't what she had come to reveal her knowledge of.

"Before I was taken, there was a stranger at our door." Maya noticed the way the woman's breath hitched. "She sounded like you."

She was you.

"The agent, Mr. Hue, told me they had known for years about Broth's treatment of us," she continued. "I guess... you knew too?"

Mrs. Fondal was clearly uneasy as she sat more upright in her seat. "I did. Don't ever mistake me, it was never our intention to leave a young girl like yourself in the hands of such a monster, but there were numerous factors working against us."

"So what *were* you doing there that day?"

If Maya hadn't been paying close attention, she wouldn't have noticed the brief hesitation in her response. "I was sent there as a warning to force him into better behavior. He was ordered to turn you in, but he must have gotten spooked, as he left with you shortly after."

The answer followed a careful tightrope between half-truths and blatant lies so smoothly that it chilled Maya to the depths of her bones. Though what was even more terrifying was the sudden remembrance of Broth's final words as he was pulled away: *"I was trying to save ya!"*

If Chance was SCRO, then the greasy man really *had* been trying to help her escape.

Even if it was for his own, selfish reasons.

"And my sister?" Maya knew she was pushing, but the curiosity festered inside her. "You knew about her too, and how she escaped."

Mrs. Fondal's eyes darkened and the table creaked as she leaned forward. Maya's palms grew sweaty, knowing she had overstepped.

There was malicious intent in her tone as she asked, "What are you *really* doing here, Maya?"

The woman's gaze had locked with hers, and Maya's brain struggled to focus. Lip trembling, she forced herself to look away from her and to the photos on the walls. "I miss my sister." The words came out with a squeak from the emotions embedded with it. Even if it wasn't the reason why she was there currently, the statement still rang true. "I just want to see her again."

Mrs. Fondal's gaze softened and she reached to place her hand on Maya's shoulder. "I understand, and I don't blame you for this desire. I wish every single day that I could be reunited with my loved ones, and I promise that you will see your sister again. Right now, however, the world is too dangerous for you to leave just yet. When you turn eighteen, everything will be much better, and you will be able to live wherever you please, if that still be with your sister. Chance Refuge is here to keep you *safe*, that's all we want.

"I'll tell you what, I'll make sure to give Mr. Hue the job of watching after your sister so she remains safe as well. Then you two can reunite strong and healthy. Does that sound good to you?"

Maya nodded, though inside she was shouting. *No, I want you all to stay far away from her!* "I'm really sorry for bothering you. I know you must be busy."

Standing up, the woman brushed her off. "Oh, it's not a problem at all. I told you to come to me, and you have. Anyway, it is my time to leave, and I'm sure you want to have some dinner before it ends."

"That would be great, thank you."

She walked to the door and held it open for the school administrator, letting her pass first before going through it herself. Slowly closing it, she slid the paper clip between the door gap and hustled back next to the woman as they walked to dinner.

She silently cheered as the door didn't lock.

She went only with her socks. Her bed was still squeaky, as well as the door, but it was with ease that she managed to slip out of the bedroom.

It was near midnight, and every single one of the students were in a deep sleep. It wasn't the utter silence that notified her of this fact, but the screams that echoed in the darkness from kids all around experiencing the most horrid of nightmares.

She followed the light pouring through the window of the metal door at the end of the hall and kept her head down low. When she got there, her heart pounded in her chest as she slowly turned the door handle, hearing the click of it unlocking.

Gratefulness surged through her that the door happened to be silent as it swung open. Sliding through the gap, she slowly closed it behind her. Maya had only gotten a few steps before the sound of the lock shutting shot through the hall, and she grew pale as she realized she had been trapped outside of the corridors. But it was too late to turn back now.

With a slight jog, she ran down the hall, slowing at the turns. She'd peek around the corners to make sure there was no one else awake roaming the halls, then move onward. It was when she reached the nursing office that she saw the first sign of life. Slowing down, Maya pressed her back against the wall next to the glass, inching her way slowly closer to the window. The room's bright lights burned her retinas. The shadows of working nurses stretched onto the tiles. While tempted, she didn't dare reach her head around to see what they were working on so late.

There was the sound of the decompressor. Her breath caught and she rushed around the corner, crouching down just before the door swung open.

The footsteps were getting louder. She brought her knees closer to herself and didn't dare breathe as a nurse's silhouette made its appearance. It was the one who had wielded the bloody towelette, and was now holding her used scrubs. The nurse stopped just before her, and Maya held herself as still as possible.

"What did you say?" The woman sounded like she was on a call. A groan followed it. *"All right, all right. I'm coming."*

Maya melted in relief when the nurse's footsteps grew quieter as she headed the opposite direction. Standing back up, she walked softly, keeping to the sides. Faint yellow bulbs on the ceiling were the only sources of light as she got closer to the office door. Her hand gripped the cold metal handle, and she slowly pulled it towards her.

The paperclip had done its job, falling to the ground with a *clink* as it prevented the door from relocking. Maya slid in silently and didn't dare turn on the light, even though visibility was low.

Making her way around the desk, she bent over and gently pulled open the drawer. Disappointment hit her at the unimpressive objects that lay inside. There were more tablets, pencils and pens. No papers were to be found, so she went over to the shelves against the walls and flipped through the files there. Nothing piqued her interest. Not the shelves at the very top or those at the very bottom. She had all but given up when she noticed a clipboard at the back, with papers still attached to it. Pulling it out, she went to sit down on the hard floor as she caught the name at the very top, reading *Project Lucid*. And in the corner, a date: 07/11/2114. Last week.

A list of all the kids that inhabited the refuge, as well as names she did not recognize filled the pages. Each of them had the letter A, B, or C next to their name. Brian and Lilith both were A's, meaning the letter probably corresponded with their color bands. As for the rest, most were B's, but as she turned more and more, C became frequent. In italicized font beside the letter was written *"unsuccessful."* Student after student, the word was repeated, no matter the person's assigned letter.

She was almost to the very end of the packet when she stopped. Highlighted in the middle of the page was her name with the letter C, and beside that read the only *"successful"* in the entire list.

In the large jigsaw puzzle that encompassed her current life, two of the pieces clicked into place.

The project was about Lucids.

She was lucid. Maybe everyone else in Chance was one as well.

But the one difference between her and the rest of them was that she was no longer trapped inside her nightmares. She was omniscient as well, and maybe that was their goal. Maybe *that* was what they wanted! After all, it had only been when she shattered through her dreams when her life started going off the rails.

One thing was for certain—her two lives were no longer separate.

Whatever Project Lucid was, it involved Kalpana as well.

Placing everything back just as she left it, Maya looked over the room one last time. Despite the revelation, a peace of mind overtook her. She understood. Even if for just an instant, something in her life made sense.

The walk back to the corridor was eerie but quiet. Only the muted sound of her socks against the hard tiles was heard. The nurses had packed up and left the decompression room and Maya allowed herself to relax, which proved to be a mistake when she heard the steps of feet that were not her own. She ran to the next hall and crouched down, praying her presence would go unnoticed.

She hadn't known what to expect, but the red-headed bully was most definitely on the bottom of her list.

Holding a tablet in his hand, Brian snuck by her and walked down the hallway. With brimming curiosity, Maya followed until the boy eventually stopped by the door with the computer sign and message banning students from entering. In awe, she watched as he fiddled with his tablet, pressing a number of buttons before the red light of the lock turned green. Placing down his shoe to stop the door from shutting, he entered the dark computer lab.

She didn't seem to be the only one rebelling.

Chapter Twenty-Eight

"Humanity"

"Not this one, not this one, no..."

Step 3: learn what The Man of Light wants.

Maya made her way deep into the Whispering Woods, where visibility continued to lessen. It was nearly impossible to recognize anything in the darkness, but she searched for a familiar path anyway, hoping something would guide her to the tree the spirit had shown her. The being was her only lead in understanding what Hypnos had called the battle between Lucis and Tenebris. If a spirit directed her to a tree, she had to know why.

The fog hovering over the leaves covered the ground, so Maya had to use her foot to feel for the curved stick she had placed as a marker. When she would make contact with a fallen branch, she'd lower down the lantern she carried from the camp. She had melded it herself from one of the Passives in the dome while no one was there to see. Time and time again, the dim light revealed a false stick, but Maya kept looking with intense vigor and commitment. Maybe it didn't make sense, but she felt no doubt; she would find the tree.

A chill blew by her, causing goosebumps to travel across her limbs. She wrapped her arms around herself. It was too dark to see, but Maya thought she could make out shadows flying across her. One, she was convinced, brought about a surge of wind with its closeness, and she instantly brought up the lantern. Nothing.

Then she heard the whispers. Though, they were nothing like how one would imagine. It sounded inhumane, the soft sound reverberating deep inside her mind. At the very least, nothing that was spoken resembled English, but even so, Maya believed she understood, as if the language was humanity's native tongue. They grew louder, and the shadows' words became more clear. *"Undeserving. Lucis won't protect her. The Anima Genus is ours."* Maya tried her best to ignore it, but the voices continued to torment her. Her eyes scanned the ground for the stick as the air grew colder and the fog became thicker.

Out of nowhere, something jumped on her back and knocked her to the ground. Maya instantly knew it wasn't a nightdweller, since they didn't have physical bodies. Rolling around, she loosened its grip and hopped onto her feet to face it, but it pushed her down again, her back hitting against a stiff root. She felt around for anything to help defend herself as the creature pinned her with sharp claws. None of its features could be seen except for the shine of fangs dripping with slime that fell onto her shirt. Gagging, Maya's fingers finally got hold of a stick and she flung it around, thumping it against the side of the creature's skull. A terrifying howl came from the beast as she crawled away, her heart pounding against her ribcage. Her hands trembled as she held the stick in front of her. She could no longer see the creature, so she blindly swung it around. The voices continued to chant, *"You are ours. You are ours. You are ours."*

"No I'm not," Maya whispered. " I'm not!"

But they continued.

The voices grew closer, their shadows swarming around her. She stepped backwards and tripped on a root that jutted out, falling on her hands. Keeping her eyes forward, she scooted until her back hit a tree. Her breathing was labored as the air became as cold as ice. That was when another voice spoke in her mind. It was gentler than the shadows, but still held tremendous power as it said, *"Call upon Lucis."*

A few feet in front, the creature who attacked her began to reappear, growing until it was twice her size. Maya closed her eyes. The word came out with a shake: "Lucis!"

The chanting stopped. The wind slowed. When she opened her eyes, the monster of darkness was gone. And the fog thinned, allowing her to see her surroundings. With a breath of relief, Maya drooped her head before looking at the stick she held on to, which brought about a spurt of wonder when it happened to be the marker of the tree.

Maya got up and grabbed the lantern, lifting it up to the trees around her. Tenebris had bowed so quickly to the mention of the Light. And if those monsters were Tenebris, how powerful was Lucis? Out of fear more than anything, she thanked The Man of Light repeatedly, hoping the voice's claim, *"I'll be here to clean up your messes,"* didn't come with an expiration date.

Eventually the lantern revealed the familiar tree as she caught sight of the charred piece of mulch. Placing the curved branch on the ground, she brought the light closer. Maya skimmed her hands over the tree's trunk, not noting anything un-ordinary besides the discoloration. This, however, suddenly changed when the tip of her finger made contact with the black mark. In an instant, there was a flash of white. Time seemed to slow as a vibrant, unfamiliar scene formed before her.

Birds chirped above as humanity cultivated the ground below, the soil growing the most beautiful and delicious plants and foods. Colors not existing in the world today were painted on flowers of magnificent gardens. The people glowed with the light of Eternity. And they were happy, because they dwelt in the Light.

But Tenebris was envious of the blessings given to humans. Cursed to dwell in the shadows by Lucis, he vowed to maim the creator of all good in any way he could. Tenebris knew he stood no chance against the Light, so instead he attacked Light's children.

Humanity had never known evil and was oblivious to its strings that twisted and corrupted. All it took was a whisper. Then their purity was gone, darkness seeping into their hearts. Rebellion formed in the hearts of humans. The crops they used to cultivate died, and the animals that roamed the land grew wild. Light was no longer the only knowledge they harbored.

Because of their betrayal, Lucis was left heartbroken, knowing Light and Dark could not coexist in Eternity. The corruption must be eradicated. Banishing humanity from their home, Lucis created another realm bounded by the powerful grasp of time, where even mountains would weather down into nothing. As they slept in this realm, a human's mind would briefly travel home to regain strength, but hallucinations would hide it from their conception.

But humans were still His children, and Lucis loved them dearly. He knew the true enemy was Tenebris and longed to walk among His creation. So He would give bits of warmth in their world, sending rain, joy, hope. Messages from the space beyond time would be transmitted through dreams, and occasionally, Lucis would come into their world to comfort the hurting. Shadows only stretch so far before the light shoos it back, and with this Lucis made a promise: when darkness appears to have consumed everything, He will come back for His children.

A tear between worlds. A war of eternal proportions. The disappearance of a billion, and trials for the rest. Tenebris sowing. Sickness growing.

A choice.

Maya jerked away with a jolt, the vision vanishing in an instant. Her mind swam from the whiplash and she applied pressure to her forehead in hopes of it fading. Once her vision came back, she noticed a bright light. Her first thought was it being a spirit, but she soon realized it was something worse—fire.

Gasping, she found the lantern shattered beneath the tree. From the candle inside, the flames trailed up the tree. It grew into six lines, lapping over each other. As she stood farther from the fire, Maya clearly identified the pattern the flames were making. Or rather, the symbol.

The mark of Tenebris.

His sowing has already begun.

And I have absolutely no idea what that means.

THE PROPHECY BOOK STILL sat on the library table, and Maya rushed to it. She flipped it open before realizing she couldn't read it, so she grabbed a pamphlet stuck to the chalkboard that translated each symbol. Sticking the translator into the book, she shut it and began to make her way out of the library into a more secure place.

Her plan to sneak out proved futile when she saw Kai standing at the door-way, and Maya quickly hid the book behind her back. Of course, Kai noticed. A teasing glimmer arose inside his eyes as he said, "What you have there?"

Maya shrugged. "Have where?"

"Behind your back?"

"I don't have anything."

The boy raised his eyebrows and grinned. "Oh yeah? Then what's...this!" Instantly, he reached behind her, but Maya held her hand up high. Kai jumped to reach, but she stood on her toes, laughing at his poor attempts. *I love being tall.*

But to his credit, Kai did happen to have a brain inside his bony skull. With a smirk, he began to poke her sides, and Maya would flinch each time. "Stop!" she said through giggles as her arm unwillingly lowered to brace herself.

She cried in protest as the boy snatched it away, sticking out his tongue before studying the book. "Prophecies, huh? Didn't think you were the faith–type, Maya."

Smiling at the use of her real name, Maya crossed her arms. "What, I can't change my mind?"

"You *can*, but it seems unlikely, since people seeing past and future isn't 'logical.'" He then turned to where she had stuck the pamphlet inside, and started chuckling again.

Maya groaned. "What now?"

"Were you really gonna try to translate this all by yourself?"

Raising an eyebrow, she said, "You don't think I can?"

Kai grinned. "Oh believe me, I know you can. It just might take a few years to learn." Before she could object, he continued. "You can't just look at the letters for each symbol and put them together. The language of Kalpana was designed to be unreadable for anyone who didn't study it. Not only do you have to translate the symbols, but then you have to translate the languages that come from various parts of the world."

She sighed and sat on one of the comfy chairs, allowing her body to sink into it. "There goes that plan."

"Woah woah woah, don't be getting all mopey on me now, lioness. You happen to know an extremely handsome and capable guy who excels at Kalpanian reading."

"Extremely handsome? I don't think I've met this man."

"Haha, so funny." Kai sat down across from her and flipped open the prophecy book. "Now, what do you want to know?"

Maya bit her cheek, deciding to ask the question that would help answer the rest. "Why does Kalpana exist?"

"Well, I wasn't expecting that." Kai closed up the book. "I don't need this thing to tell you but...are you sure you want to know? Everything you thought you knew, it would change all of it. There's no going back."

It's too late for that. "Yes. I'm sure."

And so he told her a story similar to what she had seen, where human rebellion led to the splitting of worlds. The darkness that had corrupted Terra continued to spread in Kalpana in order to destroy Light's children once and for all.

"And The Man of Light? Who is He?"

Leaning back on his seat, Kai answered, "He's the reason we all exist. The creator of all things good in every dimension. The only reason we exist is because He allows us to, same for the reason why you are able to see both realms at once. This man is literally light, whether it be brightness from the stars, the sun, or the souls."

A tingling sensation ran up her arms, signaling her time was nearly up. But before she left, she had one more question to ask. "If The Man of Light does all of these good things and helps his 'children'...then why did He kill a billion innocent people?"

Kai's eyes widened and he shook his head. "You got it all wrong. The Man of Light didn't kill them, Maya. He *saved* them."

Then her body disappeared, leaving her with the boy's claim ringing in her ears.

Chapter Twenty-Nine

"Puzzles Have Solutions"

TODAY WAS THE 14TH Anniversary of The Harvest, and so classes were cancelled for the day—not that it disappointed Maya in the slightest. In fact, she felt reinvigorated with hope. No distractions. Today was the day she would find a way out of this place.

The maze appeared different. Looking at the numerous paths, she didn't feel the same sense of hopelessness that usually undermined her attempts and instead had her curiosity brimming. As she traced her fingers around the edge of the board, Maya came across the screws that had been used to attach the glass covering over. She had seen it many times, paying it no mind. But this time, she thought back to that first day she entered Kalpana, escaping from her dream. Sometimes, you need to think outside the box. Or better yet, get rid of the box entirely.

She felt the tip of the metal wand and eyeballed its size before placing it into the hole, finding it to fit perfectly.

"I think our friend has finally lost her marbles," Carlos said from behind her, Camila standing by his side.

Maya ignored his comment and handed him the other stick. "Go around the opposite side and stick this into the small hole."

The boy raised an eyebrow. "Why?"

A sigh came from the twin and she grabbed it, handing her brother her tablet and following Maya's instructions.

"Okay, when I hold up a fist, twist the stick forward." Carlos turned the tablet over for Camila to read it and she nodded. She waited for her to get in position, then held her hand up. "Now."

The two girls turned the metal rods forward, and the covering fell off, causing Carlos to jump back. They stepped back and watched the ball roll to the edge and into the small hole at the end of the maze. When it finally stopped, it flashed green, an automated voice saying, *"Maze solved. Congratulations."*

"Woah," Carlos said. "How did you know to do that?"

A number of other kids had gathered around, trying to decipher how someone could have solved the impossible maze.

"You cheated." Brian's accusation reached over the other awes as he stepped forward into view. "You broke the whole maze."

"I didn't *break* anything," she retorted. "I don't see any rules against what I just did, do you?"

His face grew as red as his hair. "If unscrewing the whole thing was known to be an option, we all would have solved it."

"If everyone knew how to solve the maze, it wouldn't be a maze at all."

He moved toward her, but Carlos stood in his way. "What's your problem, man? Jealous someone here's smarter than you?"

"Get out of my way before I make that gap in your teeth twice as large."

"That's enough."

Mrs. Fondal's voice cut through the bickering, bringing all the student's voices to a screeching halt. They cleared the way as the head administrator walked past Brian and gave him a disapproving glare. He hung his head down, and Maya straightened as she saw the woman focus on her, the heart in her chest pounding.

Mrs. Fondal glanced at the maze, then looked back at her. "Impressive."

That's all the woman said before walking back out, but Maya chased after her, calling, "wait!" Mrs. Fondal turned around, and she made a request.

The administrator sighed. "Maya, we've talked about this—"

"Please," she pleaded. "This will be the last time I ever think of it. But I *need* to do this."

After a brief moment of silence, the lady nodded. "After dinner, come see me."

WHEN LUNCHTIME CAME AROUND, Maya quickly got her food and went to the table, interrupting the twin's exchange. "If a person wanted to leave Chance, what would they have to do?"

Carlos stared at her and blinked. "Hello to you, too."

"Are you okay, Maya?" Camila asked her. *"Did Brian do something to you?"*

She took a bite of her pasta. "I can't really explain right now, but I'm not safe here. I have to go."

Maya had pondered the idea of whether or not to tell them about Chance being an experiment and what it had to do with their nightmares, but ultimately decided that, as of now, the facility didn't seem to have any intention to use the two of them in any way. In this case, ignorance did happen to be bliss.

Camila gave her a pitying look. *"I'm sure the workers won't allow–"*

"They will. So, what do I need to do to get out of here? Break a desk? Punch a kid? Something else to get myself expelled?"

"I think your purple band is for *coco loco*," Carlos said.

Holding onto her tablet, Camila said, *"If you're really that desperate, there is one way to leave without having to be kicked out."*

"Camila–" Carlos interrupted.

"What, haven't you told her? You were supposed to explain to her how Cataball worked."

"There was no need to mention that because it's *impossible*. No one has ever managed to get the Cataton."

"We're talking about the same girl who just managed to solve the 'impossible' maze."

"What are you two talking about?" Maya interjected. "What's the Cataton?"

With an exaggerated sigh, Carlos explained. "The Cataton is a little golden ball by each team's entrance. They say if you get the ball in the middle hole, you're granted a vacation outside of the refuge."

Maya felt hope swell in her chest. "That doesn't seem too hard."

The boy scoffed. "Yeah, you'd think so. That's until you take a step with the ball and it teleports somewhere else. No one can move with it, so there's no way to place it in the middle."

"But maybe you can find a way," Camila added on.

Teeth biting down on her meal, she savored the flavors in her mouth. Her life had been through so many obstacles recently, and this felt smaller than them all.

There was always a solution.

"After my tutoring session with Jeff, I'm going to need you guys to help me," she told the group. "We're gonna find out what Chance really wants from us."

As she walked to Jeffery's office, Maya tried to figure out how to bring up the topic to the elderly man. She would be telling him about Chance's ties to Kalpana. She had to, for he was the only one that would believe her. At least, that was what she hoped.

When she saw Jeff, she sat on her seat and asked quietly, "Hey, Hypnos. Are there any cameras in here? Any recording devices?"

"Why hello, little one. Not that I know of...but I can ask one of the admin—"

"No!" she shouted, and backtracked as she saw the tutor's shocked expression. "I mean, thank you, Jeff. But this cannot be brought up to anyone, especially the heads of Chance."

"I'm afraid I don't quite understand."

Maya leaned back in her seat, tearing her hands through her hair, which had remained untended to after waking. The man looked upon her in concern, and she blew out a deep breath. "Chance isn't what it seems."

With a chuckle, Jeff said, "I admit, it definitely is different, though different isn't always a bad thing."

"Well, in this case it is." Her paranoia was yelling at her to keep her realizations to herself, but she told him anyway, explaining her discovery of the experiment, and SCRO's participation in it. Then she went on to tell her theory of Chance's ties to Kalpana. When she was finished, Jeff had become pale, spinning in his desk chair.

"This is not good," he mumbled. "Not good at all."

"I... had to tell you," Maya admitted. "I couldn't handle keeping it to myself anymore, especially knowing it has something to do with Kalpana. Do you think someone in our camp might have something to do with it? If Chance knows about the realm, then someone must be omniscient, right?"

"That is true," Jeff said. "But I couldn't imagine it being anyone in Neshama. There are other pockets inside Kalpana, and based on the nightmares you have brought into light, it is more likely to be in one of the more dangerous regions. Personally, I am more terrified of the government's knowledge of Kalpana. War in Terra is one thing. War in Kalpana however..."

"Especially if the fighters are lucid," she finished quietly, reminded of the vision she had the night before, where dark and light fought in a battle for the human race, Tenebris consuming their minds with darkness and fear.

"That's their goal, you say. And if they succeeded with you, then they can do it again. Lucids fighting in Kalpana..." Resting his head on the top of his cane, Jeff repeated, "This is not good."

Wrapping her arms around herself, Maya said, "I promise I won't hurt any of you."

"I know you won't." Jeff sighed and rubbed his forehead. "But you need to be careful, little one. They must be monitoring you, and they may have ways to make you do their bidding. I don't want you to get hurt."

"They won't hurt me. They need me."

"There are more ways to torture a soul than physical harm to oneself."

Her mind instantly went to her sister. Those here have mentioned her more than once. Would they hurt her to get Maya to comply? Would they really swoop that low?

"You need to leave, too," she said to the old man, then groaned at herself. "I shouldn't have said anything. I've put you in danger too now. You have to quit before they find out!"

A sad laugh came from Jeff. "I'm not going anywhere. I have a contract to continue working for two more years, and even if that weren't the case, I would never leave you and the other children here to suffer through such a cruel experiment."

"But–"

"I will continue doing my job, but while searching for new information. In such a facility, there's bound to be more secrets."

With this, Maya teared up and she failed to meet his stare. "Don't get caught. *Please.*"

Jeff rubbed the top of her head. "The same for you, young lady. If anyone needs to escape from here, it's you, and I'll give it my all to find you a way."

"Thank you."

Chapter Thirty

"A Cross To Bear"

Next step: make an escape plan.

"Did you find it?" Maya called out to Carlos. The boy disappeared from her eyesight as he ran forward.

"Over here!" he said, and Maya and Camila followed him. Around the corner was the golden Cataton, which had teleported once again. On the map of the Cataball maze, she drew another X to mark the ball's pattern of movement.

They had broken off from the main group, who were practicing more Cataball tactics, and had been playing a game of cat and mouse with the Cataton for hours. So far, its movements appeared to be random, and only once did they get it near the middle, though not the middle hole. Frustration was beginning to pile up as no clear answer came into light.

"Maybe we should stop for now," Camila suggested. *"Review what we have. There could be something there we didn't notice before."*

"I'm down with that." Carlos picked up the ball and pressed the button, causing it to teleport back to its starting position.

Maya didn't feel like stopping, even being just as tired as they were, but she nodded in agreement anyway, tucking the map into her pocket.

Together, they headed to the cafeteria. Maya didn't get dinner and went straight to the table, studying the X's profusely, drawing lines to each sequential mark, just like connect-the-dots. A child's mindless scribbling could have held more predictability than the Cataton's random movements. Leaning her head against the table, she tiredly poked at the map and spun it around with her finger. Carlos and Camila walked over to the table with their trays and sat down silently. Camila handed Maya an apple, which she gratefully accepted.

"You've been stressing about that for hours. Maybe if you stopped for just a *few* seconds, you'd actually figure something out," Carlos said, and Maya rested her chin on her arm.

"It doesn't make any sense. There's no pattern of any kind. No formula. Nothing." Maya huffed and Camila put a hand on her back to offer her reassurance.

She sighed in defeat when suddenly the sheet was snatched from underneath her fingers. Carlos released a cry in protest while Maya flipped around, coming face to face with Brian.

"You really are crazy enough to try to figure this out," the boy mocked as he held the paper out in front of him. "You gonna cheat your way through this too?"

"Give it back, Brian," Maya said, and cringed internally at her pitiful pleading. But he wasn't listening, tracking the X's with his eyes with an ever-changing expression before finally settling on realization. Without permission, Brian sat down heavily at their table, flattening out the paper and grabbing ahold of their pencil. A feverish energy had taken over him, and suddenly he was tracing lines, mumbling numbers under his mouth.

"What the–" Carlos started, but Maya stopped the boy from interrupting him. Carlos leaned over to her and whispered, "You think he's possessed?"

Quietly, Maya responded, "I wouldn't be surprised. Something evil is clearly in him." *Maybe he's a Tenebris slave.*

Camila lifted her head over Brian's shoulder and her eyes widened. The three of them watched in silence as the boy drew numerous X's in a seemingly random pattern around the map, circling some and erasing others. Next to her, Carlos slowly bit into his own apple and chewed obnoxiously loud as they waited for Brian to finish... whatever he was attempting to do.

The twins had nearly finished their food when Brian placed down the pencil and stepped back with his hands on his head, a look of accomplishment on his face. Carlos quickly reached across the table and snatched the sheet, zeroing in on the X directly in the middle section.

"I did it," Brian said, almost to himself.

Maya swallowed. "You did it. How..."

It took a moment for the boy to snap out of his surprise, but with a shake of his head, he was instantly back to his old self and crossing his arms in a self-absorbed way. "It's the most basic method of random assignment for computers. Programming can't really be random, so you gotta fake it. I'm disappointed in them. Anyone with a simple understanding of electronic engineering could figure it out." He smirked as he turned his gaze towards Carlos, who was still studying the sheet in astonishment. "You're welcome for solving it for you. Still not gonna win."

Maya could only open her mouth before Brian turned on his heel and walked back to his table. A shrill bell rang, signaling the end of dinner. And as she stood up, an agent opened the cafeteria door.

"Ms. Shaffer," the man said. "It's time."

I'm really going to see Broth.

Her palms were clammy as she sat in the back of the truck, Mrs. Fondal by her side. Two agents were placed across from them, one she recognized as Mr. Hue, whom she now realized was probably in on the experiment the entire time. It was becoming overwhelming how many of the people around her weren't who they seemed to be.

And it was becoming increasingly difficult to hide her disdain for all such people.

The truck slowed down, the ride being so incredibly short that Maya wondered if they had left the facility at all. She almost started to regret asking the head administrator for this meeting, but she needed to see him. She needed to know if what she had done in Kalpana affected the man in Terra.

"We're here." The back doors swung open and the officers who wore blue uniforms gestured them forward. One offered her a hand as she hopped down, taking in the scenery around her. Everything was gray and metallic, with no sign of any natural light. Just like when she entered Chance, there was a heavy door with a chip scanner to open it. With his wrist, Mr. Hue unlocked the door, leading them inside.

"I have to warn you," he said deeper into the hall. "You picked a very bad time to visit the old crude. The head officer of this sector just told me that since two nights ago, he's been completely still. No eating, no sleeping, nothing. He just keeps whispering your name, over and over. I have no idea what happened. It's like he completely lost his mind."

Maya froze as chills ran down her back.

"—but don't worry. I'll be in there to make sure he doesn't do anything to hurt you."

Mrs. Fondal looked at her, not with worry, but pure curiosity. "Do you still want to go and see him?"

Shaking off the nausea Mr. Hue's statement had caused to arise, Maya held her chin up. "I just want to get this over with."

They passed by a number of prison doors she couldn't see through. Mr. Hue led them farther along before stopping by one, knocking on the door. "Mr. Deidre, you have a visitor." There was no response. Mr. Hue gave Fondal a glance before scanning his chip again, slowly creaking the door open.

Broth's position was uncanny to how he'd been in Kalpana: sitting on the floor, rocking back and forth. But instead of his wife's name emitting from his mouth, it was her own.

A single tear ran down the side of her face, not nearly worthy of everything she was feeling.

"Mr. Deidre~" Mr. Hue said in a sing-song voice. "Don't be rude, greet your kid." Not even a catch of his breath signaled he had registered their presence.

"I want to talk to him," Maya said. "Alone."

Mr. Hue shook his head. "Not a–"

Mrs. Fondal stopped his response with her hand. "Of course."

Running a hand through his hair, he said, "With Broth in this current state, I do not think that to be wise."

"Since when does your opinion dictate the outcome, Mr. Hue?"

That statement got the man's mouth to shut as he bent his head down in surrender. With a hand on Maya's shoulder, the woman said, "We'll give you some space." She squeezed gently and directed herself and the soldier out of the room, shutting the door behind them.

Her swallow turned thick as she watched the man from behind, still having yet to see his face. She took a shaky breath and walked around to sit in front of Broth, whose glassy eyes lacked any sense of consciousness. Drool dribbled out from the sides of his mouth. Snot ran from his nose. Sweat greased his clothes. And, very faintly, her name escaped his lips as he rocked.

"Mr. Broth?"

At her voice, his mumblings went silent and his rocking ceased. Her own hands trembled as awareness came back ever so slightly, though not quite enough for him to appear conscious.

"I really messed you up, didn't I?"

This time, there was no reaction as he stared mindlessly at the wall. Maya scooted to it, leaning her back against its cold surface.

"I know I should be feeling terrible for what I've done, putting you in this lifeless state. I *did* feel terrible for it—but, seeing you now? Like this? All I feel is *relief.* You can't hurt me anymore."

She let out a bitter laugh.

"But that's the sad part, isn't it? Because it isn't true. Even with your mind shattered beyond all repair, I'm still living the same nightmare. Still having my life controlled, trapped in another prison, unable to strive for anything of my own. I never escaped you."

The warmth of her tears burned with her anger.

"And Halo said I *love* you. How could I love you? I don't! I *don't.* You are a terrible, terrible person, and this is the least you deserve–" A hum then came from the man, a familiar tune that stole her voice, with the words ringing in her mind, *"nick nack, patty whack, give the dog a bone. This old man came rolling home."*

The humming grew louder with each second, and Maya covered her ears. But that didn't stop it. The words echoed inside her skull, repeating with every knock against bone. Her breathing grew shorter, every breath coming out as a gasp. One came out as a whisper. *"What have I done?"*

She kept her hands over her ears and closed her eyes, with the salty taste of tears hitting her tongue.

I'm a monster. I'm a monster. I–

Then, like a breeze, a sudden warmth came over her, bringing along a calm she shouldn't have been feeling. Slowly, her eyes opened, as well as her ears. That was when Maya saw the light. It should have only been seen in Kalpana, but here it was in Terra, just as clear. Floating in front of her, it rested on her chest and gentled her breathing, with that same voice speaking to her.

"Judgement will fall on this man. Forgive him, so it shall not fall on you also."

"How?" Maya pleaded. "You're Lucis, right? So you must know everything he has done to me. How can I forgive?" Not a moment later, she was reminded of all the times she had fallen short. She saw her lies, her manipulations, and the way she hurt others. She was part of the trials, just like everyone else still on Earth. Maybe Maya hadn't done the things Broth had, but she wasn't perfect either.

"Holding on to the hatred will only allow him to corrupt you as well."

With a deep breath, Maya felt the light that had landed on her chest give her strength. "You have hurt me and my sister, in more ways than one. You don't deserve any grace. But...I–" She struggled to release the words, but when they fell from her lips, her shoulders instantly felt lighter. "But I forgive you. Because I don't deserve grace either."

Then she turned away.

Chapter Thirty-One

"Sometimes, One Needs A Helping Hand"

Her stomach was queasy, and the nausea made her stay in bed long after the initial alarm rang, waiting as long as she could before eventually forcing herself to stand on shaky legs. Despite desiring to return to Kalpana, sleep continued to evade her, which only served to heighten her stress. But these worries continued to swarm her mind like a scourge of mosquitoes.

Tomorrow was the day she'd have to win the game.

Get the Cataton into the hole.

And, by the power of everything above, leave Chance Refuge forever.

Reaching underneath her pillow, she pulled out the sheet marking the Cataton's patterns and shoved it in her pocket. Everyone in her corridor, besides Lilith, were on team Phoenix, and the last thing she needed was for one of them to take it.

Brian made eye contact with her from his bed and smirked, causing her to get up completely and begin to get ready. He was the one Maya was truly scared about. He knew the pattern, and was bound to have already told his team. She only hoped her own team would manage to get the Cataton in the hole first. And if that were to happen, much more practice was needed.

Her mind didn't want to focus throughout her first or second class. In her third, they were given human fingernails to examine again by dipping them in some chemical solution she couldn't be bothered to remember the name of.

She picked an especially nasty one with the tongs, only to drop it when Brian came to sit next to her, bringing his personal bag of nails.

Maya sighed. "What are you doing here?"

"We're partners, Mayo. May I use your solution?" He didn't wait for an answer before pulling it to himself.

She huffed at the nickname and leaned on her arm, maneuvering the fingernails with the tongs. It was silent for a while and nearly looked like the boy was going to leave her alone, until he said, "For someone that's not supposed to know anything, you sure seem desperate to escape this place."

Maya's head shot up. Her blood ran cold.

"What do you know?" she asked him.

"I'm surprised. I thought you'd try to deny wanting to leave. But to answer your question, I know a lot more than you and whatever you think to understand."

"You don't even know what I know."

"True, but if you were as omnipotent as you believe you are, you'd know that trying to escape this place is hopeless. And if it isn't me that prevents you from doing so, then you can bet it will be Chance itself."

She pulled the solution back to her side and dipped her nail in. Theories swelled in her mind about the extent of Brian's knowledge, whether he was bluffing to intimidate her or actually knew about the experiment and Kalpana.

"Fine." She decided to play it safe. "You're right, I have no idea what's going on here, just that I don't trust it. So what's your problem with me? What have I done that so greatly offends you?"

With his own set of forceps, he scratched the metal lab table, creating an unbearable sound. "What makes you think I need a reason? Maybe I just like being rude."

"You know what? That does check out. So sorry I asked."

Brian suddenly stopped the squeaky noise. "Okay, fine. You want a real reason? Do you?"

With a roll of her eyes, Maya said, "Please, enlighten me."

His cheeks flushed in anger. "Your presence here has ruined my life. I'm the one that's been here since I was ten. I'm the one that has worked every day to be the one that breaks free into Kalpana. And then you, a girl that comes out from the middle of nowhere, is the success. You. A nobody. You're the reason I'll never leave."

He didn't speak to her during the rest of the class, getting up to sit next to Lilith. Maya's hands gripped the tongs to the point where her knuckles became white. He knew about Kalpana. He knew about the experiment. And, scariest of all, he knew she was omniscient.

There was heartbreak in his outburst to her, and a sense of empathy relaxed her. He wanted out just as much as her. As Maya's eyes darted to the other blue bands in the class, she wondered if that was what the color stood for. Maybe all of them in the room were aware of Chance's secret, and all have accepted their fate.

The science class left her rattled; both Carlos and Camila noticed it. But, to her gratitude, they chose to ignore it while remaining even more cheerful and hopeful than usual.

"We got the plan down to a point," Carlos told her. "We stick to it, and the other team won't be able to stop us."

Camila smiled widely. *"We've got this. You'll be free in no time."*

After all the courses, Maya met back with the twins in front of the pseudo-Cata-ball maze. Beside them was Hailey: Carlos's crush that had been practicing with them for the last few days. Like usual, Maya handed each of them sheets of their marks where they needed to stand.

"Everyone knows where they have to go?" Maya asked. They all nodded. She started to count down. "3...2...1. Go!"

Each of them ran into the maze, save for herself. She waited for a minute and then, picking up the Cataton, Maya called out, "Hailey, you in position?"

"Yup!" When Maya heard the answer, she took a step forward, the ball instantly disappearing from her hand. Distantly, Hailey's "Got it!" reached her ears.

"Carlos, ready?" Maya yelled.

"In position, sergeant!"

There was the popping sound of the ball teleporting once again, and Maya stood still, chewing on her cheek. A breath released from her lungs as Carlos said, "Got it!"

"Camila?"

After the popping sound, there was a longer stretch of silence, which caused Maya to sweat. She looked at the timer on her tablet. *Three minutes.*

"Got it," Camila's automated voice said, and Maya wiped her forehead.

"In position!""In position!"

"Got it!"

"Got it!"

"In position."

After many more rounds, the ball finally made it to the middle, where Maya had positioned herself. She picked it up and lined up with the hole. Behind her, the other three contributors stood watching. Taking a deep inhale, Maya let the ball loose, watching it as it rolled slowly across the section until eventually landing in the hole.

"We did it!" Hailey exclaimed with a cheer, hugging Carlos, who looked a shade redder than usual. Camila clapped and jumped, running over to Maya's side and embracing her. She offered her friend a smile before having it drop as she looked at how long it took. *Ten minutes.*

"We took too long," she said as she watched the rest celebrate. They calmed down and turned to her.

"It doesn't matter how long it takes, as long as we get it in the middle," Camila said.

Maya looked upon her in exasperation. "Of course it matters! The average round takes around seven minutes, right? That means the game could be over before we even manage to get the Cataton into the middle. If we even want a chance to succeed, we need to do this in under five minutes!"

"No need to get all *loco* on us," Carlos told her. "This is the first time we've run successfully over the whole thing. We just need some more practice."

But as they went through it round after round, it became clear that much more practice was needed. Whether it be a misstep, a roll off target, or an extended time, they never succeeded in getting a time faster than eight minutes.

In their current round, however, they were on track to beat their past high score. Maya had the Cataton in her hands and bent down, closing one eye to focus on the hole. She reached her arm back, ready to roll, when Carlos's, "You got this!" caused her to jump, the ball leaving her hands at a strange angle and missing the hole entirely.

The rest of the group stood around her in deafening silence. Maya's nails dug into her hands as she made them into fists. With a shout, she crumpled her map into a ball and threw it across the section.

"I'm sorry–" Carlos tried to say, but Maya pushed right past him, leaving them surely staring at her in shock and confusion.

SHE LAID DOWN WITH her back on the bed, watching the top of the bunk absent-mindedly. On her chest, she rested her hands, pulling at a piece of fabric she'd ripped from the top mattress. Her previous snapping at her friends left her in a state of guiltiness. They were just trying to help, Maya knew that. But it was just so difficult to stay calm when failing to win the game would cost her freedom.

The door squeaked open and she sat up. In walked Carlos, bringing a hand up to cover his yawn. Swinging her legs around the side of the bed, Maya faced him. "Carlos? What are you doing here?"

The boy crossed his arms. "Camila told me to come and make sure you were okay and not, I don't know, ripping the room to shreds?" He glanced at the piece of fabric in Maya's hand and she shoved it into her pocket.

"That's the extent of what I've done." The boy snorted. She offered what hope-fully looked like a smile before looking down at her hands. "I'm sorry for getting upset. None of you deserved that. I truly am grateful for the help, really."He sat down on the bed next to her, bouncing on the mattress. "We all know you are, and everyone's glad to. But it would be nice to know exactly why you want to leave so badly, you know. Gives us an actual reason to try so hard."

She turned away in shame. "I can't–"

"You can, you just don't want to." He stopped bouncing. "I'm going to be completely honest with you here, Maya. No one likes secrets, and it only gets worse the longer you hold it in. If you don't want to tell all of us, fine, but the one thing I hate more than math is liars."

"Keeping something a secret isn't lying."

"It might as well be."

He met her eyes with a hard stare, and Maya sighed, chewing on her cheek. "Okay, fine. I'll tell you, but you have to promise not to tell anyone yet, not even Camila."

Catching his attention, Maya started by explaining the realm of Kalpana, the realm that existed beyond dreams. At her explanation, the boy laughed, and she dug her fist into the mattress.

"I'm not lying!" she stressed. "If you don't believe me, then you are in for a rude awakening, because this safe haven you're living in right now? It's an experiment that's trying to make you, a Lucid, aware of that realm. Why do you think you and everyone else here have nightmares? It's to try to get you to break out of your dreams so you can be like me, aware of Kalpana."

"*Or* maybe we all have trauma from surviving the war?"

Maya sighed, his disbelief the exact reason why she kept it to herself. "I *need* to get out of here, Carlos. They've already started to put me through tests. I don't know what their plan for me is, but whatever it happens to be, I don't want any part of it. If I get the Cataton into the hole and am granted the vacation, I'll have a better chance at escaping."

After absorbing all the information, the boy pinched the bridge of his nose. "Okay, say I believe you and we're all part of this child project. Shouldn't we all be trying to escape? Aren't we all in danger?"

Maya shook her head. "Not you guys. Not yet. Everyone gets to leave when they're eighteen, right? So they only need kids, and as long as you aren't successful, you'll be let free then. It would be safer for you guys to wait and not have to worry about being hunted down."

Carlos started bouncing on the bed again, lost in thought. "Okay."

Maya tilted her head. "That's it? You believe me?"

"Well, I don't think any sane person would make up a story that crazy to get out of telling the truth. And while I might need a few years to process, I'll work as hard as I can to get you out of here and into the terrible outside world."

She reached over and hugged him with repeated thank yous. "Yeah, yeah." He pushed her off and Maya laughed. "See? Was it that hard to tell the truth?" She rolled her eyes, shoving him roughly.

There was an awkward silence as the joyfulness wore off and reality started to set in. Carlos stood up, appearing a bit dazed by all the information.

"Remember, you can't tell anyone," Maya told him, and he nodded.

"I get why you wanted to hide it now. You had a good reason, don't get me wrong, but I'm glad you told me. It's not fair to have to deal with something like that all by yourself. We got this tomorrow. And—uh, have fun tonight in Kapanah or whatever."

"Kalpana," she corrected, then she smiled, truthfully this time. "See you tomorrow, Carlos."

Chapter Thirty-Two

"Where Reflections Are Hidden"

No one likes secrets.

It only gets worse the longer you hold it in.

Carlos's words stayed circulating throughout her brain until the night. She tugged on her hair as she filled out a crossword puzzle inside her book. Anything she could do to distract herself, she did.

Even still, before it came time to go to sleep, Maya had made up her mind.

That night, she would reveal the truth to Kai.

Halo and Hypnos (and maybe Jane, if she put the pieces together) knew she was lucid, and it had gone fairly well. Plus, she trusted Kai just as much, so telling him her secret shouldn't have been a problem. But for some reason, the prospect of it scared her more than both of the previous reveals combined, and if he happened to turn against her because of her lucidness, it would hurt twice as much.

But that pain would only multiply the longer she held it in.

"Kai?" Maya called into the field. The boy was tending to a unicorn that was nuzzling its head against his chest. At the sound of her voice, he looked up, the unicorn adorably turning its head with him. Kai let the creature walk away as he headed towards her.

"Hey, Maya," the boy said, and the sound of her real name out of his mouth gave her a rush of adrenaline. Kai's eyes were darting around, as if to spot someone watching them in the distance.

She shook off her flusteredness. "Do you have time? I need to talk to you about something."

He bit his lip and rubbed the back of his neck. "I don't know if that would be a good idea..."

"Griffin's not here."

"What did you want to talk about?"

Maya chuckled at his sudden change of attitude and grabbed his hand. "Not here. Follow me." He did what she asked, and Maya made sure to keep on her nonchalant expression that threatened to fall. She could feel her pulse thumping in her neck. Her body felt cold and her legs were wobbly as they crossed the grass and went around the vines that covered the castle walls. They pushed through the purple-leaved bushes until they reached the crystals that, even in her current stress-filled state, didn't fail to take Maya's breath away.

The crystal forest seemed to Maya like a fitting place to have the conversation, not just because of its beauty. Some of the prisms had started to melt away, and the black shells had almost completely disappeared.

Beside her, Kai gripped onto the necklace around his neck again, worry in his features.

"Are you okay?" Maya asked him, and he shook it off.

"Of course. Lead the way, captain."

When they reached the formation they had thrown rocks at all those weeks ago, Maya sat down, Kai doing the same.

"So, any particular reason you've taken me here to talk?"

Fear finally caught up with her, and her hands trembled. She had imagined this conversation many times so she'd know her lines by heart, but as she sat there with Kai listening expectantly, her mind froze.

"Woah, are *you* okay?" It was the boy's time to ask as he grabbed her hand.

"What do you think of me?" The words escaped her mouth before she could stop them.

Kai bit his cheek and said, "What do you mean?"

She hugged her shoulders, an involuntary flinch wracking her body. This wasn't how the conversation was supposed to go. She was supposed to explain everything, her lucidness, her lies...but she was scared.

Before she possibly ruined their friendship, she *needed* to know.

"Do you like me?" she squeezed out.

The boy's face then went a shade paler than usual, and he pulled his knees against himself. "Why do you ask?"

"I think you know why."

At her response, Kai tucked his head between his legs, pulled at his hair and mumbled, *"Oh no."*

Maya's face burned with embarrassment and confusion. "Hey, it's okay if you don't like me. I mean, I thought you did, but–"

"That's the problem!" Kai exclaimed, stunning her silent. "I do like you!"

"Then why–"

"Because I *can't.*"

His eyes avoided her gaze as he reached around his neck to take off his necklace to hand it to her.

"I... don't understand."

Kai played with his hands as he said, "Look at the ground. What do you see?"

It took Maya a few seconds for her to process what he wanted from her before she turned her attention to the reflections, only to gasp at what she saw. A shimmer of a maroon shirt and black hair. *He's not supposed to have a reflection.*

"I see you," she said softly. "How-how can I–"

"Because I'm not like you, Maya."

His mind became distant, lost in the threads of the past. She put a hand on his shoulder to prompt a response, but he removed it gently.

"Seventeen years ago, my parents wanted a child, but it turned out my mother was infertile. They couldn't afford to adopt, so it left her desire festering in her mind. She had dreams of a little baby boy she'd love and feed and cherish.

"My dad was an Omni—though you already knew that. He liked to travel into her dreams and see the baby. After a while, I guess he started to see it as his own. Even so, he knew the kid wasn't real, so he decided to break one of the biggest rules in Kalpana: he melded a living being, not worrying about the consequences."

"You were the baby." The words were so gentle, she barely registered herself speaking them.

Kai then grabbed her shoulders. "You see now, Maya? You can't feel anything for me because I don't exist in the other world. I'm not real!" The boy's shoulders were slack as he hung his head, quiet sniffles coming from him. His hands covered his face in shame.

Hesitantly, Maya moved closer and took his hands, clearing them. She grabbed his cheeks. "Kai? Kai—look at me."

The boy's red eyes met hers and her heart broke for him, but she made sure he saw nothing but certainty in her face.

"A little while ago, someone kind—and handsome—once told me that reality only depends on how we define it." Kai sniffled again and she brushed away a fallen tear with her thumb. "My definition of real? It's what I can feel." She reached down to stroke the back of his hand. "What I can touch. What causes me to... see and experience things I've never imagined experiencing. And based on that description, you are the *realest* person I have ever met. Do you understand? You are real to *me*."

Maya let the boy dig his head into her chest while she held him tightly in her arms. "I should have told you earlier," he whispered. "I was just so scared it would ruin everything. I've never met someone like you, and I don't want to lose this."

"You won't. This changes nothing. So what if you're not from Terra? Trust me, this world is so much better. All you're missing are gray skies, dead plants, and pointless war."

He lifted himself up and wiped his eyes. A sad but truthful laugh escaped his lips. "You mean it?"

"Of course I do."

"No, I mean, you think I'm handsome?"

The question took her off guard and she snorted. "Of course. It would be a shame if your mom dreamed her baby up to look ugly, dream-boy."

He gasped and knocked her to the ground, falling forward with her and laughing all the while. Their laughter however cut off shortly after, and their faces were dangerously close as she said, "Was that too soon?"

His grin reached both sides of his face. "You can insult me all you want, lioness."

She grunted at the nickname and pushed him off before sitting up. In her hand, she still held Kai's necklace, which she handed back to him. He studied it and Maya said, "Was that necklace what hid your reflection last time?"

He smiled softly, a reminiscent look in his eyes. "Yeah. My dad gave it to me a while ago. It's from a journey with Talon where they found a tiny tear between the two realms. He was able to transmit a purely Terran necklace into Kalpana. When I put it on, I guess it tricks this realm into thinking I'm not from here, so it blocks my reflection. Never really thought about using it for that purpose until I met you, and, well…"

"You got scared. I understand."

More than you could ever know.

Maya allowed herself to rest her head on his shoulder and close her eyes, the rhythmic filling and emptying of Kai's lungs relaxing her. How could this boy think he's not real? Maya could feel his beating heart. His warm skin. To her, it didn't matter if he happened to be a robot or an imaginary friend. She would've spent every single moment by his side for as long as she could.

I'll tell him my secret later. But not yet.

Chapter Thirty-Three

"A Game Of Twists And Turns"

IF YESTERDAY CAUSED HER stress, it was nothing compared to how she felt the next day.

The Cataball game was today.

And it was practically impossible to focus on anything but it.

Providentially, all classes for those participating in the game were canceled, which allowed Maya to spend her time reviewing the map and talking over the plan with the group. Although each of them knew the plan down to a tee, there were countless ways it could fall apart. A missed timing. A Phoenix interception. A failed roll. The closer the game got, the more impossible their goal seemed to be.

But Maya *had* to succeed. Failure wasn't an option. Not that this eased her nerves in the slightest.

After lunchtime, an announcement came overhead, directing all the students to head down to the basement. Maya shared the elevator with the twins and Hailey, who all studied their designated spots.

"How are you feeling?" Camila asked Maya, and the latter tucked her map away while pulling on a tuft of hair.

"Nervous. It doesn't matter how I feel though, as long as the Cataton ends up in the hole."

"And we'll make sure it gets there." At the statement, Carlos's gaze met hers, conveying a sense of understanding. She was no longer alone in this.

The doors slid open, and instantly they were met with blaring music and flashing lights. While the beat shook the ground, it was barely audible over the voices of the kids, and Maya struggled to make out any of their faces in the scattered lighting. She pushed her way through the crowd that hovered right over the entrance of the elevator and went towards a section that was mostly empty. All the noises made her head pound with a ferocity that made her vision spin. Abruptly, the music stopped, the multicolored lights freezing in place.

"*Ladies and gentlemen.*" Mrs. Fondal's voice boomed overhead, and Maya could barely decipher the woman's silhouette as she began to speak. "*The day has finally arrived... Cataball day!*" The children broke out in wild cheers. Maya plugged her ears. Fondal waited a moment for the noise to settle down before starting back up again. "*Now, if I can have everyone who is not playing sit on the bleachers, and we can get started.*"

Much of the crowd dispersed to the sides after the last announcement, leaving only what looked to be no more than thirty kids remaining.

"*For those playing, may I please have team Phoenix stand on the left, and Alicorn on the right. There, you will be given your vests and life bands.*"

Maya stayed by the twins' sides as she walked up to the right table, where two workers were handing out purple buckle-up vests to each of the kids. After grabbing hers, she stepped back as Carlos fastened his own.

"Why do you think they make us play this game?" he whispered in her ear. Clicking the band onto his wrist, he continued. "And reward us with a trip outside when they're so hellbent on us staying here our whole childhood? Kind of a weird experiment, if you ask me."

Maya copied his action. "I don't know. But nothing they've done here follows my logic, so when it comes to opportunities, I've learned to accept them."

The conversation fell silent when Camila moved next to them, and based on her raised eyebrow, she most likely noticed their sudden cease in conversation. However, she didn't say anything, and when Hailey finally met up with them, they reviewed their plan one last time.

"If you don't get a response in twenty seconds," Maya told them, "send it anyway. If you run as fast as you can to your mark, it shouldn't take longer than that."

The three of them nodded, but Hailey raised her hand. "What if one of us gets out?"

As though it had been on cue, there was a buzzing noise. Peering through the maze's entrance, laser beams started to fire out of the walls. It was the one thing Maya couldn't account for.

She clicked the buckle on her vest and tightened it with a strap. "Don't get out."

"We each have three lives," Camila said. *"If we work fast, we won't go through all of them."*

"We got this." Carlos patted Maya's back, but the worry in his eyes revealed his true state of mind. Motivational speaking wasn't exactly the honest boy's strong suit, but Maya appreciated the effort.

"Teams, in your positions!" Mrs. Fondal announced. After the Phoenix kids diverted from the mass, the Alicorn team leader summoned their team to pile around the purple-rimmed entrance.

"You all know the plan?" the teen leader asked, and Maya nodded along with the crowd, despite not paying a single mind to whatever plan he had created. Her fellow teammates positioned themselves in an orderly fashion, the leader standing in the middle. A countdown sounded, and Maya tapped her fingers in anticipation.

"Three.

"Two.

"One.

"Let the game begin."

Those around her vanished into the maze instantly, but Maya kept her arm up, gesturing for her group to stay put.

"Everyone knows their first spot?" she asked and watched until each of them nodded. "Okay. Go!"

Her hair shifted as they rushed past her. Maya held the golden Cataton in her hands, it being heavier than the one she practiced with. Shifting it between her hands, she counted in her head twenty seconds, waiting for the first call from Hailey over the loud commotion.

"Here!" Her voice was barely audible. Without hesitation, Maya ran into the maze and felt the ball vanish from her hands.

The walls made it nearly impossible to see. Using neon lights that lined the crease on the ground was the only way she could direct herself. That, and the lasers that kept on shooting from the walls.

One of the beams of light shot right in front of her, bringing her to a halt. Her heart pounded in her chest as it narrowly missed her, its bright light blinding her momentarily. Distantly, she heard Carlos shouting his readiness.

Maya hustled faster down the path, taking a right at the fork. She flinched every time a laser shot near her. The dark atmosphere disoriented her so completely that she didn't even see a purple-vested boy sprinting forward before he rammed into her, knocking her body to the ground.

"What are you doing over here?" the masculine voice exclaimed, holding the purple Cataball under his arm. "Everyone's supposed to be–"

From behind her, a red vest snatched the ball from him, changing the color and running the opposite direction, met with a shout from the boy who groaned and turned to chase him.

Maya pulled herself up from the floor and headed to her spot. She heard another pop from the Cataton, relief filling her chest that the plan was still going smoothly.

Taking a left turn, a sharp pain from her shoulder suddenly erupted as a bright light filled her vision. Maya bent over in pain, mumbling a curse. On her wrist, she checked her lives; only two hearts glowed. She'd been shot by a laser. *And no one said getting hit would hurt.*

She bit her lip to distract from the pain and forced herself to keep moving. Surely it would almost be her turn. Her designated spot caught her sight, motivating the legs beneath her to increase speed. When she reached the mark, she stood still and yelled, "Ready!"

Just then, a heavy weight dug itself into her side, the floor once again meeting her face. Maya looked up, fuming as she saw who had done it.

"Hey, Mayo." Brian crossed his arms, sneering before attempting to move to her spot, where the Cataton was now situated. Flipping over, she grabbed onto his foot, causing the boy to tumble down, but then he kicked his leg and hit her in the nose. Cradling it with her hands, she let go, while Brian reached the Cataton quicker than she could get up.

The boy mocked her, holding his own nose and fake-sobbing. With a grunt, Maya ran full throttle towards him, watching his eyes go wide. She rammed herself into his chest and he took a back forward from the impact, the ball disappearing from his hands.

Maya let go of him. Licking her lips, she tasted the blood that dripped from her nostril. "Oh, I'm sorry," she told him. "Did you need that?"

Brian growled and Maya took a step back, but instead of attacking her, he suddenly smiled. Then he ran down the path. The direction *she* needed to go to reach the next marking.

She immediately ran after his silhouette, smearing the red liquid from her nose. Adrenaline fueled her while she chased Brian, ducking under the lasers that shot across. The boy turned back to stick his tongue at her, but the action was stopped when a beam of light shot through him and he quivered in pain, yelling obscenities as she passed him while waving goodbye.

When she reached the spot, her voice was breathless as she called out, "Ready!" Faster than the previous time, the ball appeared in front of her and she picked it up. From down the maze path, she could vaguely make out a black shadow she assumed to be Brian and held onto the Cataton until the last second when she took a step to avoid him, the ball disappearing once again.

However, even though Maya no longer had the ball, Brian didn't pass by her like the last time. Instead, he grabbed her arms roughly and held them behind her back.

"What are you doing?" she exclaimed, wiggling in his arms.

He leaned closer to her ear. "Making sure you don't win."

Pushing her forward, he trapped her in his grasp, walking straight into one of the lasers.

Maya yelled in pain and the boy holding her did the same as the laser hit them, but his grip still didn't lessen. When the beam went away, he smirked. "Only one heart left, Mayo."

Panic came over her as she saw the last flashing heart. She needed to leave.

As hard as she could, Maya jutted her elbow into his chest, causing Brian to gasp for air. With the action, his hold momentarily lightened and she ripped herself away. Her body shook from the pain, but she shook it off as she sprinted forward, aware of the boy on her heels. She was terrified. The emotion took over everything in her mind. Before, Maya had room for a misstep. No more. One more laser, and she was done.

One of the beams shot underneath her and she jumped, keeping her focus forward. Her hair bounced against her shoulders as she passed both red and purple-vested children. There were numerous different pops of the Cataton teleporting. Different voices echoing, "Got it!" until it was finally her turn. The rainbow-lit middle was in her sight. Her steps became larger. Her breaths became faster. The golden Cataton was already there.

She lunged forward, the carpet floor burning her knees. Her hands were nearly at the ball when she heard Carlos's voice yelling, *"Maya, no!"*

Her hands grasped it. Someone's boot was placed on the Cataton. Looking up, Maya made eye contact with Lilith, who stared at her with her ever stoic gaze. "Maya."

"Lilith?"

Suddenly, she was grabbed by the legs and pulled backwards. Maya recognized the duel friends from their laughs. Her nails dug into the carpet floor, but it didn't stop her. In front, she obscurely caught sight of Carlos pushing Lilith to the side and kicking the ball.

Everyone glued their eyes to the Cataton as it rolled into the middle hole ever so slowly, landing inside with a *clink*.

Then the lights turned on, and commotion from all of the kids sounded.

Maya shielded her eyes from the sudden illumination, waiting for her vision to adjust. In the middle section she recognized Camila and Hailey standing across the way. All the blue bands stood on her side, as well as Carlos, who ran over to help her stand up.

"Woah, are you okay?" he asked her. "Your nose is bleeding."

"Yeah." She rubbed it, looking at her hand that came back red. "You... did it."

Carlos looked down and Maya played with her vest's buckle.

"I'm so sorry," he said. "You were supposed to do it, not me. I just didn't want the other team to win, and I wasn't thinking—"

"May I have everyone's attention," Mrs. Fondal's voice interrupted his apology. *"By managing to get the Cataton in the middle hole, Team Alicorn has won the game!"*

Shouts of protests carried through the maze, and people started to pile into the middle section.

"And this was accomplished by none other than our very own Carlos! Give him a hand everyone. He has become the very first student to achieve such a feat, and therefore will be granted a vacation outside of Chance!"

Maya's chest sank before numbness took over as Carlos wrapped his arms tightly behind his own head. "I'll fix this," he told her. "They'll give it to you once they know it was your idea. They won't give it to me. They'll give it to you."

A hologram then emitted from the middle hole, revealing Mrs. Fondal's face. *"Carlos Aguirre, please step forward."*

The boy stayed put, and Maya nudged him forward. Giving her a determined look, he grabbed her hand and pulled her in front with her.

"Mrs. Fondal, this is a mistake," Carlos said. He pointed at Maya. "She's the one that came up with the plan. She told us where to stand and where to go. I wouldn't have even gotten a chance to get the Cataton in the hole if not for her. Maya deserves the vacation, not me!"

The administrator didn't seem fazed. *"And who was the one that rolled it into the hole?"*

"Kicked," Carlos corrected. "And me, but–"

"The rules specifically state that the one that manages to put the Cataton into the hole is the one granted, so it is you."

"Then I won't accept."

"It's not a choice."

The boy's mouth gaped and his eyes swarmed with retorts, but Maya placed a hand on his shoulder to stop him. He watched her with overwhelming amounts of sympathy, though Maya couldn't feel one ounce of it. She couldn't feel anything at all.

"Once again, congratulations to Team Alicorn. Ice cream will be served for the victors here in ten minutes."

The hologram cut off, leaving in its absence instantaneous chattering filled with confusion, frustration, and dissatisfaction.

Maya barely registered the group that had surrounded her, shaking her arms. Camila hugging her. Hailey reassuring her. And Carlos, begging for her forgiveness. Her mind was far away as she walked to the elevator, pressing the upwards button.

"I need a break" was all she managed to say before stepping inside the metal chamber, the last thing she heard was Carlos's voice, riddled with regret and guilt.

"What about the ice cream?"

Chapter Thirty-Four

"Misery Dwells In Us All"

Hope is like a breeze on a smoldering day.

When the wind first comes, the sun's rays no longer sting your skin. There's momentary relief as leaves, dust, and trees suddenly burst with life. Everything has movement. And with it, you forget the heat.

But then, when the breeze ceases, you are reminded of the sun's power. Everything is still. The rays burn again, this time feeling as though they hold more force. Your body becomes tired under the weight, and you wallow in the stillness of it all, longing for another breeze to pass by in order to ease the scorching heat.

Maya found herself in that moment after the breeze.

The substantial weight of her current situation seemed to grow with every passing second. Wallowing in her own hopelessness, she pulled out the crossword booklet and turned its pages. As she flipped to a puzzle her sister had once filled out, she traced the lines of Amarie's handwriting. Her vision became blurry and she put it down, closing her eyes.

I might never see her again.

The door swung open. Maya didn't bother to wipe away the tears as the group walked by. Lilith only spared her a glance before climbing up her bunk and she scoffed at the girl who had turned against her own team just to punish her. She'd thought Lilith was the better one of the bunch. Apparently, she had been wrong.

Snickering, the two boys went over to their beds, pulling out a set of cards.

Brian stood in front of her bed with his arms crossed. "I told you," he said. "There's no way to escape this place."

The words didn't hold the typical "I told you so" tone. The way Brian said it was layered with sadness, as if he hated it just as much as she did, despite being the one to prevent her plan from working. Maya looked away from the boy. Staring at the top bunk, she watched from her peripheral as Brian sauntered back to his cot.

When it became clear the group wasn't going to leave the room any time soon, she sighed and got up, going to the restroom to clean her face. Her reflection in the mirror wasn't a sight she was proud of. Maya hadn't looked completely put together in years—life on a farm had never required it—but at least there, the sun tinting her skin would give the impression that she was more than a corpse. Now, soaking in the bandages on her wrist, the blood stains on her shoulder, the redness of her eyes, and the hollowness of her cheeks, she appeared to be withering away as she stood. The longer she stayed at Chance, the more her soul sank into despair, and her body reflected it.

The least she could do was take a shower and wash her hair, rinsing off the stink of her failure. Her soaked hair reached her mid-back after she stepped out and combed it, trying to tame its curls. She splashed her face with water from the sink, and when she looked up, she almost looked normal.

Almost.

CARLOS WAS LEAVING THAT night. Maya listened with an absent expression as the boy informed their table. He looked worse for wear, and his glossy eyes made it obvious he had been crying too. Behind his chair, he had a packed bag of necessities, as well as a container of hand sanitizer.

"Everyone's sick out there." Carlos explained, resting his elbows on the table. Camila watched him with a near mournful expression, as if the boy had already caught an illness.

"I'm sure they won't place you anywhere where you're exposed to that," Maya said.

"They could, if..." He trailed off, but by the look they shared, Maya understood the meaning. *If it was a part of the experiment.*

"How long will you be gone?" Hailey asked; she had been sitting with them since the beginning of their Cataball mission.

The boy shrugged. "They haven't told me."

All of their appetites were lacking, if the full plates in front of each of them implied anything. Carlos had apologized repeatedly ever since she retreated out of her corridor, and only after her twentieth reminder that he had done no wrong did he finally simmer down. Maya did, however, recognize the fear that remained hidden inside his eyes for himself. A fright of being alone. A feeling that had familiarized itself within her. And, more than anything, it made her wonder just how terrible his experience was with the outside world.

None of them took so much as a bite before Mrs. Fondal made her entrance, interrupting their farewell dinner. Two soldiers stood behind her, holding weapons in their arms, and Maya felt Carlos tense next to her.

"Carlos," the woman said. "It's time."

"So much for preparation," the boy muttered, standing up and pushing in his seat. The three of them stood up with him to say their last goodbyes.

Camila wrapped her arms around Carlos, squeezing the boy so tight that Maya started to worry he wouldn't be able to breathe. She pulled away, giving her brother one last look and, lifting up her hands, Camila made a series of hand motions—sign language. She punched her brother lightly on the shoulder. Carlos smiled sadly in return, speaking in Spanish, and while Maya couldn't understand the exact words, she could feel the love emitting through them.

That's when Maya realized that the fear in the boy's eyes wasn't for himself. It was for the girl in front of him. The girl he would be leaving behind.

Carlos hugged Maya quickly, but not before he leaned toward her ear and whispered, "I don't care what you have to do, but don't let *anything* happen to my sister while I'm gone."

"I won't."

"You promise?"

She closed her eyes. "I promise."

Releasing her, Carlos walked up to Hailey and, without hesitation, pulled her close and kissed her on the lips. They stayed interlocked for a while, and when he pulled back, the girl's face had gone red. She wore a dopey grin and licked her lips.

The three of them followed Carlos as far as they could. Mrs. Fondal led him down the hall to the elevator, where she finally stopped them.

"We must take Carlos alone from here," she told them. "Enjoy the rest of your dinner."

They didn't head back immediately. Maya stood as the boy stepped into the machine, the soldiers piling in after him. The door slowly slid closed, and Maya kept eye contact with Carlos, who held a silent terror in his features, like a scream blocked by a soundproof wall, unheard by those that passed the padded room. Time only slowed momentarily, and he finally disappeared from her sight.

The remainder of dinner had an uncomfortable waft of silence over it. No one knew what to say; Carlos was always the talker of the group. It was five minutes until the end of the meal when Camila eventually broke. She sniffled and wiped her nose, but soon it turned into loud, uncontrollable sobs. Maya didn't hesitate to walk around the table and hold the girl in her arms. None of her attention went to the crowd that was watching them curiously.

"It's okay," she tried to soothe. "You'll see him again."

Camila's tablet blurted out, *"You of all people know that might not be the case."*

Maya sucked in a breath, meeting her gaze. "What do you mean?"

Taking out her tablet to read what was said, she responded. *"Carlos told me everything."*

Face going pale, Maya sucked on her cheeks. No words formulated in her mind.

"What did Carlos tell you?" Hailey interjected. "Why wouldn't that be the case?"

"It's nothing," Maya quickly answered before Camila could. "Carlos was... really worried about getting sick. He could easily catch something, but there really is no reason to be terrified of it. Chance will watch after him, and even if he does get some sort of illness, they have treatments for him. I've been out there, so I know how it can be, but I'm still here, so there's no need to worry."

Maya ignored the way Camila squinted her eyes at her, giving her attention to Hailey, who had accepted the story entirely. "I knew he was scared," she said, "but I didn't realize it was *that* bad. I should have said something to comfort him!"

"You did everything you should have done," the deaf girl told her. *"You saw how he kissed you, though I personally wish I could bleach my eyes."*

Hailey relaxed and rested her head on her hand, swooning. "He was a very good kisser."

Camila made a sound of disgust while Maya smiled softly, an image of Kai popping up in her brain, which she quickly shoved away.

The final bell of the day rang, marking the end of dinner. Their chairs scratched the tile floor. Hailey broke away from the table to head with some of her other friends, and Camila did a small wave, but before she could leave, Maya grabbed a hold of her arm.

"Tomorrow," Maya said. "We're talking about what exactly you know."

She scanned over the text on her tablet. *"Your lie made Carlos look weak,"* the girl told her. *"Now all Hailey's going to think of him is a wimpy little boy terrified of germs."*

"Would you rather me tell her the truth?" Maya retorted. "Look, I'm really sorry if I made him sound that way, but I'm trying to keep you, your brother, and Hailey safe. And if I have to spin a few stories and shatter a few egos to do so, then I will."

Camila turned away, using her finger to trace the appearing words. *"I know you are,"* she said. *"But you have no idea what life was like out there for us. Every day, we were on the brink of death. We needed food, but had to hide. We needed medicines, but there were none to be found. I was bleeding out of my ears. Everything was so quiet it hurt. Carlos would stand in front of me and yell at the top of his lungs for hours until I assumed his voice went raw.*

"He could have given up there, but he didn't. He snuck into shops for snacks, blankets, anything he could find. Sometimes he'd come back with cuts and bruises, but I didn't say anything. I couldn't say anything, and that was the hardest part. He would always give me his blanket and would shiver through the night, but I couldn't tell him I was fine. That I was warm.

"I could tell he was breaking, so I pretended to have fallen ill. It hurt to see him so scared, but I knew that was the only way he'd finally take us to the hospital."

Water welled up in her eyes. *"Don't pretend to know us, Maya."*

She pulled her arm out from her grip and walked off, leaving her alone.

Maya remained in the cafeteria as long as she could, sitting at one of the back tables while the room emptied out. The cafeteria workers cleaned in the back, not paying her any mind, which she was eternally grateful for. The lights soon went off, and a hand on her back caused her to jump.

"Time's up, kid," the cafeteria lady told her. "Head off to bed."

Quietly, she headed slowly to the bedroom corridors, scanning her chip on the blue door's handle to be let in. Lilith was by the door when she opened it, and Maya looked her up and down, an arm leaned against the door.

"Looking for something?" the girl asked.

"Just for a bit of loyalty, but it seems you don't have any." She pushed past her and jumped into her bed, pulling out the tablet.

"I have loyalties," Lilith said. "But not for you."

"Or your team, if today showed anything." She scrolled to a brain game. "It does make sense, though. You do follow Brian around like a puppy."

The bright flush on the girl's face told her that she had struck a nerve, but Maya couldn't bother herself to pay any mind. Lilith reached and grabbed the tablet from out of her hand.

"I don't know why you felt the need to stop me," Maya told her, "but I know why Brian did. And that's probably all that matters, for me and for you. So do whatever you want to me. Do whatever Brian tells you to do. We're all miserable here, and if you like sharing that misery, then you'll find that inflicted pain tends to ricochet right back at you."

Lilith flipped the tablet around and threw it at her. "You finally grew a backbone." She walked to the other side of the room to the ladder where Brian was lying down. "Be careful. A broken back kills."

Crawling into her bed, Lilith turned her back away from her, and Maya huffed. She turned on the tablet and turned down the brightness. Sliding her finger to get to the brain game, her attention was drawn to a message that suddenly appeared on her screen. Her curiosity was brimming as she pressed on the icon in the left corner and it expanded.

At the top of the message read, *To Maya Shaffer.*

She read on.

I discovered something terrible, little one. You were right, Chance is not safe, and you need to leave as soon as possible. Meet me in the library at camp tonight.

Henry L. Jeffery.

Chapter Thirty-Five

"What Exists Beyond The Veil"

Wind that entered from the cracked glass windows screamed her internal anxiety. The white cloth that covered the castle furniture waved like ghosts, kicking up the dust particles that rested on its fabric.

In her arms she held Revere, its heat warming her chest. Maya rubbed its belly, but the action didn't settle her nerves. Hypnos hadn't arrived yet, though he should have. After waiting for a while, she began walking around the camp, trying to find the old man, which led her to one of the empty rooms used for storage. He must have gone to bed around the same time she did, so at most they should've been a few minutes apart.

But it had been around an hour.

No trace of the man had been found.

And a sinking feeling in her chest kept on saying that something had gone terribly wrong.

"Maya?" Kai came walking in a little while after, looking around the room. "What are you doing here?"

He appeared better than the previous day. His shoulders were relaxed and a loose smile played on his lips as he came in. This expression, however, changed as he noticed the stress on her features. "What's wrong?"

Her heart warmed at his concern, which slightly surprised her. She had meant what she said to him the night before; it didn't matter that he wasn't Terran. But even so, it would've been foolish to pretend that everything would be the same—she wasn't sure how far his humanity went. If he could grow, if he could eat, or even die of natural causes. And yet, her chest still burned for the boy. A feeling so physically close to fear, and yet the complete opposite.

"Have you seen Hypnos?" Maya asked. "I really need to talk to him about something."

Kai shook his head. "It's been really quiet today."

A new thought came to her. "It must get lonely, being here while everyone's gone."

He ran a hand through his hair. "Sometimes it does, but it's been like this ever since I could remember. Guess I'm used to it."

Rubbing her arm, Maya said, "How do you do it? Accept being alone?"

The boy chuckled. "I don't *accept* being alone. The only way I make it through the day is knowing that I never am truly alone. And knowing that when you all sleep, I'll see you guys again."

Revere ran over to Kai and rubbed against his leg. "Do you sleep?" Maya couldn't help but ask.

Kai snorted. "Of course I—what, you think that just because I was born in a dream that I can't sleep?"

"How am I supposed to know? When we sleep, we enter this world, so do you momentarily enter the other world? Do you dream? While on that topic, do you eat? Is there even food here?"

He rubbed his temples. "Seriously. What is up with you and questions?"

She gently knocked him in the shoulder and bent down to pick up the hybrid. "Fine. Don't answer my questions. Just say that I'm Revere's favorite."

Tsking, Kai said, "No can do. I couldn't utter such a despicable lie."

"A lie? It's true! Isn't that right, Revee?" Her voice increased in pitch while she petted it, bringing it closer to herself. Noticing Kai watching her with a smile, she said, "What?"

The boy shook his head side to side, the grin staying plastered to his face. "You're crazy."

"Only around you."

Their gazes tied together, keeping them in a game of tug of war, where each of them were equally strong. Locked in his eyes, Maya almost forgot all her failures and miseries. She got lost in the boy's emotions that swirled like the clouds of Kalpana in his irises.

A chirp from Revere then snapped the knot, allowing her to look at the creature instead. The pleasantry of the moment wore off and Maya sobered, petting down the hybrid's ears. "I'm going to look outside and see if I can find Hypnos."

The boy stuttered. "Okay, yeah. I need to do some dweller-hunting anyway. If I see him anywhere, I'll tell you."

"Thanks, Kai."

Moving closer to her, he quickly bent over and pecked her on the cheek. "Anytime, Maya."

She brought her hand to the side of her face, feeling where the boy had kissed her and felt her face go hot. Before a word could escape, the boy had disappeared to tend to his duties.

"Hypnos!" Maya shouted. "Jeff! Are you there?" She had explored everything, from the crystal forest to the field and stream. No sign of the old man appeared, and every second of searching brought her closer and closer to panic.

The last place she dared to look was at the top of the hill that blocked the view of the valley. Not once since she first became aware of Kalpana had she made the climb. It was steep and tall and was riddled with orange rocks. Rainbow-colored birds laid claim to it, covering every boulder.

She reached up to one of the rocks, and a swarm of birds flew into the air, vanishing behind the clouds. Wiping a bead of sweat away, she pushed her way up. The top seemed to get farther away as she climbed, but eventually she reached over the last rock and ran to the top, only to be stopped in her tracks when she had done so.

Nothing could have prepared her for the sight that met her over the tip of the hill.

Fields occupied by unrecognizable creatures extended for miles on end, only for the view to be stopped by the pale purple clouds that swirled in the sky and reached to the ground, spreading like a wave and darkening into a deep bluish color with dark massive holes embedded inside, lights of distant civilizations twinkling like stars beyond. Lightning shot through the sky like a great storm, but never dared to aim its electricity at the ground. The birds that flew around seemed to be on fire, and some of the flying creatures were a little too big to be birds.

Maya could only watch in star-stricken awe at the beautiful horrificness of it all. A wonderful sight it was, but its massive size and unfamiliarity sent chills through the bottom of her spine. The unknown always appeared to call her. And yet, while she peered into the gaps in the clouds, she could find no ounce of herself desiring to leave the valley she had come to call home.

"Maya."

Her head snapped around to see the spirit that had spoken her name. It stood mere feet beside her, glowing with an intense brightness. She didn't dare take a step towards the being, in case it scared it off.

"Lucis?" she said softly. "Do you know where Hypnos is?"

To no surprise, the soul didn't directly answer. But then it glowed brighter and floated down the hill, Maya running after it.

With agility she didn't know she possessed, Maya slid down the rocks and pushed through the bushes, making sure to keep the spirit in her sight. It flew past the unicorns, causing them to lift up their heads in curiosity. She slid through the tall blades of grass. Her heart beat in her ears, but she did not slow down until the being eventually stopped in front of the Whispering Woods once again.

"In there?" she whispered. "Why would Hypnos be–" Her question was cut off when a glowing light suddenly emerged from her mouth, making her mute. She grabbed at her mouth while staring wide-eyed at the spirit in front of her. It moved in front of her face. After taking a deep breath, the glow disappeared and her voice returned.

She tugged on her hair. "No questions. Got it."

Letting the soul lead the way, she dodged the trees as she ran. Maya instantly knew where they were heading, the path being the same one the spirit had taken her last time. Her brain tried to come up with theories to understand its goal, but no thoughts came to mind.

The spirit suddenly stopped, somehow pulling her around one of the dark trees. The glow was around her mouth again, and she glared at the being, not appreciating the way she was being controlled. Its light dimmed. From the corner of her eye, she noticed another glow from behind the tree and she peeked around its bark, the sight baffling her.

Omitting from the Tenerbris symbol on the tree she visited last time was a swirling brightness that grew inside. Within the span of a blink, the light flattened out into the shape of a door. And from the other side, she heard the sound of screaming.

Her fingers started to tingle, and she cursed internally when she noticed them fading away. She tried to get a better view to see what exactly lay on the other side. Her entire arm had disappeared at that point and the spirit floated up to her, whispering, *"Resist it, Maya."*

How? I'm not controlling this!

The one thing she managed to see before vanishing completely was the foot of a stranger, and then she was transported back to the world she hated dearly.

Chapter Thirty-Six

"Grief"

Hypnos was still her main focus as classes continued in their normal fashion—the word "normal" to be used lightly. She was in her second course of the day and she had sat herself next to Camila; Mrs. Fondal thought it would do the girl good to have more classes with a friend after the "recent loss" of her brother. And it was the specific word choice that set Maya on edge.

She tried her best to convince Camila, as well as herself, that there was no possible way they would keep Carlos away forever. After all, he was one of their test subjects, and it would be a waste of resources if they separated him from the rest. But even so, her mind couldn't help filling with "what ifs."

Maya had come to the conclusion that Carlos really had told his sister everything. She clearly knew about the experiment, and to explain that, he needed to tell her about Kalpana. All things considered, Camila held up quite well, at least in front of her.

Staring absently at the paper lying on the desk, she doodled little suns in the free spaces, tuning out the rest of the world. Time seemed to slow the more she desired it to be lunch so she could find Jeff. Her leg shook restlessly in impatience.

It was about halfway through class when the beep of the intercom snapped her out of her distracted state. There was the sound of crackling. Then, Mrs. Fondal's voice rang loud and clear.

"Children of Chance." The woman's tone held a sense of artificial solemness. *"I have grave news."* Everyone, including herself, placed down their pens. *"Unfortunately, as of this morning, our beloved tutor Mr. Jeffery has passed away."*

All of the students collectively gasped as Maya's vision went dizzy. The words echoed in her ears, over and over, as if said in a never-ending echo chamber.

"He suffered a massive heart attack," Mrs. Fondal continued, but Maya had already tuned her out, standing up abruptly. Camila grabbed her arm as though to hold her back. The action didn't stop her. With a turn, she darted out of the classroom.

Maya's breathing became more labored as she ran down the bare halls and the plain tiles. The journey was a blur. Her hands pressed against the walls in a blind panic. She darted towards the direction past the nurses' office and computer lab until she finally reached the door of Jeff's office, which had been left open.

Peering over the desk, she half-expected the balding man to be situated on the other side in his spinning chair. She stood on the dark red rug and wrapped her arms around herself. The top of his desk was covered with loose papers. The shelves remained unorganized. Nothing appeared odd, except for the absence of warmth the office had previously possessed.

She shook her head to jumble the thoughts in her mind, preventing the words from latching on to each other and spelling out her worst fears.

Maya made her way around the other side of the wooden desk, each step feeling like she was intruding in someone's personal life. The loose pages lying around were shifted by Maya's hand as she read what was written on it. Something seemed off about the papers, but she couldn't put her finger on what it was until she finally realized what they were: test scores.

She knew for a fact that Jeff wouldn't be examining such scores.

From behind her came the sound of a door creaking open and she flipped around, coming face to face with Mrs. Fondal. All she saw was red.

"What did you do to him?" Maya accused, her voice reaching a low pitch.

The head administrator showed no reaction as she stepped closer. "Maya, I understand how much Mr. Jeffery meant to you–"

"What did you *do* to him?" she said again.

The woman took another step toward her. "You're clearly not in the right state of mind–"

"Stay away from me!"

"–I just want what's best for you. All of us do. If you need to take a few days off of classes to recover–"

"Where are you holding him? Is he with Broth? What did he discover that has you so scared?"

Another step. "Take a deep breath–"

She grabbed Jeff's metal name stand and held it out in front of her. "I told you to stay away from me!"

The woman sighed as though she was a young toddler throwing a temper tantrum—a notion that made her blood sizzle, which transformed into an entire boil when Mrs. Fondal gestured one of the nurses by her side to Maya's direction.

A large syringe was uncapped by the nurse who ran toward her, needle pointed straight in her direction. Maya didn't think as she swung the metal stand, it making a loud crunching sound when making contact with the woman's head. She fell to the ground with a *thump*. Blood pouring from the nurse's head. Staining the cloth of her scrubs.

The stand dropped from Maya's hand. Her eyes wouldn't turn away from the graphic sight. She didn't flinch as the other nurse jabbed the syringe into her arm. She didn't blink as Mrs. Fondal ran out, shouting for a doctor. She didn't panic as the world around her started to go dark and drowsiness started to take over.

She only stared at the mess she had created.

And felt nothing at all.

HER ARMS WERE TIED. Her legs too. The bed she lay on wasn't particularly comfortable and couldn't even be adjusted to a better position. Her hands were cold. Something wet stuck to the tips of her fingers, warm like blood, but as she forced her neck around to see, there was nothing there.

The broken face of the nurse stayed at the forefront of her brain. The twisted nose. The soulless eyes. The blood that dripped halfway down her face from the deep gash on her cheek.

They had placed her in an empty room, with nothing but a metal door to stimulate her. The walls were a light gray. The ceiling was made up of white tiles. It was cold. She was cold.

The door opened, and Maya lifted her head. By the door stood Camila, studying her with a sympathetic expression as she closed the door behind her. When the girl saw that Maya's limbs were tied, she ran to her side and released her bondages.

Maya offered her gratitude, rubbing her sore shoulder from where the syringe had injected her.

"They told me I could come in," Camila explained. *"That you wouldn't hurt me."*

Guilt took her words captive, and tears swarmed her eyes. "They told you what happened?" The girl nodded. Maya looked away. "The nurse, is she..."

"She's alive," Camila said, and Maya let out a cry of relief, burying her head into her hands.

"They're treating her now. She's going to need a few stitches, but they have faith she'll be fine. It was an accident. You were scared. No one blames you."

Reaching around the bed, her friend pulled her into an embrace, holding her there, allowing the tears and snot to stain her uniform. *"You're okay. You're okay."* Camila's tablet relayed, and Maya was finally able to relax herself, if just slightly.

Eventually, the girl backed away, but then she pulled out a paper and started writing. Maya's curiosity stirred as she scooted around the bed to sit up next to her. After writing, Camila held it up, allowing her to read.

Do you really think Chance is responsible for Mr. Jeff's death?

Maya flinched at the reminder. "Well–" she started, but Camila quickly stopped her with a finger put to her mouth and wrote something else.

Write it down. They can see what is said and what I say.

With a nod, Maya took the paper and pen, wrote her piece, and held it up. *Jeff was gonna tell me something he learned, and the next day this happens. That can't be a coincidence.*

Do you think he's still alive?

Maya's vision blurred again. *I don't know.*

Camila grabbed the pen with an expression of fear and determination. Her writing was dark and shaky, but the words were clear. *Then we need to leave.*

Maya's turn with the pen. *How? We lost the game.*

Then we'll have to create our own way out.

She looked into the girl's eyes, who held her own tears, and then understood the weight leaving held for her. Chance was her everything. It was easy to leave when there was nothing to stay for, but this was Camila's safe place. Leaving meant she may never feel that sense of safety again. But when the safe place becomes compromised, the only hope is to try to find another one.

Maya's hand produced rushed handwriting. *I'll try to come up with a plan.*

We need to bring Hailey, Camila wrote down.

Only her. The more we bring, the lower our chances of escaping.

The girl's shoulders slumped forward. *I don't want to leave anyone behind.*

"I know." Maya said it out loud, rubbing the side of her arm. "But we have to."

With that, Camila stood up, crumpling the paper in her hands. *"Whatever they gave you put you out for a while. I think you missed dinner. I probably have to get back to my room, but... don't blame yourself. Okay? Before The Harvest took her, my grandma always said that grief's an emotion humans weren't ever supposed to experience. Life is already hard enough without hating yourself for things you can't control."*

"Thank you for being here," Maya said. "It's nice to have a friend in this world."

She smiled at her softly. *"I should be thanking you. You being here has saved me."*

Chapter Thirty-Seven

"The Ties That Strangle"

No one in Kalpana knew of Hypnos's death. That was the thing about the realm that didn't quite cure the loneliness: the people that inhabited Kalpana—aside from Kai—had other lives completely separate from this one. You never knew how their day was in Terra. What they did. Where they went. Who they were friends with. If they were injured. If they were grieving. If the reason they hadn't appeared that night was because they no longer had a conscience to transport.

Maya made her way back to the castle. Neither Jane nor Griffin had made their appearance yet, as far as she could tell. Kai was nowhere in sight either, though he was most likely wandering around the fields and petting a unicorn or lassoing a wanderer between the trees. But Halo was there, and she was just the person she needed to talk to.

The woman was walking around the dome, checking the bands of those who were standing in the glowing circles. She noticed Maya come in and beckoned her over with a wave.

"Hello, Amie. Lovely to see you." Clicking a button on one of the headbands, she turned her full attention towards her. "You're early."

Maya tucked a curl behind her ear. "When we first met and you found out I was lucid, you told me that I could come to you if I ever needed to talk."

She stood up straighter. "I do recall saying something like that, yes."

Maya swallowed and put a hand behind her neck, the words sticking to her tongue. Halo gave her an empathetic smile and placed her hand on her back. "Here, let's talk outside."

They sat on a black metal bench situated in the garden, blue and red flowers covering the ground beneath them. Maya's feet dragged over the petals and she picked one of the red ones with her shoes.

"Amie?" Halo prompted, and Maya sighed.

"I think... I'm in trouble. And I don't know what else to do."

Taking her hand, Halo looked at her intensely. "What makes you think you're in trouble?"

She stared at the clouds above, stars woven into their cotton and birds flying underneath. "It's in Terra. I was put into this refuge—at least, I *thought* it was a refuge, but it's not. It's part of something bigger. Something related to Kalpana. I don't know how, but I think they're the reason I'm omniscient and probably are planning to use me for some grand plan, and after seeing what they did to—" She hesitated. "—my friend when he found out a secret, I don't want any part of it."

Halo sat with a hand on her chin, a leg crossed over, and her brows ruffled. "And I'm assuming they won't let you leave?"

"I tried," Maya admitted. "There was this game that supposedly lets the winner go, but I failed. There's no other way."

"There is always another way." Halo reached out and gripped her hands. "Rarely are you going to be given an easy way out. You must find your own way, and only then will you be able to accomplish what you desire. I thought you of all people would understand that."

"I *do*. But I'm still trying to think of a plan that guarantees a safe way out *with* my friends that doesn't require us to be on the run our whole lives *or* be homeless *or* get killed on our way out. I just... can't find one."

Releasing her hands, Halo leaned back. "Can I tell you what I think, Amie? I don't think you're hesitant because you are still thinking. I think you're hesitant because you are afraid of the lack of control you have over the outcome. There will always be risks. There will always be unknowns. No one can know everything. All you can do in those times of uncertainty is take a leap of faith and make adjustments when it is necessary. Use what is around you; your surroundings always hold the answers to adaptability."

Use what is around you.

But what in Chance could help her in her journey to escape from said place?

Maya couldn't think of a way to respond, but moments later proved she didn't need to, a disturbance bringing both of their attentions to the front gate. Kai was calling out for help, a figure tied around his back loosely. His knees buckled from the weight.

Both of them running forward, they unloaded the limp person from his back and laid him gently on the ground. From inside the castle ran out Jane, Griffin, and Talon, all of whom gathered around the stranger who was placed onto the grass.

Stranger, at least for them.

However, Maya's soul was shocked in recognition. The straight dark hair. The warm-colored skin. The mole above his left brow. There was not a moment of a doubt that the boy that lay in front of them was Carlos, making an appearance in the last place she would have expected to see him.

Griffin grilled Kai with questions, and the latter put his hands up. "Look, I don't know, okay? He was walking around aimlessly, so I thought he was a wanderer, but then he said something to me before passing out. He's an Omni!"

Kneeling by her friend's side, Maya shook her head. It was impossible for the boy to be omniscient. Everyone in the experiment was lucid. The only way Kai's claim could be true was if Carlos escaped through his dream like her, but internal turmoil and desperate circumstances had motivated her, and the boy was alternatively on vacation.

Unless it wasn't vacation, and Carlos is in more danger than he ever had been before.

"Could he have possibly been sleep-talking?" Talon inquired; Kai shot the idea down immediately.

"I know what I—"

He stopped. The brown eyes of the boy beneath them snapped open, instantly grabbing Maya's arm and digging his nails into her skin.

"Help," he struggled out. Locking gazes with her, his breath hitched before continuing. "Third floor. Please, help me. It hurts, Maya, it hurts—*Maya*—"

His awareness slipped away. Grip releasing, his arm fell to his side in dead weight, a soft up and down movement of his chest being the only proof of life. And Maya—Maya couldn't breathe. Couldn't speak. Couldn't think of anything but the boy who lay before her, and the pain lacing his words.

"Maya?" Jane whispered, half to herself, as if testing the sound of the name on her lips.

Kai scooted next to her, placing her hand in his.

"What is your connection to this boy?" Griffin demanded. "You two are working together, aren't you? What have you—"

"Griffin, quiet!" The shout from the tall black man echoed throughout the hills. The outspoken man immediately dipped his chin, the accusations being stolen from his throat. Talon sighed deeply before muttering, "Bring him inside."

Carlos was placed on a large king's bed in one of the back rooms, the red velvet curtains that hung above tied to the corner poles. Jane adjusted his head to situate it comfortably on the pillow, but then she jumped back, eyes shot wide.

"What is it?" Maya asked, and the girl ran her trembling fingers through her blond hair.

"The boy. He's dreaming."

Halo was the first one to confirm Jane's claim. She reached for Carlos's temples, frustration evident as she pulled back. "She's right."

"That's... not possible," Kai muttered under his breath as he remained by her side. "We all saw he was aware, right?"

They all did, which made the situation all the more terrifying. Whatever Chance was doing to him, it worked; Carlos had broken free of his dreams, if only momentarily. And since he proved it was possible, there was no doubt in Maya's mind that they would push the boy even harder.

They had their next potential success.

The conversation continued around her, but all Maya focused on was forcing herself to wake up. It wasn't as simple as pulling the strings of a consciousness, but she channeled the feeling she had encountered that night with the nightdwellers. It was *her* mind. *Her* reality. All sense of control belonged to *herself*.

Her limbs started to tingle in numbness, and Griffin was the first one to notice. He pointed a finger at her. "Tomorrow. When you get back. You're going to tell us *exactly* how this kid relates to you."

The opportunity to respond never came.

Chapter Thirty-Eight

"BITTER TRUTH"

I DON'T THINK YOUR brother ever left.

It was a sentence she knew would bring hurt, but the foresight didn't stop the soul-crushing pain that encompassed her as she watched her friend trace the words on the note, tears slowly gathering in her eyes. There was no surprise in her expression, however, which made Maya wonder if Camila had the curse of foresight as well.

She wrote down what Carlos had said in Kalpana—at least, the mention of the third floor. It was the place where she assumed the refuge was holding him. Even while avoiding mentioning the pain the boy had expressed, she still noticed the resolution of his sister. If there hadn't been motivation to leave, there certainly was now.

And Maya was going to take Halo's advice. A similar sentiment her sister had left her with the day she ran away: she would create her own way out.

The cafeteria was unusually empty. Most of the kids had eaten their food relatively quickly, not staying too long after. The only subjects that remained were herself and Camila, as well as Hailey's table. The latter engaged in conversing with her other friend group, but chairs soon squeaked as even they decided to leave. With a wave goodbye to the crowd of five, Hailey moved over to their table and sat beside them.

Maya had explained the situation to the girl early that morning in the simplest way she could put it. To say she accepted it with difficulty would be an enormous understatement. Even with her claiming the support of Camila, Hailey was still resistant to the idea that Chance had any sort of hidden agenda, an ideology that was only dispelled with the mention of Carlos being in danger.

"Do we have a plan?" Hailey asked as she studied Camila, probably for any sign of a breakdown because of the situation.

Maya played with the sharp knife in her hand. "I'm working on it." She squeezed the handle, and mentally prepared for what she was about to do next. With a grunt, she brought it down, slicing her arm and letting out a shout of pain.

The girls at the table shot up with shouts of their own. Hailey gagged with her hands on her head. "Oh my gosh, Maya!" Camila wasted no time running out to get a nurse, and it was only a matter of seconds before one came running in after her.

Maya clutched her arm to her chest, bright red blood covering her hand and leaking to the floor. The nurse swung a medical kit onto the metal table before putting on a pair of blue gloves. An assortment of bandages, gauzes, and other ointments filled the bag and she pulled out a wipe, dabbing the wound gently.

"How did this happen, Maya?" the nurse questioned her, and she shrugged.

"My hand must have slipped."

With a shake of her head, the nurse threw the dirty wipe in a plastic bag and grabbed another one. "Well, you're lucky. An inch to the left and you would have severed an artery. It isn't as easy to stop the bleeding then. You'll need a lot more of this." She pulled out a red bottle, shaking it up. "Hold out your arm for me." Flipping over her forearm, the nurse pulled it towards herself and coated a white solution onto the laceration, which caused it to burn with a fierceness. Wincing, Maya blew out a breath as she waited for the pain to subside. When it finally did, the solution had become pasty and clear, the bleeding stopping entirely.

"There, as good as new." Stepping back, the nurse removed her gloves. "About time we have those knives taken out of the hands of kids."

Maya muttered a thank you. As the nurse began packing up, she held out a hand to stop her. "Ma'am, do you think I could keep the spray? Just in case it opens up again."

With an eyebrow raised, the woman said, "It shouldn't."

She looked down at her arm. "Maybe not, but I'd just feel a lot safer. If that's at all possible."

The nurse sighed, but placed the bottle in her hand. "Just make sure you give it back."

"I will."

I won't.

After packing up and walking out of the cafeteria, the two other girls at the table turned to face her.

"What was that about?" Hailey exclaimed. Camila appeared just as exasperated.

"Like I said, I'm working on it." Placing the bottle next to herself, Maya leaned up to Hailey's ear and whispered, "What's the loudest place accessible here? Is there a washing room? An air conditioning vent?"

"There's a back room with a large fan that's practically deafening," she answered. "But no one's supposed to be in there, and I don't know why you would–"

Maya cut her off. "Tomorrow morning, meet me there. Five o-clock."

"Maya–"

She wasn't listening. With the same note she had written on previously, Maya passed on the message for Camila to meet at the same spot. The girl's confusion was palpable. However, she still nodded with little hesitation.

They left shortly after and parted ways, but before Maya could make it down the hall, Hailey's voice stopped her.

"I'm not leaving."

Maya turned around. Stared her down. "You've just learned what Chance is, what they've done, and you want to *stay?*"

"It's not like I *want* to stay, but... I have friends here, Maya. What kinda person would I be if I left them with the knowledge that they're guinea pigs? I wouldn't be able to live with myself. And anyways, you need someone on the inside you can trust if you want a chance of taking this experiment down."

"'Taking it down?'"

"I mean, yeah. You wouldn't just leave everyone here to fend for themselves, would ya?"

Maya gazed away in shame. She didn't know Hailey for very long, or very well. When the girl had first mentioned her choice to stay, her first thought was it being an act of cowardice, as it had been for her. But no—Hailey's decision to stay was braver than anything she'd ever done herself. Because it wasn't out of self-preservation, but out of selflessness. Hailey had more love for others than Maya could ever imagine having, and it left her wondering when she had grown so cold. Where that innocence of her childhood had gone.

"I don't know if that's possible."

"You've asked me to believe in interdimensional travel and government experimentation. All I'm asking is for you to believe in yourself. So promise me. Promise me you won't stop until Project Lucid is destroyed."

"I don't–"

"Look, Maya. I don't know you very well. I just know that you've done the impossible ever since you've gotten here. If you can't do it, none of us can. So promise you'll at least *try*."

No matter how tempted she was to leave the experiment and run away forever, the blind faith the girl's gaze encompassed wilted her instinct of self-preservation and she nodded. "Okay. I promise."

MAYA HUSTLED DOWN THE hall. The students passing by her gave her off-handed glances, but it didn't serve to affect her in any way besides increasing her pace. In front stood the group of blue bands, and Brian stood a little farther back, messing with his tablet. They were heading into their corridors, but right before Brian could enter, Maya jumped forward, slamming the door in front of him and pressing her back against it.

The boy looked up with a snarl. "What do you think you're doing, Mayo?"

She tilted her chin up. "I've come to ask you something."

"You truly must be insane if you think I'd do anything for you."

"You won't have much of a choice."

Slowly, he placed down his tablet to meet her gaze, and she crossed her arms. "I saw you the other night, going into the computer room. To be honest, the way you somehow managed to unlock the door was really impressive. It would, however, cost quite a load of punishment if you were caught. Or if someone were to tell…"

He stepped forward and pressed her against the wall. His voice was low as he whispered in her ear, "Are you blackmailing me, Mayo?"

Maya pushed Brian back. "Maybe. But by helping me, you'll be saving yourself too."

The boy's eyes narrowed, a blazing fire behind them. "And what were *you* doing there, huh? This can work two ways."

"I'm not stupid. Do you really think I'd blackmail you with something I'm also guilty of? I was told to meet up with Mrs. Fondal that night."

She didn't think it possible, but somehow the boy's eyes narrowed further. "You still haven't said what you want. You want something, do you? Or do you just enjoy making empty threats?"

Looking all directions to make sure there was no one around them to hear, including through the window in the heavy door, Maya lowered her voice. "I need you to hack into Chance's security."

A snort came from Brian, followed by a demeaning laugh. "Still looking for a way out, aren't you? Even if I can do that, the soldiers will stop you before you make it to the first floor."

"But you can, can't you? I saw the way you unlocked that door. And if you're using the computers, you must have a way of hiding your activity."

He pinched his nose and what almost sounded like a growl came from the back of his throat. "You'd get us both in trouble."

"Not if my plan works."

"And what is that, exactly?"

"It starts by contacting someone to make sure I have somewhere to hide, but that won't do any good if someone can trace my call."

"And after that?"

"Won't matter if you don't help."

For the first time during the whole conversation, the boy looked away, which allowed Maya to relax her shoulders. The halls had gone quiet, save for the distant pattering of footsteps. The plain walls had smudges of dirt that could've been years old. Maya wondered what had been the fate of the mark-maker.

"Fine," Brian finally stated. Her eyes widened slightly from the shock of him agreeing, only for it to be followed with, "But I have one condition."

"And what may that be?"

He leaned closer, his breath felt on her cheek. "You're going to take me with you."

Chapter Thirty-Nine

"An Angel That Guards Herself"

To say Camila wasn't happy with the prospect of Brian tagging along would be an enormous understatement, and Maya couldn't help but share her bitter feelings. He was the last person she desired to be an accomplice in her escape mission. A bully. A hothead. Almost destined to be a backstabber. The last person she needed in order to form a trustworthy team. But he was the only option. They needed a hacker. He needed a way out.

Part of Camila's grumpiness could've also been related to Hailey's choice to stay, that being another friend the girl would have to leave behind, and there was no doubt Carlos would be severely distressed and furious when he discovers their failure to save his lover. Maya had explained how the girl's choice to stay was conversely a courageous act, and yet, Camila still resented her for it.

Even after all that, however, Maya somehow managed to convince Camila to be joined by her side as she prepared to face the daunting task of calling her sister in order to have a safe destination when they escape. Sure, the girl's presence wasn't exactly needed, Brian's monitoring of the security cameras and hiding of her activities pretty much covered all of their bases, but for once, it was nice to feel not so alone in this mission. To have company just for the sake of company alone. Maybe she didn't have to take on the world by herself. Maybe trusting others to carry her burdens wouldn't cause those same burdens to fall back on her. Maybe—by trusting her *friend*—something she desperately needed in this world of secrets and lies.

"This better be the right number," Brian's voice resounded from Camila's tablet. He had changed its settings to block information from reaching the heads of Chance (he said it was easy, but it took the boy forty minutes to complete). Calling from the security room, the sound of typing fingers reached through the tablet's speakers.

Maya rolled her eyes. "You were the one who traced my previous call. I'd think you'd know if it's right better than anyone."

"Shut up, Mayo." He pressed a few more keys. *"You're only gonna have a two-minute gap before the call will be in the record. This needs to be short and concise. It's not sisterly-bonding time."*

"I'm aware." Taking a deep breath, Maya curled a strand of hair around her finger to release her stress. Next to her, Camila placed a hand over hers and rubbed it with her thumb. She slowly brought her hand down and met the grounding eyes of the dark haired girl, who appeared more calm than she, and distantly listened to Brian's countdown.

"Time starts... now."

Maya pressed the call button and watched as the phone icon vibrated, the ringing sound repeating over and over. Camila had tightened her grip on her hand, and Maya found herself holding her breath.

The ringing stopped.

"Hello?"

An outburst of relief escaped through her lips. "Amarie! Thank God you answered!"

The phone speaker crackled. *"Maya? What–why are you calling me? What's going on?"*

Maya tapped her foot to release her anxiousness and looked back at Camila to calm herself. "I don't have a lot of time to explain, but something's happened. You were right to suspect something wrong with the people who took me from Broth. I'm doing it. We're running away, and we need a place to stay. Where can we meet you?"

There was an extended period of silence before her sister spoke. *"Maya... I don't think you should leave."*

Maya reeled. "What? But–"

"The world out here isn't good, Maya. I've seen... terrible things I wish I could claw from my memory. There's this sickness going around, people's eyes are falling out of their heads and—you don't want to be here."

Maya swallowed. "I can't be *here.*" Camila rubbed her back.

"They're feeding you, aren't they? You're protected from the outside world. So what if it's an experiment? At least you're safe!"

The last part of Amarie's statement froze the blood coursing through her veins. Her sister trailed off, as if waiting for her to make the connection. Maya's face must have gone pale as she said, "How—how do you—"

"One minute." Brian said, but Maya's brain didn't register. Her sister had gone silent again, and Maya's lungs constricted as a waft of dread headed her way.

"You know." The two words didn't do nearly enough to represent her feelings, but they were the only ones that managed to escape from her jumbled thoughts. Amarie's breath could be heard on the other side of the phone, panting unevenly. She was scared.

"Maya, please, you have to listen to me. You don't want to come out. They have too much power. You won't be able to escape, and if the sickness doesn't kill you, they will."

Maya's hands gripped the sides of the communication pillar, the fibers in her fingers cramping inside. "They've threatened you, haven't they? You're in trouble! They have you–"

"I'm not the one in danger. They want *you*, not me. Gosh, Maya, what have you done? What happened to keeping a low profile? Everything we've learned..."

"Thirty seconds," Brian said. *"Hurry up."*

"Amarie." A slight tremor weaved its way into her voice. "Please. I don't know what they've told you, but I have to get out of here. Together we can stand up to them." Her sister stopped talking for far too long, the time slowly ticking by. She bit her lip and was tempted to scream for a response. She didn't need to.

"Head to where you first learned the consequences of putting others first."

Maya instantly knew where her sister meant, but that didn't stop her confusion. "But that's nowhere near the city. And you said we'd never return, unless it was against your will–" The revelation stole her voice.

"Ten seconds."

Her sister's words were thick as she said, "Keep fighting, Maya. We're survivors. If you can't find a way out, create one."

"Amarie?" Her sister didn't respond and Maya shook the stand. "Amarie! What have they done to you? Answer me!"

"Time's up, Mayo!"

"Amarie! Please don't leave me! Don't leave me–"

The call shut off. Camila watched her with pitiful eyes, a finger pressed against the end call button. Maya's body went limp as she rested her head on the screen. Part of her wanted to scream at the girl for ending the call. Part of her wanted to burn Chance to the ground. The rest of her wanted nothing more than to curl up into a tightly wound ball and cry for years on end.

Camila tried to console her, but Maya pulled back, punching the dark blue screen with all her might. A crack formed from the impact that extended from the top corner to the bottom. It probably should have sent an excruciating pain through her fist, but the fury inside of her numbed all other pain.

Brian came running through the door, prepared to curse her out, but was silenced when he saw the damage done to the stand and the redness of her left hand.

"Five o-clock, tomorrow morning." She told him. "Camila already knows where we're meeting. I'll lead you there." Stomping towards him, she jammed a finger into his chest. "And if you even *think* about telling someone else about this, I'll make sure nightmares torment you for the rest of your life."

Chapter Forty
"The Secrets That Blind Us"

CARLOS'S LIMP BODY WAS still situated on the bed when Maya got back. His skin was glossy with sweat, his tan color a shade lighter. He whimpered as he pulled his knees into a fetal position and she sat on the mattress, stroking his damp hair.

She had to get his sister out safely. Fulfilling this promise was the least he deserved.

"Good, you're here." Griffin shuffled in with his typical frown, but there was no accusation in his eyes like there had been the previous day. The gray circles beneath his gaze were darker than usual, and his body dragged as though covered in tar. He stayed back with his arms folded over each other, watching the boy in the bed softly. It was there when Maya realized why Griffin had been so against the idea of her becoming emotionally attached to Kai and felt slightly more empathetic.

"Kai told me what he is," she told the gruff man, and he showed a flash of an unreadable emotion. "I understand now. Why you treated me the way you did."

A low growl came from the back of Griffin's throat. "If you treat him with any disgust–"

"I'd never. He's one of the few guys I've met that haven't had the intention of hurting me. It doesn't matter where he's from."

Her response soothed his expression, but his words were still laced with suspicion as he said, "You understand you can't have a relationship with him, right? You're only a visitor here. This is the only place he exists."

"I know."

Griffin sighed, sauntering over to sit on the bed next to her. He gazed at the sleeping boy one last time before speaking to her. "Look, *kindertjie*, I'm not going to sit here and pretend we get along, or that I trust you. That's just who I am. Terra taught me to be that way."

It was overwhelming how much Maya could relate to the man. In a post-apocalyptic world, the only way to make it through another day was to be suspicious of everything. And yet, absorbing the guilt and tiredness that encompassed his frame, she wanted nothing to do with that way of life. To end up like the bitter man beside her.

But maybe it was too late.

"However," Griffin continued, "if we're going to help this boy, we need to work together and be honest with one another. So tell me, where do you know this kid from?"

Maya sighed and turned to the boy, who was wincing in imaginary pain. "His name is Carlos. We met in Terra just a few weeks ago, in a refuge of some sort. He was taken away yesterday, and I have a feeling that's related to his condition here."

Griffin's brows ruffled. "And how could that cause him to become omniscient?"

"Well, I became an Omni from an abnormally stressful situation." *With help from The Man of Light.* "If his current predicament is that terrible, it might cause him to break free of his dreams too."

Lost in thought, the man stared at the boy on the bed and rubbed his arm. It was the first gentle action Maya had seen Griffin do, and seeing his inner humanity softened the wall of dislike she had created for him.

It was only a moment later that the rest of the Omnis entered the bedroom. Halo walked in first, Talon and Jane following suit. From behind them ran in Kai, who looked worse for wear with his curly hair wilder than usual and the sunken nature of his eyes.

"He hasn't left Kalpana ever since we brought him here," Kai sputtered out. "He hasn't woken up once."

"That doesn't make any sense!" Jane said. "Our minds are only supposed to be in REM sleep for two hours. Anything more than that... it just isn't natural!"

Talon shifted closer to the sleeping boy. "This definitely is not a natural occurrence. Whatever is happening here, someone placed him in this sleep."

Griffin tensed up next to her.

"Isn't that a bit of a stretch, Talon?" Halo tried to reason. "Why would anyone want to make someone dream for hours on end?"

"I don't know," Talon said, but he brought his gaze to Maya, an accusation clear in his stare. "Maybe someone discovered a way to turn one into an Omni."

The taste in her mouth went bitter. "You think *I* have something to do with this?"

"You clearly have relations with the boy. No one is claiming you have ill intentions, but it is clear that whatever is happening here connects to you."

Kai then stood up to be by her side, gripping her hand to show his loyalty. "If she knew of something that could harm anyone, she would tell us."

"Possibly." But the silence that followed made Talon's suspicions clear. He didn't trust her anymore. Would he banish her?

"Are we sticking to the plan, Talon?" Griffin asked, and the man nodded.

"Amie—or Maya, I presume. You and Griffin will be entering your friend's mind to gaze at his memories. Then we will be able to see what is the true cause of this situation."

Something inside of her wanted to argue, but the tumultuous thoughts and emotions in her mind caused it to be nearly impossible to articulate why the idea terrified her so much. The one thing that scared her more than anything was having to leave. What would become of her?

"Are you okay with that?" Kai whispered in her ear. Despite her despise towards the idea, she nodded, if only to ease the nerves of the boy. It didn't seem to convince him, however, and he said, "Why does Maya have to go with Griffin? I could go in her place."

"Griffin won't let anything happen to her," said Talon. "Isn't that right?"

The man twisted the recouper on his wrist. "Nothing that I won't allow to happen."

His claim offered her little solace. Nonetheless, Maya checked to make sure her own recouper was on and prepared to enter her friend's mind.

"Ready?" Griffin asked.

"Yes."

"Be careful in there," Jane warned them. "It looks like he's having a nightmare. Wherever Kai found him, he's had lasting effects from a nightdweller."

"We will." Moving his hand to the boy's temple, Griffin waited for her to do the same. On the count of three, they both made contact, and Maya felt her consciousness enter the boy's dreamscape.

There was not much walking needed to reach the dream. The dark scene was in the forefront of his mind. Beneath her feet were a series of familiar cold white tiles, but as for walls, they vanished in the distance.

"Get down!" Griffin grabbed her back and pushed her to the ground moments before a wall came flying from the sky, dropping just in front of them. The force blew back her hair and she gagged as her nose was met with an unrecognizable putrid smell.

The soles of her feet felt wet. She peered down, expecting to see water. The deep red of the liquid proved her prediction false.

Griffin covered her mouth with his hand, stopping the scream that had been rising in her throat. The blood leaking from the stone wall sloshed in her shoes, the warmth of the liquid depicting its freshness.

"Camila?" It was a soft, calm voice, pre-adolescent, calling timidly into the expansive setting. Distantly, the figure of Carlos stood, smaller. Younger. He gazed around with interest, like the seeker in a game of hide and seek. Calling for his sister once more, the little boy trudged over to a white chair, sitting down and resting his elbows on his knees.

"Have to get past him," Griffin whispered.

Gazing around, Maya couldn't help but ask, "How?"

Just then, there was another voice, more distant as it said, *"Carlos?"* And while she may have never heard the voice before, Maya had no doubt in her mind that the voice was that of his sister as he shot from his seat, attempting to catch sight of Camila. He said something in Spanish, and his sister appeared out of thin air with a smile of tenderness and relief.

"Come on." Grabbing her hand, Griffin pulled her behind the twins, their footsteps silent despite the hard floor beneath them.

This dream carried an odd set of emotions with it. Loneliness was reflected in its barren setting. Love was illustrated in the presence of Camila. Impatience was lifted in the atmosphere, the stillness of it all serving as a calm before the storm.

Up ahead were the voids leading to the depths of his memory, spinning with an assortment of colors. Although, his entrances appeared different from the woman's mind she had entered. It wasn't an open passage like the previous woman's had been, where it was a deep, endless hole. No, his entrances had a pure darkness around it, threatening to shut. A door, like Maya's had been.

Griffin either didn't notice, or paid it no mind. But her mind pieced together the reality. The reason behind her reluctance to enter his dream before.

Carlos was lucid.

The dream's mood shifted, terror palpable and reeking from every crevice of his mind. Goosebumps formed along her arms and she dared to look back, seeing the blood gushing from Camila's eyes before she fell to the ground. Carlos screamed. Maya felt nauseous.

Still attempting to enter his memory, the gruff man didn't notice the growing negativity of the dream. He was about to reach his hand into the hole when Maya yelled, "Griffin, wait!"

The voids closed shut, the darkness covering the way deeper into the boy's mind. Griffin turned around and muffled her mouth. From across the room, Carlos turned around, his eyes settling directly on top of them.

The man gazed up, realizing the gravity of the situation when there were no cracks to be found. For the first time, Maya saw true terror in his eyes. "What have you done?"

"Press your recouper, quick!" she told him, but he remained unnervingly still. Ahead, Carlos started heading towards them, a hunter with one target. "Hurry!"

"I can't." His expression went blank, void of any hint of emotion. She shook his arm. Shoved his side. Yelled his name. No reaction.

It was then when Maya noticed the strings. They weren't from her, not this time. They ran from Carlos's subconscious to Griffin, the former tugging on its strands. She watched the manipulation of the invisible fibers move Griffin's body, forcing him to his knees. Then Carlos tugged her own.

Maya pulled back, trapping them in their own mental game of tug-o-war. Sweat dripped from her forehead as she forced herself not to give in to the lucid power. Carlos's subconscious struggled as well, confusion evident as to how a dream could be out of his control.

"Carlos!" Maya said. "Please, we're not here to hurt you!"

It was no shock when a response didn't come, and the energy expended on saying those few words caused her grip to slip. She was forced to the ground next to Griffin, head forced to the ground.

"He can't hear you," Griffin managed to mumble in a dejected tone. A liquid oozed from his fingers, flowing through the granite of the tiles.

Lucids could even turn you into a pile of goo if they so desired.

"You killed my sister." Carlos's voice reverberated in the empty space, somehow making itself heard without him ever opening his mouth. Maya could sense the liquefaction of her feet as they both grew cold.

She yelped at the sight of her hands melting before her, barely managing to look at Griffin, whose ear had started to go as well. Choking on a sob, Maya shut her eyes.

She was lucid too.

Her eyes opened, and the network of webs made itself known. They formed the setting. Carried through the air. Twisted and swirled around Carlos's consciousness. She grabbed a hold of those in front of her, snapping their ties, which sent Carlos flying back. Her extremities reabsorbed the liquid and she shot up shakily. Turning to Griffin, she closed her eyes again, feeling the pop as his own ties snapped.

Carlos had gotten up again. His consciousness appeared even more furious as the atmosphere darkened. The walls that had fallen from the sky were raised from the ground, shifting shape until they had a sharp point trained on her. Then they shot forward.

Maya took cover, pressing her back against the ground as the wind from its speed ruffled her hair. She rolled to the side, the next one narrowly missing her. Griffin's body was still reconstructing as Carlos fired one final one, aimed at him.

She put an arm forward and the spear stopped mid-air, hovering six feet from Griffin's face. Standing between the instrument of death and the man, Maya felt for the ties around Carlos's mind and transmitted, *"You don't see us."*

He fought the claim, shaking his head and reached the strings toward them again. She repeated, *"You don't see us."*

His consciousness grabbed his head, taking a wobbly step back. He blinked at them. Once. Twice. And turned away.

Then Griffin grabbed her arm and pressed his recouper, pulling them both out of the boy's mind.

The recoil of coming out of the mind sent a sharp pain through her head and she rubbed her temples. Carlos remained on the bed, laying still, as though nothing had happened. Next to her, Griffin leaned back and took a deep breath, a hand squishing his stubbled cheeks together.

"What happened?" Kai asked immediately.

Maya stared at the floor before shutting her eyes. Griffin stayed quiet for a while, requiring another prompting from Talon to snap out of his own thoughts.

Griffin made eye-contact with her, and that same terror settled inside his gaze, but not because of the dream. Because of *her*.

Maya's vision became blurry. She knew the outcome, even before Griffin shot up, taking a few unchoreographed steps back. His finger pointed toward her, and she shut her eyes, though that didn't clog her ears from hearing, in his frightened tone,

"She's lucid."

Not waiting to witness their reaction, she barged out of the room and didn't dare look back. Her feet moved without her command, only having a singular goal of exiting the castle. She dashed through the halls. Took various different turns. Saw the door ahead of her.

A hand grabbed hers.

Holding her back.

It was Kai.

Horror in his eyes.

Betrayal on display.

It was like he was looking at a stranger.

The boy didn't say a word. Or move. He might not have even blinked.

She choked on her own words as she jerked away her hand. They came raspy and thick: "I'm sorry."

The strings. The damned strings were there. Everywhere. They entirely encompassed Kai—it was the difference between him and everyone else in the world of Kalpana. She didn't want to *ever* tug on those.

The ones that reached above her were stretched subconsciously by her mind. They spun around her, wrapping themselves around her until she was in a cocoon.

I'm sorry. And instantly, she was transported someplace else.

MAYA SAT BESIDE THE Pit, legs dangling from its edges. Whatever she had done in the castle teleported her deep into the Whispering Woods, where the treetops and their leaves grew so thick that they blocked out the sky.

The Pit didn't scare her anymore, nor did the nightdwellers inside its dark caverns. As she pondered the reality of her situation, she came across the epiphany that the nightmare-causing creatures and herself were the same. Just like her, they took advantage of those around them in order to satisfy their desires. Their hunger. She was just as much a monster as they were. Maya was safer in the dark than in the light.

No, the Pit didn't scare her. Her fear came from waiting for the Omnis to find her, and for them to instill whatever punishment they had in store for someone as terrible as herself.

She could've run away, sure. It might have saved her all the loss the future held. But once you start running, you never stop. Every stop is another threat. Another reason to run. Maybe by leaving, she would have found another group to belong to, but then she'd have to hide the secret again. Over and over. Never resting, and worse, never belonging.

Which were all good reasons, but the true justification was that she was so tired of running. That tactic belonged to her Terran life, not this one. She didn't want it to belong to this one.

There was the crack of a tree branch, and Maya snapped around. In front of her stood Halo, appearing as ethereal as ever, with her brown wavy hair reaching to her waist. She sported a sad smile and rested a hand on the tree. "There you are," Halo said. "I thought you must have woken up by now."

Maya didn't answer, ripping out the grass by her side and rolling it between her fingers. Eventually, she said, "Are you going to take me back?"

With a sigh, Halo held out her arm. "Come over here, Maya. You are too close to the edge of that Pit for comfort."

"It's where I deserve to be."

"Maya," her voice held more strength, "Please, come by my side."

Reluctantly, Maya stood up and sauntered over to the woman, who seemed pleased by her action. "How mad are they?" she asked her. Halo sighed once more.

"They're... confused. The truth of the matter is that you saved Griffin, even if he doesn't want to accept it just yet. Even so, you lied to them for quite some time."

"You told me to lie," Maya mumbled.

"I know." Warmth spread over her skin as Halo embraced her, Maya's heartbeat thumping against her sternum. The woman smelled like flowers—not wild ones that occasionally managed to force their way through the barren fields, but fresh ones like her mother used to get on her birthday, a memory so distant, and yet surfaced just as fresh as the floral smell.

"You don't deserve this," Halo said as she stroked her hair. "And I'm forever sorry. With the recent loss of Hypnos and the revelation of your secret, there must be a million thoughts and emotions spiraling out of control. But I'll be here to keep you safe, okay?"

Maya squeezed the woman back, but as soon as she did, the revelation hit with the force of a powerful wave.

Maya backed out of her arms just enough to look Halo into her eyes. Her mouth had gone dry. She swallowed. "I never told you he died."

Her eyes widened, surprise only there for a second before she gave that same sad smile. "Well, I just assumed..."

Maya wasn't listening. There were only a select few that knew of his passing: herself, the other kids at Chance, and the workers. *She couldn't have known. Unless...*

Without thinking, she reached her hands to Halo's temples, sinking into the woman's mind before she could stop her.

With Halo being omniscient, Maya sank directly into her memories, the scenes flying past her at such a pace that it was nearly impossible to discern a single one. She held out a hand and it froze it all as she landed on one specific image.

It was Halo gazing in a mirror. But... it *wasn't* Halo. There was not an ounce of resemblance in the woman in her reflection. She did not have long flowy curls or gentle features. They were hard. Tough. And held such vibrant familiarity that Maya was compelled to do another take.

The weight of the betrayal swept her so far under that it took her too long to realize the black tentacles that reeked of darkness. They caught a hold of her feet. Then her left arm. Halo's mind was attacking her in a way that only a Lucid could.

It wrapped around her neck and she brought the recouper to her face. Pulling her head back, she jutted out her chin and brought the bracelet close. With the click of the button, she was brought back and she instantly broke out of Halo's grasp.

No. Not Halo.

The visitor.

Mrs. Fondal.

"You—" Maya stumbled over a root as her gaze remained on the woman before her, whose reach in her life extended farther than she ever thought possible.

Now, studying the cause of all her pain, Maya noticed the facade that made up her appearance. She was too beautiful and perfect, trying so hard to appear as kind and motherly as possible. And the name, "Halo." She was such an idiot! Such a blatant way to get others to see her as angelic. And of course, *of course* she wanted to keep Maya being lucid a secret. How else would she be able to conduct her stupid, soul-stealing experiment?

"Maya, if you would just listen…" She was still trying to convince her of her own innocence. There was no more proof needed; she knew this monster, and for once, it wasn't herself.

Her heart jumped as the back of her foot slid off the edge of the Pit, sending down speckles of dirt into the darkness. She turned to face Fondal with all the hatred she could fathom, the betrayal bleeding from her eyes in hot, angry tears.

"You can't run from me," Fondal said, moving closer, like a cat stalking its prey. "Not in this life or the other. Just come with me, and we'll talk."

The frigid air from the Pit blew against Maya's back, and she made her decision.

Without a word, she jumped back, letting the home of the nightdwellers absorb her entirely.

Oh Light, have mercy on me.

Chapter Forty-One

"Just Keep Going"

THE FAN. THE SOUND of its blades and their circular orbit around the center. It spun around and around and around. Over and over and over again. A cycle never-ending as it continued its job of supplying the refuge with all of its cooler air. A job given to it, cursed in the pattern. Inescapable.

The cold metal of the three kitchen knives pressed against her side beneath the fabric of her shirt. She only dared to pull them out when the other two refugees were in the air conditioning room with the door shut and locked.

"And *what* are those for?" Brian said when he caught sight of the sharp kitchen utensils. On the floor next to her was a large white towel spread across the floor along with the bottle of medical spray.

Laying the three knives flat, Maya said, "As long as we have these chips in our wrists, Chance will be able to track us."

His eyes widened. "You're absolutely insane, Mayo."

"*This is a terrible idea,*" Camila's automated voice argued. "*The chip is placed next to the radial artery on purpose. One slice, and you'll have blood shooting out of your arm. That amount of blood loss would leave you dead in minutes.*"

With a sigh, she said, "Look, if we want to have any chance at escaping here, we need to do this. So we'll have to be careful."

Maya picked up the knife she had cleaned earlier and brought it to her skin, only for Camila to grab her wrist and say, "*Stop.*" The girl sighed. "*I've had to do my brother's stitches in the past. I have steady hands. Let me do it.*" Maya didn't resist as Camila took the knife from her hand and took a deep breath before sinking the sharp edge in. She heard Brian groan in disgust as the red liquid dribbled from the incision. Maya grunted from the pain, but didn't flinch. She accepted it. *I deserve this.*

"I see it," Camila's tablet said. Her shoulders hunched over and she leaned closer to her forearm. Maya felt it as the knife reached beneath her major blood vessel, its blade dangerously close to tearing it.

"The wire of the chip wraps around the artery," Camila said out loud. *"I can't get it out with this large of a knife. I need a small pair of scissors, or a smaller knife. Did you bring anything else, Maya?"*

Maya grunted from the pain and her own incapability. "I should have thought about that."

Camila took another deep breath to center herself. *"Okay. I guess I'll just have to use what I have. Brian, stand by with the medical spray."*

Brian looked like he would have rather been anywhere else, but he obeyed, holding the spray up. Maya closed her eyes as Camila turned the knife and pressed it against the wire.

"Got it," she said, and Maya blew out a breath. Slowly, the girl pulled the knife out, the microchip at its tip. She turned around and placed it down on the towel, the blood staining the white material. With Camila's order, Brian coated the wound and Maya displayed no reaction, even as the spray burned her skin.

As Camila rubbed the blood off her hands, she turned to look at her. *"What happened last night, Maya?"*

Maya quickly looked away. "What makes you think something happened?"

"You're not as good at hiding your emotions as you seem to think you are."

"Yeah," Brian felt obligated to add on. "You wear every single inconvenience on your face. No wonder you always look miserable."

Maya sensed her face had flushed as Camila tilted her head. *"Ignore him. I'm here to listen. Or, read."*

She brought her knees up and kept her eyes on her wound, cursing the way her eyes teared up at the recollection of the events that unfolded in Kalpana. The reveal. The betrayal. That sadness, however, quickly turned to anger. "Someone in the dream world wasn't who I thought they were. It... it was Mrs. Fondal. She's lucid too and she's been manipulating my other life." Maya scoffed. "She made me believe she *cared* for me. After we get out of here, I'm gonna make sure she pays for all the lies she's told me."

"So Mrs. Fondal knows you in Kalpana?" Brian said. "Then isn't this all for nothing? Can't she just pick out where we are from your memories?"

Camila's eyes widened. *"She can do that?"*

"Theoretically, yes," Maya answered before Brian could comment. "But I have to be in Kalpana for that to be possible. And where I am there, she won't be reaching me." Brian seemed interested in where she was hiding, but she changed the subject. "We need to hurry. The first workers get up at six, and we've already wasted fifteen minutes. Camila, are you ready to do it to Brian?"

After reading the tablet, she nodded, and Brian squirmed as the girl held his arm in her lap. "You don't have any numbing cream? Any spray?"

"This isn't a hospital," Maya said. "If I could handle it, you can too."

"Yeah, well, not everyone is as crazy as you, May—*ow!*" The boy jumped and Camila's grip slipped, slicing deeper into the skin. They all fell silent. Blood gushed from the wound, but none shot up, which would have indicated a severed artery. Then Camila slapped him across the face.

"Sit still." The monotone voice from the girl's tablet was almost amusing in contrast to the fury in Camila's expression. *"You're lucky I only hit a vein. Do not flinch again."* Brian complied, watching her as she cut deeper into his skin, biting her own cheek. With a remarkable gentleness, she cut the wire, ignoring the groans from the boy. Even faster than with her, Camila pulled the chip out, placing it next to Maya's. Spraying the incision, Maya made sure to coat it in its entirety. Brian hissed as it burned his skin, but after a few seconds, the pain seemed to subside.

"You are strangely good at that," Brian said, catching Maya by surprise. She wasn't aware he could give anyone a compliment.

Camila leaned over to read what he had said and smiled. *"I've wanted to be a surgeon since I was very little. Chance got in the way of that dream."*

"When we get out of here," Maya said, "you'll be able to become anything you want to be."

"I hope so." After cleaning her hands with the towel, she took her own knife, gasping at the pain when she reached into her wrist. After a few minutes, she pulled out her own chip, placing the last of the three onto the stained towel.

When they were all as clean as they could be, Maya folded the towel around the knives, chips, and medical spray. Then she tied it up before placing it in the nook between the fan and the wall.

The halls were silent in the early hour, save for the blowing of the vents. The three of them made their way to the elevator, where Brian pulled out his tablet. "You need a chip to enter all floors but the top one and the basement."

"But you can hack into it, right?" Maya asked him.

"Well, yeah. But unlike a simple lock on a door, these ones are heavily monitored. I've already blocked the cameras, but if we do this, they're gonna know we're here. Are you 100% sure your buddy is in here?"

"Yes." *Unless they moved him,* she thought, but didn't dare say out loud.

"Well then, I hope you're right, Mayo." With a click, the fourth button on the elevator glowed green and Brian pressed it. The ground started to sink beneath them as it took them down, the screen above the sliding doors counting each floor they passed. When it reached three, the elevator stopped with a *ding.* The doors slowly opened.

The first thing Maya noticed was the cold of the room. Its white waxed flooring was clean enough to reflect their footsteps, as if no one had ever set foot on it before. But this claim was shortly extinguished as she noticed the rows of wires and screens reaching to the back of the room. And hung from each of these contraptions were people, not much older than she. Their eyes remained shut, but none of them appeared peaceful. Bodies twitched underneath the braces that pinned them down at a vertical angle, and many of their cheeks were stained wet with unwiped tears.

"I know him," Camila said as she walked up to one of the figures dangling. Gazing at the boy's face, she realized she did as well. It was the boy who she had first witnessed being taken away to supposedly live a free life. *"They never left. None of them did."*

"You both really believed they'd let us go?" Brian asked from behind them. Unlike the two of them, he didn't appear surprised by what was in the room. He seemed sad. "Anyone here that has learned of the program is a leak. Those that leave will mention how they were taken in by Chance Refuge. An unknown organization like this would lead to examinations. Then they're out of business. All their hard work. For nothing."

"You knew," Maya told him, "that day this boy was taken, you and the other blue bands..."

"Yeah, we knew." Brian glared at the sacs of drugs hanging by the side, most likely what was keeping them under. "Us blue bands are cursed with knowledge."

Camila wandered off to look for her brother, but Maya's attention was brought to something else. The small screens next to each person were glitchy, and the quality was terrible. Even so, as she moved closer to see, she finally realized what the screens were revealing. It was their dreams. Nightmares. Something she didn't even know was possible to exhibit.

Camila's robotic voice carrying a somber message then sounded in the silence.

"Carlos isn't here."

Chapter Forty-Two

"Bittersweet Endings"

Maya and Brian ran around to meet her, where the girl's eyes watered and she sat on her knees. *"What did they do with you?"* She asked no one in particular.

"He's on this floor somewhere," Maya said, partially to convince herself. "Let's keep looking." However, they only managed to make it down one aisle before there was the silent *ding* of the elevator opening. In walked two of the soldiers and Mr. Hue, with Mrs. Fondal tailing closely. At the sight of the woman, Maya's hands clenched. Camila placed a hand on her shoulder to keep her in check.

"Check everywhere," Mrs. Fondal's darkly feminine voice ordered. "They're in here." The soldiers broke off in opposite directions, while Mr. Hue stayed by her side.

"What is this?" Mr. Hue's disbelief was barely audible, and despite her intrigue of the man's unawareness, they didn't have time to wait around. Maya pointed to the back door just a little in front of them, and Brian understood, clicking around his tablet to unlock it. It turned green, and they stood up. Camila initially resisted Maya's prompting, crying on the ground, but Maya bent down and grabbed her shoulders.

"We'll find him," Maya promised.

"You will not be finding anyone."

Mrs. Fondal faced the three with Hue by her side, the two soldiers blocking the door.

"Halo." Maya spat out the name as if it was poison given to her to drink. The woman tilted her head, that same demeaning smile stretching unnaturally across her unfeeling face.

"Maya, please," Mrs. Fondal said. "I know I might not have been the most truthful, but we trusted each other, didn't we? I care for you. I don't want to see you get hurt."

A bitter laugh sputtered out from Maya's throat. "Is that what you told all of them before you tied them up to experience nightmares for the rest of their lives?" She gestured to the victims in the rows.

"Their sacrifice was necessary for the greater good, just like yours. With you, we have the opportunity to end all future conflicts. To win the war in a way that none of our people get hurt. You can be a hero, Maya."

"I'll never do anything for a slave of Tenebris."

The woman sighed, but didn't appear surprised as she moved her gaze onto Brian. "And you. I thought you knew better."

The boy crossed his arms and shrugged. "I saw an opportunity to leave, and I took it."

"Where is my brother?" Camila demanded. *"Did you hurt him? You said the winner gets to go on a vacation. Why would you lie, Mrs. Fondal? My brother and I trusted you."*

Fondal's agitation grew more apparent. "Enough. Each of you are going to return to your beds and not say a word to anyone. You will be closely monitored. Maya, we'll start your official training. And none of you will ever try to escape again, do you understand?"

Silence encompassed the room, the three of them pondering what would be their new reality. It was a future none of them could live with.

Maya and Brian made eye contact. The latter gave her a nod. Then, with a click, the lights switched off and the sound of commotion arose.

Blindly, Maya felt her way down the aisle. The only source of light illuminating the room was the red exit sign above the door. She saw the shadow of Camila run down the row next to her, the tablet screen lighting up her face. Maya followed, ignoring the disoriented voices as they struggled to catch them in the dark. Camila reached the back door and started tugging on the door handle when she was yanked back, a scream escaping from her. The soldier holding her had his elbow pressed against her neck as she squirmed. In a quick decision, Maya ran after them and punched the man in the nose, allowing him to loosen enough for Camila to slip out. The girl held onto her, chest heaving. Keeping herself upright, Maya dashed back over to the door. Brian was already there, ushering through the door.

"Let's go," Brian said just before another one of the soldiers ran towards them from the end of the row, making them out in the dim light. Pulling Camila inside, they hustled to shut the door, shoving their bodies to hold back the soldiers. Brian frantically put in commands on his tablet and the door clicked, its lock turned red once again. Maya slid down the metal door, resting her head between her knees in relief until a scream came from Camila, and Maya instantly shot up to see what she was pointing at.

Her own hand came over her mouth, gagging noises coming from Brian. A cot sat in the middle of the room, with a body spread across it, banded against it. There was no mistaking it for someone other than Carlos, but there was no joy in finding the boy in such a state. Six thick, one-inch tubes pumped a murky liquid into his body—two into his head, two in his chest, and two into his abdomen. His veins bulged out, sporting a dark color that made his skin appear white. Even unconscious, the boy's body trembled in pain, the buckles around his limbs preventing him from hurting himself. On a screen above played the dream of his that she had entered, restarting each time at the same spot. It was a strange thing to see what she had done from another perspective. Her voice echoed over the screen: *"You don't see us."*

"That's freaky," Brain said as Camila stared at her brother, lip trembling.

A banging sound against the door reminded them of their predicament, and Maya moved up to the boy's medical machinery. "We have to find a way to get him out of these tubes."

"And then what?" said Brian. "We trapped ourselves in here."

The boy was right; the room was no bigger than her bedroom at Broth's, and the only exit was currently being pounded on by three officers. Maya took a few deep breaths to center herself. "How long can you keep it locked?"

"Considering someone is actively trying to override my order?" He scrolled on his tablet. "Five minutes."

"Okay," Maya said, mostly to herself. "Okay. Camila, do you think you can find a way to get Carlos loose?" The girl was bent over her brother's body, moving his hair out of his eyes. After a glance at her tablet, she looked at her with cloudy eyes, but nodded. Maya then directed Brian to bring up a map of the ventilation system.

"Will we even fit?" Brian said skeptically.

"You have a better idea?"

And so the boy pulled it up, and sure enough, there was a duct leading to the main hall. While the other two continued their tasks, Maya took a chair that was placed right next to the bed and stood on it, gripping between the shutters. She pulled and pulled until the screws finally loosened enough to pull out the covering. Brian was jostled as a large shove came from behind the door. "Three minutes," he wheezed out, and Maya went over to help Camila. The girl's hands were shaking tremendously, making it nearly impossible to pull out the tubes from her brother's body.

Maya put a hand on her shoulder and pointed to the machinery. "You check the machines," she said. "I got your brother." Camila got the message, instantly moving over to where the screen was. Tugging on the tubes, Maya struggled to loosen them without causing blood to pour out of the gaps. Suddenly, there was the sound of draining, and the murky liquid was emptied out. Camila's hand was over a lever as she wore an exhausted expression. After the draining was completed, the tubes snapped loose, leaving behind a mark that caused Maya to turn pale.

Six symbols. Six lines of Tenebris.

She decided not to dwell on it, and instead grabbed the boy's clothes so that Camila could cover him. The pounding grew louder. Once the boy was redressed, Maya stabilized the chair and ushered Camila over. She looked over her brother one more time before stepping on Maya's knee. Maya directed her to step on her hands, and she hoisted her up. Brian had stuffed the tablet in his pants and was pulling Carlos' hands over his shoulders to carry him up. Maya lifted herself up and reached her arms down, wincing as she was handed the limp boy. With a grunt, she pulled him up, then did the same for the red-head.

The minute Brian's foot was lifted up into the shaft, Maya heard the lock bust open and a soldier shouted, *"They're in the vents!"* She hurried Camila forward, all three of them crawling on their elbows. Camila doubled her speed, and Maya trailed just behind. Momentarily looking back, she saw Brian pulling Carlos along with all his might, cursing all the while.

"Why did I get stuck with the corpse?" He growled as he kicked back a pair of hands trying to grab him.

Maya ignored his complaining and focused on visualizing the map of the vents. In front, the shaft split in two. "Left!" she whispered to Camila, who quickly changed direction. Seeing that Brian was falling behind, Maya turned around as much as she could and helped to pull Carlos forward. Commotion came from behind them as one of the officers managed to squeeze through the entrance. Her heart pounded as the man came faster, gaining on them. They slugged around the corner. Goose-bumps traveled up Maya's arms as cold air shot through the vent. Clouds of heat came from their breathing, which all were above normal pace. Five steps further, and Maya told them to halt. Between her elbows was the exit into the hall, and she tightened her hands around the bars to push it out, the cover falling to the ground with a *clank*. Camila jumped down first before holding out her hands. With the help of Brian, they lowered Carlos down to the girl and watched as she held him in her arms. Brian hopped down next, and Maya was just about to follow before she felt a hand grab her ankle.

She let out a yelp and tried kicking herself free, but the hand was too strong. Distantly, she heard Camila scream as she was pulled away. Her body slid against the cold tile and she reached out to grasp the duct's edge. The border was sharp, and she cried out in pain the harder the man pulled. Her fingers started to slip. The man reached higher on her leg. *Oh Lucis, help me!*

She screamed when it felt like her fingers were being sliced off. The pain, however, brought about a surge of energy, which allowed her to loosen the man's grasp and kick him in the chin. Hands reached up through the duct, and Maya grabbed onto it. It pulled her through the exit, headfirst, but when she started to fall, Camila and Brian caught her, standing on a chair to reach her.

They didn't have time to dwell. The soldier who had almost gotten her was already trying to get through the duct, and so the three of them darted down the hall, Brian carrying Carlos like a bride. But once they reached the end, they skidded to a stop, seeing a soldier blocking the door.

Mr. Hue was guarding it. His stance exuded confidence, but, in the brighter red light of the exit sign glowing above, Maya could see the concern peppering his face.

"Mr. Hue," Maya begged. "Please. You've seen what will happen if we stay."

The man gazed around the room before looking back at them, pity creasing his brows. Then, out of his pocket, Mr. Hue pulled out a key. He creaked open the door. "Be fast."

Not having time to take in the surprise, they ran through the opening. However, before Maya got through, the man stopped her and handed over the keys. "Go to the first floor. Take the car."

Maya nodded, hoping her eyes conveyed her level of gratitude. She ran after the others, barely registering the click of the door locking behind them. Following Brian, they moved as fast as they could while dragging Carlos's limp body. Above, she read each sign to find the elevator. Distantly was the sound of boots hitting the ground. The soldiers had made it through.

They neared the elevator, and the keys jingled in Maya's hand. Camila pressed the button. The three of them waited impatiently for the elevator to open as the footsteps of the soldiers grew closer, and as soon as the doors opened, they shoved themselves in, pressing the button to allow the doors to close. At the end of the hall, the two soldiers made their appearance. The one that she had kicked now had a bloody nose and watched her with anger-filled eyes. Maya pressed the button repeatedly, but that didn't make the door close any faster. She heard herself say a prayer to Lucis under her breath as they neared, despite never saying a prayer in her life. They collectively held their breath when the soldier reached out his hand.

Then the door shut.

At the first floor, they ran through the parking lot. Maya pressed the keys, following the sound of the beeping car. It was a green minivan that hovered at a foot above the ground. She unlocked it and helped Brian place Carlos in the back, with his head resting on Camila's lap. Afterwards, she went and sat at the front, putting the keys in the slot.

"You're gonna have to open the gate," Maya told Brian, remembering the large garage door from when she first arrived. He had taken the passenger's seat while she drove, reversing out of the parking spot and pressing on the pedal which shot them forward. Checking the side mirrors, Maya saw five soldiers pour out from the backroom, pointing guns at them. She barely had time to yell "Duck!" when they were showered with bullets.

The large garage door grew closer and Maya shouted, "Anytime now, Brian!"

"Okay, okay! Give me a second!" came from beneath his seat. He worked through his tablet, pressing multiple buttons before saying, "Got it!"

Light flooded in from the opening, and she accelerated. The bullets had stopped, but Maya refused to look back until they broke out, zooming through the open entrance. There wasn't any outward cheering after this feat, herself too overcome with relief.

She checked back for the last time. In front of the soldiers stood Mrs. Fondal, arms blocking them from firing. Even at their increasing distance, Maya still felt herself make eye-contact with the woman as if she was still there by her side.

In that moment, she understood the power of darkness.

And she knew she'd be returning to end its reign.

"AMARIE? IT'S ME, MAYA." She sat in a message booth, locking the glass door as she held the speaker to her ear. The screen before her printed her words. "I can't call you right now, but I just wanted to say that... we made it out. We're safe. Well, as safe as we can be with what might be the entire Western government chasing us. I don't have a lot of time—Brian can only keep them from tracking us for two minutes. We're heading to where you said to meet you. We should be there in about three days."

Maya brought her knees up onto the booth. "I can't wait to see you. We can eat those Iceplops and whatever else you have and explore—have you been to one of those crater sites? I've heard they're amazing–" Brian tapped on the glass, breaking her train of thought. He pointed to his wrist and she sighed.

"I hope whatever happened between you and Chance was something you were able to escape from. It had to have been, right? Otherwise, you wouldn't have told me to meet you there." Maya fell silent for a bit. "Just... be careful, okay? See you soon. I love you."

She pressed the end button and watched as the words were wrapped in an electronic seal to be sent to her sister. A green check mark came over the screen to confirm it being sent, and Maya leaned her head back on the glass wall.

She meandered out of the booth and plopped back into the car, where Brian was chewing on a bag of potato chips, and Camila was swiping Carlos's hair to the side. The two of them had disposed of their tablets earlier to prevent any possibility of their actions being traced. After her stomach growled loudly, Brian sighed and handed her one chip, and she took it gratefully, though it didn't do much to soothe her anxiety.

"You know they can find that message you sent, right?" Brian told her. "They know you're going to meet with her."

"I know." Maya wiped the oil from the chip on her Chance uniform. "They're keeping track of my sister, so what I told them won't be news to them. But my sister's smart. If she wants to meet where we're heading, we must have an advantage there."

"And where exactly are we going?"

Maya turned the car back on and put it into drive. "Where I first got my tattoo."

Turning around, she ignored Brian's astonished "You have a *tattoo?*" and offered Camila a thumbs up to see if she was ready. Camila returned the gesture.

She turned back and changed the gear, the minivan working a similar way to how the lawn mower had. That life felt so far away now, but she didn't mind its distance. She was no longer trapped by Broth, or SCRO, or Chance. Maya had made her own freedom, and she would fight for it as long as she breathed. Starting now, she would make her own boundaries and limitations. She'd explore everything this world had to offer, and would use that knowledge to make her own decisions. Whether it be an evil experiment or a dark prophecy. Whether it be within Terra or Kalpana.

Maya wouldn't let any world take that freedom away from her.

Epilogue

WALTER CHANCE WAS A grouchy, perturbed man. It did not take much to come to this conclusion. One didn't even need to be aware of his obsession with human fingernails to sense that something was off with the way he carried himself. Being a member of the presidential Cabinet, one would think, would satisfy a man's desire for power, but for a person such as him, power acted like a magnet, its pull growing stronger the closer the distance.

Even so, he had money. Lots and lots of money. Mrs. Fondal understood that the only way to sponsor her program would be through him, and he was the only one insane enough to even consider her idea without dismissing it completely. However, as they sat in the familiar, recently-remodeled coffee shop, Charlene Fondal was starting to wonder if maybe there had been a possible alternative.

Mr. Chance sipped on his mug of black coffee, large rings on each of his fingers. He released a sigh before trapping her in the dark pits of his pupils.

"Explain this to me, Mrs. Fondal." The man rubbed the top of his bald head. "After years of pouring money into this project without any progress, we finally have a success. And then, just weeks later, not only do we lose her, but you encouraged her to do so?"

He brought his coffee back to his lips to take another sip, then slammed it down. The hot liquid splashed onto his skin, but he made no indication that he'd felt it.

"We haven't lost her, Mr. Chance." Charlene sat up straighter and crossed her legs to illustrate her confidence. "We have ways to track her. Weaknesses to exploit. Even in Kalpana, I know exactly where she is, and while she might be out of my reach for now, she won't be staying there for long."

"And yet, she shouldn't have escaped *at all.*"

Mrs. Fondal spun the wedding ring on her finger to steady her nerves. "Being lucid is as much about willpower as it is mental strength. Maya must not become compliant. If I had not encouraged her, we would have extinguished the one thing we need from her the most: power."

"*Controllable* power, Mrs. Fondal. Otherwise, she's no better than all the other failures. Worse—she'd be capable of collapsing this entire project from the inside-out."

Wringing her hands together, she said, "Trust me, Mr. Chance. Maya Shaffer will help us, and we will win the war."

Mr. Chance took a breath to relax his shoulders and traced his finger around the cup's rim. "This disease spreading around... such one like it has never been, leaving many to believe it's an attack from the Eastern World, an idea I find myself believing. They are the strongest they've been since before the war. The minute they see just how weak we are, we will have lost. Now, you said you have a solution. Do you?"

"Of course."

The man leaned forward. "You must control Ms. Shaffer by any means necessary, do you understand? Or else, Project Lucid will cease to exist."

"As I said"—Charlene picked up her own cup of coffee—"Maya Shaffer will help us. She won't have a choice."

Mr. Chance then stood up, chugging the remaining coffee inside the cup before placing it next to her own. With a nod, he said, "Well, then. You may continue with your success."

Right before he exited the small shop, Mrs. Fondal called out to him for one last question: "And the others?"

There was no sympathy in the man's voice. "Put them under with the rest."

Acknowledgements

Before I indulge in a poor attempt to convey my gratitude to the overwhelming amount of friends, family, and acquaintances who made this book possible, I'd like to take a moment to acknowledge the Lord and Savior of my life, Jesus Christ, who was with me every step of the way. There were many times I questioned His will for me and this story, but in hindsight, it is easy to see His intentions through every struggle I encountered in my writing journey. He is Almighty, the Alpha and Omega, who ordains everything, the good and the bad, according to His will. His love for humanity surpasses all understanding as He clothes His people in righteousness, not because we deserve it, but because of grace. Amen.

A big cheer for the team at Twisted Words Publishing, who decided to take a chance on my book, despite the enormous amount of rejections I got from literary agents. You all truly did make my dreams come true, and I cannot thank you all enough.

To my dad, who, despite not knowing anything about writing, was my #1 supporter and somehow always managed to give the perfect advice. To my mom, who also had faith in me, though she probably wishes I'd write about happy couples and cute puppies instead. To my sister, who never read this book despite my multitude of bribes, but I forgive her (I'm going to glue it to her pillow). To my grandma, who stalked my instagram and found the embarrassing videos I made to promote this book. To the rest of my family, both in the USA and overseas, who were always so curious and supportive of my dreams. And to my cousin Alyssa. A few of your beautifully worded sentences from your editing years back are still in there:)

To the enormous amount of friends who motivated me, some of whose names I am bound to forget. Abigail Freudenberg and Taylor Miller, thank you for hyping me up with your amazement when I showed you my roughly drawn book cover. Asha Freeman and Hannah Harper, while you guys never got to finish beta-reading, I am forever grateful for your willingness to help despite a busy schedule. To both of you: keep writing! Micalah Reed, David Qualley, and Wanda Squeponer, you three were absolute life savers and the best beta readers anyone could ask for, giving honest yet supportive advice that made OMNISCIENT what it is today. Sonia Abddallah, you are the kindest, most patient person, and your cover-making skills are incredible. While your design didn't end up being the final one, you helped so much in influencing the current version and your gentle nature made you such a pleasure to work with! You keep writing too; if you ever need anything, feel free to reach out.

To the even more ginormous amount of online friends I have made. I could not name all of you even if I tried, but you are truly what kept me going, knowing there were people interested enough in my writing to follow my journey. The connections made between the readers are what makes writing so special to me. More than anything, I pray this book touches hearts and brings someone a sense of peace, and so this online community means more than any sort of recognition.

To all those I have coached, played tennis with, and who have coached me. Coaches Tracey, Dave, and Brad, thank you for listening as I'd rant about my writing when I should have been teaching. All of you children who somehow discovered I was making a book, your sweet questions always warmed my heart. Manu, as one of the few kids who actually read, keep at it! Ethan, that one day you bombarded me with questions over what it took to be an author despite not being a reader still brings so much joy and laughter to my heart. Not going to list you all, but to my friends on and off the tennis court. Though most of you were more interested in my content on Tiktok, the support always meant a lot to me.

To Ray Brady. You may have only been our substitute teacher for a few days, but the impression your kindness made goes much deeper. Despite your busy schedule, you agreed to read a desperate teenager's extremely rough and unfinished manuscript. You led me down this publishing path, and motivated me to make a finished story I am proud of. I hope you get the opportunity to read this. I dedicate this book to you.

I am forgetting a lot of people I am sure, but the truth of the matter is that writing a book is never just a one person job. It is a conglomerate of many different people who inspire, shape, and ultimately make its story. And now, I end it off by thanking you, the reader, for taking a chance with this book. I hope you were able to enjoy it as much as I enjoyed writing it.

Peace be with you all.

About the Author

Alaina Gray

Since stapling a short story together at the ripe age of four, Alaina Gray has always felt the desire to create original ideas. She is a college student and author, with OMNISCIENT being her debut into the writing industry. In whatever she does, she strives to serve to the best of her ability, whether it be by going out into the community, or teaching important lessons through her writing. When she is not typing away, Alaina loves volunteering at her church and coaching tennis to sassy 5-year-olds. She currently lives in Florida and attends her local community college.

GLOSSARY

gat Afrikaans. Def: the fleshy part one sits on; butt. (Ch. 8, 15)

maatjie Afrikaans. Def: a buddy or close friend. (Ch. 8)

trasero Spanish. Def: the fleshy part one sits on; butt. (Ch. 13)

kind Afrikaans. Def: a child. (Ch. 15)

kindertjie Afrikaans. Def: a small child, usually used in an endearing way. (Ch. 40)

www.ingramcontent.com/pod-product-compliance
Lightning Source LLC
Chambersburg PA
CBHW021406110726
47901CB00008B/2074